Praise for Marta Perry

"Abundant details turn this Amish romantic thriller...into a work of art." —*Publishers Weekly* on *Where Secrets Sleep* (starred review)

"Crisp writing and distinctive characters make up Perry's latest novel. *Where Secrets Sleep* is a truly entertaining read." —*RT Book Reviews*

"Perry skillfully continues her chilling, deceptively charming romantic suspense series with a dark, puzzling mystery that features a sweet romance and a nice sprinkling of Amish culture." —*Library Journal* on *Vanish in Plain Sight*

Praise for *New York Times* bestselling author Lee Tobin McClain

"Lee Tobin McClain dazzles with unforgettable characters, fabulous small-town settings and a big dose of heart. Her complex and satisfying stories never disappoint." —Susan Mallery, #1 *New York Times* bestselling author

"[An] enthralling tale of learning to trust.... This enjoyable contemporary romance will appeal to readers looking for twinges of suspense before happily ever after."

Low Country Hero

MARTA PERRY

Second Chance Amish Bride

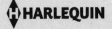

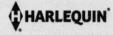

ISBN-13: 978-1-335-66253-8

Recycling programs
for this product may
not exist in your area.

Second Chance Amish Bride
First published in 2017.
This edition published in 2023.
Copyright © 2017 by Martha Johnson

Small-Town Nanny
First published in 2016.
This edition published in 2023.
Copyright © 2016 by Lee Tobin McClain

For questions and comments about the quality of this book,
please contact us at CustomerService@Harlequin.com.

Harlequin Enterprises ULC
22 Adelaide St. West, 41st Floor
Toronto, Ontario M5H 4E3, Canada
www.Harlequin.com

Printed in U.S.A.

CONTENTS

A lifetime spent in rural Pennsylvania and her Pennsylvania Dutch heritage led **Marta Perry** to write about the Plain people, who add so much richness to her home state. Marta has seen over seventy of her books published, with over seven million books in print. She and her husband live in a beautiful central-Pennsylvania valley noted for its farms and orchards. When she's not writing, she's reading, traveling, baking or enjoying her six beautiful grandchildren.

Books by Marta Perry

Love Inspired

Brides of Lost Creek

Second Chance Amish Bride
The Wedding Quilt Bride
The Promised Amish Bride
The Amish Widow's Heart
A Secret Amish Crush
Nursing Her Amish Neighbor

An Amish Family Christmas
"Heart of Christmas"
Amish Christmas Blessings
"The Midwife's Christmas Surprise"

Visit the Author Profile page
at LoveInspired.com for more titles.

SECOND CHANCE
AMISH BRIDE

Marta Perry

Do not judge, and you will not be judged.
Do not condemn, and you will not be condemned.
Forgive, and you will be forgiven.
—*Luke 6:37*

This story is dedicated to my husband, Brian,
with much love.

Chapter One

The hospital van bounced over a rut in the farm lane, and Caleb King leaned forward to catch the first glimpse of his home. At last—those four weeks in the rehab hospital after his leg surgery had seemed endless, but finally he was coming back to his central Pennsylvania farm. If only he could jump down from the van, hug his kinder and plunge back into the life of being a dairy farmer.

But he couldn't. His hands tightened on the arms of the wheelchair, and he glared at the cast on his leg. How much longer would he have to count on the kindness of his family and neighbors to keep the farm going?

Caleb glanced toward the Fisher farm across the fields. The spot where the barn had been before the fire was cleared now, and stacks of fresh lumber showed a new barn would soon rise in its place. For an instant he was back in the burning structure with Sam Fisher, struggling to get the last of the stock out before the place was consumed. He heard again Sam's shout, saw the fiery timber falling toward him, tried to dive out of the way...

He should have thought himself blessed it had been only his leg that suffered. And doubly blessed that Sam had hauled him out of there at the risk of his own life.

The van stopped at the back porch. Caleb reached for the door handle and then realized he couldn't get it open. He'd have to wait for the driver to lower the wheelchair to the ground. How long until he'd be able to do the simplest thing for himself? He gritted his teeth. He was tired of being patient. He had to get back to normal.

By the time Caleb reached the ground, Onkel Zeb was waiting with Caleb's two little ones, and his heart leaped at the sight of them. Six-year-old Becky raced toward him, blond braids coming loose from under her kapp, which probably meant Onkel Zeb had fixed her hair.

"Daadi, Daadi, you're home!" She threw herself at him, and he bent forward to catch her and pull her onto his lap, loving the feel of her small arms around him.

"Home to stay," he said, and it was a promise. He hugged her tight. His young ones had lost too much with their mother's desertion and death. They had to know that he was always here for them.

Reminding himself that whatever Alice's sins, he must forgive her, he held out his hand to Timothy, who clung to Onkel Zeb's pant leg. "Komm, Timothy. You know Daadi, ain't so?"

Little Timothy was almost four, and his blue eyes

had grown huge at the sight of the lift and the wheel-chair. But at the sound of Caleb's voice, he seemed to overcome his shyness. He scrambled into Caleb's lap, managing to kick the heavy cast in the process.

Onkel Zeb winced at the sight. "Careful, Timmy. Daadi's leg…"

Caleb stopped him with a shake of his head. "It's worth it for a big hug from my boy."

Nodding, Onkel Zeb grasped Caleb's shoulder, his faded blue eyes misting over. His lean, weathered face seemed older than it had been before the accident, most likely from worry. "Ach, it's wonderful gut to have you home again."

The driver slammed the van door, smiling at the kinder. "Don't forget, I'll be back to pick you up for your therapy appointment next week." He waved as he rounded the van to go back to the driver's seat.

Caleb grimaced as the van pulled out. "I wish I could forget it. I'd like to be done with hospitals."

"Never mind. You're getting well, ain't so? That's what's important." Zeb started pushing the wheel-chair toward the back door, where a new wooden ramp slanted down from the porch. "Sam Fisher and Daniel put the ramp in last week so it'd be all ready when you came home."

"Nice work." Of course it was. His brother Daniel was a skilled carpenter. Caleb tried to look apprecia-tive, but it was hard when he kept seeing reminders of his helplessness everywhere he looked. "Is Sam still helping with the milking?"

"I told him not to come in the morning anymore. With Thomas Schutz working every day, we're get-ting along all right." Zeb paused. "I was thinking it might be gut to have Thomas stay on full-time even after you're back on your feet. We could use the extra pair of hands."

Caleb shrugged, not willing to make that decision so quickly. Still, Thomas seemed eager to earn the money for his widowed mother, and he was a bright lad. They could do worse than take the boy on until Timothy was of an age to help.

"At least for now we'll keep him full-time," he said. "And we'll have Edith Berger continue with the house and the young ones."

Onkel Zeb stopped pushing when they reached the door. Caleb glanced up and was surprised at the look of discomfort on Zeb's face.

"About Edith…her daughter has been having some health troubles and needs her mamm. So Edith had to go to her. She isn't coming anymore."

Caleb's hands clenched again as the chair bumped over the doorstep into the house. He could hardly care for the kinder when he couldn't even go up the stairs. "We'll have to find someone…"

His words trailed off as they entered the kitchen. A woman in Plain dress stood at the stove, taking a pie from the oven.

"Here's a blessing arrived this morning that we didn't expect." Onkel Zeb sounded as if he forced a note of cheerfulness into his voice. "Look who has komm to help us out."

The woman turned as he spoke. Her soft brown hair was drawn back into a knot under a snowy kapp. She had on a dark green dress with an apron to match that made her hazel eyes look green. The woman wasn't one of the neighbors or someone from the church. It was Jessie Miller, cousin of the wife who'd left him, and the last person he wanted to find in his kitchen.

For a long moment they stared at each other. Jessie's oval face might have been a bit paler than normal, but if she was uncomfortable, she was trying not to show it. Caleb's jaw hardened until it felt it might break. Jessie had offered her assistance once before, just after Alice left, and he'd turned her down in no uncertain terms. What made her think she could expect a wilkom now?

"Caleb." Jessie nodded gravely. "I'm sehr glad to see you home again."

He could hardly say that he was happy to see her, but a warning look from Onkel Zeb reminded him that the kinder were looking on. "Yah, it's wonderful gut to be here." Becky pressed close to the chair, and he put his arm around her. "What are you…how did you get here?" *And why have you komm?*

"Jessie took the bus and got a ride out from town." Zeb sounded determined to fill up the silence with words, probably because he was afraid of what Caleb might say. "It'll be wonderful nice for the kinder to get to know Cousin Jessie, ain't so?"

Caleb frowned at his uncle, unable to agree. He supposed, if he were being fair, that Alice's family deserved some chance to get to know her children, but not now, not like this.

Before he could speak, Zeb had seized the handles of the chair. "I'll show you the room we fixed up for you so you could be on this floor. Becky, you and Timothy give Cousin Jessie a hand with setting the table for supper. Daadi must be hungry, and Onkel Daniel will be in soon."

Becky let go of Caleb reluctantly and went to the

drawer for silverware. Timothy raced to get there first, yanking so hard the drawer would have fallen out if Jessie hadn't grabbed it.

"Ach, you're a strong boy," she said, a bit of laughter in the words. "Best let Becky hand you the things, ain't so?" She smiled at Becky, but his daughter just set her lips together and proceeded with the job. Even at her young age, Becky had a mind of her own.

Zeb pushed Caleb's chair to the back room that had been intended as a sewing room for Alice. The hospital bed looked out of place, but Caleb knew it would be easier to get into and out of than a regular bed.

Once they were inside, Caleb reached back to pull the door closed so no one could overhear. He swung to face his uncle.

"What is she doing here?" he demanded.

Onkel Zeb shrugged, spreading his hands wide. "She just showed up. Seems like word got to Ohio about your getting hurt, and Jessie said she thought she was needed."

"Well, she's not." Caleb clamped down on the words. "We'll do fine without her, so she can just take tomorrow's bus right back again."

"Ach, Caleb, you can't do that." His uncle's lean, weathered face grew serious. "Stop and think. What would folks think if you turned your wife's kin out of the house? What would the bishop and ministers say?"

"I don't want her here." He spun the chair to stare, unseeing, out the window. "I don't need any reminders of what Alice did."

"What Alice did, not Jessie," Zeb reminded him. "It's not Jessie's fault. She wants only to help, maybe thinking she can make up a little for what her cousin did."

"She can't." He bit out the words. It was easy telling himself that he had to forgive Alice. It wasn't easy to do it.

"Even so, you'll have to agree to let her stay for a short visit, at least." His uncle pulled the chair back around to give Caleb the look that said he meant business. "I'll not have you hurting the woman for someone else's wrongdoing."

Onkel Zeb hadn't often given orders to Caleb and his brothers, even though he'd shared the raising of them. But when he did, they listened.

Caleb clenched his jaw, but he nodded. "All right. A short visit—that's all. Then Jessie has to go."

With Caleb out of the room, Jessie discovered that she could breathe again. She hadn't realized how hard this would be.

Caleb had changed over the years, just as she had. She'd first seen him on the day he'd met her cousin, and a lot of years had passed since then. His hair and beard were still the color of a russet apple, and his cheeks were ruddy despite his time in the hospital.

But the blue eyes that had once been wide and enthusiastic seemed frosty now, and lines etched their way across his face. Lines of pain, probably, but maybe also of grief and bitterness. Who could wonder at that, after what Alice had put him through?

Guilt grabbed her at the thought of the cousin who had been like her own little sister. She'd been meant to take care of Alice, but she'd failed.

A clatter of plates brought her back to the present

with a jolt, and she hurried to the kinder. "Let me give you a hand with those," she said, reaching for the precarious stack Becky was balancing.

"I can do it myself." Becky jerked the plates away so quickly they almost slid onto the floor. She managed to get them to the round pine table and plopped them down with a clank. "I don't need help." She shot Jessie an unfriendly look.

Had Becky picked up her father's attitude already? Or maybe she saw herself as the mother of the little family now that Alice was gone. Either way, Jessie supposed she'd best take care what she said.

"We can all use a bit of help now and then," she said easily. "I'm not sure where there's a bowl for the chicken pot pie. Can you help me with that?"

Timothy ran to one of the lower cabinets and pulled the door open. "This one," he announced, pointing to a big earthenware bowl. "That's the one for chicken pot pie. Ain't so, Becky?"

He looked for approval to his big sister, and when she nodded, he gave Jessie an engaging grin. "See?"

"I do see. That's just right, Timothy. Do you like chicken pot pie?"

Still smiling, he nodded vigorously. "And cherry pie, too." He glanced toward the pie she'd left cooling on the counter.

Jessie took the bowl, smiling in return at the irresistible little face. Timothy, at least, was friendly. Probably he wasn't old enough to remember much about his mother, so her leaving and her death hadn't affected him as much as Becky.

She began ladling out the fragrant mix of chicken and homemade noodles. The men would doubtless be back and hungry before long. Even as she thought it, Jessie heard the door of Caleb's room open and the murmur of voices.

"Let's get those hands washed for supper," she told Timothy. "I hear Daadi coming." She reached out to turn on the water in the sink, but Becky pushed her way between Jessie and her brother.

"I'll do it." She frowned at Jessie. "He's my little bruder."

Jessie opened her mouth, found herself with nothing to say and closed it again. Her mother's voice trickled into her mind, and she saw again the worried look on her mother's face.

"I wish you wouldn't go. You'll be hurt."

Well, maybe so, but she couldn't let that stop her from doing what was right. She had to atone for the wrongs Alice had done, and if she was hurt in the process, it was probably what she deserved. Given Becky's attitude, she didn't doubt that Alice's daughter was hurting inside, too.

The hustle of getting food on the table was a distraction when Caleb and his uncle returned to the kitchen. Zeb went to the back door and rang the bell on the porch. Almost before its clamor had stilled, Caleb's brother Daniel came in, pausing to slap Caleb on the back.

"So you're home at last. I thought I would have to sneak you out of that hospital."

Caleb's face relaxed into the easygoing smile Jessie remembered from his younger self. "You just want to have more help around here, that's all."

"Can't blame me for that. I've got the carpentry

business to run, remember? I can't spend all my time milking cows."

Daniel's gaze landed on Jessie, and he gave her a slightly quizzical look. He'd already greeted her when she'd arrived, so he wasn't surprised to find her there as Caleb had been. Maybe he was wondering how Caleb had taken her arrival. If so, she didn't doubt he'd soon see the answer to that question.

She'd have known Caleb and Daniel were brothers even if she'd never seen the two of them before. Their lean, rangy bodies and strong faces were quite similar, though Daniel's hair was a bit darker and of course he didn't have a beard, since he'd never married.

That was strange enough to be remarked on in the Amish community. At twenty-eight, Daniel was expected to have started a family of his own. She'd heard from the talkative driver who brought her from the bus station that folks around here said the three King brothers had soured on women because of their mother's desertion. If that were true, she couldn't imagine Alice's actions had helped any.

There was another brother, too, the youngest. But Aaron's name was rarely mentioned, so Alice had told her once. He'd jumped the fence to the Englisch world a few years ago and hadn't been back since as far as she knew. Nothing about the King boys was typical of Amish males, it seemed.

Jessie found herself seated between Zeb and Timothy, and she scanned the table to be sure she hadn't forgotten anything. Silly to be so nervous about the first meal she'd cooked in this house. It wasn't like she was an inexperienced teenager.

Caleb bowed his head for the silent prayer, and everyone followed suit. Jessie began to say the Lord's Prayer, as she usually did, but found her heart yearning for other words.

Please, Lord, let me do Your will here. Give me a chance to make a difference for Alice's children.

For a moment after the prayer, no one spoke. The dishes started to go around the table, and Jessie helped balance the heavy bowl while Timothy scooped up his chicken pot pie. Warmed by his grin, she passed the bowl on to Caleb. He took it with a short nod and turned away.

Zeb cleared his throat. "It looks like you found everything you needed to make supper." He passed the bowl of freshly made applesauce.

"The pantry is well stocked, that's certain sure. Lots of canned goods." She couldn't help the slight question in her tone, since Alice hadn't been here to do the housewife's job of preserving food last summer.

Zeb nodded. "The neighbors have been generous in sharing what they put up. Some of the women even came over and had a canning frolic when the tomatoes and peppers were ready in the garden."

"That was wonderful kind of them." The King family didn't have any female relatives nearby, so naturally the church would pitch in to help. "And someone made this great dried corn. That's a favorite with my little nieces and nephews."

Before anyone could respond, Becky cut in. "You don't have to go back to the hospital anymore, right, Daadi? So we can get along like always."

Zeb's face tightened a little, and he glanced at Caleb as if expecting him to correct Becky for rudeness. But if Caleb caught the look, he ignored it. "I'll have to go for just a few hours each week. It's what they call physical therapy, when they help me do exercises to get my leg working right again."

Becky's lips drew down in a pout that reminded Jessie of her mother. "I thought you were done."

"The therapy will help your daadi get rid of that heavy cast and out of the chair," Daniel said, flicking her cheek with his finger. "You wouldn't want him to skip that, ain't so?"

Becky shrugged. "I guess not. But only for a little while, right?"

It wasn't surprising that Becky wanted reassurance that her father would be home to stay. She'd certainly had enough upheaval in her young life.

"Don't worry," Caleb said. "We'll soon be back to normal. I promise."

Jessie rose to refill the bowl with pot pie. Caleb glanced her way at the movement, and his intent look was like a harsh word. She knew what he meant by *normal*. He meant without her.

By the time the uncomfortable meal was over, Jessie was glad to have the kitchen to herself while she washed the dishes, though a little surprised that Becky didn't insist on taking over that job, too. The little girl certainly seemed determined to convince everyone that Jessie was unnecessary.

Jessie took her time over the cleaning up, half listening to the murmur of voices from the living room. It sounded as if Caleb was playing a board game with the young ones, and Daniel was helping Timothy keep up with his big sister. The play was punctuated now and then by laughter, and the sound warmed Jessie's heart. Obviously everyone was as glad to have Caleb home as he was to be here.

She was just hanging up the dish towels to dry when Daniel and the children came back in the kitchen and started putting on jackets. "Going someplace?" she asked.

Daniel nodded. "These two like to tell the horses good-night. Timothy says it makes the horses sleep better."

"It does," Timothy declared. "Honest."

"I'm sure you're right," Jessie said. "Do you take them a treat?"

"Carrots," he said, running to the bin in the pantry and coming back with a handful.

"Share with Becky," Daniel prompted, and Timothy handed her a few, obviously trying to keep the lion's share.

Jessie had to smile. "Your mammi used to do that when she was your age," she said.

Timothy looked at her with a question in his eyes, but Caleb spoke from the doorway.

"Best get going. It's almost time for bed."

"Komm, schnell. You heard Daadi." Daniel shooed them out, and the door closed behind them.

"Don't talk about their mother to my children." Caleb's voice grated, and he turned the chair toward her with an abrupt shove from his strong hands that sent it surging across the wide floor boards.

For a moment Jessie could do nothing but stare at him. "I only said that—"

His face darkened. "I know what you said, but I don't want her mentioned. I'm their father, and I will tell them what they need to know about her."

Her thoughts were bursting with objections, but Jessie kept herself from voicing them. "I didn't mean any harm, Caleb. Isn't it better that they hear people speak about Alice naturally?"

The lines in his face deepened, and Jessie felt a pang of regret for the loss of the laughing, open person he'd once been.

"I won't discuss it. You'll have to do as I see fit during your visit."

He'd managed to avoid speaking Alice's name thus far, and that should have been a warning in itself. Arguing would do no good.

"Whatever you say. I'm just here to help in any way I can."

Some of the tension seemed to drain out of Caleb, but not much. She suspected there was more to come, and suspected, too, that she wasn't going to like it.

"Since you're here, you may as well visit with the kinder for a few days." Instead of looking at her, he focused on the National Parks calendar tacked to the kitchen wall. "I'll arrange for you to take the bus back to Ohio on Friday."

"Friday? You mean this Friday? Two days from now?" She hadn't expected this to be easy, but she also hadn't anticipated being turned away so quickly.

Caleb gave a short nod, still not meeting her eyes. He swung the chair away from her as if to dismiss her.

Without thinking, Jessie reached out to stop him, grabbing his arm. His muscles felt like ropes under her hand, and the heat of his skin seared through the cotton of his sleeve. She let go as if she'd touched a hot pan.

"Please, Caleb. I came to help out while you're laid up. Obviously you need a woman here, and your uncle mentioned that the person who had been helping couldn't any longer. Please let me fill in."

A muscle twitched in Caleb's jaw as if he fought to contain himself. "We'll get along fine. We don't need your help."

He sounded like Becky. And arguing with him would do about as much good as arguing with a six-year-old.

Would it help or hurt if she showed him the letter Alice had written a few days before she died, asking Jessie to do what she could for the kinder? While she struggled for an answer, he swung away again and wheeled himself toward the door.

"Friday," he said over his shoulder. "You'll be on Friday's bus."

Chapter Two

Jessie lingered in the kitchen until Daniel and the kinder returned. Becky and Timothy ran straight to the living room, as if they couldn't bear to be parted from their daadi for more than a few minutes. Daniel, with what she thought might have been a sympathetic glance at her, followed them.

She stood, irresolute, watching the red glow in the western sky over the ridge. It turned slowly to pink, fading as dusk crept into the valley. She wasn't used to being surrounded by hills this way. Her area of Ohio was fairly flat—good farmland. These enclosing ridges seemed to cut her off from everything she knew.

Caleb made good use of the land on the valley floor, and his dairy herd of forty head was apparently considered fairly large here. Where the ground started to slope upward toward the ridge, she'd spotted an orchard, with some of the trees already in blossom. Too bad she wouldn't be here to see the fruit begin to form. Caleb would see to that.

She turned abruptly toward the living room. Best make what use she could of the little time he seemed willing to grant her with the kinder. As she entered, she heard Becky's plaintive voice.

"But isn't Daadi going to help us get ready for bed?" She stood in front of her father's wheelchair, and her look of dismay was echoed by the one on Caleb's face.

"Ach, Becky, you know Daadi won't be able to go upstairs for a bit," Zeb gently chided her. "That's why we fixed up the room downstairs for him."

"I'm sorry." Caleb cupped his daughter's cheek with his hand, his expression so tender it touched Jessie's heart. "You go along now, and come tell me good-night when you're ready."

Timothy was already rubbing his eyes. It had been a big day for a not-quite-four-year-old.

"Komm. I'll help you." When Jessie held out her hand, Timothy took it willingly enough.

But Becky's eyes flashed. "We don't need your help."

The sharp words were so unexpectedly rude coming from an Amish child that for a moment Jessie was stunned. She realized Zeb was frowning at Caleb, while Caleb was studiously avoiding his eyes.

"Becky, I'm ashamed of you to speak so to Cousin Jessie." Zeb had apparently decided that Caleb wasn't going to correct the child. "You go up at once with Cousin Jessie, and don't let me hear you talk in such a way again."

Becky looked rebellious for a moment, but at a nod

from her father, she scurried ahead of Jessie and her brother, her cheeks flaming. Jessie, clutching Timmy's hand, hurried after her.

She was quick, but not quite quick enough. Behind her, she heard Zeb's voice.

"Caleb, I should not have had to speak to Becky. It's your job to teach your kinder how to behave."

Caleb's response was an irritable grumble that faded as she reached the top of the stairs.

"That's me and Becky's room," Timothy informed her, pointing. "And that's where Daadi sleeps. Onkel Daniel has that next one."

"Onkel Zeb is sleeping in the little front room," Becky said. "He had to move to make room for you." She shot a defiant look at Jessie.

But Jessie had no intention of responding in kind. Becky must see that rudeness wouldn't drive her away, if that was what the child had in mind. It had been a natural thing in a houseful of men for Zeb to put her into the adjoining daadi haus.

"It was nice of Onkel Zeb to let me use the daadi haus," she said. "He's a kind person, ain't so?"

Becky was forced to nod, and Timothy tugged at Jessie's hand, his sister's rebellion clearly passing over his head. "I'll show you where everything is."

With Timothy's help, Jessie soon figured out how he expected to be gotten ready for bed. She had to smile at his insistence on doing everything exactly the same way as always, according to him. Her brother's kinder were just like that. His wife always said that if they did something once, it immediately became a tradition they mustn't break.

The bathroom was as modern as those in any Englisch house, save for the gas lights. And she'd noticed a battery-powered lantern in the children's bedroom—a sensible solution when a light might be needed quickly. Caleb had done his best to make the farmhouse welcoming for Alice and the kinder, but that hadn't seemed to help Alice's discontent.

Alice had been too young, maybe. Not ready to settle down. She'd thought marriage and the move to Lost Creek, Pennsylvania, would bring excitement. But when life had settled into a normal routine, she hadn't been satisfied.

Jessie had seen her growing unhappiness in her letters. Maybe she'd been impatient with her young cousin, thinking it was time Alice grew up. If she'd been more comforting...

But it was too late for those thoughts. Jessie bent over the sink to help Timothy brush his teeth, but Becky wedged her little body between them to help him instead. *Fair enough*, Jessie told herself. A big sister was expected to look after the younger ones. Maybe if she ignored Becky's animosity, it would fade.

A line from Alice's last letter slid into her mind. *"You were right. I never should have come back here to die. Please, if you love me, try to repair the harm I've done to these precious little ones."*

Jessie's throat tightened. She had begged Alice to stay with her for those final months instead of returning to Caleb. But Alice had been determined, and Jessie hadn't been able to stop questioning her own motives. Whose interests had she had at heart?

Pushing the thought away, she reached over their heads to turn off the water. "All ready? Let's go down and say good-night."

Bare feet slapping on the plank floor, the kinder rushed down the stairs. Following more sedately, she saw them throw themselves at Caleb, and she winced at the kicks his cast took. But he didn't seem to notice.

Caleb cuddled each of them, apparently as reluctant to send them to bed as they were to go. It must have seemed like forever to him since his life had been normal, but she knew him well enough to understand he'd never regret risking injury to help a neighbor. That's who he was, and she admired him even when she was resenting the cool stare he turned on her.

"Go on up to bed now." Caleb helped Timothy slide down from his lap. "Sleep tight."

Smiling, Jessie held out her hands. Once again, Timothy took hers easily, rubbing his eyes with his other hand. But Becky pushed past her to grab Daniel's hand.

"I want Onkel Daniel to tuck me in," she announced.

"Sounds gut," he said, getting up and stretching. "Cousin Jessie and I will see you're all tucked in nice and snug. Ain't so, Cousin Jessie?"

She smiled, grateful that he'd included her. "That we will."

"Let's see how fast we can get upstairs." Daniel snatched up Becky and galloped toward the steps.

"Me, me," Timothy squealed, holding his arms up to Jessie.

Lifting him and hugging him close, she raced up the stairs, and they collapsed on Timothy's bed in a giggling heap. Timothy snuggled against her, seeming eager for a hug, and her heart swelled. If circumstances had been different, he might have been her child.

The unruly thought stuck to her mind like a burr. She remembered so clearly the day she'd met Caleb.

He'd come from Pennsylvania for the wedding of a distant cousin, and she'd been asked to show him around. They'd hit it off at once in a way she'd given up expecting to happen to her.

And he'd felt the same. She was sure of it. That afternoon was surrounded by a golden haze in her memory—the beginning of something lovely. A perfect time—right up to the moment when they'd gone in to supper and Caleb had his first look at Alice. She'd turned from the stove, her cheeks rosy from the heat, strands of cornsilk-yellow hair escaping her kapp to curl around her face, her blue eyes sparkling and full of fun.

Jessie wrenched her thoughts away from that long-ago time. No sense at all in thinking about what might have been. They could only live today, trusting in God's grace, and do their best to make up for past mistakes.

Caleb expected Onkel Zeb to chide him again about Becky's behavior once the others had gone upstairs. His defenses went up at the thought. Becky was his child. It was his responsibility how she behaved.

Unfortunately, that wasn't a very comforting thought. He'd let his own reactions to Jessie's presence influence his daughter's behavior. Besides, Onkel Zeb was as close as a father to him…closer, in some ways, than his own daad had been. It had seemed, after Mamm left, that all the heart had gone out of his father. Onkel Zeb had been the one to step up and fill the role of both parents for him and his brothers.

The unfortunate King men, folks said. Mamm had left Daad, and then Alice had left him. Onkel Zeb's young bride had died within a year of their marriage.

Daniel was definitely not looking for a wife, and as for Aaron—well, who knew what he was doing out in the Englisch world?

He darted a look at his uncle. Onkel Zeb was studying him...patient, just waiting for him to realize himself what should be done.

"Yah, you're right. I'll try to do better with Becky."

"And with Cousin Jessie," Onkel Zeb pointed out. "She is not to blame for Alice's wrongs."

"And Cousin Jessie." He repeated the words dutifully. "At least she's nothing at all like Alice was. She's plain, not pretty and flirty."

"To the *Leit*, plain is gut, remember?" Zeb's lips twitched. "I'd say Jessie has a face that shows who she is...calm, kind, peaceable. Funny that she's never married. It wonders me what the men out in Ohio were thinking to let her get away."

Truth to tell, Caleb wondered, too. If anyone seemed meant to marry and have a flock of kinder to care for, it had been Jessie. His mind flickered briefly to the day they'd met and winced away again. He had no desire to remember that day.

But Onkel Zeb's thoughts had clearly moved on, and he was talking about how things had gone while Caleb was in the hospital.

"...working out fine, that's certain sure. Sam just can't do enough for us, though I keep telling him we're all right. Guess he feels like he wants to repay you, seeing it was his barn where you got hurt."

"That's foolishness, and I'll tell him so myself. As if any of us wouldn't do the same for a neighbor. Sam's got plenty with his own farm to run. They'd best be getting his new barn up soon, ain't so?"

"Barn raising is set for Saturday." Onkel Zeb grinned. "The buggies have been in and out of Sam and Leah's lane all week with the women helping to clean and get the food ready. Nothing like a barn raising to stir folks up."

Caleb was glad Sam's barn would soon be replaced, but Zeb's words had reminded him of something else. "Maybe Leah would know of someone I can hire to help out with the kinder. What do you think?"

Onkel Zeb shrugged. "Not sure why you want to go looking for someone else when you have family right here eager to do it."

Frustration with his uncle had him clenching his hands on the chair. Before he could frame a response, he heard Daniel and Jessie coming back down the stairs. They seemed to be chuckling together over something, and Caleb felt himself tensing. Irrational or not, he wanted his uncle and brother to share his own feelings about Jessie's arrival.

They came in smiling, which just added to his annoyance. Onkel Zeb glanced at them.

"What funny thing did young Timothy say now?" he asked.

"Ach, it wasn't Timmy at all." Daniel grinned. "Cousin Jessie just didn't agree with my version of the story of the three bears."

Jessie shook her head in mock disapproval. "Even Timothy knew there wasn't a wolf in the story of the three bears. That was the three little pigs."

"Maybe you'd best stick to telling them stories about when you and their daadi were small," Zeb suggested. "And not be confusing the kinder. Or better yet, let Jessie tell the bedtime story."

Caleb could feel his face freeze. Zeb made it sound as if Jessie would be around more than a few nights to tell them stories. She wouldn't.

Jessie seemed to sense the awkwardness of the moment. She turned toward the kitchen. "What about some coffee and another piece of pie?"

"Sounds wonderful gut about now." Onkel Zeb seemed to be answering for all of them.

Caleb almost said he didn't want any. But he caught Jessie's gaze and realized how childish that would sound. So he nodded instead. Jessie's guarded expression relaxed in a smile, and for an instant she looked like the girl he'd spent an afternoon with all those years ago.

It was disconcerting. If he hadn't gone to that wedding, if he hadn't met Jessie and through her met her cousin Alice…what would his life have been then?

Jessie cleared up the plates and cups after their dessert, satisfied that her pie, at least, had met with universal approval. She'd have to take any little encouragement she could get.

Zeb and Daniel had gone to the bedroom to set up a few assistance devices the hospital had sent, leaving her and Caleb alone in the kitchen for the moment. She sent a covert glance toward him.

Caleb had his wheelchair pulled up to the kitchen table, and at the moment he was staring at the cup he still held. She suspected that he didn't even see it. His lean face seemed stripped down to the bone, drawn with fatigue and pain. Today had been a difficult transition for him, but he wouldn't want her to express sympathy.

No man wanted to admit to pain or weakness—she knew that well enough from being raised with six brothers. And clearly Caleb would resent it even more coming from her. The hurt she felt for him, the longing to do something to ease his pain...it would have to stay, unspoken, in her heart.

But the silence was stretching out awkwardly between them. "Becky is..." she began. But the words slipped away when Caleb focused on her.

"What about Becky?" He nearly snapped the words.

That didn't bother her. When folks were hurting, they snapped, like an injured dog would snarl even when you were trying to help it.

"She seems so grown-up for her age. Very helpful, especially with her little bruder."

The words of praise seemed to disarm him. "Yah, she is gut with Timothy. Always has been, especially since..." His lips shut tight then.

Especially since Alice left when he was just an infant. Those were the words he didn't want to say. She could hardly blame him. But if only they could speak plainly about Alice, it might do everyone some good.

"I know how Becky feels. I always felt responsible for Alice after her mamm passed."

Caleb's strong jaw hardened. "I don't want to talk about her. Not now. Not ever. I thought I made that clear."

She wanted to tell him that she understood, but that hiding the pain didn't make it go away. It just let it fester. But she couldn't, because he wouldn't listen. If she had more time...

"I'm sorry. I promise I won't say anything about Alice." *Until the day you're willing to talk.* "But please, think twice about sending me away. The kinder are my own blood, like it or not. I want to care for them, and they need me. You need me."

But she could read the answer in his face already. He spun the wheelchair away, knocking against the table leg in his haste. Impulsively she reached out to catch his arm.

"Please…"

The anger in Caleb's eyes was so fierce she could feel the heat of it. He grabbed her wrist in a hard grip and shoved her hand away from him.

"No." Just one word, but it was enough to send her back a step. "We don't need you. I can take care of my kinder on my own. You'll go on the bus on Friday."

Jessie looked after him, biting her lip. She should have known better than to start her plea by referring to Alice. She'd been trying to show that she understood how Becky felt, but she'd approached him all wrong.

Resolutely she turned to the sink and began washing the plates and cups. If a tear or two dropped in the sudsy water, no one would know.

Caleb might not want to hear it, but she did feel responsible for Alice, just as Becky felt responsible for Timothy. She could only hope and pray Becky never went through what she had.

"You're the older one," her mother had always said. *"You're responsible for little Alice."*

Most of the time she'd managed that fairly well. But when she'd grown older, she'd sometimes become impatient with Alice always tagging along behind her. She'd been about eleven when it happened, so Alice had been only eight. She'd tagged along as always when

Jessie and her friends had been walking home from school.

They'd been giggling, sharing secrets, the way girls did when they were just starting to notice boys. And Alice, always there, always impatient when she wasn't the center of attention, had tried to burst into the conversation. She'd stamped her feet, angry at being rejected, and declared she was going to run away.

Jessie's shame flared, as always, when she thought of her response. *"Go ahead,"* she'd said. *"I won't come after you."*

She hadn't meant it. Everyone knew that. But Alice had run off into the woods that lined the path.

"She'll come back," the other girls had said. And Jessie had agreed. Alice was afraid of the woods. She wouldn't go far. She'd trail along, staying out of sight until they were nearly home, and then jump out at them.

But it hadn't worked out that way. Alice hadn't reappeared. Jessie searched for her, at first annoyed, then angry, then panic-stricken. Alice had vanished.

Jessie still cringed at the memory of telling her parents. They'd formed a search party, neighbors pitching in, combing the woods on either side of the path.

Jessie had followed, weeping, unwilling to stay at the house and yet terrified of what the adults might find. She didn't think she'd been quite so terrified since.

It had been nearly dark when the call went up that Alice had been found. Alice wasn't hurt. They'd found her curled up under a tree, sound asleep.

Alice had clung to Jessie more than ever after that experience. And Jessie hadn't dared let herself grow impatient—not once she'd learned what the cost of that could be. She was responsible for Alice, no matter what.

Jessie tried to wipe away a tear and only succeeded in getting soapsuds in her eye. Blinking, she wiped it with a dish towel. She heard a step behind her.

"Ach, Jessie, don't let my nephew upset you."

She turned, managing to produce a slight smile for Zeb.

Zeb moved a little closer, his weathered face troubled. "You think it would be better to talk more openly about Alice, ain't so?"

She evaded his keen gaze. "Caleb doesn't agree, and they are his kinder."

Zeb didn't speak for a moment. Then he sighed. "Do you know why I was so glad to see you today?"

"Because you are a kind person," she said. "Even Alice…" She stopped. She'd promised not to mention Alice.

"Even Alice liked me, ain't so?" His smile was tinged with sorrow. "This business of not talking about her—Caleb is making a mistake, I think. You can't forgive if you can't be open."

"Some things are harder to forgive than others."

"All the more important to forgive, ain't so?" He patted her shoulder awkwardly. "Don't give up. Promise me you won't."

She didn't know how she'd manage it, but she was confident in her answer. "I didn't come this far just to turn around and go back home again."

Renewed determination swept through her. It seemed she had one person on her side, at least. And she wasn't going to give up.

Chapter Three

Caleb woke early, disoriented for a moment at not hearing the clatter of carts and trays. He wasn't in the hospital any longer. He was home. Thankfulness swept through him, replaced by frustration the instant he moved and felt the weight of the cast dragging him down.

He was home, and those were the familiar sounds of going out to do the milking. He heard the rumble of Onkel Zeb's and Daniel's voices, and then the thud of the back door closing.

The source of the sound switched, coming through the back window now. Thomas Schutz must have arrived—he was calling a greeting to the others, sounding cheerful despite having walked across the fields in the dark.

Onkel Zeb was right about the lad. They should keep

him on, even after Caleb was well enough to take on his own work. That would free Daniel to spend more time with his carpentry business instead of being tied to so many farm chores.

Caleb sat up and leaned to peer out the window. Still dark, of course, but the flashlight one of them carried sent a circle of light dancing ahead of them. Caleb's hand clenched. He should be out there with them, not lying here in bed, helpless.

Stop thinking that way, he ordered himself. He might not be up to doing the milking or going upstairs to put the kinder to bed, but for sure there were things he could do. The sooner the better.

Using his hands to move the cast, Caleb swung his legs out of bed and sat there for a moment, eyeing the wheelchair with dislike. He didn't have a choice about using it, so he'd have to figure out how to do things with it.

First things first. If he got up and dressed by himself, he'd feel more like a man and less like an invalid. His clothes were not far away, draped on the chair where Onkel Zeb had put them the previous night. That clamp-like gripper on a long handle was obviously intended for just such a situation. Maybe he should have paid more attention to the nurse who'd explained it to him.

Getting dressed was a struggle. He nearly ripped his shirt, and got so tangled in his pants he was blessed not to end up on the floor. But when it was done, and he'd succeeded in transferring himself from the bed to the wheelchair, Caleb felt as triumphant as if he'd milked the entire herd himself.

A few shoves of the wheels took him out to the

kitchen. Fortunately Zeb or Daniel had left the light fixture on, since he'd never have been able to reach that. Well, he was here, and a few streaks of light were beginning to make their way over the ridge to the east.

Jessie hadn't appeared from the daadi haus yet. The small separate house was reached by a covered walkway. It was intended to be a residence for the older generation in the family, leaving the farmhouse itself for the younger family. When he and Alice had married, Onkel Zeb had moved in. Now Jessie was staying there, at least temporarily.

Definitely temporarily. Given how irritable she made him, the sooner she left, the better.

"The kinder need me. You need me." That was more or less what Jessie had flung at him last night. Well, he was about to prove her wrong. He'd get breakfast started on his own. Even if he couldn't go up the stairs, he could still care for his own children.

Oatmeal was always a breakfast favorite. Fortunately, the pot he needed was stored in one of the lower cabinets. Maneuvering around the refrigerator to get the milk was more of a challenge.

Feeling pleased with himself, he poured milk into the pot without spilling a drop. Now for the oatmeal. This would need the gripper, but he'd brought it out of the bedroom with him. Congratulating himself on his foresight, he used it to open the top cupboard door. The oatmeal sat on the second shelf. Maybe he ought to have someone rearrange the kitchen a bit to make the things he'd need more accessible. In the meantime, he could make do with what he had.

Caleb reached with the gripper but found it wavering with the effort of holding it out with the whole length of his arm. A little more… He touched the cylinder of oatmeal, tried to get the prongs open and around it. Not quite… He leaned over the counter, focused on the elusive box, determined to get it down.

He reached, grabbed at it, lost his hold, sent the oatmeal tipping, spilling down in a shower of flakes. The chair rolled with the imbalance of his body. He tried to stop it, and then he was falling, the floor rushing up to meet him. He landed with an almighty thud that felt as if it shook the house.

For an instant he lay there, stunned. Then, angry with himself, he flattened his palms against the floor and tried to push himself up.

"Wait." A flurry of steps, and Jessie was kneeling next to him, her hand on his arm. "Don't try to move until you're sure you aren't hurt."

The anger with himself turned against her, and he jerked away. "It's not your concern."

"Yah, yah, I know." She sounded, if anything, a little amused. "You are fine. You probably intended to drop down on the floor."

Apparently satisfied that he was okay, she reached across him to turn the chair into position and activate the brake. "Next time you decide to reach too far and overbalance, lock the wheels first."

Much as he hated to admit it to himself, she was right. He'd been so eager to show her he could manage that he'd neglected the simplest precaution. While he was still fumbling for words to admit it, Jessie put her arm around him and braced herself.

"Up we go. Feel behind you for the chair to guide yourself." Her strength surprised him, but no more than her calm reaction to what he'd done.

It took only a moment to settle himself in the chair again. He did a quick assessment and decided he hadn't damaged himself.

Jessie, ignoring him, was already cleaning up the scattered oats. He had to admit, she was quick and capable, even if she was bossy.

"Aren't you going to say you told me so?" he asked.

She glanced up from her kneeling position on the floor, eyes widening as if startled. Then her lips curled slightly. "I have six brothers, remember? I've dealt with stubborn menfolk before. There's no use telling them."

"I suppose one of them broke his leg, so that makes you an expert."

"Two of the boys, actually." She finished cleaning the oatmeal from the floor and dumped a dustpan full into the trash. "Plus a broken arm or two. And then there was the time Benjy fell from the hayloft and broke both legs." Jessie shook her head. "He got into more trouble than the rest of them put together."

He watched as she started over making the oatmeal. Yah, *capable* was the right word for Jessie. Like Onkel Zeb said, it was surprising no man had snapped her up by now. She was everything an Amish wife and mother should be. Everything Alice hadn't been.

Caleb shoved that thought away, even as he heard voices. The others had finished the milking.

Jessie darted a quick glance at him. "No reason that anyone else needs to know what happened, ain't so?"

He had to force his jaw to unclamp so he could produce a smile. "Denke."

Jessie's face relaxed in an answering grin.

Onkel Zeb came in at that moment—just in time

to see them exchanging a smile. He cast a knowing look at Caleb.

Caleb started to swing the chair away, only to be stymied because the lock was on. Still, he didn't have to meet his uncle's gaze. He knew only too well what Zeb was thinking.

All right, so maybe Jessie wasn't as bad as he'd made out. Maybe she was deft and willing and good with children. But he still didn't want to have her around all the time, reminding him of Alice.

Jessie's heart had been in her mouth when she'd heard the crash in the kitchen, knowing Caleb must have fallen. She'd been halfway along the covered walkway, and she'd dashed as fast as she could for the house door. When she'd entered the kitchen...

Well, it had taken all the control she had to put on a calm exterior. Even so, her heart hadn't stopped thumping until he was back in the chair and she could see he was all right.

She set a bowl of oatmeal down in front of him with a little more force than necessary. He was fortunate. Didn't he realize that? He could have ended up back in the hospital again.

A stubborn man like Caleb probably wouldn't admit it, even to himself. Any more than he'd admit that he could use her help. Apparently it would take more than a broken leg to make him willing to have her near him.

She slipped into her chair as Caleb bent his head for the prayer. Then she started the platter of fried scrapple around the table. Timothy took a couple of pieces eagerly, but she noticed that Becky didn't serve herself any until she saw her father frown at her. Obviously Jessie wasn't going to win Becky over easily.

Jessie's heart twisted at the sight of that downturned little mouth. Becky looked as if she'd been meant by nature to be as sunny a child as Timothy, but life had gotten in the way. If only Jessie could help...but there was no sense thinking that, unless she could change Caleb's mind.

The men were talking about whether or not it was too early to plant corn, all the while consuming vast quantities of food. Jessie had forgotten how much a teenage boy like Thomas could eat. He seemed a little shy, and he was all long legs and arms and gangly build. Tomorrow morning she'd fix more meat, assuming Caleb didn't intend to chase her out even before breakfast.

"Sam says he'll komm on Monday and help get the corn planted," Zeb said. "Told him he didn't need to, but there was no arguing with him."

Jessie noticed Caleb's hand wrapped around his fork. Wrapped? No, *clenched* would be a better word. His knuckles were white, and she guessed that the fork would have quite a bend in the handle when he was done.

Caleb wouldn't believe it, but that was exactly how she felt when he refused to let her help.

Timothy tugged at her sleeve. "Can I have more oatmeal?"

"For sure." She rose quickly, glad there was something she could do, even if it was only dishing up cereal.

"I love oatmeal." Timothy watched her, probably to

be sure she was giving him enough. "Especially with brown sugar. Lots of brown sugar," he added hopefully.

"A spoonful of brown sugar," Caleb said firmly, coming out of his annoyance. Jessie met his eyes, smiling, and nodded, adding a heaping spoonful of brown sugar that she hoped would satisfy both of them.

"Shall I stir it in?" she asked, setting the bowl in front of Timothy.

He shook his head vigorously. "I like it to get melty on top." He sent a mischievous glance toward his uncle. "Onkel Daniel does, too."

Daniel laughed. "You caught me. But I'll need lots of energy at the shop today. New customers coming in to talk to me about a job." He looked up at the clock. "Guess I should get on my way."

With Daniel's departure, everyone seemed ready to finish up. Soon they were all scooting away. Left alone with the dishes, Jessie looked after them. She'd think Becky was old enough to be helping with the dishes. Probably her desire to take over didn't extend to the dishes. She'd certain sure been doing that at Becky's age. But she wasn't going to be here long enough to make any changes.

When she'd finished cleaning up the kitchen, Jessie followed the sound of voices to the living room. Becky stood backed up to the wheelchair, a hair brush in her hand. "It's easy, Daadi. Just make two braids, that's all."

Jessie stood watching, oddly affected by the sight of the vulnerable nape of the child's neck. Caleb had managed to part Becky's long, silky hair, and now he clutched one side, looking at it a little helplessly.

Gesturing him to silence, Jessie stepped up beside

him and took the clump of hair. For an instant she thought he'd object, but then he grudgingly nodded. Jessie deftly separately the hair into three strands and began to braid.

Caleb watched the movement of her fingers so intently that she imagined them warming from his gaze. If he were going to be doing this he'd have to learn... but of course he wouldn't. He'd find some other woman to take her place once he'd gotten Jessie out of the way. Maybe he already had someone lined up.

But it couldn't possibly be anyone who'd love these children more than she did. She'd come here loving them already because they were all that was left of Alice. Now she'd begun to love them for themselves... Timothy with his sparkling eyes and sunny smile, Becky with her heart closed off so tightly that she couldn't let go and be a child.

Feeling Becky's silky hair sliding through her fingers took her right back to doing the same for Alice, laughing together as she tried to get her wiggly young cousin to hold still. From the time Alice's mother died, she'd been a part of Jessie's family—the little sister Jessie had always longed for. To help raise Alice's kinder, to have a second chance to do it right this time...that was all she wanted. But with Caleb in opposition, apparently it was too much to ask.

The braiding was done too quickly. She showed Caleb how to do the fastening and then stepped back out of the way while he took his daughter by the shoulders and turned her around. "There you are. All finished."

"Denke, Daadi." Becky threw her arms around his

neck in a throttling hug. "I'm wonderful happy you're home."

"Me, too, daughter." He patted her.

The thump of footsteps on the stairs announced Timothy. He jumped down the last two steps and ran into the living room. "I brushed my teeth and made my bed," he announced. "Can I show Cousin Jessie the chickens now?"

"She'll like that," Caleb said solemnly. Then he gave her a slight smile. He turned to Becky. "You go along, too."

For an instant Becky looked rebellious, but then her desire to please her daadi won, and she nodded. Timothy was already tugging at Jessie's hand. Together they went through the kitchen and out the back door.

"The chickens are this way." Timothy pulled her toward the coop. "Reddy is my very own hen. I want to see if she has an egg for me."

"In a minute." She tried to slow him down. "Look. Is that someone coming to see us?"

Jessie pointed across the pasture toward the neighboring farm. A woman and a little boy walked toward them, the boy carrying a basket by the handle. He couldn't have been much more than four or five, and he held it carefully as if mindful of his responsibility.

"It's Jacob and his mammi." Timothy dropped her hand to plunge toward the new arrivals. "Look, Becky." His sister nodded and joined him at a trot.

Jessie stood where she was and waited, unsure. This was obviously the wife of the man who'd been helping so much. It was in their barn that Caleb had been injured, and Jessie had formed the opinion that Leah and

Sam were close friends of his. That being the case, she wasn't sure what kind of reception she was likely to get.

Leah and Jacob drew nearer. Caleb's kinder had reached them, and Timothy was chattering away a mile a minute to Jacob, who just kept nodding. Taking a deep breath, Jessie went to meet them.

"You'll be Jessie. Alice's cousin." The woman's smile was cautious. She was thirty-ish, probably about Jessie's age, with a wealth of dark brown hair pulled back under her kapp and a pair of warm brown eyes. "Wilkom."

"Denke." It was nice to be welcomed, even if Leah sounded as though she were reserving judgment. Jessie smiled at the boy. "And this must be Jacob."

The boy nodded, holding out the basket to her. "Shoofly pie," he announced. "For you."

"I wasn't sure what you needed," Leah explained. "But I thought a couple of shoofly pies were always of use."

"They surely are," she replied. "Denke."

A lively controversy had already broken out between Timothy, who wanted Jacob to look for eggs with him, and Becky, who thought he'd rather play ball.

"You should do what your visitor wants," she informed her brother loftily.

"Chickens first," Jacob said. "Then ball."

Jessie couldn't help smiling as the three of them ran off toward the chicken coop. "Jacob is a man of few words, I see."

Leah's face took on a lively, amused look that Jessie suspected was more normal to her than her cautious greeting. "Especially when he's around Timothy. Does that boy ever stop talking to you?"

"Only when he's asleep." She looked after them. "I wish Becky…"

"I know." Leah's voice warmed. "If only Becky would loosen up and talk about things, she'd be better off."

"You see it, too, then. It's not just me."

Leah shook her head, and that quickly, the barriers between them collapsed under the weight of their common concern for the child. "No, it's not just you. She may be worse with you, though, because…" She stopped, flushing.

"Because of my relationship with her mother. I know. I don't blame her."

"Still, she must learn to forgive her mother, or she'll be carrying the burden around with her for the rest of her life."

Leah's insight touched Jessie to the core. "That's what I think, too." Unfortunately, Caleb didn't see it that way.

Leah seemed to measure her with a serious gaze. Finally Leah gave a brisk nod. "Maybe you'll be able to reach her while you're here."

"I won't be here long enough, I'm afraid. Caleb… well, I am leaving tomorrow."

"You mean Caleb is insisting you leave tomorrow, ain't so?" Leah frowned. "I've known Caleb King all my life, so I guess I understand. Everyone knows the King men have always been unfortunate with women. It's turned him sour, I fear."

Jessie stared at her. "I heard something like that from the driver who brought me out from town, but I wasn't sure whether to believe it."

"They've had a string of unhappy situations with

women, that's certain sure," Leah said. "Zeb losing his young wife, and then Caleb's mammi running off and leaving the three young ones. And after what happened with Alice…well, it's not surprising folks think so. Or that it's made Caleb bitter."

She hadn't realized just how deep that belief ran from the way Leah spoke of it. Poor Caleb. She knew full well that his attitude wasn't surprising. She just wished she could make a difference.

Leah was watching her, and Jessie had to say something.

"You are wonderful kind to care so much about your neighbors. I just wish we could get to know each other better."

"Yah, I wish it, too." Leah clasped her hand, smiling. "Maybe you could dig in your heels and refuse to leave. Then what would Caleb do? He couldn't carry you out."

They were still laughing at the image when the kinder came running up to them. "Can we help with the barn raising on Saturday, Leah?" Becky looked more enthusiastic than Jessie had ever seen her. "Please?"

"You'll have to ask your daadi. If he says so, we'd certain sure like to have your help. There's lots you can do." Leah held out her hand to her son. "Now we must be getting home to fix lunch. We'll komm again when we can stay longer." She gave Jessie a warm glance. "I hope you'll be here."

"It was wonderful gut to meet you, anyway. And we appreciate the shoofly pies."

Timothy grabbed the basket handle as they walked away. "Can we have some shoofly pie, Cousin Jessie?"

"I'll help carry it," Becky said. "Let's ask Daadi about the barn raising."

They headed for the house, the basket swinging between them, and Jessie followed, smiling a little. For a moment there, in her enthusiasm for the barn raising, Becky had looked like any happy little girl. Somehow the glance gave Jessie hope. That child existed in Becky, if only she could bring her out.

Caleb sat at the kitchen table with a cup of coffee, looking a little startled at the excitement of the children. They swung the basket onto the edge of the table and rushed at their father.

"Daadi, we saw Leah and Jacob." Timothy rushed the words, wanting to be first.

"Leah says we can go to the barn raising on Saturday if you say it's all right." Becky wasn't far behind. "We'll help."

Caleb seemed to have mixed feelings about the barn raising. Was it the fact that he'd been injured when the old barn burned? Or maybe just the thought that ordinarily, he'd be up on the beams with the rest of the community, making sure the barn was finished for his neighbor?

"Barn raising is for grown-ups. I don't know how you'd help," he said.

"Jacob says he's going to carry water. I could do that." Timothy straightened as if to emphasize how tall he was.

"We could carry the food Cousin Jessie fixes. Leah said they could find something for us to do." Becky didn't look at Jessie when she said the words, but apparently she didn't mind using her if it meant she'd be allowed to help.

Apparently Caleb hadn't told them she was leaving tomorrow.

She touched their shoulders. "Why don't you give Daadi a minute to think? You go and wash your hands, and I'll cut the shoofly pie."

When they'd stampeded toward the bathroom, she turned back to Caleb. "I guess the young ones don't know I have to leave tomorrow. I'll explain to them."

"You don't have to do that."

She frowned slightly. "You mean you'd rather explain it yourself?"

"No." His voice was gruff. "I mean I've been thinking about you leaving. Maybe I was a bit hasty. If you want to, you can stay. But just until I get back on my feet again. That's all."

It wasn't the most gracious of offers, but she was too relieved to boggle at that. She felt as if an intolerable pressure had been lifted from her heart.

"Denke." Jessie struggled not to let her emotions show in her voice. "I would like that, Caleb."

Her time was still limited, but at least she had been given a chance. A quick prayer of thanks formed in her mind.

Please, dear Father. Show me what to do for these precious children.

Chapter Four

Following the noise late Friday morning, Caleb rolled himself into the kitchen. It had turned into a beehive of activity since breakfast, with racks of cookies cooling while Jessie pushed another pan into the oven. Both Timothy and Becky were intent upon baking projects, Timothy with a dish towel tied around him like an apron. Young Thomas leaned against the counter, seeming right at home with a handful of snickerdoodles.

"What's going on?"

His voice brought all the activity to a halt for an instant. Thomas straightened up, flushing and trying to look as if he didn't have his mouth full of cookies.

Jessie straightened, as well, closing the oven door. She was flushed and smiling, and with her eyes sparkling, she didn't look as plain as he'd thought. "We're

baking for the barn raising tomorrow. All those workers need plenty of fuel."

"Look, Daadi." Timothy waved a fistful of dough in
the air. "I'm making the little balls, see? When Cousin
Jessie bakes them, they'll be snickerdoodles."

Caleb wheeled himself closer to the table. "I see.
What's Becky doing?"

"I'm rolling them in cinnamon and sugar." Becky's
attention was grabbed by the dough Timothy had in
his hand. "That's not how to do it, Timothy. They're
supposed to be round. Let me."

Timothy flared up instantly. "This is how I do it.
You do your own."

Becky reached out to take the dough from him, but
before it could turn into a fight, Jessie was there.

"Becky, can you help me? I need these cookies
moved to the cooling tray to make room for the next
batch. You're old enough to be careful not to touch the
hot pan, I know."

Distracted instantly by the thought of doing something Timothy wasn't allowed to do, Becky abandoned
the battle over the shape of Timothy's cookies, and
peace reigned.

Thomas seemed to sidle toward the door, and Caleb
waved him back. "Stay and help if you want." He
pushed his chair through the doorway and out onto
the back porch.

The sun's rays warmed his face, and he inhaled the
familiar aroma of the farm, overlain by the baking
scent coming from the kitchen. He should have been
grateful just to be home instead of fretting about all
that he couldn't do, but it was hard to be helpless.

Still, if he could manage a little more each day, he'd

see progress. He just had to make up his mind to it. The sooner he was back on his feet, the sooner life would return to normal. Without Jessie's disruptive presence.

Hands on the wheels, he rolled himself carefully down the ramp, pleased when he reached the bottom without incident. He turned toward the barn and spotted Onkel Zeb and his brother coming toward him.

"You're out and rolling!" Daniel exclaimed. "Gut work." He grabbed Caleb's shoulder, his face creasing in pleasure.

Maybe Daniel's pleasure was mixed with relief. If the past weeks had been hard on Caleb, they'd been hard on everyone else, too.

"I had to get out," Caleb said. "If you wander into the kitchen, you might get sucked into helping with all the baking that's going on for tomorrow."

"That doesn't scare me off." Daniel headed for the steps. "I'll talk Jessie into a bag of cookies to take to the shop with me." He waved in the direction of his carpentry shop, located in its own building about twenty yards beyond the barn.

"Don't say I didn't warn you." He turned his attention to his uncle. "Thomas is in there, but he looks like he's doing more eating than helping."

Onkel Zeb shook his head. "I don't know where that boy puts it all. He's as skinny as a rake, and he eats all the time." He put his hand on the chair handle. "Headed for the barn?"

"Seems like a gut jaunt. The doctor said to keep busy."

"He probably also said to be careful not to overdo." Zeb moved as if to push the chair toward the barn.

Caleb tried to turn the wheels on his own, but it was

a lot harder than he'd expected on the gravel lane. He gritted his teeth and put more muscle into it. He'd have to try harder. Zeb grasped the handles and pushed, too.

For a moment they didn't speak, but then Onkel Zeb cleared his throat. "Seems like you decided Cousin Jessie can stay."

"For a while," Caleb said quickly. He didn't want any misunderstanding on that score. "Just until I get back on my feet."

"What made you change your mind?"

He couldn't see his uncle's face since he was pushing the chair, but he should have known Zeb would want an explanation. And he didn't have one, not really.

"I got to thinking about what you said. About her being kin to the young ones." He hesitated, remembering how he'd felt when Jessie had interceded to braid Becky's hair and then stepped back to let him take the credit. "I have to admit, she seems to care about them."

"She must, giving up her business to komm all the way from Ohio to help, ain't so?"

Caleb blinked. "Business? What business? I thought she just lived with her brother and his wife."

"She does. She helps out a lot there, too. But she has a business of her own, making baked goods to take to the Amish markets in a couple of towns. Way I hear it, it's turned into quite a success."

Caleb stopped pushing and swung to face his uncle. "How do you know all this?"

"All you have to do is talk to get to know a person." There was a chiding tone to Zeb's voice that made itself heard. He meant that Caleb should have done the same.

Caleb ducked away from the implied criticism. "I

guess that's why she looks like she does about all that baking she's doing," he muttered.

"How does she look?"

Caleb shrugged. "I don't know. Happy, I guess." Pretty. Not beautiful, the way Alice had been when they'd met, but appealing in her own way.

"If she's used to baking for market, I guess she'd take a little thing like a barn raising in her stride." Onkel Zeb frowned a little. "As for the barn raising, are you wanting to go over for it?"

Caleb's jaw tightened, and he slapped the chair. "Not likely I can be much help, is it?" Besides, he wasn't sure he wanted to visit the site of his injury so soon. He'd relived the accident enough times already.

But Onkel Zeb's frown had deepened. "Sam's been doing a lot for us while you've been laid up. Seems like it's only neighborly to go over for a spell. Visit with folks, anyway. I was thinking you could use the pony cart. It's low enough that it wouldn't be hard to get in, and the chair could go in the back."

When Caleb didn't answer right away, his uncle shrugged. "Think on it, anyway."

It wasn't easy to hold back when Zeb gave him the look that said he'd be disappointed in Caleb if he didn't go. So he supposed he'd be hauling himself into the pony cart tomorrow.

But as for his uncle's other expectation—well, why should he be interested in finding out more about Jessie's life? She'd be gone soon enough, anyway, and he wouldn't have to think about her at all. That would suit him fine, wouldn't it?

Jessie brought the pony cart up to the bottom of the ramp on Saturday. She'd been wryly amused at the expression on Caleb's face when he'd realized he'd have to let her help him get to Sam and Leah's, since Zeb and Daniel, along with Thomas, had gone as soon as they'd eaten breakfast.

She stopped the black-and-white pony so that the cart was directly in front of Caleb waiting in his wheelchair. Timothy and Becky were on either side of him, Timothy bouncing up and down in excitement.

"Here we are." Jessie hopped out of the cart and scooted around the wheelchair. "I think it will work best if the chair is right next to the cart seat." She moved it into position as she spoke and then set the brake.

Caleb didn't say anything, but he looked as if he held quite a few words back. He reached out for the cart. She intercepted him.

"Better let Becky get up there first, and she can steady the cast and help lift it in. Right, Becky?"

"For sure." She was already scrambling in, eager to help her daadi.

"Me, too." Timothy pouted.

"We need you to hold the chair steady so it doesn't wobble when Daadi pushes off it. You think you can?" Jessie asked.

"Sure. I'm strong." He seized the arm of the wheelchair and planted both feet, gritting his teeth.

"I can swing myself over." Caleb sounded for all the world like his son. He grasped the rail on the cart seat. It was lower than a buggy, but still higher than the wheelchair.

"A little extra help never hurts." Before he could object, Jessie slid her arm around him. "Ready? Go."

She hadn't given him time to argue, but she felt him stiffen, probably not liking her so close.

And they were close, very much so. Caleb grasped her shoulder with his free hand, his body pressing against hers for what seemed a long moment. Fighting not to react, Jessie concentrated on lifting him. Becky grabbed the cast, and in a moment Caleb was seated in the pony cart, breathing heavily.

She was breathless, too, but not from the exertion. She hadn't expected—well, whatever it was she'd felt when she'd held him against her.

Nothing, she told herself fiercely, and knew it wasn't true. It seemed the feelings that had been aroused that long-ago afternoon were still there, ready to flare up. Maybe that was why her mother feared coming here would hurt her.

While the kinder argued about who was going to sit next to Daadi, Jessie folded the wheelchair and lifted it into the back of the cart. Then she placed the tins of cookies in with it.

"Just hush," Caleb said. "One of you should walk over with Cousin Jessie since there's not room for all in the cart. Who will it be?"

Neither of them wanted to, she thought with a stab of pain. Of course they'd both rather go with Caleb. "It's all right," she began, but before she'd finished, Timothy had hopped down.

"I'll walk with you, Cousin Jessie." He took her hand. Her heart gave a thump at the feel of his small hand put so trustingly in hers. Mamm had been right—being here hurt, and leaving would hurt even more.

But that didn't matter. Nothing mattered except helping Alice's children face life happily again.

Timothy beguiled the short walk by talking about what kind of barn he'd build when he was big enough. Jessie encouraged him even while she was keeping an eye on the pony cart and hoping Caleb wasn't overestimating his strength. But the cart arrived safely, and she could see several of the men helping him down and establishing him in the wheelchair. He was probably delighted that he didn't have to rely on her this time.

They had barely reached the fringe of the crowd of helpers when a smiling teenage girl appeared. "I'm helping to look after the kinder. Timothy, why don't you come along so your cousin can help the women with the food?"

Timothy switched over happily enough, spotting his friend Jacob with the other children. Jessie wasn't surprised that the girl knew who she was. Everyone in Lost Creek probably knew it by now. How they felt about it was another matter. Everyone here had known Alice. They had known what she did to her family. Would their attitude toward her carry over to Jessie?

Another teenager had gathered up Becky, and Caleb was surrounded by a group of men, so Jessie headed for the pony cart to get the cookie tins. Leah would probably want them brought to the kitchen, and the sooner she managed to face these people, the better.

The kitchen buzzed with activity. Women unpacked food and tried to put just one more casserole in an already crowded oven. Jessie hesitated inside the screen door, searching for Leah, and spotted her wedging a dish onto the refrigerator shelf.

Jessie made her way to Leah, aware of furtive glances from the other women. "Leah?"

Leah turned, her face warming with a smile even

though she looked as distracted as any homemaker would who had a few too many people in her kitchen. "Jessie, I'm wonderful glad you came. Did Caleb make it, as well?"

Jessie nodded. "He used the pony cart. Easier to get into with his cast."

"Gut, gut. He'll be wanting to be outside after all that time in the hospital." Leah glanced around as a pan clattered in the sink.

"You're busy," Jessie said quickly. "Where do you want these tins? They're snickerdoodles and whoopie pies."

Leah looked for an available flat surface and didn't find one. "Let's put them in the pantry for now." She led the way. "My shelves are getting empty now that the winter is over."

The pantry still looked very well stocked with Leah's canning, but Jessie found an empty shelf and slid the tins onto it. "Is there something I can do to help?"

Leah rolled her eyes. "Everyone asks that, but just now, I need to get organized. Once it's nearly time to serve the men, I'll need everyone's hands. Until then..."

"You'd prefer our space to our presence," Jessie said, smiling. "I understand. I'll be back."

When she returned to the kitchen, she saw that most of the other women, having deposited their offerings, were scattering outside. Leah would have organized some reliable workers, probably kinfolk, to be her aides, and they'd work best without interference. Jessie was too used to the routine of this sort of work frolic to have any doubts.

Outside, Jessie paused on the back porch to get her

bearings. Long tables, probably the same ones that would be turned into benches for worship on Sunday, were already set up, and the teenage girls had the young ones corralled a safe distance from the barn going up. She caught a glimpse of Becky and Timothy chasing around with other kinder in some sort of game.

The barn was already taking shape, as the men had been hard at work since dawn. They swarmed over it like so many purposeful bees, each worker knowing the task assigned to him. Sam and Leah must be sehr happy to see their whole community contributing to their new barn. She could well remember the day the new barn had gone up on her brother's farm—he hadn't been able to stop smiling all day.

Jessie searched for Caleb almost without planning it. His wheelchair was placed next to a long wooden table that held supplies the workers would need. Even from here, she could see the tension in his figure— the way his hands gripped the arms of the chair as if he'd propel himself out of it. Watching the work go on without him must have made him feel more helpless than ever. Maybe it would have been best...

"Don't worry too much about Caleb." The unexpected voice came from behind her, and Jessie swung around to see an older woman watching her with sympathy in her face. "There, my husband is talking to him. Josiah will keep him from fretting."

Jessie suspected her cheeks were red. "I didn't... I mean..."

"Ach, I know." The woman patted her arm. "I'm Ida. Ida Fisher, Sam's mother." She gestured toward the addition to the farmhouse. "We moved into the daadi haus a few years back to give Leah and Sam's family more space. And you are Alice's cousin, komm all the way from Ohio to help out."

Jessie nodded cautiously. This woman, at least, didn't seem to harbor ill will toward her because of Alice. "I arrived on Wednesday."

"I know," she said again, chuckling this time. "The Amish grapevine works wonderful fast here in Lost Creek. Are you finding your way around all right?"

"It's fine. Onkel Zeb is a big help. And Timothy isn't shy about telling me how things should be done."

"He's a talker, that one. Such a sweet child. He and our little Jacob are growing up gut friends, just like his daadi and Caleb always were. So you don't need to worry that Caleb will get into mischief trying to help. Josiah is looking out for him, and Sam will, too. The two of them have taken care of each other more times than I can count—even when the barn was burning."

"That was when Caleb was hurt, ain't so?" She'd heard only a brief reference to the accident since she'd been here.

"The Lord was watching over both of them that day, that's certain sure." Ida's blue eyes misted with tears. "They were getting the animals out when they saw a burning timber coming toward them, Sam says. Caleb jumped, but it came down right on his leg."

Jessie touched Ida's arm in quick sympathy. "I'd guess Sam got him out, ain't so?"

Ida nodded, blotting the tears away with her fingers. "Yah, he did. I'm being foolish, crying when they're both safe. But that's how those two boys always were, getting into trouble together and pulling each other out."

"Caleb's fortunate to have such gut friends and

neighbors to help him, especially since Alice…" Jessie stopped, not really wanting to talk about Alice with someone she hardly knew.

"Poor Alice." Ida shook her head. "The way I see it, she's paid for whatever mistakes she made. It's way past time for forgiveness."

Jessie's throat was tight. "I wish everyone felt that way."

Ida studied her face as if searching for answers. Whatever she saw seemed to satisfy her, because she gave a short nod.

"Maybe your visit will help. Make Caleb and the rest of the community face what they're feeling. The gut Lord forgives us in the same measure that we forgive others. That should give all of us pause, ain't so?"

Jessie nodded, and Ida gave her hand a little pat. "I see Josiah has gone off to check on something. May be a gut time for you to see if Caleb needs anything."

Was that a hint? If so, maybe she'd best follow it. Sam's mother seemed the kind of wise woman her own mother was, who always saw beneath the surface of other folks.

At least Ida was ready to be friendly, as was Leah. Perhaps Jessie's acceptance here wouldn't be so difficult after all.

She stopped a step or two short of Caleb's chair. He hadn't noticed her, probably because his gaze was intent on the workers busy erecting the framing for the barn's loft. Well, she couldn't just stand here.

"They're working quickly." A foolish comment, but at least it drew Caleb's attention.

He glanced at her and then gave a short nod. Impossible to tell what he was thinking when he wore that stern expression.

"It's going to be a bit larger than the last one, according to Sam," he said just when she thought he wasn't going to speak. "He's been impatient to get it up."

Jessie's tension eased. At least he was talking to her. Maybe she could distract him from thinking that he ought to be up there, balancing on a beam, hammer in hand.

"Close to a month they've been waiting, so Onkel Zeb says. No wonder he's eager to see it done."

"Yah, he says it was one thing after another—first delays at the sawmill, then bad weather, then Elias Stoltzfus down with the flu."

"Elias Stoltzfus?" Stoltzfus was a common enough name among the Pennsylvania Amish, but she hadn't heard of him since she'd been here.

"He's planned every barn in Lost Creek in the last forty years. No one would think it right to start building without him. Especially Elias." There was the faintest twinkle in Caleb's eye.

"I see. Moses Miller is the barn planner out in our community. If he doesn't walk it out first, no one will start to build." In fact, folks were starting to wonder what would happen when Moses, already eighty-four, couldn't go on.

Caleb glanced at her in a way that was almost friendly. "Guess there are as many things the same out in Ohio as there are different."

"I guess so. I keep expecting to see bicycles, but I gather that's not part of your tradition."

Caleb shrugged. "I've heard tell bicycles are allowed

out in the Ohio communities because folks tend to live farther apart."

That hadn't occurred to Jessie before, but maybe it was the reason. There certainly seemed to be a big concentration of Amish farms along this road, whereas in Ohio, they'd more likely be interrupted by Englisch homes.

"Probably that's why." She saw that he was staring at the men working the very top of the barn. "I suppose you're one of those who likes to work up top."

He actually chuckled at that. "I guess. The first time I was a bit scared, but when I got up there, it felt pretty good. And Sam… Sam was never afraid of heights. He was climbing to the top of the big oak tree when he wasn't much more than Timothy's age."

"Better not let Timothy hear you saying that, or we'll be coaxing him down, ain't so?"

"You've noticed he's a bit sure of himself."

"You could say that." Relief bubbled up in Jessie that they were actually talking together as though they were kin, maybe even friends.

"He's always been that way. Crawling out of his crib at ten months, he was." Caleb's smiling gaze met hers—met and held for a long, breathless moment.

They both looked away, and Jessie prayed that color wasn't flooding her cheeks. "Well, I… I came over to ask if there is anything you need."

"No. Nothing." Caleb grabbed a box of nails from the table next to him and began counting them as if the success of the barn raising depended on knowing how many nails were used.

"I'll go along and help with the lunch, then."

Jessie went hurriedly toward the house, imagining

she felt people looking at her. Watching her every move with critical eyes.

Nonsense. Folks had better things to do than to think about her. Some teenagers put plates and napkins on the tables, and women were starting to head into the kitchen. She'd be needed to help carry things out.

They'd feed the workers first, of course. That was always how it was done. That way the builders could have a bit of a break to let their food digest before getting back at it. If it was like most barn raisings, they wouldn't want to leave today until the barn was under roof, if not completely ready to use.

After the men had eaten, the women and children would take their turn at the tables, enjoying the plentiful food. Always enough and more—that was the Amish table. And then there'd be all the cleaning up to do.

She searched for Timothy and spotted him still running, maybe a little slower than before. The boy had plenty of energy, but he was likely to tire out before too long. That might be a good excuse to get Caleb to go home, as well. He'd been out of the hospital only a few days, and he'd probably been told to take it easy, although he wouldn't want to admit it.

Taking a deep breath, she prepared to plunge into the maelstrom of activity in the kitchen. All of the other women seemed to have the same idea, but the service was surprisingly orderly. Each person picked up a dish handed over by Leah or one of her helpers and then filed out with it, passing those still waiting in line.

With the assembly line working at full speed, it wouldn't take long to have everything out to be served. Jessie's thoughts fled back to Caleb. He might need someone to help the wheelchair across the grass. But of course one of the men would assist him. He didn't need her.

Jessie grabbed the dish of whipped potatoes that was handed to her and hurried back out the door, following the lead of the woman ahead of her in placing her dish. Then she started back, not sure whether there would be a second round of deliveries.

The entry line seemed to have slowed to a crawl, so Jessie stopped on the porch. A glance back told her that the men were already taking their places on the long benches, and she spotted Caleb with his wheelchair situated at the end of one table. So that was all right.

She tore her attention away from him in time to hear the conversation of the women ahead of her, who were just inside the screen door.

"...terrible, having the nerve to come here and move in on Caleb after what her cousin did. I'm surprised Caleb let her stay."

Jessie was frozen in place, cold hands clasping one another.

"Caleb had better watch out, that's all," the other woman said. Jessie caught just a glimpse of her when she moved—an older woman, sharp-featured, wearing black. "A helpless widower with two young children... She's out to trap him, that's what. Did you see her watching him? Not content with her cousin breaking his heart...now she's after him herself."

Jessie took a step back, then another. She had never been so mortified in her life. How could anyone possibly think that about her?

Well, she'd wondered how she'd be accepted here, hadn't she? Now she knew.

Chapter Five

Caleb didn't want to admit how much the barn raising had taxed his strength, but by Sunday morning he had no choice but to face it. He wasn't the person he'd been before the accident, and there were days he feared he never would be.

He tried to shake off the feeling as he struggled into the wheelchair. That process was getting easier, he reminded himself. The doctors had been right to insist he spend two weeks in the rehab hospital. Without that time, he wouldn't have been ready to come home.

Now for today's challenge—going to worship. This was church Sunday, and folks would expect to see him there. Their community, like most in Pennsylvania, held worship every other Sunday. He wheeled himself out to the kitchen.

Jessie was already at the stove while Onkel Zeb,

Daniel and the kinder sat at the table eating. Jessie's smile looked a little strained as she spooned up oatmeal for him and poured a mug of coffee.

Now that he thought about it, she'd seemed unusually quiet after they'd returned home from the barn raising yesterday. He gave a mental shrug. He didn't understand what made Jessie tick, and that was just fine. He'd been pushed by circumstance into accepting her help, but that didn't mean he wanted to be friends.

Daniel gave him a sidelong look as he took his place at the table. "You sure you should be going to worship today? Nobody would blame you if you stayed home."

He glared at his brother. "I'm fine." He bit out the words. Daniel shrugged, not impressed by his ill humor. Or maybe thinking it showed he wasn't fine at all.

"I want to be at church," he added, modifying his tone so nobody could accuse him of being cranky. "I've missed it. Anyway, that's where we belong on a church Sunday, ain't so?"

"That's certain sure." Jessie put a bowl of scrambled eggs on the table and then took her seat. "I suppose a lot of the folks who were at the barn raising were from your church district?" Her tone made it a question.

"Most of them," Onkel Zeb said. "Some were from the next district over. Here, each bishop has two districts. Is it that way out in Ohio?"

Jessie nodded, her mind seeming to be on something else. Whatever it was, it had taken the sparkle from her eyes.

Caleb frowned. But he worried how he would manage just getting to worship. He didn't need to be wondering about Jessie.

Daniel and Onkel Zeb had obviously given some thought to the problem of transporting him to worship. They'd rigged an improvised ramp to lift him to the level at which he could move over to the buggy seat. He and Daniel would go in the smaller buggy, while Onkel Zeb took Jessie and the kinder in the family buggy.

He barely suppressed a sigh once he was settled on the buggy seat. Daniel picked up the lines and released the brake before he spoke. "I don't want to get my head bitten off, but don't push yourself too hard."

Caleb pushed down the frustration that wanted to release. "Sorry," he muttered. "I hate seeing everyone else carrying my load."

"Guess I'd feel that way, too," Daniel admitted. "But you'd do the same for every one of us, ain't so?"

Caleb grunted. "It's easier to be on the giving end."

His brother grinned. "Maybe the gut Lord decided to teach you some humility."

Was that true? If so, the Lord had surely found the hardest way of doing it—forcing him to depend on Jessie, of all people. The idea was enough for him to chew on the rest of the short ride to the Stoltz farm, and he still hadn't finished with it when they arrived.

Daniel took the buggy right up to where folks were gathering outside the barn—men and boys arranging themselves in one line while women and girls did the same in another. Soon they'd be filing into the Stoltz barn for worship, going from oldest to youngest, as always.

Several men hurried forward to help, and Caleb was lifted down and installed in the wheelchair almost before he had time to brace himself. Becky and Timothy came running over, trailed by Onkel Zeb and Jessie.

Funny. He took another look. Jessie's strained expression seemed to have intensified. Was it possible she was nervous about meeting all these people who were as close to him as family?

"I'll sit by you, Daadi." Timothy grabbed the arm of the wheelchair, bouncing up and down.

"No." Becky's pout had returned. "I want to sit next to Daadi."

"You'll sit on the women's side, like you always do," Onkel Zeb said firmly.

"No, please, Daadi. I want to sit with you."

Jessie didn't speak. She just looked at him, and Caleb knew she was waiting for his verdict. But there couldn't be any question, could there?

"Becky, you always sit on the women's side. Go with Cousin Jessie now."

Jessie held out her hand, smiling at his daughter. "Komm. I need you to show me where to go in the line."

Becky folded her arms mutinously, and Caleb's patience snapped. "Rebecca Jane, stoppe! Go to your cousin this instant!"

He'd spoken so sharply that several people nearby turned to look at him. Becky's lips trembled. Annoyed with her and disgusted with himself, he spun the chair away.

What kind of father was he turning into? What was wrong with him?

"Komm." Jessie's voice was soft, but it reached him, and he felt sure she'd taken Becky's hand. "Folks are cross when they're in pain, ain't so? We just have to understand and love them, anyway."

If it was possible for him to feel any more ashamed than he did already, Jessie's words would have done it.

Jessie breathed a silent prayer that Becky would understand. Then Becky took her hand and led her toward the lineup of women and girls. As they passed the single young women, Becky hesitated, glancing up at Jessie.

Jessie answered the question in the child's face. "At home I sit with the women who are about my age, even though they're all married but me." Becky obviously hadn't known where to put her, which wasn't surprising. Everyone from her rumspringa group was long since married, and it had seemed foolish to sit with younger and younger unmarried girls. She had no plans to be married, so the day she'd joined them had been a silent announcement, if any were needed, that she considered herself a spinster.

Not a pretty term, but it was true. She'd given up the idea of marriage a long time ago.

Now the question was how to avoid the women she'd heard talking about her yesterday at the barn raising. She cringed inside at the memory of those hurtful words. *Forget them*, she ordered herself, but since she'd been saying the same thing all night, the command didn't seem to be working.

She'd had only a quick glimpse of one face, so how would she know them for sure? And for all she knew, everyone here was thinking the same thing, even if they weren't so outspoken about it.

Fortunately, before Jessie could sink any deeper, she saw Leah gesturing to her. Relief lifted her heart.

She had one friend here, at least. That was something to thank the gut Lord for.

Leah greeted her with a smile. "Komm, sit with us."

"Denke." Leah couldn't know how thankful she really was. "Becky is showing me around this morning."

"Gut." Leah touched Becky's cheek lightly. "I'm glad you're taking care of your cousin. And everyone will be sehr happy to see your daadi back in worship this morning."

Becky nodded without speaking, still looking on the edge of tears. Jessie could almost believe the child pressed a little closer to her. Maybe it was possible to break through the barriers Becky had put up between them, but she certain sure didn't want it to be at the cost of Becky's close relationship with her daadi. This was proving much trickier than she had imagined when she'd left home so full of hope.

The line started to move then, so there was no time for more. But Becky's hand stayed in hers all the way into the barn and while they filed into the rows of benches on the women's side of worship.

The two rows of mammis and small children were so placed that they had the rumspringa-age girls in front of them and then the row of young girls who were deemed old enough to sit together in worship. Their older sisters and mothers would keep a close eye on them. Jessie smiled a little, remembering the day her brother's oldest had begun to giggle in worship and been escorted, face flaming, back to sit with her mamm.

Sitting on the hard backless benches for three hours could be a challenge. Jessie let her gaze slide covertly to the men's side, where she saw with relief that Caleb was in his wheelchair, pulled up to the end of a bench next to his brother and little Timothy. At least he hadn't stubbornly insisted on moving to the bench, where his cast would have had little or no support.

"I hope Caleb is not overdoing it." Leah had mastered the gift of whispering just loudly enough to be heard by her neighbor.

Jessie nodded. "Me, too. But he's…" She let that trail off, not wanting to seem critical.

"Stubborn." Leah supplied the word, the corner of her mouth twitching. "I know."

The song leader began the long, slow notes of the first song, with the rest of the worshippers joining in. Jessie had no need to consult the book of hymns to join in the familiar words. Next to her, Becky sat very straight, adding her small voice to the song of praise.

Jessie was relieved that the service was familiar from her own church district. There were always differences in custom from one district to another, but from what she had seen so far, Caleb's was very similar to hers in Ohio except for some minor differences in what technology they accepted.

Had that made Alice feel at home when she came here? Or would she have felt stifled by it, with her longing for change and adventure unmet?

Jessie discovered her fingers were twisting together in her lap, and she forced them to be still. Everyone had been happy when Caleb started courting Alice. Apparently Jessie had been the only one to question whether Alice was actually ready for marriage. If she had spoken out then, might it have made a difference?

But she hadn't. She'd been hamstrung by the undeniable fact that she had thought she would be the one

Caleb wanted. Anyone might think she was speaking out of her own disappointment.

Jessie didn't think other people's opinions would have stopped her, if only she hadn't feared in her own heart that it might be true that she felt jealous.

Probably the result would still have been the same. *Accept*, the faith counseled. *Accept what God sends as His will*. She'd tried. She was still trying.

Halfway through the long sermon, given today by the bishop, Becky began to sag. Leah eased her arm around the child, wishing with all her heart that Becky would relax against her and accept the love she had to share.

The bishop was talking now of the love the shepherd had shown, leaving the ninety-nine behind to seek and save the one who was lost. Love for his people seemed to shine in Bishop Thomas's face as he spoke, and Jessie warmed to him. She felt for a moment as if he talked directly to her. She wasn't exactly lost, but she was alone in a strange place. Maybe Bishop Thomas was someone she could turn to if necessary.

Becky jerked upright when Leah's two-year-old, Miriam, kicked her legs fretfully as she sat on her mamm's lap. As if it were catching, Becky began kicking her feet.

Jessie pulled her attention away from the bishop's preaching on the lost sheep and exchanged looks with Leah. Both of them were obviously familiar with the efforts involved in keeping small children quiet during a long worship service. And Jessie couldn't help wondering how many people were watching her with critical eyes, ready to seize on the slightest mistake on her part.

Drawing out a white handkerchief, Jessie began shaping it into, if you used considerable imagination, a bunny. She slipped it over her fingers and made it hop over to Becky. Her attention captured, Becky made the bunny hop along her own lap.

Little Miriam made a grab for it and was thwarted by her mother. Smiling, Leah hushed her small daughter and passed another handkerchief over to Jessie so that she could produce a second bunny. In two minutes the kinder were happily…and silently…playing. Peace reigned until the end of worship.

As they rose from the final prayer, Leah turned to her, smiling. "That was a lifesaver, Jessie. You must show me how to do it."

"For sure. But they fall apart pretty fast, I'm afraid."

Becky was tugging at her, so she moved out of the way of the men and boys who were rapidly changing the benches into the tables that would be used for lunch. Later they'd be loaded onto the church buggy, ready to be taken to the next host residence for worship.

Leah was saying something about her fretful daughter when Jessie's attention was drawn away by a voice that was only too familiar. An older woman, filing out of a seat a few rows behind her, spoke to the woman next to her. The words didn't matter, but the voice… the voice was that of the woman who'd said those hurtful words yesterday at the barn raising. When Jessie looked closer, she recognized the sharp-featured face.

Jessie waited a moment before turning to Leah. "Who is the woman just going out two rows behind us?"

"The one in the black dress with the gray hair? That's Ethel Braun. Bishop Thomas Braun's wife."

Jessie's heart sank to her shoes. The bishop had preached about love and forgiveness, and she'd been drawn to him, eased by his words. All the while his wife spread hateful rumors about Jessie. It didn't look as if she could expect any understanding from the bishop.

Why does it matter what anyone else thinks? Jessie, sitting in the living room rocker with a stack of mending that evening, tried to dismiss the reactions of Caleb's community from her mind. She had made a friend in Leah, and some of the other young married women had cautiously approached her, so the prospect of being accepted wasn't entirely bleak. Besides, her job here was to make things better for Caleb and the kinder, not to worry about her own popularity or lack of it.

How Alice had expected her to do that was another question. The last letter from Alice had laid a burden on her, but not even Alice had suggested how Jessie might make things right with the family she'd left behind. Alice probably hadn't known—she'd just had a glimmer of hope that her older cousin would solve her problems, as Jessie so often had.

Jessie picked up one of Becky's dresses from the mending basket. The hem had pulled out—a simple enough fix, but it made her wonder who had been taking care of the mending and sewing for the family. Neighbors or relatives, she supposed, but if so, they'd allowed it to pile up fairly high. She'd have several evenings' work just to catch up.

Caleb cleared his throat, and she glanced at him. He'd seemed engrossed in the newspaper, so she'd respected his silence. But now he was frowning, glancing first at her and then down at his hands.

"About Becky..." He came to a stop, frown deepening.

"What about her?" Jessie kept her voice even, wondering if this would be another warning about what she should or shouldn't say to his daughter.

"I heard what you told her this morning. After I was so short with her."

"I'm sorry if I spoke out of turn." She swallowed a number of things she would have liked to say.

"It's not that." He looked directly at her, and she was startled by the pain in his face. "You were right in what you said. Becky shouldn't question doing what she's told, but there was no reason for me to tell her so harshly."

What could she say? He was right, of course, and yet she understood. "Being sick or in pain does make a person a bit short-tempered."

"It's important that Becky listen." He seemed to be arguing with himself. "But I... I wonder if I should say anything to her about it. If I should..."

"Apologize?" she finished for him. Jessie made several stitches in the hem to give herself time to think. "It's a hard decision. But I remember a time when my daad and one of my brothers were at odds most of the time." Her lips curved upward, remembering. "Joshua was fourteen, and thought he knew all the answers about everything. He got sassy with Daad at a time when Daad was worried about the milk tank leaking. He was afraid we were going to lose a whole day's production and maybe risk the contract with the dairy.

Anybody smart wouldn't have butted in at a time like that."

"Joshua wasn't smart, I take it." Caleb's interest had been caught.

"Not as smart as he thought he was, anyway. Josh was the last straw, and Daadi blew up at him." She paused. "He was sorry afterward, that was certain sure. He'd always been fair, and it was like he'd let himself down, as well as Josh."

"Yah, it does feel that way." Caleb ran his hand through his hair in a frustrated gesture. "What did he do about it?"

"At first I didn't think either of them was willing to be the first to speak. But then Daad said he was sorry, that he shouldn't have taken his worries out on Josh. Josh just stood there for a minute. Then a couple of tears spilled over, and the next thing he was crying and saying it was his fault." She grinned. "Which it was, but he finally grew out of being so obnoxious."

Caleb's smile flickered. "Yah, I have little brothers, too. Denke, Jessie."

For once it seemed they were really communicating, without all the barriers between them. Something that had been tied up in knots inside Jessie began to ease.

There was a clatter at the back door as Onkel Zeb, Daniel and the kinder came in from doing the evening chores. Not that the little ones would be much help, as small as they were, but that was how children learned—by standing beside an adult, first watching, then helping, then finally doing it all by themselves.

Jessie folded the mending. "I'll go up and get things ready for bed."

They'd fallen into a routine already in the few days

she'd been there. By disappearing upstairs to prepare for the kinder's bedtime, she gave Caleb a few minutes alone with them. He'd need it tonight if he intended to tell Becky he was sorry for his anger.

Jessie understood his hesitation. It wasn't easy to admit you'd been wrong, especially when the other person had been wrong, as well. Caleb wouldn't want Becky to get the idea that it was all right for her to disobey, but he wanted to be honest with her, too.

Taking her time, Jessie got everything ready. Then she started downstairs quietly, ready to retreat if it seemed Caleb was still having a private talk with Becky. But when she reached the spot from which she could look into the living room, all seemed fine. Timothy was on the floor, showing his daadi something about his farm animal set, while Becky cuddled on Caleb's lap.

Relieved at the sight, she went on to the living room, smiling. "This looks like a happy group."

"I was showing Daadi the brown-and-white cow I have. I named her Brownie. Do you think that's a gut name for a cow?" Timothy's blue eyes were very serious.

"Very gut. It describes her, doesn't it?"

He gave a decided nod, and she suppressed a grin at his determination.

"If I had a cow, I'd name her Buttercup," Becky said, leaning against her daadi's shoulder. "Do you think I could have a calf to raise all by myself, Daadi?"

"In a year or so," Caleb said. He smoothed back the strands of blond hair that had slipped out of her braids, and the tender look on his face told Jessie everything was all right between them now.

Even as she thought it, Caleb's gaze moved to her face with a smiling acknowledgment that her words had helped. Her heart swelled. They seemed to have reached a truce, and that was surely enough to be going on with. Perhaps they could even be friends one day.

Caleb glanced at the clock. "Time you young ones were in bed. Put the farm set away now, Timothy."

For an instant Timothy pretended not to hear. Jessie knelt next to him. "Should Brownie go into the barn for the night?" She "walked" the cow toward the barn.

"I'll do it," Timothy said, his smile instantly restored. He set about putting the pieces away, and in a moment Becky slid down from her daadi's lap.

"I'll help."

Jessie stood, smiling. That sort of cooperation was sweet to see between sister and brother. In a normal Amish family, there might be another baby or two by now, and they'd be sharing time and attention, but for Becky and Timothy, there was no other sibling. Or cousin, either, for that matter, and Daniel showed no sign of getting serious about anyone. Maybe he, like everyone else, believed the King brothers to be unfortunate in love.

She waited while Becky and Timothy kissed their daadi. When she bent over to detach Timothy, who had a tendency to use Caleb's cast to climb on, Caleb caught her wrist. She raised startled eyes to his, wondering if he could feel her pulse pounding.

"Denke," he said again, softly.

He let go, looked away, and time moved on at its usual pace. But for a moment, it seemed to have stopped indefinitely.

The kinder were already scrambling up the stairs,

and Jessie hurried after them with more speed than dignity. She couldn't let Caleb imagine she had any feelings for him. She just couldn't.

Timothy was already at the bathroom sink, brushing his teeth, but Becky lingered in the bedroom.

"Cousin Jesse, could I have my hair in one braid for the night? So it won't get tangled?"

"For sure." She tried to keep her elation from filling her voice. Becky was actually letting her do something. This was a red-letter day indeed.

They sat side by side on the bed while Jessie unpinned the silky soft hair and ran the brush through it, careful of any tangles. As she started winding the strands into the loose braid that would be comfortable for sleeping, Jessie found herself slipping backward in time.

Wasn't it just yesterday that she'd done the same thing for Alice? She'd been so glad to have a small girl cousin, since Mamm and Daadi hadn't provided her with any sisters. Alice had been a pleasant change from the boys, who never wanted to sit still for a minute and certain sure wouldn't let her brush their hair.

"There we go."

The bottom of the braid was well below Becky's shoulder blades, and Jessie rested her hand against the child's back as she found the band to secure the braid. How small and fragile Becky seemed in this quiet moment, with the vulnerability of her nape exposed. Jessie was swept with an intense wave of protectiveness.

After Jessie fastened the band, Becky shook her head so that the single braid swung from side to side. "Feels gut."

"Your mammi used to say that, too. You look very

like her." The words were out before Jessie remembered that she wasn't supposed to mention Alice to the kinder.

But she didn't have time to worry about that, because Becky's reaction was too violent to let her think of anything else.

"I'm not! I'm not like her!" Becky burst into a storm of weeping and threw herself onto the bed, her whole body shaking.

For an instant Jessie froze, aghast at the reaction to her simple words. Fortunately it seemed no one else had heard. At least, no one came hurrying to see what was wrong.

She bent over Becky, almost afraid to speak for fear of saying the wrong thing again. "I'm sorry, Becky. I didn't mean to upset you. Please forgive me." She kept her voice soft and gentle, praying silently for guidance.

Oh, Lord, help me know what to do for this troubled child.

Becky's sobs eased. "I don't look like her. Not one little bit." Her voice had returned nearly to normal, interrupted only by a little hiccup.

"If you say so." Jessie hesitated, wondering how much she dared to say. "Is it bad to look like her?" She carefully didn't speak Alice's name.

Sniffing a little, Becky sat up, nodding. For an instant, Jessie thought that was all she'd get by way of explanation. Then Becky blinked away the tears. She stared down at the floor.

"Daadi might not like me if I look like her," she whispered.

Jessie felt as if Becky had grabbed her heart and squeezed it. She couldn't seem to get her breath. How could the poor child have come up with this idea?

But she knew how, didn't she? Caleb, and his determination never to speak of Alice.

She focused on Becky, praying she might feel the love in Jessie's heart. "Your daadi loves you and Timothy more than anything in the whole world, no matter what you look like. I promise you."

Becky pierced her with an intent stare. "Are you sure?"

"I'm sure," she said. "If you were purple with blue-and-white stripes, your daadi would still love you just the same."

That brought the smile she'd hoped for to Becky's face. But it didn't solve the problem.

Caleb should be made to know and understand the harm his attitude was doing to Becky. If Jessie tried to tell him, though, he would turn on her with all the anger bottled up in his heart. The brief truce between them would be over.

He wouldn't listen to her words. But somehow he had to be made to see the truth.

Please, Lord. I don't think I can do this. Please, help me.

Chapter Six

Getting ready for the visiting therapist to arrive on Monday morning, Caleb found he was still a bit uneasy about Jessie. The plan was to have the therapist come every week, while he went to the clinic periodically. Not that it was any concern of his, but she was, in a sense, his guest, and she'd seemed distracted, almost worried, since they'd come home from worship on Sunday.

Even now, while she cleaned up the kitchen after breakfast, Jessie acted as if she was preoccupied with something other than the job in front of her. Maybe she was bored. The thought slid into his mind. After all, Alice had become bored with this life quickly enough.

That was probably unfair. Jessie had spent many years as an adult helping with her brother's children and doing all the things any Amish woman would take for granted. She wouldn't have expected anything else here.

But at the moment he'd rather think she was bored, illogical as it was, than assume he was in some way responsible for her feelings. He hadn't invited her here.

That justification didn't seem sensible, even to him.

The sound of a car pulling up next to the house put an end to his fruitless imaginings. "That'll be the therapist," he said.

Jessie swung around as if she hadn't realized he was in the room. "Ach, yah, that's who it will be." She dried her hands on a dish towel. "I'll get the door."

The kinder came stampeding down the hall at the sound of the vehicle. "We'll go," Becky said. "We'll get it, Cousin Jessie."

Jessie smiled and nodded, but she followed them. Just as well, since even Becky didn't have much Englisch yet. In September, when she started first grade, she'd begin learning the Englisch an Amish person needed to get along in the world. But around the house and with other Amish folks, Pennsylvania Dutch was spoken.

Becky pulled the door open almost before the man had finished knocking, but then, as Caleb had expected, she was struck dumb with shyness, stepping back and blushing. Thankfully Jessie had reached them by then.

"Please, komm in. Caleb is expecting you."

"I'm Joe Riley." He was young, with reddish hair and freckles, and he grinned at the kinder in a friendly way. "Who are you?"

"This is Becky, and this is Timothy." Jessie touched them lightly as she said their names, and then she switched from Englisch to Pennsylvania Dutch. "Give the gentleman room. He's here to help Daadi with his exercises."

Still speechless, the children backed into the kitchen from the entryway.

The therapist raised his eyebrows at Jessie. "And you are?"

"Cousin Jessie," she said. "Caleb is here." She ushered him into the kitchen, and Joe came over to shake hands with Caleb.

"We met before you were released from rehab, didn't we? I bet you're enjoying being back in your own house after all that time in the hospital. And having some good home cooking, too, right?"

Caleb nodded, wondering why all the therapists he'd run across were so unwaveringly cheerful. "Yah, that's so. It's good of you to come to the house."

"That's my job." Joe set a duffel bag on the table. "We can't just let you sit in that chair when you get home. Have to help you build up your strength so this leg won't be as weak when the cast comes off."

"Yah, I know." Caleb took himself to task for sounding unwelcoming. The man was here to help him, and the more Caleb worked at it, the faster he'd get back to doing the things he wanted.

"Just remember that the leg will be wasted some after all this time in a cast. Even after it comes off, you'll still have to work on getting the strength back in it."

Maybe the therapist thought he needed the cautionary words. He probably did, since he'd seen the cast as the enemy.

"Where would be the best place to work?" Caleb asked.

Joe looked around. "This would be a good spot. Nice smooth floor and not much to trip on. If it's okay to move the table and chairs, that is." He glanced at Jessie as if rearranging the kitchen was up to her.

"Yah, it's fine," Caleb said. This was his house, not Jessie's.

"I'll take the chairs into the dining room." Jessie suited action to words and the kinder, catching on even though Joe had spoken in Englisch, hurried to help.

It was quickly done, and then Joe grabbed one end of the table while Jessie took the other. They put it against the far wall.

"Great! Now we can get to work." Joe was relentlessly happy, and Caleb expected he'd be relentless about pushing him, as well.

"The children and I will get out of your way." Jessie shooed the children gently toward the other room. "Just call if you need anything."

They began with some of the simple routines he'd done in the rehab hospital. After a few minutes Joe called a halt.

"Okay, obviously I don't need to start with building upper body strength. I guess a farmer already has plenty of that, not like somebody who sits at a desk all day."

Caleb hadn't expected to find this process amusing, but he was returning Joe's grin. "Yah, when you're tossing hay bales around, you build up a few muscles."

"Let's get on to the hard stuff, then." Joe bent to check the cast and the pulse in Caleb's ankle. "See, what happens is that this leg is losing muscle all the time it's in the cast. Right?" He glanced at Caleb's face to make sure he was following. "So we want to keep the muscles working as much as possible. That's going to help you move around more easily with the cast on, and also keep you from losing too much. Okay?"

He always seemed to want agreement with his statements, so Caleb nodded. Maybe that was the therapist's way of ensuring that his patient was on board.

"I want to get back to my regular work," Caleb said, "so whatever you say to do, I'll do it. I'm needed here, and I can't run a dairy farm from a wheelchair."

"You might be surprised at what people can do from a wheelchair," Joe said, his face serious. "I worked with a farmer up north of here who couldn't get around without a chair, and he did all right. He even rigged up a lift he could work himself to get from the chair to his tractor."

Maybe Joe meant that to be encouraging, but Caleb didn't care to picture that kind of a life for himself. He would get his strength back, and everything would be as it had been.

"All right," Caleb said. "Let's get to work."

Caleb almost regretted his words over the next half hour. Joe worked him every bit as hard as he'd expected, and Caleb felt convinced that the cast was getting heavier with every repetition.

By the time Joe stepped back with a satisfied nod, he was breathing about as hard as Caleb was. He stood for a moment and seemed to be considering something.

"I'm going to give you a bunch of exercises to do on the days I don't come." He pulled a couple of printed sheets from his bag. "But they're not things you can easily do on your own. What we really need is someone to help."

Before Caleb could respond, Joe had spun and walked into the living room. "Hey, Jessie? Could you come and give us a hand?"

"For sure."

Caleb's jaw tightened at Jessie's quick assent. If Joe expected him to accept Jessie's help with the exercises, he was mistaken.

Jessie and Joe came back to the kitchen, the kinder trailing along behind, their eyes round with curiosity. "Caleb will have to do this routine on the days I don't come, and it's not something the client can do alone. Can I count on you to help?"

Jessie's face didn't give anything away, but Caleb thought she didn't like the idea. Still, she'd never say so. He knew she'd consider it her duty.

Jessie answered as he'd expected. "I'm wonderful glad to help any way I can. What do you want me to do?"

Caleb had to stop this before it went any further. "Jessie has enough to do with the kinder and the house. I can work on my own."

"Sorry." Joe's smile flashed, but he sounded firm. "You really can't. Not and do what needs to be done. This definitely requires another person."

"Then my uncle can help," Caleb said impatiently.

"Is that the older man I saw working outside when I came in? Looks like he already has plenty to keep him busy."

"He does," Jessie said. "I'm the logical person to help Caleb." She turned to the children and spoke quickly without giving him time to argue. "You'll help me with Daadi's exercises, ain't so?"

"We'll help. We'll do a gut job, Daadi. We really will." Becky was solemn in her assurances, and Timothy ran over to scramble up into his lap.

"Looks like you're outvoted," Joe said. He gestured with the papers to Jessie. "Here are diagrams that show exactly how the exercises are supposed to be done. I'll demonstrate them to you, just to be sure."

Jessie nodded, her head bending over the papers. Her soft brown hair was parted in the center and swept smoothly back under her kapp, and the column of her neck was slim and strong. There was determination in the firm line of her jaw. If Jessie thought she was going to give Caleb orders…

But was that really what bothered him about this idea? Or was it the fact that he wasn't sure how he felt about working so closely with her?

"I want to help plant the garden!" Timothy ran alongside Jessie that afternoon, while Becky trailed behind.

"For sure you're going to help," Jessie assured him. "And Becky, too."

Becky's face gave her feelings away so readily. She wanted to participate, and yet she was resentful of each new chore Jessie took over. "Onkel Zeb planted the garden last year," she pointed out.

"He'd like to do it this year, but he's been wonderful busy since your daadi got hurt, so I said we'd help." Jessie glanced at Becky. "He got it all ready for us, and he said you were a big help last year."

Becky's face brightened. "I was. And I'm bigger this year, so I can do even more."

"We'll make a gut job of it, then, with such gardeners." They'd reached the plot not far from the kitchen that had been plowed and harrowed. "Onkel Zeb says we should wait a week or two for the tomatoes and peppers, but we can already plant a lot of the vegetables."

Using the corner of a hoe, she marked out a furrow for each of the kinder and gave each one a seed packet. "Drop just a seed or two at a time," she cautioned, remembering her small nephew planting by the handful.

But these two seemed happy enough to follow directions. Jessie moved along with them. "Not too deep," she cautioned when Timothy poked a hole with his finger. "Remember, when the seed sprouts, it has to work its way clear up through the soil so it can reach toward the sun."

"How long will it take?" Timothy eyed the seeds he'd just planted. "I want to see it sprout."

"Some seeds take a week. Some take two or even longer." Thinking of her nephew's activities, she added, "You can't dig it up to see if it's sprouting, you know. If you do that, it will never grow."

Timothy's mouth turned down. "But I want to see it."

"You will," she assured him. "When it's ready, it will pop up through the ground. A couple of little leaves will start to open. Then you can watch it grow bigger every day."

"Then we'll water it," Becky added. "That will help it grow."

"Yah, that's so." Jessie smoothed the soil over a few more seeds. "Jesus said that our faith is like a tiny seed planted inside us. He helps it grow just like the sun helps the plant grow, until it's strong and healthy and able to do good things."

She wasn't sure Timothy was getting it, but Becky seemed to mull over her words. "Good things like helping other people," she said finally. "Onkel Zeb says a good deed is like a lighted candle in a dark room. It helps folks see."

"Onkel Zeb is a wise man," Jessie said, relieved. She had wondered who was teaching them the gentle examples of faith from everyday life that an Amish mother imparted without even thinking about it. It sounded as if Zeb had sensed that need in Becky and Timothy and was trying to fill the gap.

They'd reached the end of the third row of planting when Timothy leaped up. "Daadi's coming out!" He charged toward the porch, closely followed by Becky, their feet making small prints on the row of newly planted seeds.

Jessie got up slowly. She and Caleb hadn't spoken to each other since the physical therapist left, and she hesitated to bring up the subject. Clearly Caleb hadn't wanted her to be the one to assist him, and she hadn't really wanted to, either.

But she felt quite sure that their reasons were very different. Caleb didn't want to be beholden to her because he resented her presence—or maybe more accurately, he resented the fact that she was a reminder of Alice.

Her reasons were much more complicated. Over the years, she'd convinced herself that she couldn't be blamed for having feelings that had started before Caleb had even so much as seen Alice. And anyway, those feelings had long since faded to the vanishing point.

Unfortunately, she wasn't quite as sure of that fact as she had been. And being close to him, helping him with his exercises, touching him…that could be very dangerous to her emotions. To her heart, which still seemed vulnerable where Caleb was concerned.

The kinder were helping Caleb down the ramp in the wheelchair. Or at least, he was letting them believe they were helping him, which amounted to the same thing in making them feel useful. Her mother always said that a useful child was a happy child, and Jessie agreed. It seemed to her that the worst thing a parent could do was to do everything for a child.

She watched as they approached the garden, Becky very intent and serious as she pushed the chair and Timothy holding on to the arm to ease it along. This opportunity to be with Alice's kinder and help them might be as close as she ever got to parenthood, and she was determined to do it well.

She still had her many nieces and nephews, she reminded herself. But each of them had two parents, and none of them had Becky and Timothy's desperate need.

The chair came to a halt at the edge of the plowed earth. "Look, Daadi." Timothy darted along the row. "I planted all these seeds. They'll grow into carrots."

"We put the seed packet on a stick at the end of each row so you can tell what's planted there." Becky tapped the one closest to her. "They're like little flags, ain't so?"

Caleb nodded and then glanced at Jessie. "Zeb usually takes care of the garden. You didn't have to do it."

He sounded like his daughter, resisting any change in the order of things.

"Zeb has plenty on his hands right now," Jessie said lightly. "He was happy to let us take over the planting. Besides, I love planting the garden. At home, my nieces and I always take care of the vegetable patch and the flowers."

Caleb's hands tightened on the arms of the chair. "Yah, you're right. Onkel Zeb is taking on too much for a man his age."

"Better not let him hear you say that about him," Jessie said lightly, hoping to distract him.

But Caleb just glared at the cast. "I'd like to take a saw to this thing."

A quick glance assured Jessie that the children were at the far end of the garden, out of earshot. "Then you'd never get back to the way you were, ain't so?" Could he feel her sympathy? "It's wonderful hard to be patient."

"It is." His hands eased as if he'd needed someone to recognize how difficult this was for him. "Where's Zeb now? Do you know?"

"In the barn. He said something about fixing a few weak stall boards." She made her tone casual. "Maybe he could use someone to help hold the boards."

Caleb's smile flickered briefly. "Trying to make me feel useful, Jessie? I've seen you do that with the kinder, distracting them from being quarrelsome."

She couldn't help laughing. "I was just remembering something my mamm always says…that a useful child is a happy child."

Surprisingly enough, he took that well. "Maybe grown-ups aren't so different." He raised his voice. "Becky! Timothy! Komm help me out to the barn."

The kinder ran down the lane between the rows. "I'll push," Becky declared, getting there first.

"No, I will." Timothy's face puckered.

"You are both needed to push," Caleb said. "The chair doesn't go so well on the rough ground."

"We can do it," Becky said. She made space for her brother, and they both began to shove.

Jessie hurried to keep pace with them, suspecting another hand might be needed to get up the incline to the barn door. Caleb rolled the wheels with his hands. He must be tired after this morning's hard workout, but he didn't show it.

Caleb darted a quick look at her, and then his gaze dropped. "You never told me about your business out in Ohio."

It took a moment for Jessie to process the unexpected words. Finally she shrugged. "There didn't seem to be a reason to."

"Or an opportunity?"

She shook her head slightly, but it was probably true. They hadn't had many casual conversations, and she tended to pick her words carefully with him.

"Zeb told me about it. He said you gave it up to come and help us."

"I couldn't be there and here, could I? It seemed more important to be here."

"Why?" His eyes met hers, challenging. "Why was this important to you?"

Jessie hesitated. She glanced at the kinder, but they didn't seem to be paying any attention to the adults' conversation. "I grew up being responsible for...for my little cousin."

She wouldn't say the name, afraid of provoking an

explosion, and as it was, she was dangerously close. Still, Caleb was the one who'd forced the question.

"I guess I still feel responsible. If I can do something to right a wrong, then I want to do it. I need to do it."

Jessie couldn't bring herself to look at his face, afraid of what she'd read there. He reached out suddenly to grab her wrist, covering her hand on the chair, and her breath caught.

"You aren't…" he began.

But she wasn't to know what he might have said. Becky gave the chair a big shove. "We can take it the rest of the way. We don't need any help."

Jessie let go and watched the children struggle to get the chair into the barn. She wanted to assist, but not at the cost of upsetting Becky.

What had brought on that sudden reaction on the child's part? The fact that Caleb had been momentarily occupied with Jessie? She wasn't sure. But each time she took a step forward with Becky, it seemed to be followed by a plunge backward.

As for where she stood with Caleb…she didn't even want to think about that problem.

Caleb grasped the wheels, helping propel the chair onto the barn floor. It began to roll faster once it hit the worn wooden floor boards.

"Stop pushing now or you'll send me right into Beauty's stall."

For some reason, the kinder seemed to find that hilarious, and they scampered into the barn, giggling. Jessie followed a few paces behind. It took a moment for his eyes to adjust to the dimness after the bright sunshine outside.

He'd wanted to say something to Jessie, but clearly now was not the time, not with Zeb and the kinder around. Later, maybe. Or was it best to leave the whole subject alone? She couldn't atone for what Alice had done, if that was what she'd meant. Nobody could.

"Ach, you've made it all the way to the barn." Beaming, Onkel Zeb rose from squatting by a stall door. "Looks like you had some helpers."

"Yah, I did." He rolled the chair toward the stall. "Now it's my turn to help. I can reach the stall bars from the chair, anyway."

Zeb gave Jessie a questioning look as if wanting reassurance that he could manage. Caleb tried not to let it annoy him. Onkel Zeb was only acting out of love.

Whatever Zeb saw on Jessie's face must have satisfied him, because he nodded. "I could use an extra pair of hands, that's certain sure."

Becky darted forward to join them. "I'll help, too."

"You already have a job," Caleb said firmly. "That garden isn't going to plant itself. We're counting on you."

He saw the faintest suggestion of a pout forming on his daughter's face.

"Onkel Zeb and I will komm see it when you're done, ain't so, Onkel Zeb?"

"For sure," Zeb said. "Don't forget to water the seeds when you get them in."

"We won't." Timothy grabbed Jessie's hand. "Let's hurry. I want to water." They started toward the door.

"I do, too." Becky, distracted, hurried after them.

Zeb waited until they'd disappeared before he chuckled. "What one does, the other wants to do, as well. You boys were just the same when you were that age."

"I guess we were." For a moment his thoughts strayed to Aaron, his youngest brother. What was he doing out there in the Englisch world? Was he well? Did he ever regret jumping the fence?

But there was little point in worrying over something he couldn't control or asking questions with no answers. He had enough of that right here at home.

Somewhat to his surprise, Caleb found he had little trouble figuring out how to work from the chair. He and Zeb labored together as they always did, with the exception that Zeb fetched things he couldn't reach. His spirits began to lift. Maybe he wasn't so helpless after all.

Zeb hammered a nail into place. "Folks were sure glad to see you at worship yesterday. Seemed like it had been an awful long time."

"For me, too." He frowned slightly. "Jessie was quiet after we got back from church, ain't so?"

His uncle considered, lean face solemn. "Maybe folks weren't as happy to wilkom her as they were to see you."

"She doesn't know anybody, I guess, other than Leah and Sam and their family."

Zeb looked at him as if waiting for more. When it didn't come, he set a screw for the door with a tad more force than necessary. "Whenever someone brings a visiting relative to worship, folks gather round to meet them. Make them feel at home."

"So?" Maybe he knew where Zeb was going with this, but he didn't want to admit it.

"So, did you see anybody gathering around Jessie yesterday? I sure didn't. A few of the women smiled in passing, but that was about it."

"You think it's because they know she's Alice's cousin." He toyed with the nails in his hand, turning them over and over.

"Not just because she's Alice's cousin. Because most folks know how you feel about Alice and all of her kin."

Caleb tossed the nails into the toolbox. "I never said a word to anyone."

"You didn't have to. You think folks are dummies? They know you well, Caleb. Your actions speak louder than your words. Half the county probably knows you feel like Jessie pushed her way in here."

Caleb wanted to defend himself. Unfortunately, the small voice of his conscience was telling him there was something in what his uncle said.

If Jessie meant what she said to him earlier about making up for what Alice had done... But he didn't know for sure. Maybe she was trying to justify her own actions.

Or was he just trying to justify his?

Chapter Seven

Jessie sat in the rocking chair that evening, working her way toward the bottom of the mending basket. The room had a pleasant feeling of peace with the day's work done. Onkel Zeb was replacing the wheels on a broken toy while Becky and Timothy built a barn with blocks.

She shot a quick glance at Caleb. Once again he was holding a newspaper, but he didn't seem to be reading it. Did her very presence make him uneasy in his own home?

Jessie pushed that idea away. She had to be patient, and so did Caleb. Today she had referred to Alice very obliquely, and he hadn't bitten her head off. Maybe that was progress.

"We need some more pieces for the roof," Becky said. "Where are the rest of the green ones?"

"I'll find them." Timothy's method of searching involved diving into the block box headfirst, giving them a view of the seat of his pants.

Jessie couldn't help smiling. Caleb, meeting her gaze, was smiling, as well, and for a moment they shared their amusement. Then Timothy resurfaced, red in the face, clutching the long green blocks they were using for the roof. "I got them."

He was taking the blocks to his sister when he noticed the small shirt Jessie had pulled out of the basket. He hurried over to her. "Hey, that's my shirt. It was lost."

"Not lost. Just hiding in the mending basket." She held it up against him and chuckled. "I think you won't be wearing this one again."

Timothy held his arm out to see how short the sleeve was. "I grew, didn't I?"

"That's certain sure. You're getting bigger all the time." Jessie folded the shirt on her lap. "What shall we do with it? Can I use it to make patches in a quilt?"

"Whose quilt? Will it go on my bed?"

"If you want." She might not possess the artist's eye for a quilt that her sister-in-law did, but she usually had something in progress, and she took a lot of satisfaction from the quilts she made.

"Can I help?" Becky still sat on the rug by the barn, but she was watching them.

"Yah, you can. Do you like to sew?"

"I never tried." She looked at her hands as if assessing the possibility of their wielding a needle.

"Well, then, it's time you did. We'll collect some quilt patches and plan a project for you."

Jessie was ridiculously elated. It was the first time

Becky had shown any enthusiasm for doing something with her, and at six, it was time she was introduced to sewing. Normally a mother, grandmother or aunt would have done it already, but Becky was missing all of those.

And whatever memories she had of her mother must have been sad ones. She was five when Alice died—old enough to see, if not understand, those last weeks of life. If only Jessie had been able to convince Alice to stay with her instead of coming home...

But Alice was determined. She had left Caleb and the kinder when Timothy was just a baby, and she hadn't contacted anyone. The only explanation she'd left behind had been a short note saying she was sorry. Jessie had wondered about postpartum depression, but Alice had been dissatisfied with her life for a time before that pregnancy.

Jessie's family had searched, of course, but it was easy for an Amish person to hide in the Englisch world. It was only when Alice was seriously ill with the cancer that took her life that she'd resurfaced, announcing that she intended to go back to Caleb for whatever time she had left.

Jessie had tried to dissuade her. She'd written, urging Alice to reconsider, to live with her and let Jessie care for her. But Alice had thought she could reconcile with the family she'd left.

Jessie, convinced it could only cause harm, had taken an endless series of buses to get to the address in Chicago that Alice had given her, only to be too late. Alice had gone back to Caleb.

Jessie eyed him covertly. How had he taken Alice's return? He'd accepted her back into his house because she was his wife. But Jessie couldn't believe he'd been glad to see her. And under the circumstances...

It was past, and it was futile to go over it again, but Jessie longed to replace the unhappy memories Becky must have with some happier ones of Alice. She was the only person who could tell the children stories of "when Mammi was a little girl," but Caleb wouldn't allow it.

Daniel came down the stairs just then, obviously dressed to go out. Zeb raised an eyebrow.

"Are you finally using the courting buggy for its right purpose, Daniel?"

Daniel gave a good-natured grin. "If that happens, I'll be sure to tell you. Tonight I'm meeting with that Englisch couple who's talking about having me do new kitchen cabinets for them." He shrugged. "Not sure it's the best thing for me right now, though."

"That would be a big job for you, ain't so?" Caleb looked concerned, and Jessie thought she knew why. He was afraid Daniel might turn the job down because he was needed to help Caleb. "Why wouldn't you take it?"

Daniel hesitated. "It'd take a lot of time. And an extra pair of hands, most likely. I'm used to working on my own."

"If you're thinking we need you here, don't." Caleb bit out the words. "I can hire another man if need be."

Daniel shrugged again. "We'll see what happens. I'd best find out what they want first." He scurried out as if eager to escape an argument.

Jessie bit her lip to keep from offering an opinion that wouldn't be welcomed. She realized the children were staring after their uncle, so she laid the mending aside.

"It's about time for bed. Shall we put away the blocks?"

For a moment she thought she'd have a protest on her hands, but after a quick look at her daadi's face, Becky began cleaning up. Jessie helped Timothy slide the barn they'd built into a corner out of the way. As long as he didn't have to tear his barn apart, he seemed willing enough.

In a few minutes she was shepherding the kinder upstairs. At a guess, Zeb and Caleb would take advantage of being alone to discuss this possible job of Daniel's and how it would affect them.

When Becky and Timothy were ready for bed, they unfortunately didn't seem ready for sleep. That always seemed to be a problem as the days grew longer. The daylight slipping into the room around the window shades convinced little ones they should stay up longer, even when they could hardly hold their eyes open.

"Tell us a story, Cousin Jessie." Timothy paused in the act of jumping on his bed. "Tell us a story before we go to sleep."

Becky didn't seem to be listening. Or at least, she was pretending not to be interested, busy settling her Amish faceless doll under the covers.

"A story. Now, let me think." Jessie looked into Timothy's blue eyes, so like Alice's, and the idea popped into her head. She couldn't tell them about Alice—or could she? If she didn't use Alice's name, Caleb would never know. And she wouldn't really be breaking her agreement, would she?

After a short struggle with her conscience, she gave in to the temptation.

"Once upon a time there were two little Amish girls," she began. "Their names were... Anna and Barbie."

"Were they twins?" Becky's attention seemed to be caught.

"No, no, they weren't. Anna was the big sister, and Barbie was the little sister. But even though they weren't twins, they liked to do things together, and Barbie would always say, 'Me, too, me, too' whenever Anna was doing something."

"Like me," Timothy said, grinning.

"Like you," she agreed, reaching out to tickle him. "So one day, they decided to go up the hill and pick blackberries."

"It must have been summer," Becky said wisely.

"Yah, it was. August, when the wild blackberries are ripe. So they each took a pail, and they went up the path to where the blackberries grew." She noted that Timothy had stopped wiggling and settled onto his pillow.

"The berries were so big and fat and juicy that they couldn't stop. They'd picked half a pail full each in no time at all. Anna picked the ones up high, and Barbie picked the ones on the bottom. They were just talking about what to make with the berries when what do you think Barbie saw under the blackberry brambles?"

"A bird," Timothy murmured sleepily.

"No, a turtle," Becky said.

"You're both wrong. It was a great big black snake. When Barbie saw it, she let out a huge shriek, threw her bucket into the air and ran as fast as she could go down the path. And the snake, who had been taking a nice nap in the shade of the bushes, went spinning around in a big circle and raced up the hill in the opposite direction as fast as it could go."

Becky giggled. "The snake was scared, too."

"I wouldn't be scared…" Timothy's words were interrupted by a huge yawn.

Jessie tucked the covers around him. "So Anna picked up all the berries she could find and took them back down the hill. Anna and Barbie helped their mammi make a big blackberry cobbler for supper, and they each had two pieces."

His eyes were closed. Jessie bent and kissed his cheek lightly. Then she went to Becky's bed. To her pleasure, Becky let her tuck the covers in and didn't even turn her face away from Jessie's kiss.

"Good night. Sleep tight," Jessie murmured. She went softly across the room and out into the hall.

When she turned from closing the door, her pulse gave a little jump. Zeb stood a few feet away.

"Ach, you startled me," she said softly. "I didn't know you'd komm upstairs."

"Just wanted my pipe." He gestured with it and then glanced at the door to the children's room. "I was in time to hear the story you were telling the kinder."

Something about his steady regard made her nervous. "Picking blackberries. It was maybe not as exciting as Onkel Daniel's version of fairy tales."

"It's best not to be too exciting when they're going to sleep, ain't so?" He paused for a moment. "Thing is, I'd heard that story before."

Jessie's breath caught. "When…when was that?"

"A long time ago now. Alice happened to see a black snake in the garden. Scared her, I guess. She mentioned the day she went picking berries with her big cousin and saw the snake."

Jessie pressed her hands together. She'd never thought of that. "Does Caleb know?" If he did, and the kinder mentioned the story…

Zeb shook his head. "He wasn't here that day. She didn't want him to know she'd been so foolish, she said."

"I see." She tried to still her whirling thoughts. "Are you going to tell Caleb I told the kinder a story about their mammi?"

Zeb lifted an eyebrow. "I didn't hear you mention Alice, ain't so?"

Jessie felt herself relax. "I don't wish to upset Caleb, but it seems…"

"Yah, I know." Zeb's voice sounded weary. "No good can come of bottling everything up. I've tried and tried to convince Caleb of that, but he isn't ready to listen."

"No." They stood together for a moment, and she knew that they understood each other. "I haven't repeated that story to anyone in a long time. But it…it made my little Alice seem real to me again. Maybe one day, the kinder will remember it and know it was about their mother."

"Maybe one day you'll be able to tell them yourself," Zeb said.

"Maybe," she echoed, but she doubted it.

"I like scrambled eggs better than anything." Timothy was his enthusiastic self at breakfast a few days later. "Don't you, Onkel Daniel?"

Daniel considered, head tilted and eyes twinkling. "Better than chocolate cake? Or whoopie pies?"

"Well, but... I mean for breakfast. Cousin Jessie wouldn't give us whoopie pies for breakfast."

Caleb glanced at his son. Funny how quickly Timothy had accepted Cousin Jessie as the authority on what he had for breakfast. After a week, he acted as if Jessie had been here forever.

At the moment, Jessie was entering into the fun, talking about how a whoopie pie could be a breakfast food and making Timothy giggle. She seemed to have overcome whatever had depressed her spirits on Sunday.

Maybe Zeb had been wrong in what he'd thought was going on. Maybe people were sensible enough to know that Jessie wasn't responsible for what Alice had done. The thought made him uncomfortable. Why was it sensible for others to think that when he himself acted as if blaming Jessie was okay?

He risked a glance at her face again. He didn't blame her, exactly. He just didn't like being constantly reminded of Alice. That was natural enough. Not Jessie's fault, but not his fault, either.

"More coffee?" Jessie had just filled Onkel Zeb's cup, and she stood next to Caleb, the coffeepot in her hand.

He nodded and watched the hot liquid stream into the heavy white cup he used. A simple gesture, refilling the coffee cups, but one that Alice had ignored often enough. It was a silly thing to have bothered him. After all, he could pour his own coffee.

"Maybe a little slice of that shoofly pie with my coffee," Daniel said. "A man's got to keep his strength up, after all." He grinned, looking as if he expected a tart response to that.

"You'll need it, if you're going to take on that kitchen job," Onkel Zeb said. "Did you make up your mind yet?"

Daniel shook his head as Jessie put a slab of shoofly pie in front of him. "Still have to work out all the figures before we get to an agreement. And I may not have the time and manpower to do it."

"I told you I'd hire another person to help on the farm until I'm rid of this cast." Caleb knew he sounded testy, but he couldn't help it.

Daniel eyed him. "Not so easy as you might think. Thomas is a fine helper, but I'm not sure where we'd find another like him."

"We can manage," Zeb said. "If someone has two good legs, I can teach him what to do."

"Is it possible…" Jessie began, and then fell silent when they all looked at her.

"Go on, Jessie," Zeb urged. "You have an idea?"

"Well, I just wondered if maybe there were things Caleb could do to help Daniel with the project—things he could do from the wheelchair that would free up Daniel's time."

Caleb swallowed his instant response. He shouldn't reject the idea just because it came from Jessie.

Daniel brightened, but then shook his head when Caleb didn't respond. "It would be too much for him."

"No. It wouldn't." No matter where the idea came from, it was a logical one. "If you lowered one of the work benches so I could reach it from the chair, there's plenty I could do. Better than sitting here feeling useless."

"That could make all the difference." Daniel gulped down the rest of his coffee and pushed his chair back. "I'll get started on those figures. Maybe you can come out to the shop after your exercises and we'll see if we can make it work." He beamed at Jessie. "Gut thought, Jessie."

Becky's fork clattered onto the table. "I'm done." She slid off her chair and started from the room.

"Take your plate to the sink first, please," Jessie said before Becky could make her escape.

"I want to go outside." Becky's face set in the pout that Caleb was seeing too often.

"Do as Cousin Jessie says, Becky." The least he could do was back Jessie up when she was right. Becky shouldn't be allowed to develop rebellious habits.

Becky just stared at him for a moment. Then, without a word, she came back, picked up her plate and utensils, and carried them to the sink.

"Denke, Becky," Jessie said. Ignoring Becky's lack of response, she began to clear the table with quick, deft movements. "When I've finished, will you be ready to start your exercises?"

Caleb suspected she thought he'd argue, but he wouldn't. He'd do whatever was necessary to get back to his normal self, including accepting help from Jessie.

By the time Jessie had pushed him through his first few exercises, Caleb was beginning to wonder if he really was willing to do anything to regain his strength. Jessie was much more of a taskmaster than he'd expected.

He stopped, panting a little at the exertion of attempting to lift his leg multiple times. "That's enough of that one."

"Just three more. Komm, you can do three more."

Caleb's temper flared in spite of himself. "I ought to know how many I can do."

"And what do you think the physical therapist would say to that?" she chided. "Now, if you were Becky's age, I could offer you a whoopie pie for doing it all ten times."

His momentary annoyance fizzled. "Are you saying I'm acting like a six-year-old?"

"What do you think?" Her eyes twinkled. "I'll help. Just three more."

Steeling himself, he managed to push himself through three more leg lifts.

"Wonderful gut," Jessie said. "You see? You can do whatever you put your mind to."

She sounded as if she had a routine for encouraging rebellious patients. "This can't be the first time you've done this—helped someone komm back from an injury, I mean."

"You remember all those brothers of mine, don't you? If one wasn't damaging himself, another one was. Mamm was too soft on them to make them exercise. And when Daad busted his leg…ach, if you think you're pigheaded, you should have seen my daad."

Jessie hadn't often relaxed like this when she talked to him. It was nice to see the affection in her eyes when she spoke of family.

She'd had a full, rich life in Ohio with her kin and her business, and she'd left it behind out of her need to help his family. She'd come here knowing what her reception would most likely be. He thought of what

Zeb had said about the attitude of the church family and felt a prickle of guilt.

"It's gut you had a chance to get acquainted with Leah so fast. She's been a wonderful gut neighbor to us."

"I can see that. It's been nice to get to know her a little and to feel she's ready to be friends. Especially since I don't know any other women here."

Caleb hesitated, but Zeb's words still rankled. "Did you talk to some of the other women after worship?"

"A few." Jessie's gaze slid away from his, and she busied herself getting out the elastic bands for his next set of exercises.

"Some of them must have made you feel wilkom." He was pushing, because he needed to know if his uncle had been right or not.

Jessie was silent for a long moment. At last she shrugged. "I'm sure they usually do so. But folks here know I'm Alice's cousin. They're bound to be resentful. I can't be surprised that they are not eager to accept me."

Caleb's fingers tightened on the arms of the chair. "You mean it's because of me. Because I am unforgiving." He stopped, aghast at what he'd said. To be lacking in forgiveness for the wrongs done to him by another person was to live in defiance of God's law.

"I don't… I didn't mean that," he said quickly, stumbling over the words. "I've forgiven Alice." *Over and over.* So why did he have to keep doing it?

"Have you?" Jessie's face twisted in what he thought was grief and hurt. "Sometimes I think forgiveness has to keep happening again and again, each time we think of the person who has wronged us. Until one day, we finally know we are free, and can think of them without pain."

He felt he was seeing Jessie for the first time. She might act sure of herself and competent, but inside there was pain and guilt.

"Yah." He found he was reaching out instinctively, clasping her hand in his. He could feel the flutter of her pulse against his skin and hear the catch in her breath. "Have you been able to forgive her and be free?"

Jessie's eyes met his, and the barriers between them slipped away for the moment, at least. She sighed. "I'm getting better at it, I think. Maybe, one day..."

"One day," he echoed. He would like to live without this tight ball of anger and resentment inside him. He just didn't know to get rid of it.

Her lips trembled a bit. "If I can help Becky and Timothy, perhaps I will go the rest of the way."

The lump in his throat made it hard to get the words out, but they had to be said.

"I'm sorry. Sorry I've made it more difficult for you, sorry for treating you as if you were to blame." His fingers moved against her skin. "Forgive me."

Whatever she might have answered was lost in a cry from the doorway. He turned, still clasping Jessie's hand, to find his daughter standing there, staring at them.

"Daadi! What are you doing?"

The anger in her small face shocked him. Maybe Jessie was right. Maybe Becky did need help.

"I am thanking Cousin Jessie for assisting me with my exercises," he said evenly. Jessie slipped her hand from his and stepped away, bending to pick up the exercise bands. "And you are being rude, Rebecca. You had best go to your room and think on it."

Becky stared at him with angry eyes. Then, with a sharp, cutting look at Jessie, she turned and ran toward the stairs.

Chapter Eight

Jessie couldn't get the expression on Becky's face out of her mind. She had been angry, yah, but upset, too. And then there were her own emotions to contend with. Maybe Caleb hadn't felt anything. Maybe it had all been her—her longing, her imagination, creating a momentary link that hadn't been real.

Caleb had certainly been quick to get back to his exercises after the interruption. Everything they had said to each other was strictly business. The minute they'd finished, he had headed out to the workshop, waving away her offer of help.

Thankfully Daniel must have been watching for him. From the kitchen window she saw Daniel hurry from his shop along the gravel lane to intercept his brother and push the wheelchair on its way. The shop was even farther from the house than the barn. Caleb was stubborn, that was all. She just hoped he wasn't so stubborn he'd hurt himself.

Jessie turned away, occupying herself with the fabric fragments she'd been gathering for the quilt project she wanted to start with Becky. A small nine-patch quilt, suitable for a doll's cradle—that was a good beginner project. In fact, it was the one her mamm had started her on all those years ago.

Mamm would have done the same with Alice. Jessie felt sure of it, even though she didn't remember the specifics. Mamm had been determined to do all she could after Alice's mother passed.

Jessie had enough scraps to start the doll quilt. Whether she'd have any cooperation from Becky was another question.

Picking up her sewing bag, she went into the hall and called up the stairs. "Becky and Timothy? Komm down for a minute, please."

Timothy bounded down the steps as he always did, his feet thudding on each tread. Becky came more slowly, running her hand along the rail. Jessie had thought she might have been crying but could see no sign of tears on her face.

"I have my sewing bag here, and I thought maybe you'd like to start on a sewing project. There are a lot of scraps in the scrap bag, so we could make a little quilt or maybe a pot holder together."

Timothy would no doubt want to do whatever his sister did, but the project she had in mind for Becky would be beyond his abilities. Still, she could find something to keep him busy.

"I want to make something." Timothy ran over to her and tugged on the bag. "Komm on, Becky."

"No." When they both looked at her, Becky managed to ignore Jessie. "I'm going to collect the eggs. Komm with me, and I'll show you how to do it."

Timothy looked a little hesitant, and Jessie suspected she knew why. He was a bit scared of the chickens, especially the bad-tempered Rhode Island Red.

"You're not scared, are you?" Becky knew just how to prompt him to do what she wanted.

"I'm not scared of any chicken. I'll get the basket." He ran toward the back door, and Becky followed him.

Jessie set her sewing bag on the floor next to the rocker. She'd known this wouldn't be easy, especially with Becky. Maybe she should have waited a bit longer to allow time for her to get over her little snit at seeing her daadi holding Jessie's hand.

At the moment, she'd best get outside so she could keep an eye on the egg gathering from a distance. She could logically be checking on the garden, couldn't she?

Jessie was bending over a few green leaflets that were already above ground while she watched the children approach the chicken coop. Becky, carrying the egg basket, unhooked the door and stepped right in. Timothy held back for a minute as the hens rushed toward Becky in hope of food. Then Becky said something to him, and he stepped into the enclosure.

If this helped Timothy get over his fear, it would be a good thing. He followed his sister under the shelter of the roof where the laying boxes waited. If the hens had been cooperative, this shouldn't take long.

Jessie let her gaze stray toward the workshop. How was Caleb getting along? If only he could do something, even if it wasn't his usual work, he'd be happier.

Time hung heavy when a busy person suddenly had no responsibilities.

A squawk from the henhouse captured her attention. She craned her neck, trying to make out what was happening. Timothy's voice alerted her—he was yelling for his sister, and the red hen was chasing him.

Jessie got up quickly. Before she could go more than a few steps, Becky had reached her brother. She shoved him out the door and slammed it behind her. Timothy let out an anguished howl, and Jessie ran. That wasn't fear. It was pain.

When Jessie reached them, both children were outside the chicken coop. Becky was crying nearly as hard as Timothy was.

Jessie caught them, turning them toward her. Her heart pounded so loudly she could hardly hear. "What's happened? Who is hurt?"

They both tried to answer at once, and she could make no sense of it at all.

"Hush, now. I can't understand you when you're crying. Who is hurt?"

Becky managed to check her sobs. "Timmy. I didn't mean it. I slammed the door on his finger."

"Ach, now, we know you didn't mean it." She drew Timothy close against her. "Komm, Timothy. You must let me see your finger so I can tell how badly it's hurt."

"Don't touch it," he cried. Reluctantly he held his hand out, and she took it gently in hers.

"I think maybe you'll live, ain't so?" The small finger was red and puffing up a little, and an open scrape didn't make it look any better. But judging by the way he was moving his finger, it probably wasn't broken.

He started to cry again, and she picked him up, holding him close against her.

"It will be all right. I promise. Komm, Becky. Let's go in the house and fix your bruder's finger, okay?"

Tears still dripped down Becky's cheeks, but she nodded. At least they'd both stopped wailing. Jessie took a cautious look toward the workshop, but obviously the men hadn't heard the commotion. Just as well. She'd like to get everyone calmed down and cleaned up before trying to explain this to Caleb.

Becky hurried ahead of her to hold the door open, and they went into the kitchen. Still cradling Timothy against her shoulder, Jessie pulled a handful of ice from the gas refrigerator.

"Becky, will you get a clean dish towel from the drawer for me?"

Nodding, Becky hurried to obey. Having something useful to do seemed to calm her tears a little. She rushed back with the towel.

Jessie sat down at the table with Timothy on her lap, detaching him from her shoulder. "We're going to put ice on your finger. That will help it stop hurting. Will you let Becky hold your hand steady?"

Sniffling, Timothy nodded, extending his hand toward his sister. Suppressing a few sniffles of her own, Becky took his hand gingerly. She held it while Jessie wrapped the towel around the ice and put it gently against the injured finger. Timothy winced at first, but then he seemed to relax when he realized it wouldn't make matters worse.

"Gut job, Becky. Timothy is a brave boy, ain't so?"

"Is it broken? Like Daadi's leg?" Becky's voice wavered.

Timothy actually brightened at that idea, convincing Jessie that he wasn't badly hurt. "Will I get a cast?"

"No, I don't think it's broken. But it has a nasty scrape. We'll need to put a bandage on it, won't we, Becky?"

Becky nodded and ran to the kitchen drawer where first aid supplies were kept. She brought the whole box back with her.

"Gut. We'll keep the ice on just a little longer, I think." She affixed the bandage in place and held the ice against it, then tried a smile for the two of them, who still looked woebegone. "We're going to have to teach that red hen who is boss, ain't so?"

Becky's face seemed to crumple again. "It wasn't the hen. It was me. It's all my fault!" She bolted from the room before Jessie could stop her.

Jessie bit her lip. She'd tried not to interfere, but this time she had to. Becky couldn't go on like this, flaring up about things and then running off. Somehow she had to get through to the child.

But first, Timothy must be taken care of. His bottom lip was trembling again, no doubt in reaction to his sister's tears. She was reminded of her mother, saying that there were times when every mammi needed an extra pair of hands. Maybe she wasn't Becky and Timothy's mammi, but right now she was all they had.

"Becky feels bad because you got hurt, ain't so?" She smoothed Timothy's hair back from his rounded forehead. "She loves you."

Timothy snuggled against her. "Do you think Daadi cried when he got hurt?"

She suppressed a smile. "I'm sure he felt like crying, even if he didn't. Lots of times grown-ups do."

That seemed to satisfy him. After another minute of snuggling, he started to wiggle. "Maybe a cookie would make my finger feel better."

Jessie dropped a kiss on his hair. "I don't know about your finger, but I'll bet your tummy would like it. How about a snickerdoodle and a glass of milk?"

He nodded, and she set him on his own chair and got out the promised snack. He was using his hurt finger normally by the time he'd had a bite, so it was safe to assume he'd be okay. Now for Becky.

"I'll see if Becky wants a snack. You wait here for us, okay?"

"Okay," he said thickly around a mouthful of cookie.

With a silent prayer for guidance, Jessie climbed the stairs toward the children's bedroom.

Becky lay on her bed, both arms wrapped around her pillow. Her face was buried, but her shoulders still shook with muffled sobs. She looked so small and vulnerable that Jessie's heart ached.

She sat on the edge of the bed. When Becky didn't move, Jessie leaned over to put her hand on the child's back.

"Timothy is eating snickerdoodles. I think that means his finger feels much better. That's gut, ain't so?"

Becky didn't respond. Well, Jessie hadn't expected it to be as simple as that. Whatever troubled Becky, it was bigger than the question of her brother's finger.

"You feel bad because Timothy got hurt, I know. But it was an accident. Accidents happen to everyone. All we can do is try to be more careful."

That got a response from Becky. She shoved herself up on her elbows and pounded the pillow. "It's my fault! He's my little bruder. I have to take care of him."

"I know. I have little brothers, too." *And once I had a little cousin.* "But we can't always stop them from getting hurt, no matter what we do."

"It's my fault. It's always my fault…just like when Mammi went away."

Jessie's heart seemed to stop. She had to repeat the words over in her own mind before she could take them in. Becky was blaming herself for Alice leaving. Why hadn't any of them seen that?

"Becky, listen…" She swallowed her words. Careful…she had to be very careful in what she said now. "Why would you think it was your fault that your mammi left?"

"Because it was. If I'd been better, or prettier, or…"

"Ach, Becky, don't!" She put her arm around the thin shoulders, ignoring the way Becky stiffened at her touch. "That's not true. It isn't. I know."

"How do you know? You weren't here." Becky's jaw set, reminding her of Caleb.

"No, I wasn't." *I wish I had been.* "But your mammi wrote to me all the time. Every week she wrote. And you know what she said about you?"

That caught Becky's attention. She actually turned to look at Jessie. "What?"

Jessie risked stroking her hair. "She said she had the prettiest little daughter ever. She told me all about what you did…when you took your first step, when you got your first tooth, everything. She was so very pleased with you, and she loved you so much."

"Then why did she go away?" The rebellious note

was gone from her voice. Poor child. She wanted so much to know it wasn't because of her.

But how did Jessie answer her in a way that a six-year-old could understand? "I don't think even your mamm really understood why," she said carefully. "She was very young when she got married, and maybe she hadn't grown up enough yet. And sometimes she got really sad. Not because of what anyone did but just because of something inside her. It was like being sick. We don't blame people or get angry with them for being sick, do we?"

Jessie's own thoughts seemed to clarify as she tried to explain to the child. Who could say why Alice had been the person she was? Maybe having her mamm die when she was so young had started something inside her that none of them had understood.

"No, but..."

"No buts," Jessie said gently. "One thing we know for sure. It wasn't your fault that your mamm left. I promise."

Some of the tension eased out of Becky's face. She sat up, leaning against Jessie's arm for a precious moment before pulling away.

Becky wasn't entirely convinced. No one ever gave up a deeply held belief because of a few simple words.

Jessie knew that. She knew because looking into Becky's face was like looking into a mirror and seeing her own pain.

Just like Becky, she'd been telling herself that what Alice did was her fault. But Alice, no matter what problems she had, had been a grown woman, not a little girl.

There might be nothing Jessie could do about her own feelings, but there was something she had to do about Becky's. She must talk to Caleb about this, whether he wanted to hear it or not. Healing Becky's hurt would take effort on all their parts, not just on hers.

Caleb pushed the wheelchair through the back door and into the kitchen. No help needed, he told himself. There might be things he couldn't do, but he wasn't helpless, and that was a wonderful gut feeling.

He found Jessie alone in the kitchen, cutting up a chicken at the counter. "Chicken tonight, yah?"

He'd keep the talk between them light and casual. No more conversation that led to revealing emotions, and definitely no more touching. He still seemed to feel her pulse beating against his palm, and that wouldn't do.

Jessie's smile seemed a little strained. She was probably as uncomfortable about what had passed between them as he was. Not that it had meant anything.

"Chicken and homemade noodles, just like my grossmammi always made."

"I remember." Jessie's family had spread the wilkom mat on his first visit to Ohio, and her mother and grandmother had stuffed him until he was ready to burst. "Are yours as gut as hers?"

"I wouldn't go that far," she said lightly. She glanced at the clock. "You were out at the shop for two hours or more. You must be ready for a rest."

He shook his head, helping himself to a snickerdoodle from the cookie jar. "It felt great to be working again. Not that I'm anywhere near the craftsman Daniel is. He always had a feel for wood, even when he was a kid. I'm an apprentice compared to him."

"Even an apprentice can be helpful," she said, moving the heavy Dutch oven onto the stove. "This job… it's important to Daniel, ain't so?"

"Very. If he satisfies an Englisch client, he'll probably get a lot more orders. He shouldn't miss a chance like that. Even if all I can do is attach hinges and finish the wood, it frees Daniel up to do the hard part."

Jessie leaned against the sink, drying her hands. "You could reach everything all right?"

"Daniel fitted up a makeshift workbench that's just the right height for me." He slapped his palms on the arms of the chair. "Even if I'm stuck in this thing, I can still work. I…"

Caleb stopped. Here he was blabbing away about it as if he was some kind of hero for helping his brother, after all Daniel was doing for him. That was bad enough, but worse, he'd completely ignored the fact that it had been Jessie's suggestion in the first place.

Jessie was looking at him with some concern, probably because he'd stopped what he was saying in midstream. He shook his head.

"Ach, I'm forgetting the most important thing. You're the one who thought of it to begin with. Denke, Jessie."

She gave a quick shrug. "You would have, I'm sure."

Maybe, but she had first. He glanced around the kitchen, belatedly aware of how quiet it was. "Where is everyone?"

"Your uncle had to run over to the feed mill, so he took Becky and Timothy with him. They should be back soon." Now it was her turn to hesitate. "While they're out, I'd like to have a word with you about Becky."

"If it's about her being sassy this morning…" He was caught in a cleft stick. He could hardly say it was none of her business when she was taking care of his kinder.

"No, not that." A faint flush rose in her cheeks. "It's something that happened later. She told Timothy she'd show him how to gather the eggs from the chickens, so they went out to the coop."

If that was all, it hardly seemed worth her bringing it up. "I'm surprised he went. He's a little bit scared of the chickens."

"I know. But he wanted to appear brave to his sister, so he went." She hesitated. "I know Becky does that by herself, but I kept an eye on them since Timothy was going."

Caleb gave an impatient nod. Jessie was picking her words carefully over nothing, it seemed.

"I heard a ruckus and went running. I'm not sure exactly what happened, but I think that bad-tempered red took off after him. He was trying to get out, and in all the fuss, Becky accidentally shut the door on his finger."

"He's all right?" He must have been, if he'd gone off to the feed mill with Onkel Zeb.

"He's fine." Her face relaxed in a smile. "I think they were both more scared than anything. I took care of the scraped finger, and Timothy was happy again in no time."

"Well, then…"

"But Becky wasn't." Jessie looked at him, her hazel eyes dark and serious. "I found her upstairs crying her heart out. She was blaming herself, you see, for Timothy getting hurt."

He frowned. "I'm more used to boys than girls. I don't recall my brothers being upset about something like that, but Becky is more sensitive. That's all."

"You're thinking I'm making a mountain out of a molehill."

Jessie's comment was so near the truth that he had to smile. "Aren't you?"

"It was what else she said that troubles me." Jessie took a breath. "She said she was to blame for Timothy getting hurt. Just as she was to blame for her mammi going away."

The words hit Caleb like a blow to the stomach. For an instant it seemed the wind had been knocked out of him. He finally got his breath so he could speak. "She couldn't think that."

"She does." Jessie's lips trembled. "I'm sorry. I know you don't want to hear it. And you don't want me to mention Alice. But it's no use trying to handle her leaving and her dying that way. Don't you see?" She leaned toward him, almost pleading. "Becky has that guilt in her heart, foolish as it is. You can't make it go away by pretending it isn't there."

He spun the chair away from her, because he was afraid of what his own face might betray. "Didn't you tell Becky she was wrong?"

"Of course I did." Now it was Jessie who sounded impatient. "I tried to get through to her. I told her how often her mammi talked about her in letters, and how happy she was to have a sweet little daughter." Jessie's voice tightened on that. "Alice did love them, you know. Despite what she did."

Caleb wanted to push everything away, because it

hurt too much to talk about it. But Jessie... Jessie had come too far into their lives for that, like it or not.

"I'll talk to her," he said, trying to sound sure of himself. "I'll convince her it wasn't her fault."

"I know you'll try to make it better. But it's not easy to let go of the burden of guilt, no matter how irrational it may be. Becky..."

"All right!" He couldn't take any more. "I'll do what I can. Just leave it alone for now."

Chapter Nine

Had Caleb tried to talk to Becky about her mother or not? Jessie sat with her sewing basket at her feet that evening, wondering. Somehow she thought not. Caleb's stoic expression might not reveal his emotions, but Becky would be showing the effects if he'd said anything.

Becky was quiet, for sure, but it was the same quiet that she'd maintained since her bout of crying earlier in the day. Maybe Caleb had had no opportunity to get Becky alone for a serious talk. Or maybe he was avoiding the job, unwilling to open that box of trouble.

Jessie could understand. It was always tempting to pretend that nothing was wrong, sometimes even convincing yourself. After all, she'd convinced herself that she'd done everything she could to keep Alice from coming back here to die. But had she? Had she been able to disentangle her own feelings from what was best for everyone?

And then there was the realization that she and Becky were doing the same thing—blaming themselves for what Alice had done. Becky was clearly wrong. She could have done nothing. Jessie would like to say the same of herself, but she couldn't quite convince herself.

Life could be like the tangle of thread she'd discovered in her sewing basket—impossible even to find an end to pull.

She could fix the thread with a pair of scissors. The same wasn't true of relationships among people.

Smoothing out a couple of the fabric squares she'd cut, she started to pin them together for a small quilt. Timothy, deserting his toy barn, came over to see.

"What are you making, Cousin Jessie?" He fingered one of the pieces and narrowly missed pricking himself on a pin. "What will it be?"

"It'll be a quilt when it's finished." She smiled at him. "But it won't have any pins in it then to stick you."

"Gut." He gave a little shiver as if imagining himself wrapped in a quilt with pins. "Can I do it?"

She glanced at Caleb, wondering if he'd object to his son learning to use a needle. But he seemed intent on something he was jotting on a tablet.

"Sure thing. Let me get you some pieces of your own to sew." She found a couple of scraps and held them together. "The needle goes down through the material and then back up through. Try putting it in right here."

His little face intent, tongue sticking slightly out of the corner of his mouth, he managed to push the needle through and promptly dropped it so that it hung by the thread. "I did it."

"Yah, you did. Now keep pulling on the needle until the thread is tight. Next we'll come back up through the material." Experience with her small nieces and nephews had taught her that it was too much to expect him to make a complete stitch in one movement.

She took a covert look at Becky and discovered that she was watching them. Good. She was interested. Now to reel her in. "There's some material here if you'd like to try, Becky."

Becky hesitated and then came over. She stood in front of Jessie with her hands linked as if to show that she wasn't really all that intrigued.

"Why don't you pick out two pieces of different colors you think would look nice next to each other."

She handed Becky the basket and began threading a needle for her, stopping only to help Timothy in his efforts to stab the material without stabbing himself.

In a moment Becky had pulled a stool over and settled in next to Jessie. As she'd imagined, Becky's little fingers were quite nimble, and she soon got on to the idea of making small, even stitches. Her line of stitches wasn't quite straight, but it was very good for a first try.

"Look at that. You've done this before, haven't you?"

Becky smiled. "Leah showed me a little bit, and I practiced. It's fun."

"My fingers are tired," Timothy announced. "I need to put my horse in the barn." He dropped his material in Jessie's lap and reached for the horse, then paused. "Tell us another story about the big sister and little sister. Is there one with a pony in it?"

Jessie really didn't want to tell her thinly disguised

story in front of Caleb, but it seemed her chickens had come home to roost. She glanced at Zeb, who gave a tiny shrug. At least Caleb wasn't paying much attention.

"Once upon a time, Anna was teaching Barbie how to drive the pony cart. Their pony was named Snowflake. Know why?"

Timothy blinked, shaking his head, but Becky grinned. "It was white, ain't so?"

"That's right. It was a pretty little white pony, but when they drove the cart through a puddle, she got all muddy. So they decided to give her a bath."

She spun out the story, seeing that Timothy's eyes were growing heavy while he listened. He leaned against her knee, patting the toy horse.

"So when the pony was sparkling clean, Anna and Barbie led her up toward the house to show Mammi. But they didn't watch where they were going, and before you knew it, Snowflake saw a nice freshly plowed garden and thought it would be a great place to roll."

Timothy started to giggle, anticipating what the pony would do, and Becky grinned.

"So Anna and Barbie grabbed the rope and pulled as hard as they could, but they couldn't stop that determined pony. She rolled and rolled right in the dirt. And then she stood up and shook herself, and the wet dirt flew all over Anna and Barbie until they were even dirtier than Snowflake. Mammi came out, and they thought she'd be mad, but instead she laughed until the tears rolled down her cheeks."

The kinder laughed almost as much as Mammi had that day, especially Timothy, who found the image of the mud-splattered little girls hilarious.

Once again, just telling the story seemed to bring Alice alive again for her. It hurt, yes, but at the same time it was comforting. Those we lost did live on in our memories, it seemed.

"Time to get ready for bed," she said firmly when Timothy suggested another story. She shooed them toward the stairs and was about to follow when Caleb said her name.

Jessie paused, looking back at him.

"That story…" Caleb hesitated. "Would I be right in thinking it a true story?"

So he knew. Had Alice told him at some point, or was it just obvious from her own emotions?

"Yah, it was true."

He nodded, his eyes going dark with pain. "I thought so."

She waited for him to forbid it, but the words she anticipated didn't come.

"All right," he said at last. "All right." His voice was heavy, and her heart ached for him. But she knew better than to comfort him. He couldn't accept that, not from her.

Caleb stared down at the cast on his leg for a few minutes, hearing the sound of Jessie's retreating footsteps. He'd been so sure he was right to forbid any talk about Alice. That part of their lives was over, and the best thing they could do was forget.

But he'd been wrong, if doing so had allowed his daughter to blame herself. He still wasn't sure how to fix it, but perhaps letting Jessie tell her stories was a step in the right direction.

"Something is wrong," Onkel Zeb observed. "Will you tell me?"

Caleb moved his shoulders restlessly, trying to get rid of the weight of the guilt. "I'm not hiding it," he muttered, knowing that was exactly what he was doing. From himself, most of all. "Becky got upset this morning, and she told Jessie something she's kept secret from the rest of us." He forced himself to display a calm he didn't feel. "Becky says it's her fault that her mother went away."

For a long moment there was silence. Onkel Zeb shook his head slowly, his face sorrowful. "Poor child. Poor little child."

"I should have known." The truth burst out on a wave of pain. "I should have been the one to find out, not Jessie."

"Maybe it was easier for Becky to say it to Jessie instead of you."

"I'm her daad. She barely knows Jessie." Resentment edged his tone.

"How could Becky tell you?" He asked the question and just let it lie there between them. Onkel Zeb had always done that when the brothers tried to evade responsibility that belonged to them. His uncle looked at him steadily until Caleb's gaze fell.

Caleb's throat grew tight. "I never spoke of her mother. She must have thought she couldn't. So she kept it to herself. Brooded on it, most likely. And I never realized."

That was the bitterest thing of all—he hadn't realized something was wrong. Becky had lost all the laughter and sunshine she'd once possessed, and he hadn't even guessed at the cause.

"It won't be easy to change her mind," Zeb observed.

"That's what Jessie said. It will take more than just telling her it's not her fault to make her really believe it."

"Cousin Jessie has a gut heart," his uncle observed. "And a sharp eye where the kinder are concerned."

"I don't deny that. I just wish…"

He didn't know what he wished. That she'd never come here? But if he hadn't broken his leg, if she hadn't come and insisted on staying in spite of his order, how long would it have taken him to find out what was happening with his daughter?

"Your parents' failings hurt all three of you boys." His uncle's voice was heavy. "Look at the results. You married a girl who was nowhere near ready to be a wife and mother. Daniel smiles and guards his heart from love. And Aaron runs away entirely."

"You can't blame all that on Mamm and Daad. They didn't mean to hurt us."

"Not meaning to has caused a lot of trouble." Onkel Zeb sounded more severe than Caleb could ever remember. "And now you. You didn't mean to hurt Becky by your silence. But it happened. If you are not careful, your kinder will be as afraid of loving as you are."

Caleb wanted to argue. The words boiled inside him, but he couldn't let them out. If there was even a chance that Onkel Zeb was right, he must do something. Must change. And the pitiful thing was that he didn't know how.

"Onkel Daniel says he saw a few ripe strawberries in the strawberry patch." Jessie kept a firm hold on

Timothy's hand as they approached the patch that lay between the barn and Daniel's workshop. He was only too likely to run right over the plants in his eagerness.

"I want to pick lots," he exclaimed.

"It's too early for there to be lots," Becky said wisely.

"That's right." Jessie smiled at her, relieved that Becky seemed a little more herself this morning.

"Not like when Anna and Barbie picked the blackberries," Becky said, eyes already focused on the green plants. "Maybe we can have enough to eat, though."

"Or make a rhubarb strawberry cobbler. Onkel Zeb said Daadi loves that," Jessie said. Jessie stopped at the edge of the strawberry patch and knelt to capture Timothy's wandering attention. "We walk only on the path between the plants, ain't so? And we move the leaves very, very gently to look."

"And only pick the really red ones," Becky added. "I'll watch him, Cousin Jessie."

Jessie nodded. Becky still wanted to look out for her little brother, and that was how it should be. But she didn't seem quite so determined to push Jessie out of the picture.

Could Jessie say the same for Caleb? Maybe, at least a little. He could have been angry the previous night when he'd realized her stories were about Alice. He hadn't been. Grieved, yes, but he would put his own pain aside if it meant helping his children.

"I found some," Timothy shouted, and Jessie stepped carefully over the row to look.

"Yah, those are fine to pick. Yum, they'll be delicious."

"I got some, too," Becky began, and then gave a startled yelp. "Look what's here! Komm, schnell."

Jessie picked Timothy up and swung him over the row of plants he was about to step on. They found Becky squatting next to a turtle.

"Not a snake, like the story. A turtle," Becky said. She touched the shell with the tip of her finger. "Is it dead?"

"No, he's just hiding in his shell. He's afraid of boys and girls, I think. He's called a box turtle."

"Why?" Timothy wanted to know.

Jessie grinned. "I have no idea. But my daadi said that's what this kind of turtle was, and I believed him."

"Did you find one when you were my age?" Becky asked.

"Just about. My brother and I were picking strawberries when we found him. We put our initials on his shell, so whenever we saw him we knew he was our friend."

"Can we do that?" Becky jumped up. "I'll get a crayon."

"We need something more lasting than crayon. Why don't you run over to the shop and ask Onkel Daniel for a permanent marker?"

"Okay." Becky leaped over the rows of berry plants and streaked off toward the shop.

"Does the turtle eat the berries?" Timothy clutched his berry container close to his chest.

"I don't know, but I'm sure there will be enough for all of us. You could watch him and see."

Timothy squatted, staring intently at the turtle, who seemed equally intent on staying safe in his shell and peering out at Timothy.

Amused, Jessie concentrated on picking the ripe berries along the edges of the rows. If the children's attention lasted, they might get a pint or more, and the berries along the edges should be picked before they attracted the attention of hungry birds.

"Daadi's coming," Timothy said, looking up from his absorption.

Jessie's heart gave a little thump when she spotted Becky pushing the wheelchair toward them while Caleb propelled the wheels with his hands. She almost jumped up to help but caught herself. Better to let Becky do it and give them a chance to talk.

But it looked as if their thoughts were only on the turtle. Becky waved a marker in one hand. "Daadi wants to see, too."

"We'll bring the turtle to him." Jessie picked the creature up carefully and carried it to a spot on the edge of the patch where Caleb could examine it easily.

"Here we are. I suspect he'll stay in his shell until we leave. Becky, will you put a *B* for Becky or an *R* for Rebecca?"

Becky knelt, uncapping the marker. "A *B*, 'cause mostly I'm Becky. Where shall I put it, Daadi?"

Caleb gave the question serious consideration, but his eyes twinkled a little. "Why don't you do one side and let Timothy do the other?"

Becky nodded and advanced the marker toward the shell. She hesitated, the pen wavering a bit. "Cousin Jessie, will you hold it still?"

It seemed highly unlikely the turtle would venture out of its shell, but she nodded, steadying it until Becky had put a small *B* on one side.

"Now me, now me!" Timothy squished his way between them. "Hold him still, Cousin Jessie."

"Gently now," Jessie cautioned.

"You don't need to press hard," Caleb added, lips quirking as he and Jessie exchanged a glance.

Jessie's heart warmed for no good reason. But just for a moment he'd reminded her of the optimistic young man she'd spent an afternoon with a long time ago.

And lost my heart to, a small voice whispered. She did her best to ignore it.

"Sehr gut," she said when Timothy had managed a wobbly *T* on the ridged shell.

"Just like you did, ain't so?" he said, and turned to his father. "Cousin Jessie and her brother did that when they were our age."

"Did you ever put your initial on a turtle, Daadi?" Becky asked.

"No, I don't think so." Caleb hesitated, and Jessie saw his brown eyes darken a little. Odd how quickly she had learned to read his moods. He was thinking of something that saddened him.

Caleb reached out to pull Becky into the circle of his arm. "But once I put a *C* for Caleb and an *A* for Alice on that big old apple tree by the paddock. That was when I was courting your mammi." He smoothed a strand of Becky's hair back. "I'll bet you can find it if you look. Komm back and tell me, yah?"

Becky's eyes had widened at the mention of her mother. She nodded tentatively as if not sure that was the best thing to do. Then she ran off toward the apple tree, with Timothy in hot pursuit.

It took Jessie a moment or two to be sure she had

mastery of her voice. "That was gut for her to hear, I think."

"I hope so." His voice was sober. "Onkel Zeb said…"

He let that trail off, and his face closed down. Apparently she wasn't meant to know what Zeb had said. But whatever it was, she suspected it was good advice. She was almost afraid to speak for fear of ruining the step forward he'd taken.

Caleb was looking after his children, who were circling the apple tree. "I hope you…we are right about this."

Her heart clutched at the way he'd coupled them together in the responsibility. "Yah."

Finally Caleb looked at her, something a little rueful in his gaze. "Any thoughts on what to do next?"

Was he seriously asking for her advice? She couldn't quite accept that he was relying on her, but she did have an answer if he wanted one.

"Becky said once that she didn't want to look like her mammi, because you wouldn't like that." She stopped, afraid she'd gone too far.

Caleb brushed a hand at his forehead as if brushing away cobwebs. "She does look like Alice. I never realized…" He shook his head slightly. "Becky shouldn't feel that way about how she looks. But being pretty isn't everything."

Jessie forced a smile. "I'm afraid it's the first thing a young man notices."

But he didn't put it off lightly. "A gut heart is worth more than a pretty face."

Did he mean that as a compliment? She found herself ridiculously elated, even while thinking that no woman especially wanted to be praised for her plain looks. Now, if a man found beauty in the person who had the good heart—well, perhaps that was reaching for the moon.

Jessie reminded herself that she had long since become satisfied with the life she had. It wouldn't do to let being here make her long for something that was out of reach and always had been.

Chapter Ten

It was an off Sunday, so Caleb wouldn't have to sit through another worship service wondering if folks were feeling sorry for him. Like most Amish church districts, worship here was held every other Sunday. In the intervening week, a family might travel to worship with a neighboring district or spend a peaceful day at family gatherings.

Peaceful. Somehow that didn't exactly describe today's visiting. The whole family was invited to Zeb's cousin Judith's house for her usual immense family meal, giving opportunities for everyone to speculate on Jessie's presence among them.

At the moment, he, Onkel Zeb and Daniel were lingering over coffee in the kitchen, watching Jessie packing the pies she'd made into a basket.

Daniel put his mug in the sink and went to peer over

her shoulder. "You're not going to take all four pies to Cousin Judith's, are you? We'll be fortunate to get a slice. If you left them for us…"

"And go empty-handed?" She set the fourth pie on the rack in the basket. "We can't do that. And I don't think you'll go hungry if it's like any family meal I've ever gone to."

Daniel grimaced, and Caleb knew just what he was thinking. "The food will be wonderful gut, but I'd just as soon stay home if I had my way."

Before Jessie could react, Onkel Zeb chuckled. She looked at him inquiringly.

He grinned. "Ask Daniel why he doesn't want to see my cousin."

Jessie couldn't know it was a family joke, but she did as he directed. "Why, Daniel?"

"Onkel Zeb can laugh. It's not him she's after," Daniel grumbled. "Every single time I see Cousin Judith, she wants to know why I'm not married yet."

"And then she starts talking about all the young women she thinks would be perfect for him," Caleb added, grinning at his brother's discomfort. "If he's not quick on his feet, he'll find himself courting someone without even knowing it."

"You should talk," Daniel retorted. "She's starting to think about you now. She's probably lining up available widows. She says the kinder need—"

"Time to hitch up the carriage," Onkel Zeb said loudly, covering the end of that sentence.

For an instant Caleb was startled, but then he saw Becky and Timothy coming and understood. Just as well if the kinder didn't hear any speculation about him remarrying, which he wasn't going to do, anyway.

Jessie jumped into the momentary silence. "Becky, will you wrap up a couple of the oatmeal cookies for you and Timothy during the ride to Cousin Judith's?"

Becky's slight frown vanished, and she trotted over to Jessie. "Two for Timothy and two for me, yah?" She reached for the cookie jar on the counter.

Caleb nodded. "That's gut. Timmy, you go along and help Onkel Daniel hitch up. It's time we were on the road."

The awkward moment passed. Daniel sent an apologetic glance toward Caleb and went out, Timothy at his heels.

He couldn't very well blame Daniel. Or Cousin Judith, for that matter. Speculation about the marital prospects of bachelors was common in the Amish community, and the blabbermauls had been gossiping about the King brothers for years.

Jessie was supervising while Becky tucked a snowy napkin over the pies in the basket. She seemed to have an instinctive awareness of Becky's need to help, and she went out of her way to invite that assistance. Jessie was thoughtful when it came to the children. He had to give her that. She seemed to have noticed things in a little over a week that he hadn't picked up on in a year.

He didn't like that idea, but he couldn't seem to dismiss it, either.

Soon they were all assembling outside to climb into the family carriage for the ride to the farm where Cousin Judith lived with her youngest son and his family. There were sure to be plenty of cousins and second cousins there, all curious about Jessie. Did Jessie realize that?

Her expression was as serene and composed as always, but he thought he detected a hint of worry in her eyes. While he wondered whether he should say something, Onkel Zeb supervised loading everyone into the carriage. Before Caleb quite understood what was happening, he found he was driving, with Jessie sitting beside him.

"You can tell Jessie about the valley along the way," Zeb said blandly. "She hasn't had a chance to see much of anything since she came."

What Jessie thought about that, Caleb couldn't say. She was glancing across the field, and the brim of her bonnet hid her face from him.

Daniel seemed to be teasing Becky in the back of the carriage—Caleb heard her giggle. He glanced back. "Don't get the kinder all riled up before we reach Cousin Judith's," he warned. "Not unless you want to be responsible for calming them down again."

"Hey, I'm just their onkel," Daniel protested. "I'm supposed to be fun."

"How about a game of I Spy?" Jessie suggested. "You can look for signs of spring. I spy a willow tree that has its leaves out. What do you see?"

Of course both of them started naming things, trying to top each other. Since Jessie couldn't very well keep turning around, Onkel Zeb and Daniel took over the game, and they were soon completely engrossed.

"That was a gut idea," Caleb said under the cover of their noise. "Denke, Jessie. Daniel always did like to stir things up."

"When he's a father, he'll learn," she said, smiling a little.

"If," Caleb muttered, thinking of what Zeb said about the influence their parents' troubles had on them.

She shrugged, obviously not wanting to venture an opinion on the subject.

They passed two other Amish buggies headed in the other direction, no doubt on the same mission they were. Each buggy had a husband and wife in the front, of course, and he was suddenly very conscious of Jessie sitting beside him. What was she thinking? Any casual observer might assume they were husband and wife.

Onkel Zeb had no doubt thought of that. He was getting as bound on mischief as Daniel was, in his own way. What did he think was going to happen?

Caleb had been silent too long, and he saw that Jessie was looking at him with apprehension. He cleared his throat, trying to find the right way to reassure her.

"I thought maybe…" He ran out of words, not sure what he wanted to say.

"Yah?" Her eyebrows lifted.

The game was still going full blast in the back of the carriage, and he and Jessie might as well have been alone. "If you're feeling a bit nervous about being pitchforked into a lot of family…well, I don't blame you, I guess."

"It is a little scary," she confessed. "I suppose I met some of them at…at the wedding." She rushed over that part. "But I probably won't remember names."

His jaw tightened at the mention of his wedding to Alice, but he forced himself to go on. "Nobody will expect you to, except probably Cousin Judith. You won't be able to dodge her."

"Wants to have a shot at me, does she?" Jessie seemed to make an attempt at lightness, but he didn't think she felt it.

"It's certain sure she'll want to know all about you

and not be shy about asking." He should have realized it would be an ordeal for her, meeting all these people who had strong feelings about what Alice had done. "They'll be polite, I think." He hoped. "If you get caught in an uncomfortable conversation, you can always say you have to check on the kinder."

"I'll be fine." In a turnabout, she was the one reassuring him. "Denke, Caleb." She smiled, her eyes warming as she looked at him. "It's gut of you to think of it."

Her smile touched him. She was going into a difficult situation, but she wouldn't let it get her down. It seemed Jessie had a tough core of strength to go along with the tenderness she showed his kinder.

Looking back on it that evening, Jessie had to admit that the afternoon had gone better than she'd anticipated. Zeb's cousin Judith had been terrible inquisitive, that was certain, firing question after question at Jessie until she'd begun to sympathize with Daniel's reluctance to face her.

Then suddenly the inquisition stopped. Apparently she'd passed some sort of test and had gained Judith's grudging acceptance. And where Cousin Judith led, it seemed the rest of the family followed.

Jessie had come home with a copy of Cousin Judith's precious recipe for pon haus, she'd exchanged quilting ideas for youngsters with a second cousin who had daughters about Becky's age, and she felt she'd begun to make some friends.

Now the house was quiet. The kinder were long since asleep, and Daniel had gone off on some mission of his own that he'd seemed disinclined to talk about. A girl? She'd wondered but hadn't asked.

Onkel Zeb, suppressing his yawns, had headed for bed early, and Caleb had disappeared into his own room at that point. Had he been reluctant to be left alone with her? She wondered, but her relationship with Caleb was tentative at best, so she tried to take things as they came.

Besides, she enjoyed these last few moments of tidying the kitchen for the next day, feeling the house sleep around her. It was almost as if she belonged here, as if this were her own house, her kinder asleep upstairs, her...

"Jessie, surely you can stop working now. It's late."

Startled, Jessie swung around from the sink to find Caleb in the doorway. The memory of the direction her thoughts had been headed made her cheeks warm.

"Ach, I'm enjoying it. My mamm always says that tidying the kitchen the last thing at night sets it up for a fine morning's start."

"Looks wonderful tidy to me already. You should see it when it's just us and Onkel Zeb here." He wheeled himself around the table, closer to her. "If it's Daniel's turn to do the dishes, they pile up until there aren't any left to eat from."

"He can't be as bad as all that. Although I confess, my brothers are a menace when left alone in the kitchen." She dried her hands on the towel. Was he hinting that it was time she retired to the daadi haus?

But he didn't seem in any hurry. "I remembered that I hadn't told you I have an appointment with the doctor tomorrow morning. The van is going to pick me up at nine."

"I should think he'll be happy with your progress. You're getting stronger every day." That wasn't an exaggeration. In the past week he'd done things he hadn't even attempted when she'd first come.

"Yah, it's been better. It's that boss I have forcing me to exercise, ain't so?"

When Caleb's eyes crinkled in amusement, his whole face changed, warming until she hardly remembered the steely expression he'd worn that first day. Her heart lifted in response, making her think she'd best give herself another lecture about her attitude toward Caleb.

"I'm only doing my job," she said, unable to keep from smiling back. "You're the one who is working hard at it. You have the will to get back to normal, and that's the most important part."

Getting back to normal. To Caleb, that meant seeing the last of her. Ironic that the harder she worked to help him, the sooner she'd leave.

"Being at Cousin Judith's today…it wasn't bad after all, ain't so?" he asked.

Her smile widened. "I began to sympathize with Daniel when she started questioning me. I felt like she turned my head inside out to see what was in there."

"Yah, Cousin Judith has that effect on people. She claims she's old enough to say what she wants, but as far back as I can remember, she always has. What was she asking you?"

Jessie hesitated, but he seemed to want to know. "Actually, she was asking about Alice. About why we were so close."

She waited for Caleb's expression to shutter as it

usually did at the mention of Alice. But although he frowned, he didn't turn away from the subject.

"I guess she didn't know about Alice's mamm dying when she was so young. I don't think we ever talked about it."

It was a measure of success that he acknowledged that much, she thought. "Yah, well, I don't suppose it mattered. She understood when she realized that Alice was much more like a little sister to me."

She darted a cautious glance at Caleb, and found that he was studying her gravely with a hint of question in his eyes.

"There's more to it than that," he said slowly, with an air of feeling his way. "It seems like you hold yourself responsible for...well, for what she did wrong."

Jessie brushed a hand across her forehead, trying to banish the memories. "Maybe so. I guess I never got over thinking that I had to take care of her."

He didn't speak for a moment, and the old farmhouse was very still around them...so still she could hear the ticking of the clock on the shelf.

"Why?" Caleb spoke abruptly. "Tell me why, Jessie." He reached out to circle her wrist with his fingers as if he'd compel her to tell him the truth.

She found she was shaking her head. "It...it's nothing."

Caleb leaned over to grasp one of the kitchen chairs and pull it close to the wheelchair. "Sit down and tell me. I want to know why it's important to you. You don't have to atone for what someone else did wrong."

Jessie sank down on the chair, as much because her knees were wobbly as because of the pressure of Caleb's hand. "I was the big sister. That's how my mamm put it after Alice's mother passed. She would try to be a mamm to Alice, and I must be her big sister."

Caleb nodded. "You mentioned that, and I could just hear your mamm saying it." He waited as if he understood there was more she had to tell.

"I tried. I really wanted to be a gut big sister. But I failed." The taste of failure was still there. "I just... I suppose I got tired of always having to include her. One day, after school, we were walking home." The memory never really left her, but it wasn't easy to say out loud. "Alice got mad because I was talking with the other girls. I wasn't paying attention to her."

"Ach, Jessie, every big brother or big sister feels that way sometimes. Plenty of times I told Daniel and Aaron to get lost."

She couldn't smile as he'd obviously intended. "That's what she did. Really. She ran off into the woods and I... I didn't go after her. The other girls said she'd jump out at us when we got home, but she didn't. Alice was lost."

"What happened?"

"I went back. I looked in the woods, called to her, all the time getting more and more frantic. I couldn't find her. Finally I had to go home and tell Mamm and Daad what I'd done."

His fingers moved soothingly on the palm of her hand. "Somebody found her, yah? And she was all right?"

"Daadi called out all the neighbors. We searched and searched." She still remembered how terrifying it had been. "I followed along behind Daad, feeling so guilty. Someone finally found her asleep under a tree."

"So no harm was done." Caleb was obviously struggling to understand. "Maybe you were thoughtless, but that shouldn't make you carry a burden the rest of your life."

She shook her head. He didn't understand. Maybe he couldn't.

"I was responsible, but it was worse than that. When Alice flounced off into the woods, I was actually glad. I finally had time alone with my friends. Then, when I couldn't find her, I knew how wrong that had been."

"Ach, Jessie, if anybody could be too responsible, it must be you." His voice was gentle, maybe a little amused, but kind.

The trouble was that she couldn't tell him the rest of it, because it involved him too closely. How could she admit that she'd resented it when he picked Alice? How could she say that she might have kept Alice from coming back here to die if only she'd tried harder? Maybe she could have spared Caleb and the kinder if she'd been wiser and more determined.

"You want to make amends for the harm Alice might have done to Becky and Timothy." Caleb's fingers tightened on hers, and she forced herself to look at him. "I do understand that, Jessie. You came because you thought you could make a difference."

"Yah, I did." She was finding it difficult to breathe, sitting so close to him in the quiet house, feeling his hand encircling hers as if it was the most natural thing in the world. "You don't agree?" She made it a question, longing to have this much, at least, clear between them.

"At first all I wanted was to get rid of you, but..." His voice trailed off, and she felt his gaze on her face as if he were touching it. "You showed me some things about my kinder that I should have seen for myself,

Jessie. I'm grateful." He leaned toward her, his eyes intent. "This hasn't been easy for you. I'm sorry if I made it harder."

She'd never expected an apology from him...never thought he'd admit that her presence had helped. She ought to have spoken, but her lips trembled.

Caleb was scanning her face. He was so close that she could see a miniscule scar on his temple, hear the intake of his breath.

"Jessie." He said her name softly. He leaned even closer...so close that in a moment their lips would touch.

And then footsteps sounded on the outside steps, and the back door rattled. Caleb snatched his hand away, spinning the chair around so that by the time Daniel came inside, they were several feet apart.

Jessie managed to compose herself, to speak rationally to Daniel. But all the while her heart ached. Now she'd never know if Caleb would have kissed her. And she'd never know if he was glad or sorry that Daniel had stopped him.

The next day, Caleb still couldn't quite believe his actions. How had he come so close to Jessie? Another moment and he'd have kissed her.

He could only be thankful Daniel had come in when he did. If Caleb had acted on the impulse of the moment, he'd have made all their lives unbelievably difficult.

Frowning out the window of the van taking him home from his doctor's appointment, Caleb automatically noticed the greening of the pastures. The spring rains had been plentiful this year, thank the gut Lord.

Another reason for thanks was that he'd had an appointment this morning. It had given him a reason to get out of the house early, cutting short any chance of a conversation with Jessie. At the breakfast table, awkwardness had been avoided by the kinder babbling away about the spring program at the Amish school this week. They took it for granted that the whole family would be going. Becky, especially, couldn't wait. She'd been picturing herself in school come fall.

And she'd included Jessie in her imaginings, as if naturally Jessie would be there to pack her lunch and walk her to school on the first day. Jessie had answered her without committing herself, carefully avoiding a glance at him.

Which brought him right back to the problem he'd caused. He'd thought he was being generous, encouraging her to talk about her reasons for coming. He'd felt it was the least he could do, given all the ways she'd helped them.

Maybe he'd even been thinking he should tell her she was welcome in his house for as long as she wanted to stay. But then he'd turned that possibility upside down by giving in to the wave of attraction.

It might be better, safer, if Jessie left. She'd made him realize that he still had longings for a woman to spend his life with, that there might be hope of a normal relationship with someone. But not with Jessie, carrying the baggage of her involvement in Alice's life. That would be a disaster.

His gaze landed on the crutches that lay on the floor of the van. The doctor had been so pleased with his progress that he'd actually given him permission to start using them a short while each day.

It was thanks to Jessie that he'd made such progress. Once he was on crutches, he'd be on his feet, in a way. On his feet—that was what he'd told Jessie. She could stay until he was on his feet again.

He didn't have time to follow that thought to its difficult conclusion, because they were pulling up to the house.

"Here we are," the driver announced cheerfully, coming around to maneuver the lift that would lower the wheelchair to the ground. "Looks like someone is here to help."

It was Onkel Zeb who'd come out to the van. How long would it take him to start asking questions? Caleb knew perfectly well that Zeb had been aware of the strain between him and Jessie at breakfast. His uncle didn't miss much.

"Back already?" Zeb nodded his thanks to the driver and grabbed the handles of the wheelchair. "What did the doctor say?"

"That I'm doing fine." Caleb took the crutches the driver handed him. "See?"

"Ach, he's not going to let you start using crutches already, is he? He said it would be six weeks, and it's not near that."

"I won't use them all the time," Caleb admitted. He was tempted to skirt what the doctor had actually told him, but he didn't have any desire to do something stupid and ruin all the progress he'd made. "He said I could try them a couple of times a day for a few minutes at a time. Just to see how it will feel to be back on my feet again."

Zeb surveyed him severely. "How many minutes?

And where are you allowed to try it? Are you supposed to have help?"

Caleb couldn't suppress a smile. "You sound like a mother hen, ain't so?"

"Mother hen or not, you just answer me." His uncle took up a position in front of the chair, plainly intending that Caleb wouldn't go anywhere until he'd answered.

Caleb sighed. There was no getting away from Onkel Zeb when he was in this mood. "Yah, someone must be with me. No more than fifteen minutes at a time. And only in the house. Satisfied?"

Onkel Zeb gave a crisp nod. "Jessie and I will see there's no cheating, that's certain sure, so don't even think it." He started pushing the chair up the ramp to the back door.

Jessie. Caleb frowned at the crutches he was carrying. If he wanted it, he now had an excuse to send Jessie away. After what happened between them, that might be the smartest thing he could do, no matter how wrong it felt.

Chapter Eleven

"That's enough for now." Jessie put as much steel into her voice as she could, her hand steadying Caleb as he tried to balance on the crutches.

She forced herself not to quail at the angry look he sent her.

"I can judge better than you when I've had enough."

"The doctor is the one who knows better than either of us. According to Onkel Zeb, he told you no more than fifteen minutes at a time." She moved the wheelchair into position behind Caleb.

"Onkel Zeb talks too much," he muttered, but he reached back with one hand for the chair. The crutch slid from under his arm, and she grasped him to ease him into the chair.

"If you overdo, you'll just risk a setback. You don't want that, ain't so?"

For an instant he looked as if he'd snarl at her, but the expression slid away into one more rueful. "Yah, you're right. I get impatient."

"That's only natural." She set the crutches in the corner of the hall, which they'd decided was the best spot for practicing. "But look at how far you've komm just since you got home from the rehab hospital. No one would believe you could do so well in a few short weeks."

He needed the encouragement, she suspected, as well as the cautioning. He was eager to get back on his feet. She feared a big part of that was his determination to get rid of her.

Sure he was settled, she headed back to the kitchen. From the moment he'd gotten his body upright with the help of the crutches, she'd been expecting him to say they could do without her now.

She couldn't fool herself just because he'd seemed so kind the previous night, encouraging her to share her feelings about Alice. That momentary connection between them had been smashed by the wave of longing that seemed to come from nowhere.

Caleb was regretting it today—she'd seen it clearly in the way he'd withdrawn from her at breakfast. Probably he'd consented to let her help with the crutches only because Daniel and Zeb were both out this afternoon, and he had just enough sense to know he couldn't do it alone.

The back door slammed, and Becky and Timothy rushed into the kitchen, Becky carrying a few eggs in a basket.

"Leah is coming," Becky announced.

"And Jacob, too," Timothy added.

"Gut." She gestured to the containers of rhubarb they'd picked that morning. "It's time we were making a batch of jam."

"I'll help," Becky said immediately. "Timmy will play with Jacob, but I'll help."

Jessie hesitated, trying to find the right way to say she'd rather not have a six-year-old around boiling syrup. But Caleb made it unnecessary to disappoint her.

"I need your help this afternoon, Becky. I have to finish sanding those cabinets before Onkel Daniel gets home. I'm counting on you."

Becky sent one regretful glance toward the rhubarb, but the lure of working with her daadi won out. "I like to sand. I'll do it just the way you showed me." She hurried to get behind the wheelchair. "I can help push you up the ramp to the workshop."

"I can, too," Timothy said, obviously determined not to be left out. They headed out the back door, arguing about who should push the chair.

Jessie heard them exchanging greetings with Leah. In a few moments the children's voices faded and Leah came in, smiling.

She set a plastic pail of berries onto the counter. "I have enough strawberries that we can do a few jars of strawberry rhubarb, I figured. Looks as if Caleb is going to keep the kinder out from underfoot while we're making jam. It's just as well, ain't so?"

"There's nothing worse than a burn from boiling sugar syrup," Jessie said. "I've never forgotten the time my mamm and I let Alice help, and she got it on her fingers. I had to chase her across the kitchen to grab her and stick her hand in cold water."

Leah lost no time in starting to wash and cut berries, since Jessie had everything they'd need laid out and the rhubarb already prepared. "I decided I'd help when my mamm was pouring out peanut brittle. That really hurts. Poor Alice. No wonder she lost her head." She paused, looking at Jessie. "Alice was like a little sister to you. I know that makes it hard to hear how some folks here talk about her."

Jessie nodded, trying not to think of the hurtful words. "I understand how folks feel. After all, they had Caleb and the kinder to care for when she ran off. But it's still difficult." She measured sugar carefully. "I'm grateful that you understand. Alice was…" She stopped, not wanting to say too much.

"Go on," Leah said. "You can talk about her to me, even if Caleb probably isn't ready to hear it."

But Caleb had let her talk last night, hadn't he? Was it possible his bitterness was ebbing?

"Alice was always so bright and cheery. It was like having a ray of sunshine in the house, my daad said. Such a smile she had, and how she'd laugh at the silliest things. You couldn't help but be charmed by her."

"Caleb was, that's certain sure." The pile of berries grew higher in Leah's bowl. "He told me once he'd fallen in love as soon as he set eyes on Alice."

"That's so." Jessie tried to ignore the little pang in her heart at the memory. "He'd traveled out to Ohio for a wedding, and Mamm and Daad offered to house some of the overnight guests. So he came to our place."

"And saw Alice and fell hard," Leah said. She shook her head. "I can't say I think that's a gut way of doing it. Sam and I knew each other all our lives. There wasn't much we didn't know about each other when we married."

"Actually, when he got to the farm, Alice wasn't home. Mamm had me show Caleb around and keep him company." But that wasn't the part Leah wanted to hear. "When we got back to the house, Caleb walked into the kitchen and saw Alice. He stared like he'd never seen a girl before in his life."

She tried to keep her voice light, but the memory was so strong. She'd walked in happy, enjoying Caleb's presence, eager to introduce him to the rest of the family. And then she'd seen him staring dumbstruck at Alice, and all the joy had faded from the day.

She realized Leah was watching her and gave herself a little shake. "The syrup is almost ready. How are the berries coming?"

"About done," Leah said. "Jessie…"

There was a questioning note in her voice, and it was a question Jessie didn't want to answer. She'd never confided her feelings about Caleb to a soul, and she wouldn't now.

"Yah?" She smiled brightly, and Leah seemed to understand.

"I'll scald the jars," she said instead of the question that obviously hovered on her tongue.

They busied themselves with their jobs, and it wasn't until several minutes had passed that Leah spoke again.

"Funny." She glanced around the kitchen. "It must be quite a few years since anyone made jam in here. The last few years, Caleb insisted I take the rhubarb and the berries, so I made jam and brought half over here."

"I noticed someone had stocked the pantry shelves,"

Jessie said. "I should have known it was you." She poured hot jam carefully into a jar. "I suppose Caleb's mamm did a lot of canning."

"I guess." Leah began wiping jars and capping them. "I don't remember her all that well, and everything changed once she left." She shook her head. "I've wondered sometimes how the boys would have turned out if she hadn't gone away."

"They were affected, that's certain sure." She thought of Becky and Timothy. She'd just begun to make some headway with them. If only Caleb didn't insist on her going away too soon...

"And then Becky and Timothy went through the same thing," Leah said, her voice heavy. "Almost seems like it runs in families, though I guess that's silly. Still, they've been much better since you've been here."

"I hope I can make a difference for them."

Leah eyed her, speculation in her face. "Maybe you'll be here for good. It's time Caleb gave those kinder a mother and himself a wife."

Heat flooded Jessie's face. "Don't matchmake, please, Leah. It's impossible."

"Why?" Leah didn't seem ready to give up her idea. "Nobody could love those kinder more than you do, and it's plain you care about Caleb. So just tell me why not."

"I can't. It would be wrong." She felt as if she couldn't breathe. "I let Alice down. I wasn't there when Alice needed me. It would be wrong to take her place."

"Nonsense," Leah said robustly. "Alice was a grown woman who made her own choices. That's no reason you and Caleb and the kinder should suffer."

All Jessie could do was shake her head. After those

moments when they'd felt the strength of the attraction between them, Caleb probably felt just as guilty as she did. No matter what she might wish, Alice would always stand between them.

By the time he spotted Daniel's buggy pulling up to the barn, Caleb had sent the kinder out to play while he finished the cabinets. The soothing, repetitive nature of the work gave him plenty of time to think. Unfortunately, his thoughts just kept going around in circles.

One part of him kept saying that now that he was better, he had a good excuse for sending Jessie back to Ohio. And a good reason, too, given the way he'd responded to her last night. But his conscience insisted that it would be wrong to send her away just because he hadn't been able to control his desires. Her reason for coming was admirable, even if he thought she was overreacting with her guilt.

Daniel came in, arms full. He stacked supplies on one of the work tables and looked over Caleb's shoulder. "You've got a lot finished. Denke, Caleb. I don't see how I'd be able to do this job without your help."

Caleb shrugged off his thanks. "You should think of bringing in an apprentice once I'm back to work. Especially if this job leads to more. Once this client's neighbors see your work, you may have more than you can handle."

Daniel seemed unimpressed. "Sometimes I think they just want to say their cabinets are Amish-made."

"As long as they hire you, what difference does it make?" Caleb studied his brother's face, wondering at the slight frown he wore. "You and I might know that being Amish doesn't automatically make you a fine craftsman, but that's what you are."

"I guess so." Daniel's face relaxed in a smile. "I'm too picky. I want them to hire me because I'm good, not because I'm Amish."

"So you're both. They win both ways." He was relieved to see the smile. People who didn't know his brother well might have been fooled by his carefree exterior, but Caleb knew how conscientious he was. Daniel would always do his best, no matter what it cost him.

Daniel focused on organizing the supplies he'd brought in, and Caleb went back to putting the final touches on the cabinets. Even though he didn't come by the work naturally like Daniel, it was still a pleasure to feel the wood grow smooth and silky under his hand. They worked together in comfortable silence.

Then Daniel looked at him with a question in his face. "You didn't tell me about the crutches. Did you try them out earlier, or were you waiting for me to get home?"

"Already done," Caleb said. "Jessie helped me." He considered. "I'd say it went pretty well for the first time. Made me feel normal again to be standing and moving."

"Sehr gut." Daniel hesitated. "You're not going back to using that for an excuse to get rid of Jessie so soon, are you?"

Caleb evaded his eyes. "I don't know. I'll maybe soon be well enough we could just have someone in for a few hours a day to watch the kinder, ain't so?"

"No." Daniel leaned against the workbench, frowning. "Not if you mean to subject us to Onkel Zeb's cooking again."

"Do you ever think of anything but your stomach?" Caleb tried to keep his voice light. He didn't want to talk about Jessie leaving. He was already having enough trouble with the idea.

"It's important," Daniel protested. "Besides, Jessie's wonderful gut with the kinder. I'm not saying it's like having a mamm of their own, but I don't know who'd be any better. Do you?"

Caleb gritted his teeth at the direct question. It hit too close to the bone. "Why don't you think about getting married to some nice girl? Becky and Timothy would love to have an aunt."

Daniel turned away. "Just haven't run across the right one, that's all."

"Is it?" Caleb felt a sudden longing to see someone in the family make a success of love. "Are you sure it's not because of…well, because of Mamm? And because of the mess I made of marriage? You shouldn't give up on the idea because of that."

"I could tell you the same thing, ain't so?" His brother's quick gaze challenged him. "Seems to me you're the one who's given up on being happy."

The words seemed to hang in the quiet room between them. Caleb clamped his lips together. He wasn't going to respond. Not now. Maybe not ever.

Chapter Twelve

Nothing was any pleasanter than having the family sitting together in the living room as the sun slipped behind the ridge. Jessie paused in her mending to let her gaze rest on Caleb, relaxed in the easy chair he'd insisted on moving to from the wheelchair. He had a newspaper in his hands, but he looked over it at Timothy and Becky, playing more or less quietly together on the floor.

Jessie could understand his insistence on getting out of the wheelchair. Every small step he took toward recovery was important to him, even if it was as simple as sitting in his usual seat.

Funny how quickly this rocker had become hers. Onkel Zeb had gone automatically to the end of the sofa, pushing her mending basket over next to her as she reached for it.

Daniel had disappeared in the direction of his workshop after the chores were done, saying he wanted to get his materials ready for the next day. He'd shaken his head, smiling a little, when both his uncle and his brother offered to help.

"I want to plan the work out in my head," he'd said. "You'll just be a distraction."

That was probably the best way he could have picked to dissuade Caleb from going out with him. Caleb had thrown himself into work in the shop, no doubt from his need to repay Daniel for all the farm work he was doing. That determination was a measure of Caleb's personality, she suspected. He hated being dependent more than anyone she'd ever known.

Perhaps the accident was God's way of confronting Caleb with that, but she knew he wouldn't want to hear it.

Following his gaze to the two children, she found herself smiling. Timothy had reached the point of taking her presence as a fact of life, and it never seemed to occur to him that she wouldn't always be there.

As for Becky...well, Jessie couldn't entirely suppress a sigh. Becky had been much more cooperative lately, and any resentment she might have felt over Jessie's presence seemed to have disappeared that day that she'd sobbed her heart out and Jessie had comforted her.

But Becky still wasn't the happy, carefree little girl she was meant to be. She accepted Jessie, but the closeness Jessie longed for hadn't been forthcoming.

How could she reach the child and make a difference to her if Becky didn't let her guard down? They needed a situation that would encourage Becky to talk, and Jessie hadn't yet found it. She thought longingly of the hours she and her mamm had spent chatting about anything and everything while they washed the dishes each evening. But if she tried to engage Becky that way, Timothy would be right there, determined not to be left out.

She glanced down at the sewing in her lap and remembered her thought about introducing Becky to quilting. The quilt squares she'd cut were still in her basket, but she and the kinder had been busy with other things and it had slipped her mind. Maybe now was the time to introduce it.

As she tucked the mending away and began taking out the quilting squares, Becky crossed the room to her daad. "Daadi, you didn't forget going to the school tomorrow, did you?"

"No, for sure I didn't." Caleb put the paper down. "You'll be going to school every day come September. We'll go so we can all get a gut look at it."

Timothy, overhearing, pouted. "I want to go to school, too."

"You'll see the program tomorrow," Jessie reminded him. "Then you can imagine what it's like when Becky is there."

"I wish I was older," he declared, but the pout receded.

Onkel Zeb chuckled. "You won't feel that way in a few more years, young Timothy."

Timothy looked a little puzzled at that, but he noticed the patches Jessie was laying out on her lap, and that distracted him.

"What are those, Cousin Jessie?" He poked at a patch with one finger.

"These are the quilt squares. Remember? I showed you some before, and you tried sewing. When these are all stitched together, they'll make a small quilt, just big enough for a doll or a teddy bear. I'm trying to see which patches will look best next to each other."

"Can't you just make them all the same?" he asked.

"Silly," Becky said, showing off her experience. "Quilts always have different colors on each patch."

"I guess they wouldn't have to, but they're prettier this way," Jessie said, peacemaking. "It's called a nine-patch, because I'll put one in the middle and eight around it." She laid out a sample on her skirt. "Then you sew them together for the quilt."

Becky reached out tentatively and rearranged one of the squares. Encouraged, Jessie smiled at the child. "Do you want to pick out some squares, Becky? I have lots of them. You'll stitch them together just like you sewed that practice piece the other night."

Becky hesitated, and Jessie held her breath, hoping she hadn't sounded too eager. Then Becky nodded.

Jessie scooped the rest of the fabric squares from the basket and fanned them out. "Which ones would you put together?"

Timothy started to reach in front of Becky for a square, but Onkel Zeb called his name.

"Timothy, komm over here. Let's see if I remember how to make a lamb from a piece of wood."

Timmy scrambled over to his great-onkel, hanging on him as he got a penknife out. Jessie looked her thanks at him. Zeb, at least, understood what she was trying to do.

Becky quickly got into the idea of laying out the squares into a pattern, and Jessie smiled at the intent look on Becky's face. When she concentrated so hard, she very much resembled her daadi. Jessie glanced at Caleb and found him watching her. His face softened into a smile, and for a long moment they just looked at each other.

Then she felt the heat rising in her cheeks and focused on the fabric again. What did that stare mean, if anything?

"How about these two together?" She put a brown square against a black one.

Becky wrinkled up her nose. "Too dark," she said decidedly. "Maybe this." She picked up a rose-colored piece and laid it out next to the black.

"Very nice." Jessie felt a slight inward twinge. That rose piece was from a dress Alice had in her early teens. She'd looked like a flower in it.

Finally the squares were arranged to Becky's satisfaction. "Now we sew them together, ain't so?"

Jessie nodded. "I'll thread a couple of needles," she said, taking out the spool. "Why don't you match up the edges of two squares so they're just right?"

Becky pulled a stool over next to Jessie and picked up two of the squares. Her forehead wrinkled into a frown of concentration as she focused on matching them exactly. Like her daadi, she wanted to do everything perfectly.

"Now we start to stitch them together." Jessie showed Becky how to move the needle, picking up a small stitch. "It will be hard at first to sew a straight line, but it will get easier with practice."

Becky managed to get two stitches more or less in place before she pricked her finger and stopped to suck on it. She eyed Jessie. "You learned to sew when you were my age, ain't so?"

"Yah, that's right. My mamm taught me. I used to stick myself sometimes, too." She smiled at the memory. "My mamm said that my fingers would get better long before the nine-patch was finished. And she was right."

Becky stuck her needle in the fabric again. "Did you make one like this?"

"Yah, but different colors. It was in my doll cradle for a long time. Alice made one for her bear, I remember."

She was smiling until she saw the rigid look come over Becky's face. How foolish of her—she'd said the one thing that might turn Becky against the idea of quilting. But the girl couldn't go through life refusing to do anything her mother had done, could she?

Becky put the sewing down carefully and got up from the stool. "I don't want to sew anymore now." She went to Onkel Zeb, seeming instantly absorbed in what he was doing.

Frustrated, Jessie frowned at Caleb. Hadn't he said he'd work on showing Becky it was okay to be like her mammi? As far as she could tell, he'd never bothered to do it.

Caleb returned her look with one that was half ashamed and half stubborn. She ought to have been angry, but instead she felt only sorrow. Helplessness. What would break this cycle of blame and guilt that kept Caleb and his children trapped in this difficult place?

Caleb grasped the arms of the wheelchair as Onkel Zeb moved him into place at the rear of the schoolroom, Jessie following with the children. Several of Caleb's friends and neighbors got up, greeting him, making room on the benches for everyone.

He'd wanted to come to the school program on crutches, but Zeb had talked him out of it, reasoning that it would be hard to maneuver in the crowded room without tripping someone. He'd been right, that was certain sure. It looked as if the whole church was here. Everyone wanted to see the scholars put on their program—one of the few times Amish children performed for others, since that idea smacked of being prideful.

The one-room school hadn't changed, it seemed, since he'd been a scholar here. The alphabet still marched across the wall over the top of the chalkboard. Someone had put a Wilkom Friends sign on the board, decorated with flowers in colored chalk.

Becky had wiggled her way next to him on the end of the bench, and now she pulled at his arm. "Where will I sit when I'm a scholar?"

Putting his arm around her, he pointed to the small desks at the front of the room. "You'll be right up there. Teacher Mary wants the first-graders up front so she can help them."

His daughter stood to scan the front row of desks, now occupied by the schoolchildren who were waiting and eager to begin. "I want that one, on the end," she whispered in his ear.

"Maybe you'll be there, maybe not. It's Teacher Mary who decides."

Becky looked slightly mutinous for a moment, but then she nodded and relapsed into silence, her small face grave.

What had happened to the bright, sunny child she

used to be? His conscience struck him a blow, and he glanced at Jessie. She seemed to know.

They hadn't spoken about last night. In fact, Jessie seemed determined to ignore the incident.

Not so Onkel Zeb. He'd had plenty to say once he got Caleb alone. And Caleb knew he was right. It was his responsibility to help his daughter come to terms with what her mother had done. He'd told Jessie he would. But when it came right down to it, he hadn't been able to find the words.

Fortunately, the program started before he tied himself in too many knots trying to rationalize his failure. No one could think of anything else while the young scholars were saying their pieces and singing their songs.

He had to smile, remembering the school programs of his youth. There was the year he'd completely forgotten his lines and stood there, turning red, until the teacher had prompted him. To say nothing of the time Aaron had knocked over a whole display of posters by backing into it.

Timmy, seated on Jessie's lap so he could see better, was wiggling, but Becky sat rapt, totally engaged in every line. Her lips moved silently along with the songs.

Caleb smiled, watching her, and found himself automatically looking at Jessie, wanting to share the moment with her. She was looking at Becky, as well, but then she glanced at him. Her serene face curved in a smile, and it was hard to look away. How could it be that he was communicating wordlessly with her?

His gaze dropped. He didn't want to feel that comfortable with her. It was yet another reminder that he had to move forward, and he didn't know how.

When the program ended, everyone began moving outside for the picnic and games that always closed out the school year. The chatter of the crowd was immediate, and he was kept busy answering questions about his health.

Willing hands lifted the chair down the single step out of the white frame schoolhouse, and Zeb pushed Caleb toward the picnic tables where the scholars' mothers were busy putting out food. He spotted Jessie taking the kinder to the table and knew he didn't have to worry about them. Jessie would take care of them.

Zeb parked him next to a group of men. "You stay here and catch up on all the news. I'll bring you a plate."

"No need to pile it into a mountain," Caleb called after his uncle. Zeb seemed to think he would recover faster if he was stuffed with food. Just like an Amish mother, he was.

Caleb found it rejuvenating to join in the talk of the weather, the crops, who was planting what, who'd increased his dairy herd and who was having trouble with the cooperative dairy. The ordinary topics of life in a farming community were of vital interest to no one but the folks who lived there. To them, such things were crucial, and just chatting with the others made him feel a part of it again.

The group dispersed as they finished eating, some to join the ball game that was starting, others to watch and cheer.

"Looks like the kinder are done eating," Zeb observed, nodding at Becky and Timothy, who were running toward the swings.

Caleb's gaze lingered on Becky. For once she was laughing, distracted from her troubles. She ought to have been that way all the time. He glanced at Zeb and found his uncle watching him.

"Yah, all right." Caleb frowned at him. "I know what you're thinking. And you're right. I have to try harder with Becky. It's just…difficult."

Zeb took a breath before he spoke, a sure sign he was weighing his words. "You're finding it hard."

"I'm finding it impossible," Caleb said flatly. "Jessie thinks I ought to be able to talk normally about Alice to the kinder, and I can't. It keeps coming out stiff."

"You think maybe that's because you haven't really forgiven her yet?"

Caleb smacked his palms on the arms of the chair. "I've tried. The gut Lord knows I've tried. I think I've done it, and then the anger and resentment pop back up again."

"Ach, Caleb, what do you expect? That's what forgiveness is like. If you found it easy, it surely wouldn't be real. You forgive, and then the next day when the feeling comes up again, you forgive again. One day you'll know that this time it will stick."

"That's what Jessie says. I hope you're both right," he muttered with no great confidence.

His uncle gave him a stern look. "You know what to do. Take it to the Lord. He will help you. And when you understand what the next step is, take it. Whether you want to or not."

Caleb nodded, feeling the reluctance drag at him. Yah, he knew what the next steps were. To apologize to Jessie. And then to speak naturally about Alice to his daughter.

Muttering that he was getting some coffee, he maneuvered the chair toward the table where he'd last seen Jessie.

The wheels moved quietly over the grass, newly mown for the event, and probably the bishop's wife and her daughter-in-law didn't hear his approach.

"I saw how they looked at each other," Ethel Braun was saying. "They should be ashamed of themselves."

"Maybe you misunderstood…" the daughter-in-law began timidly.

"I did not! I'd never have thought it of Caleb. That woman is out to trap him into marriage just like her cousin did, and we all know how badly that turned out."

He could back up silently. Pretend he hadn't heard anything. Nobody wanted to start an argument with the bishop's wife. Bishop Thomas himself was kind and reasonable. What he'd done to deserve a woman with such a sharp tongue, nobody knew.

But he couldn't let it go. He knew how much killing a rumor of that sort took. If he didn't scotch it today, half the county would be wondering tomorrow. Jessie didn't deserve that.

"Excuse me." *Be polite*, he told himself. *No matter what you're thinking.*

The two of them swung around. The younger woman went scarlet when she saw him. But the bishop's wife just looked more sharp-featured than ever.

"Caleb." For a moment he thought she was going to ignore the whole thing, but then she gave a short nod. "I suppose you heard what I said. I suppose I hurt your feelings, but…"

"I'm not easily hurt by gossip," he said bluntly, forgetting his resolve. "But Cousin Jessie has done nothing, and it's not right to spread rumors about her."

Faint, unbecoming color stained her thin cheeks. "Are you accusing me of being a blabbermaul?"

If the shoe fits, he thought but didn't say.

"When you talk that way about an innocent woman, what am I to think? Jessie has been nothing but kind in helping my kinder and taking care of the house during this difficult time." He was building up a head of steam. He should have stopped, but he couldn't. "She knew she would be facing rejection by coming here, but she came, anyway."

She came, knowing what she'd have to contend with, and he hadn't been much help. It was time he made a fresh start.

He spun the chair around and froze. Jessie stood there, and it was obvious she'd heard the whole thing.

Chapter Thirteen

Jessie started down the stairs to the living room that evening after she'd gotten everything ready for putting the kinder to bed. She stopped abruptly when Caleb's voice reached her.

"...didn't you want to make a quilt with Cousin Jessie? I thought it would be nice to do."

Jessie froze, pressing her hands against the wall as she strained to hear what reply Becky might make.

"I don't know," Becky mumbled. "I just didn't want to."

Caleb cleared his throat as if talking had become difficult. "You know, your mamm was really good at sewing things. I think you would be, too."

If only Jessie could see their faces. Then she might know what they were thinking and how Becky was reacting. But she was afraid to move for fear of interrupting them.

Caleb was actually doing what she'd hoped. She could hardly believe he was able to speak that way to Becky. True, he didn't sound very comfortable, but at least he was trying.

"I don't know," Becky said again, and Jessie could imagine the confusion she must feel. Her mother hadn't been spoken of in this house for what would seem a long time to a child.

"Maybe you could ask Cousin Jessie to show you a little more about quilting before you decide you don't like it," Onkel Zeb suggested.

"Yah, that's a gut idea." Caleb sounded relieved at the helpful interruption.

"I'd like a doll quilt," Daniel said. "Make me one."

Becky giggled, and Jessie decided it was safe to go the rest of the way down. "And what would you do with a doll quilt?" she asked, keeping her voice light. "It would only cover one of your hands."

"Or one foot," Becky said, her face alight.

"Wrong, both of you." Daniel swung Becky up toward the ceiling, gave her a hug and set her down again. "I'd wrap it around my coffee thermos to keep it hot when I go to work." He shot a glance at Onkel Zeb. "Ready to help me load those cabinets on the buggy?"

"Sure thing. You'll want to put some padding between them. And a tarp on top to protect them overnight."

"Sounds gut. I want to make an early start tomorrow." Daniel ruffled Timothy's hair. "About bedtime for you, ain't so? I'll see you in the morning."

Timothy dropped a wooden horse in the toy box and flung his arms around Daniel in a hug. "See you in the morning," he echoed.

There was a little spell of silence when the two men had gone. Jessie smiled at the children. "I think it's time to tell Daadi good-night now. Don't you?"

Timothy shoved the toy box against the wall and went to hug his daadi. But Becky hesitated, looking at Jessie. "Can we sew a little bit more tomorrow?"

It took an effort to hide her pleasure. "For sure. I'd like that."

Apparently satisfied, Becky nodded before she trotted over to tell Caleb good-night. Above the child's head, Jessie's gaze met Caleb's. *Thank you.* She mouthed the words, and Caleb nodded. Unable to stop smiling, she walked up the stairs with Becky while Timothy scurried up ahead of them.

The usual routine of putting the children to bed seemed doubly precious to Jessie that night. The kinder had grown so dear to her. Just the fact that Caleb was supporting her made her feel more a part of the family, so much so that she couldn't bear the thought of leaving.

Maybe that was what Mamm had been thinking when she'd worried about Jessie coming here. That she'd give her heart away and not be able to take it back.

Jessie sat down on Timothy's bed, and he and Becky hopped up on either side of her. She snuggled them close. "What kind of story will it be tonight?"

"A story about a rabbit," Timothy said quickly. He'd been engrossed in the story of Peter Rabbit lately.

"Peter Rabbit?" she suggested. "Benjamin Bunny?"

"We already heard those," Becky said. "Tell us a story about an Amish girl who had a rabbit."

Becky seemed to like making her use her imagination when it came to bedtime stories. "All right, but you'll have to help me."

Thinking quickly, Jessie began a story that relied a little on the fact that her cousin had once raised rabbits. She encouraged the children to fill in details of color and place, loving the way their imaginations caught hold.

When the story had wound its way to the end, with the bunny safely back in his hutch after his adventures, she tucked them in, bending over Timmy for one of his throttling hugs. When she went to Becky she paused, as always, for any sign that an embrace would be welcome. She found Becky looking up at her solemnly.

"Cousin Jessie, am I like my mammi?" It was said in a very small voice.

Jessie's heart ached. What was the right answer to that question?

"You're like your mammi in some ways, and like your daadi in others," she said. "Parts of each, all mixed up to make a special Becky."

Apparently it was the correct response. Becky smiled and lifted her head for a good-night kiss, putting her arms around Jessie's neck in a long hug.

Jessie went back down the stairs slowly, knowing that when she reached the living room, she and Caleb would be alone. They had to talk about what the bishop's wife had said, didn't they? The fear that he'd think she was trying to trap him nagged at her. She had to face it, but what she really wanted was to go straight to the walkway that led to the daadi haus and hibernate there until morning.

But that would be cowardly. So she walked into the living room, knowing that Caleb would be waiting for her and not looking forward to it any more than she was.

She began to talk when she entered the room, afraid she'd panic if she waited any longer. "Caleb, about what happened at the school…"

"I'm sorry," he said abruptly. His jaw was like iron.

"Sorry for what? You didn't do anything."

"I don't think I honestly realized the harm I was doing by how I thought about…about Alice. I thought it was my own business. But it must have been obvious to everyone else in the community."

She took the chair next to him. "You had every right to be angry with Alice, Caleb. I know that better than anyone."

"Yah. But I hardly considered how folks would act toward you because of it."

"They haven't all been like the bishop's wife," she hurried to assure him. "Leah has been kindness itself, and many others have been friendly."

That didn't seem to make him feel any better. "I should have thought. Just like I should have seen what was happening with my Becky." He shook his head and seemed to fight for control. "Why, Jessie? Why did Alice act as she did? Why couldn't she be happy with the life we had?"

Her throat was tight with pain, and she struggled to speak. "I don't know. But I thought from the beginning that she was too young. She hadn't…hadn't settled yet, inside herself. It was like she was always looking for a place to belong."

Caleb turned a tortured face to her. "That's what I wanted to give her."

"I know. You did your best. We did, too. From the

time her mamm died, she was like one of our own, but..."

"But you failed. I failed, too."

She put her hand on his arm, helpless to comfort him. "We did our best. Somehow what we offered was never enough to fill the empty place inside her."

"No." Caleb sucked in a deep breath, and some of the tension seemed to seep out. "When she came back, I thought at first she was sorry. That she wanted to make up for what she'd done. But I guess she just wanted a place to die."

On that subject, at least, she could reassure him. But it meant revealing things she'd never intended to say.

She pressed her fingers against her temples. "It's not...not quite that way. Really. I offered to have her. We could have moved into the daadi haus at my brother's. I would have taken care of her." She paused, trying to find the truth of her emotions at that painful time. "I should have tried harder. Maybe she knew how angry I was with her, even though I tried to forgive."

"Forgiving isn't easy." He shook his head. "'t wasn't your fault."

They would each have to carry their own burden in that regard, it seemed.

"There's more," she said. "When Alice was here at the end, she wrote to me. She hadn't been writing regularly for a long time, but she did then. She...she said she came back because she hoped to put things right in the little time she had left. So, you see..."

His fingers tightened painfully around her wrist. "She wrote? You have a letter she wrote when she was dying?"

She nodded, helpless to do otherwise.

"Why haven't you shown me?" He clamped his mouth closed for a moment. "Never mind. I wouldn't give you a chance, would I?"

"No. And I didn't want to hurt you."

"Hurt me?" He said it as if it sounded ridiculous. "I want to see it. I must see it."

She looked at him for a long moment, not sure if this was wise. But what else could she do, now that he knew?

She nodded, rising. "I'll get it." She looked down at his hand, still taut around her wrist.

He grimaced, letting go. "Sorry," he muttered.

"It's nothing." She turned, heading for the kitchen and the door that led to the daadi haus, a sense of dread weighing on her heart. Would knowing what Alice wrote hurt him? Or heal him?

Caleb found he was gripping the arms of the wheelchair so tightly that his fingers were white. He relaxed them deliberately, one by one, trying not to think of anything else.

His thoughts didn't cooperate, racing ahead to what Alice might have written. Jessie had so clearly not wanted to show him. But Jessie, he'd begun to see, had a tender heart under her practical exterior. She couldn't bear to hurt anyone.

Did she imagine anything could be worse than the hurt he'd already endured? It was better to know everything.

He heard the door, and then Jessie's footsteps sounded lightly in the kitchen. He waited, praying that Onkel Zeb and Daniel wouldn't return too soon. For this he needed privacy.

He watched her come through the doorway and turn toward him. The letter was in her hand, and he couldn't tear his gaze away.

It was only a couple of seconds, but it seemed forever until she held the envelope out and sank into the chair next to him.

Now that he had it, he couldn't seem to muster the courage to look at it. He turned it over and over in his hands. "How is it I knew nothing about her writing to you?"

"I don't know."

"I wouldn't have stopped her from writing to you." The words were laced with bitterness. Was that what Alice had thought of him toward the end? That he'd have been mean enough to suppress her letters?

"I know you wouldn't. I'm sure she knew that, as well. Maybe she didn't want to talk about it."

"To me," he added to her words. "Zeb wrote the address. I know his writing."

"Does it matter?" Jessie's tone was gentle. "She'd have known how busy you were, and I'm sure things were strained enough already. It would have been natural to ask Onkel Zeb to do it."

"I guess." He knew what he was doing. He was delaying the moment when he'd actually have to read Alice's words. Being a coward.

The thought propelled him forward, and he opened the envelope.

The notepaper was worn and creased as if Jessie had read it time and again. He unfolded it and began to read.

You were right, Jessie, like always. I shouldn't have come here. I thought I could do some good.

No, I promised I wouldn't lie to myself anymore. I wanted forgiveness for myself. Selfish, I guess, but I did think it might help Caleb and the children.

I was wrong. Caleb can't forgive me. Oh, he says the words, but I can see the bitterness in his heart. I should know. I put it there. He can't forgive, and I'm only hurting the children by letting them see me this way. It's not so bad for Timmy. He's just a baby, and he'll forget.

But Becky…dear Jessie, please do what you can to help my little daughter. Don't let her grow up bitter and lonely.

I'm always asking things of you, ain't so? But never anything as important as this. Please, Jessie. I pray that you can do what I can't.

Don't grieve too much for me. It was only when I faced death that I knew what a mess I'd made of living. But I have confessed and asked the good Lord for forgiveness. I rest on His promise to forgive.

Try to remember the silly little cousin who always wanted to be like you, and let the rest slip away to dust.

Caleb's eyes stung with salty tears, and he closed them tightly, struggling to gain control as he let the letter drop in his lap. Poor Alice. Poor, foolish Alice. She had grabbed for what she thought she wanted, only to find it turn to ashes.

"All she asked of me was forgiveness." He struggled to get the words out. "But I couldn't give it." He slammed his fist on the arm of the chair as if that would help.

"Don't, Caleb." Jessie took his tight fist in her hand. "You did your best. That's all anyone can do."

He turned blindly toward her, fighting not to give way. "If only…"

"I know."

Jessie put her hand tentatively on his back, the way she would comfort one of the children. He leaned against her arm as if it were the most natural thing in the world. He could feel the caring flow from her to him, soothing his battered heart.

"There are so many things I could have done better." Speech came more easily now. "Words I could have spoken. Acceptance I could have shown."

"The same is true for me. I keep thinking there was something more I could have done to keep her from coming back here when she was dying. It would have spared you and the kinder so much."

"Don't think that." He enclosed her hand in both of his. "None of it was your fault. The responsibility was mine. I took the vows, not you. I am to blame."

"Ach, Caleb, it's a gut thing the Lord knows we're only human. We all make mistakes. Alice, too. She knew that. Didn't you see what she said? She confessed and accepted God's forgiveness. We must do the same."

"Onkel Zeb told…" He paused, not sure he wanted to go on. But who should he say it to but Jessie, who was so deeply involved? "He told me I was passing my doubts and lack of trust on to the next generation. Folks already say the King boys don't fare well in love.

If I didn't change, one day they'd be saying that about Becky and Timothy, too."

Maybe he hoped she'd deny that, but she didn't. "Onkel Zeb is a wise man," she said softly. "But you have already begun to make that right, ain't so?"

"Only because you've been here to guide me." He managed a rueful smile. "With me fighting you every step of the way."

"Not as bad as that," she said. "Becky is more open already, thanks to you."

He shook his head. "Not me. You. If we have changed, it's because of you, Jessie."

He looked into her eyes and seemed to become lost in their depths. He leaned toward her, longing filling him. Not for comfort this time, but for her. For Jessie herself.

He touched her cheek, feeling the smooth skin beneath his fingers. She flushed, her lips trembling just a little. And then he leaned across the barrier of the wheelchair arm and kissed her.

It was a long, slow kiss, gentle at first but deepening as he felt her response. He inhaled the sweet, feminine scent of her, heard her breathing quicken and felt her lips warm. Her hand touched his nape tentatively, then more surely as she leaned into his kiss. The world seemed to narrow until it encompassed only the two of them.

Slowly, reluctantly, she drew back. "I don't... I'm not sure. Is this right, for me to care about you this way?"

He put his finger across her lips. "You have been so intent on making the rest of us free to move ahead.

Now you have to do the same for yourself. It can't be wrong to hope for a better future, can it?"

He saw the doubt ebb from her face, to be replaced by the gentle smile he loved.

"No. Hope is never wrong."

Chapter Fourteen

It was still dark in the kitchen when Jessie began getting breakfast ready, but the sky was lightening in the east, and it would soon be day. Dairy farmers got up early. That was part of the business, and this morning Caleb had insisted on going out to the barn with the other men. There might not be much he could do, but he was determined to take another step toward normal life.

A smile touched Jessie's lips. Once, normal had meant getting rid of her. Now…now it meant something much different.

She cautioned herself not to expect too much, but it was impossible. Caleb wouldn't kiss her that way unless he intended marriage. They weren't teenagers, smooching with one after another on the way to finding a life partner. At their age, a person didn't get involved without it being serious.

She must convince Caleb that they couldn't rush into anything. They'd have to give the children time. But...

Daniel came in, bringing a blast of chill early morning air with him, and gave her a sharp look. "What are you smiling about?"

"I'm not," she said, schooling her face to her usual calm.

"Sure you were. What's up?" He helped himself to a mug of coffee and leaned against the counter to drink it.

She shrugged, thinking she'd have to be more careful if she didn't want everyone talking about her and Caleb. "Just thinking about plans for the day, I guess. I've filled a thermos with coffee for you, and your lunch is packed. Do you have time for breakfast, or should I wrap something up?"

Daniel glanced at the clock and straightened. "I'd better get going. Just give me a couple pieces of the shoofly pie. That'll be enough."

Nodding, Jessie wrapped up half the pie, knowing how Daniel liked to eat, even though it never showed on his lean frame. He grabbed his lunch pail, thermos and the bag into which she'd put the shoofly pie.

"Denke, Jessie. I'll have it on the way to the job."

He went out, the door banging behind him. She heard him exchange a few words with the others, so they must be on their way in. She began dishing up oatmeal from the pot on the stove as the kinder thudded their way down the stairs.

Breakfast was a time for chatter about what the day would hold. Jessie tried resolutely to keep from catching Caleb's gaze, but every time she glanced at him, he was watching her with a warmth in his face that was a sure signal to anyone studying him. She'd warn him to be more careful.

She was on pins and needles throughout the meal, sure he was going to give them away. Somehow they got through without it happening, although she did think Onkel Zeb was looking at them a little oddly.

At last the kitchen emptied out except for her and Caleb. He shoved his chair toward her.

"We're finally alone. I thought they'd never finish breakfast." He caught her hand.

She sent a quick look around to be sure they were really alone. "Ach, Caleb, you have to be more careful. I'm sure Onkel Zeb thought something was going on, the way you kept looking at me."

"But I want to look at you, my Jessie." He drew her down for a quick kiss. "It's a good morning when we're together. Ain't so?"

"Yah." She cupped his cheek with her hand for a moment. "But I mean it about being careful not to let anyone suspect our feelings."

"Why not? Why not just let them know that we're going to marry?"

"Are we?" she asked, smiling in spite of her efforts to stay sober.

"Of course we are. If you go around kissing men the way you kissed me without marriage in mind, all I can say is that I'm surprised at you."

"Silly. I don't go around kissing anyone. Except you," she added. She yanked her mind away from the joy of joking with him. "But it's best if we don't let anyone in on it, at least not yet." She could see the objection forming in his thoughts and hurried on. "For the children's sake, Caleb. We should move gradually. They'll need time to adjust."

"We doubtless won't convince anyone to marry us until fall," he pointed out, reminding her of the traditional season for weddings. "Isn't that time to adjust?"

"Yah, but I want to be positive sure that Becky has accepted me before expecting her to think of me as your future wife."

"And her mother," Caleb added. "They'll be happy. Why wouldn't they be? But I guess you're right. We don't want any setbacks now, that's for sure."

"Denke, Caleb. I knew you'd understand."

He smiled. "So long as you understand that I'll need to snatch a kiss now and then. Just to keep me going."

"I think we can manage that," she said gravely, while her eyes danced.

He lifted her hand to his lips and dropped a light kiss on it. "So much to look forward to. Soon I'll trade this big cast in for a smaller one, I'll be able to do more, and we'll be busy making plans for our marriage. I feel as if I've come out from under a dark cloud."

"I know. I feel it, too."

"Then come here and give me a kiss before everyone comes back again." He drew her down, cradling her face in his hands. "One to last through the morning," he said, kissing her lightly. "And another…"

Something…some sound…had her turning to look around.

"What's wrong?" Caleb sobered at once.

"I…nothing, I guess. I thought I heard something."

"Just the house making noises as it settles," he said, and he pulled her back to him for a long, satisfying kiss.

* * *

Caleb, trying to sweep the workshop floor, decided that sweeping was best done by someone who had two feet to stand on. It was difficult to manipulate the broom and impossible to manage the dustpan from a wheelchair.

He glared at the heavy cast on his leg. He'd be wonderful glad to be rid of it. Maybe, when he went to have it checked tomorrow, they'd decide he could make do with the small one that would let him be more mobile.

Leaning back in the chair, he gave himself up to thoughts of the future. The initial euphoria he'd felt last night when he'd realized he loved Jessie had already subsided to a quiet contentment. That was as it should be, wasn't it?

When he'd met Alice, he'd tumbled into love without a single sensible thought in his head. They'd hurried into marriage because they couldn't bear to be parted, and probably because he'd feared losing this wondrous thing that had happened to him.

How long had it taken to see that they hadn't known each other at all? By the time they did, it was too late.

Everything was different with Jessie. Not less, only different. He'd moved slowly from distrust to wariness, then to cautious acceptance and finally to love. It had been so gradual that he almost didn't realize it was happening until he'd known, for certain sure, that what he felt was love.

He'd rebelled at first at not sharing their happiness with everyone right away, but probably Jessie was right. They needed to do what was best for the kinder. They'd be happy, wouldn't they? They already loved Jessie.

But it was worth taking their time so it was the right moment to tell them. When they did…

The door rattled, and Onkel Zeb came in on a wave of warm air filled with the scent of spring. "Getting stuffy in here, ain't so? Let's see if I can get one of these windows open." He began wrestling with the front window.

"Let me help." Caleb moved the wheelchair into position, and together they managed to push the balky window up. "That's better. Smells like spring, ain't so?"

Zeb nodded. "Soon it'll be summer. The corn we planted is showing green already."

"Gut." Caleb smacked the arms of the chair. "The sooner I get out of this, the better."

"I'm thinking we should tell Thomas we'll keep him on until fall, at least. He'd be glad to know his steady work will go on." Zeb glanced around the shop. "Daniel had best get moving on finding an apprentice. He'll need someone soon."

"Any ideas?" Caleb pushed away from the window, reflecting that Onkel Zeb was never happier than when he was taking care of them.

"I hear tell that Zeke Esch's second boy, Eli, is wonderful gut with his hands. Zeke says he likes working with wood. Seems to me he'd be a good possibility. Zeke would like to see the boy settled in a trade."

Caleb smiled. Things would probably work out just the way Onkel Zeb had in mind. They usually did. The future was falling into a new pattern, it seemed. Not bad, just different.

He realized that his uncle was studying his face. "Anything you want to tell me?" Zeb asked.

"What makes you say that?" Caleb parried, playing for time. It was all very well for Jessie to say they should keep their plans to themselves, but she hadn't reckoned with Onkel Zeb's sharp eyes.

"Ach, I can see as far as the next person. You're different today. And Jessie is, as well."

He'd never been very good at keeping secrets from his uncle. At least he could tell him part of the truth.

"Last night Jessie let me see the letter she got from Alice just before she died. You knew about it, didn't you?"

"Yah, I did." Zeb's face grew sorrowful. "I went to see if she needed anything, and she was just finishing it. I helped her address it and mail it. I didn't know Jessie still had the letter."

"So you don't know what it contained?"

"No. I thought Alice probably wanted to say goodbye to Jessie. They'd always been close."

"She did." Caleb's throat felt rough. "She also said that she'd come back hoping for my forgiveness. And that she hadn't gotten it." He cleared his throat so he could speak. "It made me feel pretty small that she knew I hadn't really forgiven her."

"It's not easy. You know that. It doesn't happen all at once."

"I see that now. The letter opened my eyes to the fact that I've been holding on to my resentment. Reading it…sharing it with Jessie…it seemed as if that set me free. I could forgive…forgive Alice and forgive myself."

Zeb clapped his shoulder, his face working. "Always best to get things out in the open, ain't so?" His voice was husky. "Things heal better that way."

"Yah, they do. I'm out from under a heavy weight. Jessie…" But he'd best be careful what he said about Jessie if he didn't want to give them away.

He saw, through the open window, Jessie hurrying toward the shop. "Here she comes now."

Jessie came in, sweeping the room with a quick glance. "Becky's not here?"

"No. I haven't seen her since breakfast." Caleb's thoughts readjusted. "What's wrong?"

"Ach, nothing," Jessie said quickly, but he saw the little worry line between her brows. "I thought she had gone to gather eggs, but she hasn't come back. Timothy is busy looking for strawberries, and he doesn't know where she is."

"She'll be around here somewhere," Caleb said, vaguely disturbed but not wanting to upset her.

"Most likely she's fallen asleep somewhere," Zeb said. "I mind the time we were looking all over the place for Daniel, and he was up in the hayloft. He'd been hiding from you, and he fell sound asleep."

"That must be it," Jessie said. "I'll have a look around."

"We'll hunt for her, too." Caleb shoved his wheelchair toward the door, his fear mounting.

Jessie hurried ahead as he went out, stopping briefly to talk to Timothy. Reassuring him, most likely.

Common sense told Caleb there was nothing to worry about. Becky had to be here somewhere. Onkel Zeb was probably right, and she'd fallen asleep.

Reaching the house, he went up the ramp as fast as he could. Jessie would have looked in the house already, but it wouldn't hurt to check again.

He went through the downstairs rooms, calling

Becky's name. Nothing. He yanked open the cellar door. There was no logical reason why she'd have gone down there, but he sat at the top and shouted her name.

Useless. He was useless, trapped in this chair. He couldn't even go upstairs or down to the cellar in search of his daughter. He shoved the chair to the bottom of the steps leading to the second floor and grasped the newel post. If he could keep hold of the posts, maybe he could pull himself up.

Common sense intervened. Jessie would have looked upstairs first thing. Still, he shouted Becky's name up the steps. No response came.

Back outside again, he could see his son just coming around the corner of the barn from the strawberry patch. Caleb began pushing himself in that direction.

In another moment, Jessie and Onkel Zeb came out of the barn and stood, conferring with each other. Why were they just standing there? Why weren't they hurrying?

Frustration driving him, he tried to move faster, but the chair didn't cooperate on the rough ground. He shoved impatiently and the chair slewed to the side, caught in a rut in the grass. Angry, he yanked at it, overbalancing as he tried to free the wheel. Another angry pull and the whole chair tipped over, spilling him onto the ground.

He had a glimpse of Zeb and Jessie running to help him as he shoved himself up onto his hands. The cast had taken a jolt, but he didn't think anything was injured. He didn't have time for that now in any event.

Jessie reached him, grasping his arm, but he shoved her away. "Never mind me. Just find my child."

She took a quick step back and then busied herself

with righting the chair and holding it steady while Zeb helped him into it, scolding all the time.

"Don't be so foolish. It won't make things better if you get hurt." Zeb settled him in the chair. "Let Timothy help you to the phone shanty in case we need to call for help."

"What are you going to do?" He ignored Jessie, trying to hide the irrational resentment that was building inside him.

"I'm heading up toward the woods. Jessie will go over to Leah and Sam's place."

"If they haven't seen her, I'll ask them to help look," Jessie said as Zeb struck off toward the woods. She put her hand on the chair. "Please, Caleb, go back."

He pushed her hand away. All the darkness he thought he'd banished came storming back, flooding his mind.

"I trusted you with my children. I should have known better."

Jessie whitened. Then she spun and set off for Leah's at a run.

Somehow Jessie managed to keep putting one foot in front of the other as she crossed the field toward Leah's farmhouse. Caleb blamed her. The love he'd shown so briefly was swallowed up in anger at her failure to keep his children safe.

He couldn't blame her more than she blamed herself, though. Her heart twisted in her chest. She had lost Alice. Now she had lost Becky. What kind of person was she, to let down the people she loved?

A failure. She should have taken better care of them.

The only thing to do now was pray she could find Becky safe.

Then…then she'd have to go. She'd come here with hopes of doing good, but she'd ended up doing harm. So leaving was her only option.

Please, God, please, God. She prayed in time with her hurrying footsteps. *Please let me find her. Please keep her safe.*

Blinking tears away, she saw Leah coming toward her. Breaking into a run, Jessie reached her.

Before she could speak, Leah had clasped both her hands. "It's all right," she said quickly. "You are looking for Becky, yah?"

Jessie nodded, breathless.

"She's safe. Really." She patted Jessie's hands. "Calm down before you talk to her."

"Yah." She took a breath, thankfulness surging through her. *Thank You, Lord. Thank You.* "Where is she? How did you find her?"

"She's in our barn loft. She's okay. I saw her climbing up. She looked as if she were crying, so I thought it best to say nothing and let you speak to her. Whatever it is, I didn't want to make it worse."

"Denke, Leah. We've been searching everywhere for her. She…she ran off." It was an admission of failure. "Thank the gut Lord she's safe. You're sure she hasn't left?"

"I've been keeping an eye on the barn door. She hasn't come out. I was just going to send one of the kinder for you when I saw you coming. I'll send him to let Caleb know she's safe."

"Denke," Jessie said again. The word didn't seem enough. "I'll go to her."

"I'll walk with you," Leah said. Gesturing to her oldest boy, she gave him quick instructions as they went.

Jessie felt Leah's gaze on her face as they walked together toward the new barn. She'd have to explain it to Leah later. Now, she must concentrate on the child.

They stopped at the door to the barn, which stood ajar. Leah squeezed her hand in silent encouragement and then turned away. Taking a breath, praying for calm, Jessie walked into the barn.

It was very quiet. The barn was empty of animals at this time of day. Then she heard a small scraping sound from above, and a few fragments of hay drifted down from between the boards of the loft. Becky was almost directly above her.

"Becky," she called. "Where are you?"

Nothing. She imagined Becky freezing, scarcely breathing, like a small animal caught in the beam of a flashlight.

Jessie crossed to the ladder that led to the loft. "Becky, will you come down?"

Again there was no answer. She began to climb, knowing Becky could hear her coming.

When she reached the top she paused. Becky was curled on top of a hay bale against the front wall of the barn, her figure rigid, her face turned away from Jessie.

Relief swept over Jessie at the sight of the child. She was here. She was safe. The rest could be dealt with, surely.

Walking softly, she crossed to Becky and sat down on the bale next to her. Her prayers reached to God for wisdom, for guidance. When the silence stretched on too long, she spoke softly.

"I'm wonderful glad you're all right, Becky. Daadi was very worried about you."

For a moment there was no response. Then Becky began to cry. "I saw," she said, between sobs. "I saw Daadi kissing you this morning."

"Yah, I thought that must be it." So there had been something to that sound she'd thought she heard this morning. They should have been more careful. This was just what she'd feared—that letting the kinder know about their relationship too soon could ruin everything.

"It made you angry?" she asked.

Becky shook her head, hiccoughing a little. "Not... not angry, exactly. I was...mixed up. Mammi died. Daadi got hurt. Then you came, and I didn't want to like you, but I did. Everything keeps changing." She ended on a wail.

Jessie's heart ached for her. Poor Becky. She was just six. *Everything keeps changing.* How could she understand all the things that had been happening in her short life? It wasn't fair to expect her to.

Jessie could fill in what Becky didn't say. She'd just begun to trust Jessie, and then she'd seen Jessie with her father. No wonder she didn't know what to think. Who could she trust to be there for her?

"I know, Becky. I know." She put her arm around Becky's shoulders, feeling her tremble. But Becky didn't pull away, so Jessie drew the child against her. Sometimes everyone just needed to be held.

They sat in silence for a few moments. Jessie struggled for an answer. For the right words to say. *Gut Lord, guide me*, her heart cried.

She stroked Becky's hair. "It's hard to take so many

changes in your life. Not just for you, but for everyone. When your mamm died, I lost someone who was a much-loved little sister to me."

Becky clutched her hand. "She did bad things. Everyone said so."

It sounded as if "everyone" had been careless of what they'd said in front of a small child. "She made mistakes," Jessie said gently. "We can't stop loving someone for making mistakes." She dropped a light kiss on Becky's forehead. "I could never stop loving you no matter what."

Jessie bit her lip. What she'd said was true, but what would Becky think when Jessie left?

She tilted Jessie's face up so that she could see her expression. "Listen to me, Becky. No matter where I go or what I do, I will always love you. And Daadi will always love you…always, always, always. You can be sure of that."

Becky nodded slowly as she struggled to process Jessie's words. She was trying to believe, but her doubts and fears couldn't be cleared up so easily. They were bound to continue, and Jessie's heart seemed to break at knowing she wouldn't be here to help her.

"I think we should go home to Daadi now. What do you think?"

Becky scrambled to her feet. "Daadi. I want to see Daadi."

Together they crossed the loft and climbed down the ladder. They set off. Becky trotted ahead a few steps. Then she stopped, came back and took Jessie's hand. Together they walked toward home.

Caleb saw Becky and Jessie coming toward him across the field. Relief and joy surged through him, closely followed by anger. If Jessie had found her in Sam's barn, why had it taken so long? She should have known he'd be frantic to have his child in his arms again.

He couldn't possibly stay where he was and wait patiently for Becky. He began wheeling himself over the bumpy grass, fighting to keep the chair upright. Zeb came running to grab the wheelchair.

"What are you doing? They're coming. Becky is safe. Do you want to fall again? You won't help matters by getting yourself hurt just when you can see that Becky is fine."

Caleb ground his teeth together, but he had to admit that his uncle was right. It also wouldn't help matters to get into an unseemly tussle with Onkel Zeb over control of the chair.

It seemed to take forever, but it was surely just minutes. When they reached the mowed grass of the yard, Becky let go of Jessie's hand and raced toward him. She flung herself at him, hiding her face in his shirt.

Caleb held her close, murmuring to her. "It's all right. You're here now. It's all right."

He should talk to her about how wrong it had been to run off that way, but not now. Now he just had to hold her and rejoice that no harm had come to her.

Jessie reached them. "Caleb…" Her voice was tentative.

"Not now." He was sharp, but he couldn't help that. He couldn't talk to Jessie without losing what little control he had, so he'd best calm down first.

Regaining his control on that subject took longer than he'd have imagined. Jessie must have realized that, because she went about her usual routine without attempting to speak. The rest of the day passed, and still he hadn't made time to talk to Jessie.

It wasn't until he was lying in bed, staring at the ceiling, that he realized what was really troubling him. Before Jessie came, he'd been…if not happy, at least content with his life. He'd resigned himself to staying single, knowing he could never trust his heart to a woman after Alice. Having Jessie here had shown him how foolish he'd been. He couldn't bar all women from his life because of what Alice had done.

More than that…he couldn't completely blame Alice for what had gone wrong between them. If she'd been too young, too heedless, for marriage, he hadn't been that much better. He hadn't seen the problems for what they were when they began to arise, and he hadn't coped.

But that didn't mean he should fall in love with Jessie. He came back to the source of his anger. He'd trusted her with his children, and look what had happened. The fear he'd felt when he'd realized Becky was missing came surging back.

The sky had begun to lighten along the eastern ridge when he pushed through to what he really felt. He was afraid. Afraid that this love he felt for Jessie wasn't strong enough, afraid that he was jumping into a relationship again, afraid to trust.

You trusted her, one part of him argued. *You trusted her with the kinder, and she let you down.*

She couldn't keep her eyes on them every second of the day, he reminded himself. No one could…and no one should. No kinder could grow up properly if parents protected them that much.

The endless argument was giving him a headache.

He had to stop this, had to decide what he was going to say to Jessie. A pang struck him. Jessie must have suffered, too, when she'd seen Becky was gone. She must have told herself that it was just like the day Alice had run off.

He pushed himself upright, sitting on the edge of the bed. Ready or not, the day was beginning. He'd dress, head to the barn, try to be useful. Before he knew it, the van would be here to take him to have his cast checked.

Maybe when he returned, he'd have come to some conclusion about what to say to Jessie.

By the time Caleb left for his appointment, Jessie knew what she had to do. She'd waited throughout the early morning for Caleb to speak…to say something, anything, that would tell her what he was feeling.

But he'd said nothing. He'd avoided her eyes and talked to everyone else. She'd failed. And she knew she didn't have any choice.

Leaving the kinder in Onkel Zeb's care, Jessie walked across the field to Leah's house. She found Leah in the kitchen, rolling out pie crust.

"Jessie! What brings you here so early?" Then she got a glimpse of Jessie's face and dropped the rolling pin. She came quickly to her side, wiping flour from her hands with a tea towel. "What is it? Something has happened. Surely Becky hasn't run off again, has she?"

"No, nothing like that." Jessie hadn't intended to explain anything. She'd thought she'd ask her favor and be on her way. But the sympathy on Leah's face undid her. She blinked back tears. "Caleb blamed me for what happened with Becky. He won't even talk about it."

"You have to make him understand."

She shook her head. "I can't. He won't listen to anything I have to say." She tried to smile, but it was a miserable effort. "Funny, isn't it? Becky ran off because she saw Caleb kiss me."

"You and Caleb…well, all I can say is that it's about time." Leah hugged her. "All the more reason you have to make him listen."

"I tried to talk to him, but in a way he's right. I was responsible for Becky. She was upset enough to run away, and I never saw it."

"Ach, you can't blame yourself for everything. A child Becky's age can be gut at hiding her feelings. And poor Becky's had lots of practice, ain't so?"

Jessie had to admit that was true. Hadn't Becky been convinced that her daadi wouldn't like her if she looked like her mammi?

"There's plenty I could say to Caleb, but it's no use if he can't listen. The only thing is for me to go back home."

"Jessie, no." Leah's arm was around her, comforting her the way Jessie had comforted Becky. "Don't run away."

"I have to." She closed her eyes against the pain. "Please don't argue with me, Leah. Just…help me."

She could almost feel Leah's internal struggle, but finally Leah asked, "What can I do?"

"Will you drive me to the bus? I'll need to leave Zeb with the kinder, and Daniel is at work."

Leah clamped her lips closed. She nodded.

"Gut. Come in about an hour. I'll be packed and ready by then." Jessie made for the door, but not in time to prevent Leah from getting in the last word.

"I'll do it. But I still think you're wrong."

Right or wrong, she didn't have a choice, she told herself as she headed back across the field to the place she now thought of as home. Caleb blamed her. He hadn't trusted her. How could she imagine that they'd be able to build a life together without trust?

Caleb wheeled himself off the lift when the van brought him home again, looking ruefully at the heavy cast still on his leg. His hopes that it might be replaced today were dashed. The technician who worked with him would say only that the doctor would be in touch once he'd received the report. Still, she'd said it with a smile, and Caleb had decided to interpret that as a positive sign.

He waved goodbye to the van driver and turned toward the house. Where was everybody? Usually someone came out when he returned to see if he needed help.

No sooner had he thought it than the door opened and Becky and Timothy hurtled themselves onto his lap. With a jolt, he saw that they were crying.

"Here, what is it? What's wrong with the two of you? Are you hurt?" He glanced at Onkel Zeb, who'd followed them out, but Zeb was uncharacteristically silent.

"Becky." Caleb pulled her back so that he could see her face. "You must tell me what's happened to cause all these tears."

Becky nodded, gulping. "It's Jessie. Jessie went away. She's gone!" Her words escalated into a wail.

"Jessie left? Where did she go?" He couldn't make sense of this. "What do you mean, she's gone?"

"Leah is taking her to town to catch the bus," Onkel

Zeb said. "Jessie said she had to go home." His expression accused Caleb.

Becky cried, "She said she had to go, but…"

Timothy cut off his older sister. "She can't! Who will tell us stories and tuck us in? We need her more than anyone."

"We love her," Becky said. "And she loves us. It's all my fault for running away."

"Hush, now. Nothing's your fault." He tried to grab on to something that might make sense. "Why did you run off, Becky? That's not like you."

Becky sniffled. "'Cause I saw you kissing Jessie. I… I didn't know what to think. I just wanted to be by myself and figure it out."

For a moment he was speechless. "Becky, I didn't know."

"Jessie said you loved me and Timothy more than anything. She said she'd never stop loving us. But now she's going away."

"Daadi will stop her," Timothy declared. "Daadi will bring her home."

"Please, Daadi?" Hope kindled in Becky's eyes.

If Jessie left, he could stop asking himself difficult questions. He could stop dealing with painful truths.

Jessie was loving and honest all the way through. If he blamed her for anything, it was just an excuse not to blame himself.

Hugging his children, he looked at Onkel Zeb. "Will you bring the carriage? We'd best go if we're going to catch them before Jessie gets on the bus."

Zeb broke into a huge grin. Then he trotted toward the barn, shouting at Thomas to help him harness the mare.

They must have harnessed up in record time. In moments they'd brought the family carriage over. With the help of Zeb and Thomas, Caleb hoisted himself up into the seat.

"What are you waiting for?" he said. "Get in."

Still grinning, Zeb helped the young ones into the carriage and climbed in himself. Caleb clucked to the mare, and they were off.

He took the turn onto the road and snapped the lines, urging the mare faster. They'd have to step on it if they were to be in time.

"Faster, Daadi, faster," Becky urged, sliding off the seat to stand behind him. "Hurry."

"I'll go faster, but you sit properly on your seat and hold on. I don't want to lose you."

He'd come close to losing both of them...all wrapped up as he'd been in his own pain. If it hadn't been for Jessie, he might well have done so.

Onkel Zeb had been right all along. Jessie was probably the only person in the world who could break through to him, because she was hurting just as much as he was. Alice had broken her heart, too. And Jessie had reacted by reaching out to help him despite his rejection.

Once she'd accepted that this was no ordinary, sedate drive, the mare outdid herself, pacing along as if she were pulling a racing sulky instead of a family carriage. Caleb's pulse was pounding in time with the hooves, it seemed. If they didn't make it before Jessie left...

He could write. He could even go out to Ohio after her. But the need to catch her pushed him on. The time

for righting wrongs was now, the very minute he realized how wrong he'd been.

They rounded a bend in the road, and the children
shouted in excitement.

"There! Leah's buggy. Hurry, Daadi, hurry," Becky
said. She was leaning forward as if she could make the
buggy go faster.

He closed the gap between the buggies. Surely Leah
would hear another buggy behind her, but she didn't
slow down. He slapped the reins, the mare put on a
burst of speed, and they passed the other buggy. Caleb
signaled and pulled slowly to the side of the road, keeping one eye on the mirror to be certain Leah was doing
the same. She was, and in a moment both buggies were
parked, one behind the other.

Caleb turned, trying to get a look at Jessie's face,
but he couldn't. Gritting his teeth, he accepted what
he had to do. If only he'd thought to toss the crutches
in the buggy before they left.

Swinging his good leg over the step, he lifted the
cast, using both hands to move it over, as well.

"Caleb, wait…"

He ignored Onkel Zeb's warning and swung himself outward, grasping the railing with both hands and
swinging his legs down. He'd get his feet on the
ground, then work his way along the side…

His grip slid, he was losing control, he was falling…

Arms closed around him, supporting him, and he
knew without looking that it was Jessie. She held him
with both arms clasping him close, so that he could
feel her ragged breath.

"What are you trying to do?" she scolded, her voice
shaking. "Break the other leg?"

"No." He got one arm around her while he held on to the carriage strut with the other. "Trying to keep you from doing something so foolish as leaving us. Don't you know that we…that I…can't possibly get along without you?"

What else could he say? His thoughts spun frantically. What would show her how much he loved her? What would convince her to stay with them?

She was looking at him, a question in the clear depths of her eyes. "You didn't say anything," she said. "You wouldn't talk to me. How could I know what you were thinking?"

He smoothed his hand down the slender curve of her back. "Ach, Jessie, you should know by now how foolish I am. I had to fight my way through a sleepless night of arguing before I saw the truth for what it is. I love you. Alice's flaws were only human. I forgive her. And I ask God's forgiveness for my mistakes."

Her face softened, warmed. "I'm wonderful glad to hear it."

He found he could breathe again. He wasn't too late. "I'm not done making mistakes myself, you know. I need you, because you keep me straight about who I am. And I love you. For keeps." His heart seemed to be pounding so loudly he couldn't hear anything else. "Please, Jessie. I know you love my kinder. Can you love me, as well?"

She began to smile, and it was like the sun coming out in her face. How had he ever thought her plain? She was the most beautiful sight he'd ever seen. If only she'd speak and say the words that would put him out of his misery. He became aware that the children were hanging out of the carriage over their heads, listening to every word.

Well, why not? This was their future, too.

Jessie's smile encompassed all of them. "I love Becky and Timothy. And I love you, too. All of us belong together."

Caleb's heart was too full for speech. The doubting and anger and bitterness had been a thicket he'd hacked his way through for years, but now the struggling was over. He'd gotten there—to a place of peace and forgiveness.

He could only hold Jessie close and listen to his heart sing with joy. God had taken their broken pieces—his and Jessie's—and fit them together into something wonderful…something that would last a lifetime and beyond.

Epilogue

Spring had come to the valley again. The bulbs Jessie had put in last fall seemed eager to affirm the new life spring brought, sending green leaves unfurling tentatively in the sunshine.

"Mammi, Becky's coming. I see her. Can I run and meet her. Please?" Timothy tugged at her apron, his favorite way of ensuring her attention.

Jessie gave him a quick hug, loving the way it sounded when he and Becky called her Mammi. She looked down the path Becky followed when she walked back and forth to school and spotted her skipping along with Leah's kinder.

"Yah, you can. Mind you stay right with her and don't tease."

Without lingering to respond, Timothy darted across the yard toward the path. Caleb, fixing the pasture fence with Onkel Zeb and Thomas, waved to him and then started toward her.

Jessie walked to meet him, loving the ease with which his lean figure moved now. It had been a long haul, getting his leg back to its normal strength, but he'd made it. Now no one could tell it had ever been injured.

Recovering his strength had meant recovering his confidence, too. Like most men, Caleb could never be content until he could do all the things he expected of himself. He and Onkel Zeb had increased the dairy herd this spring, and with Thomas working full-time, they were able to manage the work among them.

A good thing, too, because Daniel's business had really taken off in the past year. The successful completion of the kitchen project he'd done for the Englischers had brought him as much business as he could handle, and he had taken on two apprentices to work alongside him.

Now, if only Daniel could find a good woman…

Caleb reached her and put his arm around her for a quick hug. "What are you thinking about, looking so serious?"

"How happy we are," she said, returning his hug. "And how I wish Daniel would find someone to love."

"Don't go making matches," Caleb warned. "He'll fall in love one day, and that will be it for him. You'll see. After all, it happened for us, ain't so?"

She nodded, wondering if he'd ever realized that she'd loved him since that first day when he'd come to her parents' farm. "Yah, and just when everyone was giving up on you."

He smiled. "It wasn't everyone's business. Just yours and mine."

"And Becky's and Timothy's," Jessie reminded him.

"Them, too," he agreed. He pressed his hand lightly against her rounding belly. "And this little one's."

Jessie put her hand over his, love overflowing her heart. "I never thought to be as happy as I am right now."

He held her closer. "Me, also. God has given us the gifts we didn't even know to ask for."

Contentment flooded through her. Caleb was right. Even when they hadn't known what was best for them, God had known. He had seen them through the pain and brought them to this joy, and she was forever grateful.

* * * * *

Lee Tobin McClain is the *New York Times* bestselling author of emotional small-town romances featuring flawed characters who find healing through friendship, faith and family. Lee grew up in Ohio and now lives in Western Pennsylvania, where she enjoys hiking with her goofy goldendoodle, visiting writer friends and admiring her daughter's mastery of the latest TikTok dances. Learn more about her books at leetobinmcclain.com.

Books by Lee Tobin McClain

Love Inspired

K-9 Companions

Her Easter Prayer
The Veteran's Holiday Home

Rescue Haven

The Secret Christmas Child
Child on His Doorstep
Finding a Christmas Home

Redemption Ranch

The Soldier's Redemption
The Twins' Family Christmas
The Nanny's Secret Baby

Visit the Author Profile page
at LoveInspired.com for more titles.

SMALL-TOWN NANNY

Lee Tobin McClain

For I know the plans I have for you, declares the Lord,
plans to prosper you and not to harm you,
plans to give you hope and a future.
—*Jeremiah* 29:11

To the real Bob Eakin. Thank you for your service.

Chapter 1

Sam Hinton was about to conclude one of the biggest business deals of his career. And get home in time to read his five-year-old daughter her bedtime story.

He'd finally gotten the hang of being a single dad who happened to run a multimillion-dollar business.

Feeling almost relaxed for the first time since his wife's death two years ago, Sam surveyed the only upscale restaurant in his small hometown of Rescue River, Ohio, with satisfaction. He'd helped finance this place just to have an appropriate spot to bring important clients, and it was bustling. He recognized his former high school science teacher coming through the door. There was town matriarch Miss Minnie Falcon calling for her check in her stern, Sunday-school-teacher voice. At a table by the window, one of the local farmers laughed with his teenage kids at what looked to be a graduation dinner.

And who was that new, petite, dark-haired waitress? Was it his sister's friend Susan Hayashi?

Sam tore his eyes away from the pretty server and checked his watch, wondering how long a visit to the men's room could take his client. The guy must be either checking with his board of directors or playing some kind of game with Sam—seeming to back off, hoping to drag down the price of the agricultural property he was buying just a little bit more before he signed on the dotted line. Fine. Sam would give a little if it made his client's inner tightwad happy.

Crash!

"Leave her alone! Hands off!" The waitress he'd noticed, his sister's friend Susan, left the tray and food where she'd dropped them and stormed across the dining room toward his client.

Who stood leering beside another, very young-looking, waitress. "Whoa, hel-lo, baby!" his client said to Susan as she approached. "Don't get jealous. I'm man enough for both of you ladies!"

"Back *off*!"

Sam shoved out of his chair and headed toward the altercation. Around him, people were murmuring with concern or interest.

"It's okay, Susan," the teenage waitress was saying to his sister's friend. "He d-d-didn't really hurt me."

Stepping protectively in front of the round-faced teenager, Susan pointed a delicate finger at his client. "You apologize to her," she ordered, poking the much larger, much older businessman in the chest with each word. She wore the same dark skirt and white blouse as all the other waitstaff, but her almond-shaped eyes and high cheekbones made her stand out almost as much as her stiff posture and flaring nostrils. Three or four gold hoops quivered in each ear.

"Keep your hands off me." Sam's client sneered down at Susan. "Where's the owner of this place? I don't have to put up with anything from a…" He lowered his voice, but whatever he said made the color rise in Susan's face.

Sam clapped a hand on his client's shoulder. He hadn't pegged the guy as this much of a troublemaker, but then, he barely knew him. "Come on. Leave the ladies alone."

The other man glanced at Sam and changed his tone. "Aw, hey, I was just trying to have a good time." He gave Susan another dirty look. "Some girls can't take a joke."

"Some jokes aren't funny, mister." She glared at him, two high spots of color staining her cheeks pink.

The restaurant manager rushed up behind them. "We can work this out. Mr. Hinton, I do apologize. You girls…" He clapped his hands at the two waitresses. "My office. Now."

"I'm so sorry, I didn't mean to cause trouble!" Crying, the teenage waitress hurried toward the office at the back of the restaurant.

Susan touched the manager's arm. "Don't get mad at Tawny. I'm the one who got in Prince Charming's face." She jerked her head sideways toward Sam's client.

The restaurant manager frowned and ushered Susan to his office.

Sam's client shrugged and gave Sam a conspiratorial grin as he turned toward their table. "Ready to get back to business?"

"No," Sam said, frowning after the restaurant manager and Susan. "We're done here."

"What?" His client's voice rose to a squeak.

"I'll see you to your car. I want you out of Rescue River."

Ten minutes later, after he'd banished his would-be client, settled the bill and fixed things with the restaurant manager, Sam strode out to the parking lot.

There was Susan, standing beside an ancient, rusty subcompact, staring across the moonlit fields that circled the town of Rescue River. He'd only met her a couple of times; unfortunately, he worked too much to get to know his sister's friends.

"Hey, Susan," he called as he approached. "I got you your job back."

She half turned and arched an eyebrow. "Oh, you did, did you? Thanks, but no, thanks."

"Really?" He stopped a few yards away from her. Although he hadn't expected gratitude, exactly, the complete dismissal surprised him.

"Really." She crossed her arms and leaned back against her car. "I don't need favors from anyone."

"It's not a favor, it's just…fairness."

"It's a favor, and I don't want it. You think I can go back in there and earn tips after the scene I just made?"

"You probably could." Not only was she attractive, but she appeared to be very competent, if a little on the touchy side. "Rescue River doesn't take kindly to men being jerks. Most of the people in that room were squarely on your side."

"Wait a minute." Her eyes narrowed as she studied him. "Now I get it. You're part owner of the place."

"I'm a silent partner, yes." He cocked his head to one side, wondering where this was going.

"You're trying to avoid a sexual harassment lawsuit, aren't you?"

His jaw dropped. "Really? You think that's why..." He trailed off, rubbed the heavy stubble on his chin, and thought of his daughter, waiting for him at home. "Look, if you don't want the job back, that's fine. And if you think you have a harassment case, go for it."

"Don't worry. It wasn't me your buddy was groping, and I'm not the lawsuit type." She sighed. "Probably not the waitress type either, like Max said when he was firing me."

Sam felt one side of his mouth quirk up in a smile as he recognized the truth of that statement. He found Susan to be extremely cute, with her long, silky hair, slender figure and vaguely Asian features, but she definitely wasn't the eager-to-please type.

Wasn't *his* type, not that it mattered. He preferred soft-spoken women, domestic ladies who wore makeup and perfume and knew how to nurture a man. Archaic, but there it was.

Just then, the teenage waitress came rushing out through the kitchen door. "Susan, you didn't have to do that! Max said he fired you. I'm sorry!"

"No big deal." She shrugged again, the movement a little stiff.

"But I thought you needed the money to send your brother to that special camp—"

"It's fine." Susan's voice wobbled the tiniest bit, or

was he imagining it? "Just, well, don't let guys do that kind of stuff to you."

"I know, I know, but I didn't want to get in trouble. Especially with Mr. Hinton on the premises…" The girl trailed off, realizing for the first time that Sam stood to one side, listening to every word. "Oh, I didn't know you were there! Don't be mad at her, Mr. Hinton. She was just trying to help me!"

Susan patted her on the shoulder. "Go back inside and remember, just step on a guy's foot—hard—if he tries anything. You can always claim it was an accident."

"That's a great idea! You're totally awesome!" The younger woman gave Susan a quick hug and then trotted back into the restaurant.

Susan let her elbows drop to the hood of her car and rested her chin in her hands. "Was I ever that young?"

"Don't talk like you're ancient. What are you, twenty-five, twenty-six?" Susan was relatively new in town, and if memory served, she was a teacher at the elementary school. Apparently waitressing on the side. Sam assumed she was about his sister Daisy's age, since they'd fast become thick as thieves.

"Good guess, *Mr.* Hinton. You didn't even need your bifocals to figure that out. I'm twenty-five."

Okay, at thirty-seven he *was* a lot older than she was, but her jibe stung. Maybe because he knew very well that he wasn't getting any younger and that he needed to get cracking on his next major life goal.

Which would involve someone a lot softer and gentler than Susan Hayashi. "Listen," he said, "I'm sorry about what happened. You should know that guy who caused the trouble is headed back toward the east coast even as we speak. And he's not my friend, by the way. Just a client. Former client, now."

She arched a delicate brow. "My knight in shining armor, are you?"

What was there to say to a woman who misinterpreted his every move? He shook his head, reached out to pat her shoulder, then decided it wasn't a good idea and pulled his hand back. If he touched her, she might report him. Or throw a punch.

Definitely a woman to steer clear of.

There didn't seem to be any sweetness in her. So it surprised Sam when, as he bid her goodnight, he caught a whiff of honeysuckle perfume.

The next day, even though she wanted to pull the covers over her head and cry, Susan forced herself to climb out of bed early. She'd committed to spend her Saturday morning helping at the church's food pantry, and honestly, even that might not have gotten her out of bed, but she knew her best friend, Daisy, was going to be there.

"Come on," Daisy said when Susan dragged herself down the steps and into the church basement, "we're doing produce. Hey, did you really get fired last night?"

Embarrassment heated Susan's face as she followed her friend to an out-of-the-way corner where bins of spinach and lettuce donated by local farmers stood ready to be divided into smaller bunches. "Yeah. How'd you hear?"

"That sweet little Tawny Thompson spread it all over town, how you rescued her from some creepy businessman. What were you thinking?"

"He practically had his hand up her skirt! What was I supposed to do?"

"I don't know, tell the manager? Honestly, I would've done the same thing, but I'm not in your position. You needed that job!"

"I know." Susan blew out a sigh as she studied the wooden crates of leafy greens. Her hopes of funding the summer respite her mom needed so desperately had flown out the window last night. "Waitressing at a nice restaurant like Chez La Ferme is definitely the best money I can make, but I get so mad at guys like that. I thought Max would back me up, not fire me."

"Can you even send your brother to camp now?"

"Probably not. I shouldn't have told him he could go, but when I landed this waitressing job and found out it could be full-time as soon as school lets out for the summer, I thought I had the fee easy. I had a payment plan, everything. Now…" She focused on lettuce bunches so Daisy wouldn't see the tears in her eyes.

"What are you going to do?"

"I don't know. And to top it off, I might have to move home for the summer." Even saying it made her heart sink. She loved Rescue River and had all kinds of plans for her summer here.

"Why? You're always talking about how you and your mom…"

"Don't get along? Yeah." She sighed, wishing it wasn't so, wishing she had a storybook family like so many of the Midwestern ones she saw around her these days. "I love Mom, but she and I are like oil and water. If I go back, honestly, it'll stress her out more. I just want—*wanted*—her to have a summer to garden and antique shop with her friends, maybe even go on a few dates, without worrying about Donny."

An older couple wandered over. "You guys okay? Need any help?"

"We've got it." Daisy waved them away and carried a load of bagged lettuce to a sorting table. "So you had a good plan. But you couldn't help what happened."

"I could have been more…refined about it." A couple of tears overflowed, and Susan took off her plastic gloves to dig in her pocket for a tissue. "When am I ever going to learn to control my temper?" She blew her nose.

Daisy put an arm around her. "When you turn into a whole different person. You know, God made you the way you are, and He has a plan for you. Something will work out." She paused. "Why would you move back home, anyway? What's wrong with your room at Lacey's?"

"Lacey's got renovation fever." Susan pulled on a fresh pair of plastic gloves. "Remember, she gave me my room cheap because she knew I'd have to move when she started fixing up the place. So now her brother—you know Buck, right?—well, he's dried out and ready to help, and summer's the best time for them to get going." She gauged the right amount of lettuce for a family of four, put it in a plastic bag and twist-tied it. "And I don't have money for a deposit on a new place. I'll need to save up."

"You can stay with me. You know that."

"You're sweet." Susan side-hugged her friend. "And you live in a tiny place with two dogs and a cat. You have exactly zero room, except in that big heart of yours."

Daisy pried open another crate, this one full of kale leaves. "We just have to pray about it."

"Well, pray fast, because Lacey asked if I could be out next week. And even if I can land a job at another restaurant in Rescue River—which I doubt, with the non-recommendation Max is giving me—I won't be making anything like the tips I could bring in at Chez Le Ferme." She sighed as she dumped out the last of the kale leaves and stowed the wooden crate under the table. "I'm such an idiot."

"I've got it!" Daisy snapped her fingers, a smile lighting her plump face. "I know exactly what you can do for the summer!"

"What?" Susan eyed her friend dubiously and then went back to bagging kale. Daisy was wonderful, but she tended to get overexcited when she had a new idea.

"You know my brother Sam, right? He was at the Easter service at church, and at Troy and Angelica's wedding."

"I remember. In fact, he was at the restaurant last night. He…actually said he could get me my job back, but I turned him down." Susan felt her face flush as she thought of their conversation. She'd still been heated about the encounter with that jerk of a businessman, and she hadn't had her guard up around Daisy's brother, as she had the previous couple of times they'd met. She had the distinct feeling she'd been rude to him, but truthfully, he'd disconcerted her with his dominant-guy effort to make all her problems go away.

He was a handsome man, no doubt of that. Tall and broad-shouldered, an all-American quarterback type with a square jaw and close-cropped dark hair.

But he was one of those super traditional guys, she

could just tell. In fact, he reminded her of her father, who thought women belonged in the home, not the workplace. Dad had wanted his wife to stay home, and Mom had, and look where it had gotten her. To make matters worse, her father had expected Susan to do the same, sending her to college only for her MRS degree, which she obviously hadn't gotten. Which she had no interest in getting, not now, not ever. She was a career woman with a distinct calling to teach kids, especially those with special needs. Susan wasn't one of those people who heard clear instructions from God every week or two, but in the case of her life's work, she'd gotten the message loud and clear.

Daisy waved her hand impatiently. "You don't want that job back. I have a better idea. Did I tell you how Sam hired a college girl to take care of Mindy over the summer?"

"What?" Susan pulled herself back to the present, rubbed the back of her plastic-gloved hand over her forehead and tried to focus on what Daisy was saying.

"Sam texted me this morning, all frantic. That girl he hired to be Mindy's summer nanny just let him know late last night that she can't do it. She got some internship in DC or something. Now Sam's hunting for someone to take her place. You'd be perfect!"

Susan laughed in disbelief. "I'd be a disaster! I'm a terrible cook, and...what do nannies even do, anyway?" She had some impression of them as paid housewives, and that was the last thing she wanted to be.

"You're great with kids! You're a teacher. Do you know Mindy?"

Susan nodded. "Cute kid, but sort of notorious for playground fights. I've bailed her out a few times."

"She can be a bit of a terror. Losing her mom was hard, and then Sam hasn't been able to keep a baby-sitter or nanny…"

"And why would that be?" Susan knew the answer without even asking. You could tell from spending two minutes with Sam that he was a demanding guy.

"He works a lot of hours and he expects a lot. Not so much around the house, he has a cleaning service, but he's very particular about how Mindy is taken care of. And then with Mindy being temperamental and, um, *spirited*, it's not been easy for the people Sam has hired. But you'd be absolutely perfect!"

"Daisy, think." Susan raised a brow at her friend. "I just got fired for being too mouthy and for not putting up with baloney from chauvinistic guys. And you think this would be perfect how?"

Daisy looked crestfallen for a minute, and then her face brightened. "The thing is, deep inside, Sam would rather have someone who stands up to him than someone who's a marshmallow. Just look how well he gets along with me!"

Susan chuckled and lifted another crate to the table. "You're his little sister. He has to put up with you."

"Sam's nuts about me because I don't let him get away with his caveman attitude. You wouldn't, either. But that's not the point."

"Okay, what's the point?" Susan couldn't help feeling a tiny flicker of hope about this whole idea— it would be so incredible to be able to send Donny to camp, not to disappoint him and her mother yet again—but she tamped it down. There was no way this would work from either end, hers or Sam's.

"The point is," Daisy said excitedly, "you're certified in special education. That's absolutely amazing! There's no way Sam could say you don't know what you're doing!"

"Uh-huh." Susan felt that flicker again.

"He'll pay a lot. And the thing is, you can live in! You'll have the summer to save up for a deposit on a new place."

Susan drew in a breath as the image of her mother and autistic brother flickered again in her mind. "But Daisy," she said gently, "Sam doesn't like me. When we talked last night, I could tell."

One of the food pantry workers came over. "Everything okay here, ladies?"

"Oh, sure, of course! We just got to talking! Sorry!"

For a few minutes, they focused on their produce, efficiently filling bags with kale and then more leaf lettuce, pushing a cartload of bundles over to the distribution tables, coming back to bag up sugar snap peas and radishes someone had dumped in a heap on their table.

Working with the produce felt soothing to Susan. She'd grown up urban and gotten most of her vegetables at the store, but she remembered occasional Saturday trips to the farmers market with her mother, Donny in tow.

Her mother had tried so hard to please her dad, who, with his Japanese ancestry, liked eggplant and cucumbers and napa cabbage. She and her mom had watched cooking videos together, and her mom had studied cookbooks and learned to be a fabulous Japanese chef. Susan's mouth watered just thinking about daikon salad and salt-pickled cabbage and broccoli stir-fry.

But had it worked? Had her dad been happy? Not

really. He'd always had some kind of criticism, and her mother would sneak off and cry and try to do better, and it was never good enough. And as she and Donny had grown up, they hadn't been enough either, and Susan knew her mother had blamed herself. Having given birth to a rebellious daughter and a son with autism, she felt she'd failed as a woman.

Her mom's perpetual guilt had ended up making Susan feel guilty, too, and as a hormonal teenager, she'd taken those bad feelings out on her mother. And then Dad had left them, and the sense of failure had been complete.

Susan shook off the uncomfortable reminder of her own inadequacy and looked around. Where was Daisy?

Just then, her friend stood up from rummaging in her purse, cell phone in hand. "I'm calling Sam and telling him to give you an interview."

"No!" Panic overwhelmed Susan. "Don't do it!" She dropped the bundle of broccoli she was holding and headed toward Daisy. There was no way she could interview with a man who reminded her so much of her father.

"You can't stop me!" Daisy teased, and then, probably seeing the alarm on Susan's face, put her phone behind her and held out a hand. "Honey, God works in mysterious ways, but I am totally sensing this is a God thing. Just let me do it. Just do an interview and see what he says, see how you guys get along."

Susan felt her life escaping from her control. "I don't—"

"You don't have to take the job. Just do the interview."

"But what if—"

"Please? I'm your friend. I have no vested interest in how this turns out. Well, except for keeping you in town."

"I…" Susan felt her will to resist fading. There was a lot that was good about the whole idea, right? And so what if it was uncomfortable for her? If her mom and Donny could be happy, she'd be doing her duty, just as her dad had asked her to do before he'd left. *You have to take care of them, Suzie,* her dad had said in his heavily accented English.

"I'm setting something up for this afternoon. If not sooner." Daisy turned back to the phone and Susan felt a sense of doom settling over her.

That afternoon, Susan climbed out of her car in front of Sam's modern-day mansion on the edge of Rescue River, grabbed her portfolio and headed up the sidewalk, all the while arguing with God. "Daisy says You'll make a way where there is no way, but what if I don't like Your way? And I can say for sure that Sam Hinton isn't going to like *my* way, so this is a waste of time I could be—"

The double front doors swung open. She caught a glimpse of a high-ceilinged entryway, a mahogany table full of framed photos and a spectacular, sparkling chandelier, but it was Sam Hinton who commanded her attention. He stood watching her approach, wearing a sleeves-rolled-up white dress shirt and jeans, arms crossed, legs apart.

Talk about a man and his castle. And those arms! Was he a bodybuilder in his spare time or what?

"Thanks for coming." He extended one massive hand to her.

She reached out and shook it, ignoring the slight breathlessness she felt. This was Sam, Daisy's super-traditional businessman of a brother, not America's next male model. "No problem. Daisy thought it would be a good idea."

"Yes. She had me squeeze you in, but you should know that I'm interviewing several other candidates today."

"No problem." Was God going to let her off this easy?

"It seems like a lot of people are interested in the job, probably because I'm paying well for a summer position." He ushered her in.

"How well?"

He threw a figure over his shoulder as he led her into an oak-lined office in the front of the house, and Susan's jaw dropped.

Twice as much as she'd ever hoped to make waitressing. She could send Donny to camp and her mom to the spa. Maybe even pay for another graduate course.

Okay, God—and Daisy—You were right. It's the perfect job for me.

He gestured her into the seat in front of his broad oak desk, and Susan felt a pang of nostalgia. Her dad had done the exact same thing when he wanted to talk to her about some infraction of his rules. Only his desk had just been an old door on a couple of sawhorses in the basement. How he would have loved a home office like this one.

"I don't know if you've met Mindy, but she has some…limitations." His jaw jutted out as if he was daring her to make a comment.

"If you think of them that way." The words were out

before she could weigh the wisdom of saying them, and she shouldn't have, but come on! The child was missing a hand, not a heart or a set of lungs.

Sam's eyebrows shot up. "I think I know my child better than you do. Have you even met Mindy?"

Rats, rats, rats. Would she ever learn to shut her big mouth? "I teach at Mindy's school, so I've been the recess and lunchroom monitor during her kindergarten year. I know about her hand. But of course, you know her better, you're her father."

Sam was eyeing her with a level glare.

"We have a sign up at school that reads, 'Argue for your limitations, and sure enough, they're yours.' I think it's Richard Bach. I just meant…it's an automatic response." *Stop talking, Susan.* God might have a nice plan for her, but she was perfectly capable of ruining nice plans. She'd done it all her life. She fumbled in her portfolio. "Here's my résumé."

He took it, glanced over it. Then looked more closely. "You've done coursework on physical disabilities? Graduate coursework?"

"Yeah. I'm working on my master's in special ed. Bit by bit."

"Why not go back full-time? At least summers? Why are you looking to work instead?"

"Quite frankly, I have a mother and brother to help support." *Hello, Mr. Rich Guy, everyone's not rolling in money like you are.*

"Doesn't the district pay for your extra schooling?"

"Six credits per year, which is two classes. I've used mine up."

He was studying her closely, as if she was a bug pinned on the wall. Or as if she was a woman he was interested in, but she was absolutely certain that couldn't be. "I see." He nodded. "Well, I'm not sure this would be the job for you anyway. I go out in the evenings pretty often."

"Really?" She opened her mouth to say more and then clamped it closed. *Shut up, you want this job.*

"I know, being young and adventurous, you must go out a lot yourself."

"Don't make assumptions. That's not what I was thinking." She looked away from him, annoyed.

"What were you thinking?"

"Do you really want to know?"

"Try me."

"I was thinking: you work super long hours, right? And you go out in the evenings. So…when do you spend time with your daughter?"

Sam stared at Susan as her question hung in the air between them. "When do I…? Look. If you've already decided I'm a terrible parent, this isn't going to work."

Truthfully, her words uncovered the guilt that consumed him as an overworked single dad. He hated how much time he had to spend away from Mindy. Half the time, he hated dating, too, but he'd promised Marie that he'd remarry so that Mindy wouldn't be raised without a mother in the home. Probably, she'd made him promise because she knew how much he worked and feared that Mindy would be raised by babysitters if he didn't remarry.

Well, he'd changed and was trying to change more, but he'd made a promise—not just about remarrying, but about what type of mom Mindy needed, actually—

and he intended to keep it. Which didn't mean this snippy schoolteacher had the right to condemn him.

"Look, I'm sorry. It's not my place to judge and I don't know your situation. Ask Daisy, I'm way too outspoken and it always gets me into trouble." Her face was contrite and her apology sounded sincere. "The thing is, I know kids and I'm good with them. If you're struggling, either with her disability or with…other issues, I could help. Build up her self-esteem, encourage her independence." Those pretty, almond-shaped brown eyes looked a little bit shiny, as if she was holding back tears. "Don't turn me down just because I'm mouthy, if you think I'd be a help to Mindy."

She was right. And he was a marshmallow around women who looked sad, especially seriously cute ones like Susan. "It's okay."

And it *was* okay. He recognized already that his burst of anger had more to do with his own guilty feelings than with her comment. But that didn't mean he had to hire her.

The doorbell chimed, making them both jump. "That's probably my next interview. I'm sorry." He stood. "Here's your résumé back."

"It's all right, you can keep it. In case you change your mind." She stood and grabbed her elegant black portfolio. Come to think of it, all of her was elegant, from her close-fitting black trousers to her white shirt and vest to her long black hair with a trendy-looking stripe of red in it, neatly clipped back.

Just for a minute, he wondered what that hair would look like flowing free.

Sam forced that thought away as he came around his desk to Susan's side. She looked neat and professional, but as soon as she opened her mouth, it became apparent that she was quite a character. Sam shook his head as he ushered her through the entryway. Why Daisy had thought he and Susan could work together was beyond him.

Thinking about her interview, he couldn't help grinning. What job applicant questioned and insulted the potential boss? You didn't see that in the business world. He was used to people kowtowing to him, begging for a job. Susan could take a few lessons in decorum, but he had to admit he enjoyed her spunk.

The doorbell chimed again just as they reached it, so he was in the awkward position of having two job applicants pass each other in the doorway. The new one, a curvaceous blonde in a flowered dress, stood smiling, a plate of plastic-wrap-covered cookies in her hands.

"Hi, are you Mr. Hinton? Thank you so much for agreeing to interview me. I would just absolutely love to have this job! What a great house!"

"Come on in." He gestured the new applicant into the entryway. "Susan, I'll be in touch.'"

"I hope so," she murmured as she brushed past him and out the door. "But I'm not holding my breath."

Chapter 2

The next Thursday afternoon, Sam arrived at the turn-off to his brother Troy's farm with a sense of relief. His sister was right; he needed to take a break from interviewing nannies during the day and working late into the night to make up for it. But he was desperate; Mindy's last day of school had been Tuesday, and without a regular child care provider, he'd had to stay home or use babysitters who weren't necessarily up to par.

Mindy bounced in her booster seat. "There's the sign! Look, it says *D-O-G*, dog! But what else does it say, Daddy?"

He slowed to read the sign aloud: "A Dog's Last Chance: No-Cage Canine Rescue."

"Cuz Uncle Troy and Aunt Angelica and Xavier rescue dogs. Right?"

"That's right, sugar sprite." And he hoped they could

rescue him, too. Or not rescue—they had too much going on for that—but at least give him ideas about getting a good child care provider for Mindy for the summer.

"There they are, there they are! And look, there's baby Emmie!"

Sure enough, his brother and sister-in-law stood outside the fenced kennel area. He parked, let Mindy out of the car and then paused to survey the scene.

Troy was reaching out for the baby, all of two weeks old, so that his wife could kneel down to greet Mindy with a huge hug.

The tableau they presented battered Sam's heart. He wanted this. He wanted a wife who would look up at him with that same loving, admiring expression Angelica gave Troy. Wanted a woman who'd embrace Mindy, literally and figuratively. Seeing how it thrilled Mindy, he even thought he wouldn't mind having another baby, a little brother or sister for them both to love.

This was what he and Marie had wanted, what they would have had, if God hadn't seen fit to grab it away from them.

He pushed the bitterness aside and strode up to the happy family. "How's Emmie? She sleeping well?"

Troy and Angelica looked at each other and laughed. "Not a chance. We're up practically all night, every night," Troy said, and then Sam noticed the dark circles under his brother's eyes. Running a veterinary practice and a rescue while heading a family had to be exhausting, but though he looked tired, there was a deep happiness in Troy's eyes that hadn't been there before.

That was the power of love. Troy and Angelica had married less than a year ago and instantly conceived a baby, at least partly in response to Angelica's son Xavier's desire for a little sister. They'd even gotten the gender right.

Sam renewed his determination: With or without God's help, he was going to find this for himself and Mindy. He didn't need the Lord to solve his problems for him. He could do it on his own.

"Where's Xavier, Uncle Troy?"

Troy chuckled. "It's Kennel Kids day. Where do you think?"

For the first time, Sam noticed the cluster of boys on the far edge of the fenced area. It was the ragtag group of potential hoodlums that Troy mentored through giving them responsibilities at the kennel. Amazing that his brother, busy as he was, had time to work with kids in need. Or made time, truth be known, and Sam's conscience smote him. He ought to give more back to the community, but he felt as if he was barely holding his own life together these days. "Who's monitoring the boys? Is that Daisy?"

"Can I go play, Daddy?" Mindy begged.

"No."

"Why not?"

"It's not safe, honey."

"But Xavier's over there."

"Xavier's a boy, honey. And…" He broke off, seeing the knowing glance Troy and Angelica exchanged. Okay, so he was overprotective, but those boys were playing rough and Mindy, with her missing hand, had one less means of defense.

And one more reason to get teased, in the sometimes-cruel world of school-aged kids.

Mindy's face reddened and she drew in a breath, obviously about to have a major meltdown.

Sam squatted down beside her, touching her shoulder, willing her to stay calm. He was so tired after another late night working, and he wasn't that great about dealing with Mindy's frequent storms. Didn't know if there even was a good way to deal with them.

"Hey!" Angelica got a little bit in Mindy's face, startling her out of her intended shriek. "I know! Why don't you and your daddy go ask Xavier to take you down to the barn? He can show you the newest puppies. You can stay outside the fence," she added, rolling her eyes a little at Sam.

"Okay! C'mon, Daddy!"

Thank you, he mouthed to Angelica, bemused by the way a little girl's mood could change in a second.

"Not sure if you'll be thanking me in a minute," she said with a chuckle.

She must mean his ongoing battle with Mindy, the one where Angelica and Troy were staunchly on Mindy's side. "We're not getting a puppy!" he mouthed over his shoulder to Angelica, keeping his voice low so he wouldn't reawaken Mindy's interest in the issue.

But as he and Mindy approached the group at the other end of the fenced enclosure, Sam wondered if Angelica might have been talking with Daisy…and if her joke about him not thanking her might have meant something entirely different.

Because *she* was there.

Susan, the firebrand waitress and job candidate he hadn't been able to get out of his mind for the past four days.

Who was she to tell him he wasn't raising his daughter right?

And what on earth was she doing here?

The answer, apparently, was that she was working with the kids, because she was squatting down beside one of the smaller boys, probably seven or eight years old. From the boy's awkward movements, Troy guessed he had some kind of muscular disorder.

And Susan was helping him to pet a pit bull's face.

Sam shook his head. Of course she was. The woman obviously had no common sense, no safety consciousness, no awareness of what was age-appropriate. If that kid's parents could see what she was doing… Of course, given the nature of Kennel Kids, the boy might not have involved parents. Still, Troy or Angelica ought to rein Susan in.

At that moment, she lifted her head and saw him. Her mouth dropped open, and then her eyes narrowed as if she was reading his mind.

"Xavier!" Mindy's joyous shout was a welcome distraction. "C'mere! C'mere!"

Susan called out to Daisy, who was, he now realized, standing guard over the overall group. Daisy came and knelt beside the boy Susan had been helping, and Susan exchanged a few heated words with her, then rose effortlessly to her feet. She followed Xavier, who was running toward the fence to see Mindy.

A knee-high black-and-white puppy bounded over on enormous, clumsy feet, barking. The kids immediately started playing with it, Mindy poking her fingers through the fence to touch its nose and Xavier jumping and rolling with the puppy on the inside of the enclosure. Which left Sam to watch Susan's approach. She wore cutoff shorts and a red shirt, hair up in a long ponytail. She looked young and innocent, especially since she'd removed her multiple earrings. "Didn't expect to see you here," he said, hoping his voice didn't betray his strange agitation.

"The feeling's mutual, and when I get the chance, I'm going to strangle your sister." She knelt down, and Xavier, along with the black-and-white dog, fell into her lap, pushing her backward.

Daisy. Oh. Susan's being here was Daisy's doing. "I never could control that girl. She always does exactly what she wants."

She flashed a smile. "And she always means well."

He watched Susan struggle out from under the dog, laughing when it licked her face. Then she handed Xavier a ball from her shorts pocket and he threw it for the dog to fetch.

"What's Daisy doing?" Sam asked. "Is she pushing us together on purpose?" If his sister was playing matchmaker, she was doing a poor job of it. She had to know Susan wasn't his type, even though the thought of going out with Susan sounded the tiniest bit appealing, probably just for the chance to argue with her.

"She wants you to give me your nanny job, which you and I both know is ridiculous."

Oh, the *job*. Heat rose to the back of Sam's neck as he realized he'd misinterpreted his sister's actions as dating-type matchmaking. And, yes, it was ridiculous from his own point of view to hire someone as mouthy and inappropriate as Susan, but why did *she* find the idea ridiculous?

"Hi, Miss Hayashi," Mindy said, looking up at Susan with a shy smile.

"Hi, Mindy." Susan's voice went rich and warm as honey when she looked down at his daughter. "Want to come in and play with the dogs?"

"No, she can't come in!" The words practically exploded out of Sam's mouth.

"Oh." Susan looked surprised, and Mindy opened her mouth to object.

"She can't…" He nodded down at her. "It's not safe."

Xavier provided an unexpected escape route. "You're too little to come in here," he explained. "But I can take you to the barn and show you our new tiny puppies. There's eight of them, and they're all gray 'cept for one spotted one, and their eyes are shut like this!" He squeezed his eyes tightly shut, them immediately opened them, grinning.

"I want to see them!" Mindy jumped to her feet, hugged Sam's leg and gazed up at him. "Please, Daddy?"

Love for his daughter overwhelmed him. "Okay, if you have an adult with you."

Xavier ran a few yards down to the gate, and with an assist from Susan, got it open. "Come on, Dad will help us," he said, and the two children rushed off toward the barn.

Leaving Sam and Susan standing with a fence between them. "You shouldn't have invited Mindy to come in without my permission," he informed her.

"Right. You're right. I just… Who knew you were *that* overprotective? She's not made of glass, but you're going to have her thinking she is."

"I think we've already established that you don't have the right to judge."

"Yeah, but that was when I was trying to get the

job with you. Now, I'm just a…well, an acquaintance. Which means I can state my opinion, right?"

"She's an acquaintance with a double certification in elementary and special ed," his sister, Daisy, said, coming from behind to put a hand on Susan's shoulder. "Sam, when are you going to realize you're way too cautious with that child? Marie was even worse. You're going to have Mindy afraid of her own shadow."

"That day is a long way off," Sam said, frowning at the idea that Marie had been anything but the perfect mother. Did everyone think he was too overprotective? Was he? Was he hurting Mindy?

"Um, think I'll go help get the kids ready to go home." Susan walked off, shoulders squared and back straight.

Daisy glared up at Sam. "What's your problem, anyway? Susan said her interview with you didn't go well."

"Did she tell you she couldn't stop questioning my abilities as a father? I hardly think that's what I want in a summer nanny."

"Come on, let's walk up to the house," Daisy said, coming out through the gate and putting an arm around him. "Sam, everyone knows you're the best dad around. You stepped in when Marie got sick and you haven't taken a break since. If you're a tiny bit controlling, well, who can blame you? Mindy's not had an easy road."

"You're using your social worker voice, and I'm sensing a 'but' in there." He put his own arm around his little sister. She definitely drove him crazy, but he didn't question her wisdom. Daisy was the intuitive, people-smart one in the family, and Sam and his brother had learned early on to respect that.

"The thing is, you're looking for a clone of your

dead wife. In a nanny and in a partner. What if you opened your mind to a different kind of influence on Mindy?"

"What do you mean, in a partner?" He'd kept his deathbed promise to Marie a secret, so how did Daisy know he was looking for a new mom for Mindy?

Daisy laughed. "I've seen the women you date. They're all chubby and blonde and worshipful. It's not rocket science to figure out that you're trying to find a replica of Marie."

The words stung with their truth. "Is that so bad? Marie was wonderful. We were happy." He'd never been like Daisy and Troy, adventurous and fun-loving; he'd always been the conventional older brother, wanting a standard, solid, traditional family life, and Marie had understood that. She'd wanted the same thing, and they'd been building it. Building a beautiful life that had been cut short.

"Oh, Sam." Daisy rubbed a hand up and down his back. "It's understandable. It was a horrible loss for you and Mindy. For all of us, really. I loved Marie, too."

Reassured, Sam could focus on the rest of what Daisy had said. "You think I need to be worshipped?"

"I think you're uncomfortable when women question your views, but c'mon, Sam. You're Mensa-level smart, you're practically a billionaire and you've built Hinton Enterprises into the most successful corporation in Rescue River, if not all of Ohio. It's not like you need reassurance about your masculinity. Why don't you try dating women who pose a little bit of a challenge?"

"I get plenty of challenge from my family, primarily you." He squeezed her shoulders, trying not to get defensive about her words. "My immediate problem is finding a nanny, not a girlfriend. And someone like Susan has values too different from mine. She'd have Mindy taming pit bulls and playing with hoodlums."

"She'd let Mindy out of the glass bubble you've put her in!" Daisy spun away to glare at him. "Look, she's the one with coursework in special ed, not you. She's not going to put your daughter at risk. She'd be great for Mindy, even if she does make you a little uncomfortable. And you did kind of contribute indirectly to her getting fired from her waitressing job."

A hard lump of guilt settled in his stomach. He didn't want to be the cause of someone losing their livelihood. He'd always prided himself on finding ways to keep from laying off employees, even in this tough economy.

She raised her eyebrows. "Think about it, bro. Are you man enough to handle a nanny like Susan, if it would be the best thing for Mindy?"

Susan sat at the kitchen table with Angelica and the new baby while Daisy warmed up the side dishes she'd brought and ordered her brothers outside to grill burgers.

"Do you want to hold her?" Angelica asked, looking down at the dark-haired baby as if she'd rather do anything than let her go.

"Me?" Susan squeaked. "No, thanks. I mean, she's beautiful, but I'm a disaster with babies. At a minimum, I always make them cry."

Of course, Sam came back into the kitchen in time to hear that remark. She seemed to have a genius for *not* impressing him.

"I used to feel that way, too," Daisy said, "but I'm great with little Emmie. Here, you can stir this while I hold her." She put down her spoon and confidently scooped the baby out of Angelica's arms.

Susan walked over to the stove and looked doubtfully at the pan of something white and creamy. "You want me to help cook? Really?"

"Oh, never mind, I forgot. Sam, stir the white sauce for a minute, would you?"

"You don't cook?" he asked Susan as he took over at the stove, competently stirring with one hand while he reached for a pepper grinder with the other.

In for a penny, in for a pound. "Nope. Not domestic."

"You'll learn," Angelica said, stretching and twisting her back. "When you find someone you want to cook for."

"Not happening. I'm the single type."

"She is," Daisy laughed. "She won't even date. But we're going to change all that."

"No, we're not." Susan sat back down at the table.

"Yes, we are. The group at church has big plans for you."

"*My* singles group? Who would run it if I somehow got involved with a guy?" Susan pulled her legs up and wrapped her arms around them, taking in the large, comfortable kitchen with appreciation. Old woodwork and gingham curtains blended with the latest appliances, and there was even a couch in the corner. Perfect.

She enjoyed Daisy and enjoyed being here with her family because she'd never had anything like this. Her family had been small and a little bit isolated, and while Donny was great in his way, you couldn't joke around with him.

She watched Sam stir the sauce, taste it, season it some more. This was another side of the impatient businessman. Really, was there anything the man wasn't good at?

He probably saw her as a bumbling incompetent. She couldn't succeed at waitressing, at cooking, at holding a baby. He thought she'd be bad for his daughter, that much had been obvious.

Too bad, because she needed the money, and Mindy was adorable. Kids were never the problem; it was the adults who always did her in.

Suddenly, the door burst open and Xavier rushed through, followed closely by Mindy. "Give it back! Give it back!" she was yelling as she grabbed at something in his hands.

"No, Mindy, it's mine!"

Mindy stopped, saw all the adults staring at her, and threw herself to the floor, holding her breath, legs kicking.

Sam dropped the spoon with a clatter and went to her side. "Mindy, Mindy honey, it's okay."

The child ignored him, lost in her own rapidly escalating emotional reaction.

"Mindy!" He scolded her. "Sit up right now." He tried to urge her into an upright position, but she went as rigid as a board, her ear-splitting screams making everyone cringe.

Sam was focused on her with love and concern, but at this point that wasn't enough. Susan knew that interfering wasn't wise, but for better or worse, she had a gift. She understood special-needs kids, and she had a hunch she could calm Mindy down.

She sank to her knees beside the pair. "Shhhh," she whispered ever so softly into Mindy's ear. "Shhhh." Gently, she slid closer in behind the little girl and raised her eyebrows at Sam, tacitly asking permission.

He shrugged, giving it.

She wrapped her arms around Mindy from behind, whispering soothing sounds into her ear, sounds without words. Sounds that always soothed Donny, actually. She rubbed one hand up and down Mindy's arm, gently coaxing her to be calm. While she wasn't a strict proponent of holding therapy, she knew that sometimes physical contact worked when nothing else could reach a kid.

"Leave me 'lone!" Mindy cried with a little further struggle, but Susan just kept up her gentle hold and her wordless sounds, and Mindy slowly relaxed.

"He has a picture frame that says..." She drew in a gasping breath. "It says, Mom. *M-O-M*, Mom. I want it!"

Sam went pale, and Susan's heart ached with sympathy for the pair. Losing a parent was about the worst thing that could happen to a kid. And losing a wife was horrible, but it had to be even more painful to watch your child suffer and not know how to help.

To his credit, Sam regrouped quickly. "Honey, you can't take Xavier's picture frame. But we can get you one, okay?"

"It might even be fun to make one yourself," Susan suggested, paying attention to the way the child's body relaxed at the sound of her father's reassuring words.

"Then it would be even more special. Do you have lots of pictures of your mom?"

"Yes, 'cause I'm afraid I'll forget her and then she'll never come back."

Perfectly normal for a five-year-old to think her dead mother would come back. But ouch. Poor Mindy, poor Sam. She hugged the child a little tighter.

"Hon, Mommy's not coming back, remember? She's with Jesus." Sam's tone changed enough on the last couple of words that Susan guessed he might have his doubts about that. Doubts he wasn't conveying to Mindy, of course.

"But if I'm really good…"

"No, sweetie." Sam's face looked gray with sadness. "Mommy can't come back to this world, but we'll see her in heaven."

"I don't like that!" Mindy's voice rose to a roar. "I. Don't. Like. That!"

"None of us do, honey." Daisy squatted before her, patting the sobbing child's arm, her forehead wrinkling. "I don't know what to do when she's like this," she said quietly to Susan.

"Mommy!" Mindy wailed over and over. "I'll be good," she added in a gulp.

Sam and Daisy looked helplessly at each other over Mindy's head.

"It's not your fault. You're a good, good girl. Mommy loved you." Susan kept her arms wrapped tightly around Mindy and rocked, whispering and humming a wordless song. Every so often Mindy would tense up again, and Susan whispered the soothing words. "Not your fault. Mommy loved you, and Daddy loves you."

She knew the words were true, even though she hadn't known Sam and his wife as a family. And she knew that Mindy needed to hear it, over and over again.

She was glad to be here. Glad she had enough distance to help Sam with what was a very tough situation.

Very slowly, Mindy started to relax again. Daisy shot Susan a smile and moved away to check the stove.

"Shhh, shhh," Susan whispered, still holding her, still rocking. Losing a piece of her heart to this sweet, angry, hurting child.

Finally, Mindy went limp, and Susan very carefully slid her over to Sam. Took a deep breath, and tried to emerge from her personal, very emotional reaction and get back to the professional. "Does she usually fall asleep after a meltdown?"

Sam nodded. "Wears herself out, poor kid." He stroked her hair, whispering the same kind of sounds Susan had made, and Mindy's eyes closed.

"She'll need something to eat and drink soon, maybe some chocolate milk, something like that," Susan said quietly after a couple of minutes. "Protein and carbs."

"Thank you for calming her down," he said, his voice quiet, too. "That was much shorter than she usually goes."

"No problem, it's kind of my job. Did she have tantrums before you lost your wife?"

Sam nodded. "She's always been volatile. We thought it was because of her hand."

Susan reached out and stroked Mindy's blond hair, listening to the welcome sound of the child's sleep-breathing. "Having a disability can be frustrating. Or she could have some other sensitivities. Some kids are just more reactive."

"Did you learn how to be a child-whisperer in your special ed training?"

Susan chuckled. "Some, but mostly, you learn it when you have a brother with autism. Donny—that's my little brother—used to have twenty tantrums per day. It was too much for my mom, so I helped take care of him."

Sam's head lifted. "Where's Donny now?"

"Home with Mom in California," she said. "He's eighteen, and…" She broke off. He was eighteen, and still expecting to be going to a camp focused on his beloved birds and woodland animals, because she hadn't had the heart to call and tell him she'd screwed up and there wasn't any money. "He's still a handful, that's for sure, but he's also a joy."

Mindy burrowed against her father's chest, whimpering a little.

"How long has it been since you lost your wife?" Susan asked quietly.

"Two years, and Mindy does fine a lot of the time. And then we have this." He nodded down at her.

"Grief is funny that way." Susan searched her mind for her coursework on it. "From what I've read, she might re-grieve at each developmental stage. If she was pre-operational when your wife died, she didn't fully understand it. Could be that now, she's starting to take in the permanence of the loss."

"I just want to fix it." Sam's voice was grim. "She doesn't deserve this pain."

"No one deserves it, but it happens." She put a hand over Sam's. "I'm sorry for your loss. And sorry this is so hard on Mindy, too. You're doing a good job."

"Coming from you, that means something," he said with a faint grin.

Their eyes caught for a second too long.

Then Angelica and Daisy came bustling back into the room—when had they left, anyway?—followed by Xavier. How long had she, Sam and Mindy been sitting in the middle of the kitchen floor?

"Hey, the potatoes are done," Daisy said, expertly pouring the contents of one pan into another. She leaned over and called out through the open window. "Troy, how about those burgers?"

"They're ready." Troy came in with a plate stacked high with hamburgers, plus a few hot dogs on the side.

Sam moved to the couch at the side of the kitchen, cuddling a half-asleep Mindy, while the rest of them hustled to get food on the table. Susan folded napkins and carried dishes and generally felt a part of things, which was nice. She hadn't felt this comfortable in a long time. Being around Mindy, she felt as if she was in her element. This was her craft. What she was good at.

Again, she couldn't help comparing this evening to those she'd spent with her own family. The tension between her mom and dad, the challenges Donny presented, made family dinners stressful, and as often as not, the kids had eaten separately from the adults, watching TV. Susan could see the appeal of this lifestyle, living near your siblings, getting to know their kids. Cousins growing up together.

This was what she'd want for her own kid.

And where on earth had that thought come from? She totally didn't want kids! And she didn't want a husband. She was a career girl, and that was that.

So why did she feel so strangely at home here?

Chapter 3

A while after dinner, Sam came back into the kitchen after settling Mindy and Xavier in the den with a movie.

The room felt empty. "Where's Susan?"

"She left." Daisy looked up from her phone. "Said something about packing."

"She's going on a trip?" That figured. She seemed like a world traveler, much too sophisticated to spend her free summer in their small town. Applying for the job as Mindy's nanny had probably been just a whim.

Then again, she'd mentioned needing to help support her mother and brother...

And why he was so interested in figuring out her motives and whereabouts, he didn't have a clue.

"No..." Daisy was back to texting, barely paying attention. "She's gotta move back home for the summer."

"Move?"

"Yeah, to California."

"What? Why?"

Daisy was too engrossed in her phone to answer, and following a sudden urge, Sam turned and walked out into the warm evening. He caught up to Susan just as she opened her car door. "Weren't you even going to say goodbye?"

"Did I hurt your feelings?" she asked lightly, turning back to him, looking up.

She was so beautiful it made him lose his breath. So he just stared down at her.

It must be the way she'd helped Mindy that had changed her in his eyes, softened her sharp edges, made her not just cute but deeply appealing.

And he obviously needed to get on with his dating project, because he was having a serious overreaction to Susan. "Daisy said you're leaving town."

She wrinkled her nose. "Yeah, in a few days. Got to go back to California for the summer."

"You're not driving that, are you?" Lightly, he kicked the tire of her rusty subcompact.

"No! I'm taking the Mercedes." She chuckled, a deep, husky sound at odds with her petite frame. "Of course I'm driving this, Sam. It's my car."

"It's not safe."

She just raised her eyebrows at him. As if to ask what right he had to make such a comment. And it was a good question: What right *did* he have?

The moonlight spilled down on them and the sky was a black velvet canopy sprinkled with millions of diamond stars. He cleared his throat. "Does this mean you don't want the job?"

"Does this mean I'm still in the running?" There was a slightly breathy sound to her voice.

They were standing close together.

"You are," he said slowly. "I liked... No. I was amazed at how you were able to calm Mindy." He couldn't stop looking at her.

She stepped backward and gave an awkward smile. "Years of experience with my brother. And the coursework. All the grief stuff. You could call a local college, find someone with similar qualifications."

"I doubt that. I'd like to hire you."

"We don't get along. I wouldn't be good at this. I mean, nannying? Living in? Seriously, ask anyone, I'm not cut out for family life."

He cocked his head to one side, wondering suddenly about her past. "Oh?"

She waved her hand rapidly. "I was engaged once. It...didn't work out."

He nodded, inexplicably relieved. "Maybe you should come work for me on a trial basis, then."

"A...trial basis?" That breathy sound again.

"Yes, since you're not cut out for family life. It's a live-in job, after all."

"I do need a place to stay," she said, "but no. That wouldn't look right, would it? Me living in your house."

Her eyes were wide and suddenly, Sam felt an urge to protect her. "Of course, I wouldn't want to compromise your reputation. We have a mother-in-law's suite over the garage. It has a separate entrance and plenty of privacy."

"Really? You're offering me the job? Because remember, I can't cook."

"You can learn."

"Maybe, maybe not. I... What made you change your mind? I thought you didn't like me." She was nibbling on her lower lip, and right now she looked miles from the confident, brash waitress who'd stood up to a businessman in front of a restaurant full of people.

He smiled down at her. "My sister. My brother. And the way you handled Mindy."

"But she's probably not going to have another trauma reaction for a long time. Whereas cooking's every day. You really don't want to hire me."

"Why are you trying to talk me out of it?" Her resistance was lighting a fire in him, making him feel as if he had to have her, and only her, for Mindy's nanny. "I do want to. The sooner the better. When could you start?"

"Well..." She was starting to cave, and triumph surged through him. "My room is going to be remodeled out from under me starting this weekend."

"Great," he said, leaning in to close the deal. "I'll have a truck sent round tomorrow. You can start setting up your apartment over the garage."

"You're sure?"

"I'm sure."

"Paying what you told me before?"

He flashed a wide smile. "Of course."

She paused, her nose wrinkling. Looked up at the stars. Then a happy expression broke out on her face. "Thank you!" she said, and gave him a quick, firm handshake.

Her smile and her touch sent a shot of joy through his entire body. He hadn't felt anything like that before, ever. Not even when Marie was alive.

Guilt overwhelmed him and he took a step back. "Remember, it's just a trial," he said.

What had he gotten himself into?

Of course, everyone and his brother was in downtown Rescue River the next Saturday morning to comment on the moving truck in front of Susan's boarding house. The truck carrying Susan to her absolute doom, if the scuttlebutt was to be believed.

"So you're the next victim," said Miss Minnie Falcon, who'd hurried over from the Senior Towers, pushing her wheeled walker, to watch the moving activities. "Sam Hinton eats babysitters for lunch!"

"It's just on a trial basis," Susan said, pausing in front of the guesthouse's front porch. "If I don't like the job, I can leave at any time. Don't you want to sit down, Miss Minnie?"

"Oh, no, I'd rather stand," the gray-haired woman said, her eyes bright. "Don't want to miss anything!"

"Okay, if you're sure." That was small-town life: your activities were like reality TV to your neighbors, and truthfully, Susan found it sweet. At least everyone knew who you were and watched out for you.

"I'm going to miss you so much," her landlady, Lacey, said as she helped Susan carry her sole box of fragile items down the rickety porch steps. "I'm really sorry about making you move. It's just that Buck seems to be serious about staying sober, and he's looking to make money, and of course, he's willing to work on this place for cheap because he's my brother."

"It's fine. You've got to remodel while you can," Susan soothed her. "And we'll still hang out, right?" She'd enjoyed her year at Lacey's guesthouse, right in the heart of her adopted town. She wouldn't have minded staying. But sometimes, she felt silly being twenty-five years old and having to use someone else's kitchen if she wanted to make herself a snack.

"Of course we'll hang out. I'll miss you!"

"I know, me, too." She and Lacey had gotten close during a number of late-night talks. Susan had comforted Lacey through a heartbreaking miscarriage, and they'd cried and prayed together.

"And it's not just me. The cats will miss you!" Lacey said. "You have to come back and visit all the time."

As if to prove her words, an ancient gray cat tangled himself around Susan's ankle and then, when she grabbed the bannister to keep from tripping, offered up a mournful yowl.

Susan reached down to rub the old tomcat's head. "You and Mrs. Whiskers take care of yourselves. I'll bring you a treat when I come back, promise."

They went outside and loaded the box of breakables into the front seat of Susan's car, only to be accosted by Gramps Camden, another resident of the Senior Towers. "Old Sam Hinton caught himself a live one!" he said. "Now you listen here. Those Hintons are trouble. Just because my granddaughter married one—and Troy is the best of the bunch—that doesn't mean they're a good family. I was cheated by that schemer's dad and now, his corporation won't let up on me about selling my farm. You be careful in his house. Lock your door!"

"I will." She'd gotten to know Gramps through the schools, where he now served as a volunteer.

"He wasn't good enough for that wife of his," Gramps continued.

"Marie was pretty nearly perfect," agreed Miss Minnie Falcon.

From what Susan already knew about Sam, she figured any woman who married him would have to be. And yet, for all his millionaire arrogance, he obviously adored his little daughter. And a man who loved a child that much couldn't be all bad. Could he?

"Is that all your stuff, ma'am?" the college-age guy, who'd apparently come with the truck, asked respectfully.

Gramps waved and headed back to the Towers with Miss Minnie.

"Yes, that's it," Susan said. "What do I owe you?"

"Nothing. Mr. Hinton took care of it."

"Let me grab my purse. I want to at least give you a tip for being so careful."

The young man waved his hand. "Mr. Hinton took care of that, too. He said we weren't to take a penny from you."

"Is that so," Susan said, torn between gratitude and irritation.

"Money's one thing Sam Hinton doesn't lack." The voice belonged to Buck Armstrong, Lacey's brother. He put a large potted plant into the back of her car, tilting it sideways so it would fit. The young veteran had haunted eyes and a bad reputation, but whenever Susan had run into him visiting his sister, he'd been nothing but a gentleman. "You all set?"

"I hope so. I'm hearing horror stories about my new boss, is all." And they were spooking her. As the time came to leave her friendly guesthouse in the heart of Rescue River, she felt more and more nervous.

Buck nodded, his eyes darkening. "Sam didn't use to be quite so...driven. Losing a wife is hard on a guy."

Sympathy twisted Susan's heart. Buck knew what he was talking about; he'd lost not only his wife, but their baby as well. That was what had pushed him toward drinking too much, according to Lacey.

"You giving this gal a hard time?" The voice belonged to Rescue River's tall, dark-skinned police chief. He clapped Buck on the shoulder in a friendly way, but his eyes were watchful. Chief Dion Coleman had probably had a number of encounters with Buck that weren't so friendly.

"He's trying to tell me Sam Hinton is really a nice guy, since I'm going to work for him," Susan explained.

Dion let out a hearty laugh. "You're going to work for Sam? Doing what?"

"Summer nanny for Mindy."

"Is that right? My, my." Dion shook his head, still chuckling. "I tell you what, I think Mr. Sam Hinton might have finally met his match."

"What's that supposed to mean?" Susan asked, indignant.

"Nothing, nothing." He clapped Buck's shoulder again. "Come on, man, I'll buy you a cup of coffee if you've got half an hour to spare. Got something to run by you."

Buck was about to get gently evangelized, if Susan knew Dion. He headed up a men's prayer group at their church and was unstoppable in his efforts to get the hurting men of Rescue River on the right path. According to Daisy, he'd done wonders with her brother Troy.

As Buck and Dion headed toward the Chatterbox Café, Lacey came out to hug her goodbye. "You'll be fine. This is going to be an adventure!" She lowered her voice. "At least, let's hope so."

An odd, uncomfortable chill tickled Susan's spine as she climbed into her car and headed to her new job, her new life.

Chapter 4

Sam paced back and forth in the driveway, checking his watch periodically. Where was she?

Small beach shoes clacked along the walkway from the back deck, and he turned around just in time to catch Mindy in his arms. He lifted her and gave her a loud kiss on the cheek, making her giggle.

And then she struggled down. "Daddy, Miss Lou Ann says I can play in the pool if it's okay with you. Can I?"

Lou Ann Miller, who'd worked for his family back in the day and had helped to raise Sam, Troy and Daisy, followed her young charge out into the driveway. "She's very excited. It would be a nice way for her to cool off." She winked at him. "Nice for you if she'd burn off some extra energy, too."

Sam hesitated. Lou Ann was an amazing woman,

but she was in her upper seventies. "If she stays in the shallow end," he decided. "And Mindy, you listen to Miss Lou Ann."

"Of course she will," Lou Ann said. "Run and change into your suit, sweetie." As soon as Mindy disappeared inside, Lou Ann put a hand on her hip and raised an eyebrow at Sam. "I was the county synchronized swimming champion eight years running," she said. "And I still swim every morning. I can get Mindy out of any trouble she might get into."

"Of course!" Sam felt himself reddening and reminded himself not to stereotype.

He just wanted to keep Mindy safe and get her home environment as close to what Marie had made as was humanly possible. Get things at home back to running like a well-organized company, one he could lead with confidence and authority.

The moving truck chugged around the corner and up to the house, and Sam rubbed his hands together. Here was one step…he hoped. If Susan worked out.

He gestured them toward the easiest unloading point and helped open the back of the truck as Susan pulled up in her old subcompact, its slightly-too-dark exhaust and more-than-slightly-too-loud engine announcing that the car was on its last legs. He'd have to do something about that.

As the college boys he'd hired started moving her few possessions out, she approached. Her clothes were relaxed—a loose gauzy shirt, flip-flops and cutoff shorts revealing long, slender, golden-bronzed legs—but her face looked pinched with stress. "Hey," she said, following his glance back to her car. "Don't worry, I'll pull it behind the garage as soon as the truck's out of the way."

"I didn't say—"

"You didn't have to." She grabbed a box off the truck and headed up the stairs.

He helped the guys unload a heavy, overstuffed chair and then followed them up the stairs with an armload of boxes.

There was Susan, staring around the apartment, hands on hips.

"What's wrong?" he asked. "Is it suitable? Too small? We can work something out—"

"It's fine," she said, patting his arm. "It's beautiful. I'm just trying to decide where to put things."

"Good." There was something about Susan that seemed a little volatile, as if she might morph into a butterfly and disappear. "Well, you need to put the desk in that corner," he said, gesturing the movers to the part of the living room that was alcoved off, "and the armchair over there."

"Wait. Put the desk under the window. I like to look out while I work."

The young guys looked at him, tacitly asking his permission.

Susan raised her eyebrows, looking from the movers to Sam. There was another moment of silence.

"Of course, of course! Whatever the lady wants." But when they got the desk, a crooked and ill-finished thing, into the light under the window, he frowned. "I might have an extra desk you can use, if you like."

"I'm fine with that one."

He understood pride, but he hated to see a teacher with such a ratty desk. "Really?"

"Yes." She waited while the young movers went down to get another load, then spun on him. "Don't you have something else to do, other than comment about my stuff?"

"I'm sorry." He was controlling and he knew it, but it was with the goal of making other people's lives better. "I just thought... Are you sure you wouldn't rather have something less...lopsided? The money's not a problem."

She walked to the desk and ran a hand over it, smiling when one finger encountered a dipped spot. "My brother made it for me at his vocational school," she explained. "It was his graduation project, and he kept it a secret. When he gave it to me, it was about the best moment of my life."

"Oh." Sam felt like a heel. "So he's a woodworker?"

She shook her head. "No, not really. He's still finding his way, but the fact that he pushed past the frustration and made something so big, mostly by himself... and that he did it for me...it means a lot, that's all." She cleared her throat and got very busy flicking dust off an immaculate built-in shelf as the college boys came in with another load.

Obviously her brother was important to her. And obviously, Sam needed to pay attention to something other than just the monetary value of things.

He didn't have any family furniture, heirloom or sentimental or otherwise. For one thing, his dad still had most of their old stuff out at the family estate. For another, Marie had liked everything new, and he'd enjoyed providing it for her.

As the movers carried the last load into the bedroom, Susan looked up at him, then rose gracefully to her feet. "I was going to spend a little time getting settled. But is there something I can do for you and Mindy first?"

"Do you need help unpacking?"

One corner of her mouth quirked up, and he got the uncomfortable feeling she was laughing at him. "No, Sam," she said, her voice almost…gentle. "I've moved probably five or six times since college. I'm pretty good at it."

Of course she had, and the fact that she looked so young—and had a vulnerable side—didn't mean he had to take care of her. She was an employee with a job to do. "I'll be in the house," he said abruptly. "Come in as soon as you're set up, and we'll discuss your duties."

As he left, he saw one of the college boys give Susan a sympathetic glance.

What was that all about? He just wanted to have things settled as soon as possible. Was that so wrong?

Okay, maybe he was pushing her a little bit, but that was what you did with new employees: you let them know how things were going to be, what the rules were. This was, for all intents and purposes, an orientation, and he wanted to make sure to do things right.

But he guessed he didn't need to rearrange her furniture. And given her reaction to the desk suggestion, she probably wouldn't welcome his getting his car dealer to find her a better car, either.

No, Susan seemed independent. Which was great, but also worrisome. He wondered how well she would fit in with his plan for a traditional, family-oriented summer for Mindy. What changes would she want to make?

He walked by the pool and saw with relief that

Mindy was happily occupied with her inflatable shark in the shallow end.

Lou Ann Miller sat at the table in the shade. He did a double take. Was that a magazine she was reading? He opened his mouth to remind her that Mindy needed close attention. When Marie had brought Mindy out to the pool, before she'd gotten too sick to do it, she'd been right there in the water with her.

But the moment Mindy ventured away from the edge of the pool, Lou Ann pushed herself to her feet and walked over to stand nearby.

"See what I can do!" Mindy crowed as she swam a little, her stroke awkward. She had an adaptive flotation device for her arm, but she didn't like to use it.

"Try kicking more with your feet, honey," Lou Ann said. "If you get tired, you can flip over to your back."

"Show me how?"

"Sure." Lou Ann shrugged out of her terrycloth cover-up, tossed it back toward the table and walked down the steps into the water, barely touching the railing. She wore a violet tank suit and her short hair didn't seem to require a swim cap.

Glad he hadn't interfered and satisfied with Lou Ann's abilities as a caregiver and swim instructor, Sam strode toward the house. He hoped Susan wouldn't take long to get settled and come down. The sooner they established her duties, the sooner things could go back to normal.

He'd just finished a sandwich when there was a tap on the back door.

"You ready for me?" Susan asked, poking her head

inside. "Am I supposed to knock or just come in? I really don't know how to be a nanny."

"Just come in." If he needed privacy, there was the whole upstairs. "I'm ready. Let me give you a quick tour so you know where things are."

"Great." She was looking around the kitchen. "Is this where you spend most of your time?"

He nodded. "It's a mess. Sorry. My cleaning people come on Mondays."

"You call this a mess?" She laughed. "I can barely tell you have a kid."

"Mindy's pretty neat. Me, I have to restrain my inner slob. Plus, Lou Ann Miller's been helping me until I find...well, until I found you. She's a whiz at cooking and cleaning."

"Why didn't you just hire her?" Susan asked as he led her into the living room.

"She doesn't want a permanent job. Says she's too old, though I don't see much evidence of her slowing down. This is where we...where I...well, where we used to entertain a lot." The room had been Marie's pride and joy, but Sam and Mindy didn't use it much, and he realized that, without a party full of people in it, the place looked like a museum.

Susan didn't comment on the living room nor the dining room with its polished cherry table and Queen Anne chairs. He swept her past the closed-off sunroom, of course. When they got to Mindy's playroom, Susan perked up. "This is nice!"

She walked over to inspect the play kitchen and peeked into the dollhouse. "What wonderful toys," she said almost wistfully. She looked at the easel and smiled approvingly at the train set. "Good, you're not being sexist. I see you got her some cars, too."

"Those are partly for my sake," he admitted. "I go nuts after too many games with dolls."

"Me, too." She walked over to perch on the window seat, crossing her arms as she surveyed the playroom. "It's a big place for one little girl."

A familiar ache squeezed Sam's chest. "We were going to fill it up with kids." He stared out the window and down the green lawn. "But plans don't always work out."

When he looked back at her, she was watching him with a thoughtful expression on her face. "That must be hard to deal with."

He acknowledged the sympathy with a nod. "We're managing."

"Do you ever think of moving?"

"No!" In truth, he had. He'd longed to move, but it wouldn't be fair to Marie's memory. She'd wanted him to continue on as they'd begun, to create the life they'd imagined together for Mindy. "We're fine here," he said firmly.

She arched one delicate brow. "Well, okay then." She stood up, looked around and gave a decisive nod. "I know a lot of kids, so we'll work on filling up the playroom and pool with them this summer. This place is crying out for noise and fun."

"Vetted by me," he warned. "I don't want a lot of kids I don't know coming over."

"You want to approve every playdate?"

"For now, yes."

She pressed her lips together, obviously trying not

to smile, but a dimple showed on her face. A very cute dimple.

"Hey, look. I'm a control freak, especially where Mindy is concerned."

"No kidding." She raised her eyebrows in mock surprise. "It's okay, Sam. We'll figure out a way to manage this. But Mindy does need friends around this summer. She needs to work on her social skills."

"There's nothing wrong—"

She cocked her head to one side and tucked her chin and looked at him.

"Her social skills are okay." He frowned at Susan's pointed silence. "Aren't they?"

"It's not a big problem," Susan said. "But she's very sensitive about her disability and her mother, or lack of one. I've broken up several playground brawls. The best way to work on it is to give her lots of free-play experience with other kids." She squatted down beside the bookshelves that lined one side of the room. "And there are books that can help. But these—" She ran a delicate finger along the spines of the books. "These are books for toddlers, Sam. She can read better than this."

Her criticism stung, but he nodded. "Her mother was the big book-buyer. That's why I'm glad you're here, Susan. I can see that you have an expertise the other candidates didn't have. I want to do right by Mindy."

"Weekly trips to the library. Fern can help us pick out some good books, including ones about social skills."

"Sure." He led the way back through the kitchen. "Now, I don't expect you to cook for us—"

"That's good," she interrupted. "Remember, I'm a disaster in the kitchen."

"I'm sure you can figure out how to make breakfast and lunch. I'll do dinner, or order it in. But I do want you to eat dinner with us most nights."

"What?" She froze, staring at him.

"It's better for Mindy," he explained. "All kinds of studies show the importance of family dinners. I'd like to have you be a part of that."

She looked a little trapped. "I'm not your family, I'm a hired—"

"Five days per week," he bargained. "You can have a couple of nights off."

Through the open kitchen window, he could hear Lou Ann and Mindy laughing together in the backyard. He leaned back against the granite counter and watched an array of expressions cross Susan's face.

Was he being unfair, demanding too much of her? He'd looked over lists of nanny duties online, and while having a sitter eat with the family wasn't common, he'd seen a few examples of it being done. He was paying her well, much better than the average.

"You have to eat," he reminded her. "It's free food."

She chuckled, a throaty sound that made all his senses spring to life. "We'll give it a try."

He pushed his advantage. "And Sunday dinner is the most important meal of all, so I'd appreciate your being there. I think we agreed that you'd work Sunday afternoons and take a weekday afternoon off, correct?"

"You mean, like, tomorrow?"

He nodded. Best to start out as you meant to go on. "Yes. Definitely tomorrow."

"We'll give it a try," she repeated doubtfully. "But I'm not... Well. We'll see."

Score one for him. But her resistance proved this wasn't going to be as easy as he'd hoped.

The next day, Susan stood at the kitchen counter scooping deli salads into bowls. Even though she'd turned down Sam's offer of an apron to protect her church clothes—which, hello, consisted of a faded denim skirt with a lime-green tee and sneakers, hardly designer duds that needed special care—she still felt uncomfortable and out of place. She was used to grabbing a bagel with friends or fixing herself a peanut butter sandwich after church. Fixing a family lunch in a big, fancy kitchen was way out of her comfort zone.

Since she attended the same church as Sam and Mindy, it had made sense to all go together. Uncomfortable with the intimacy of that, she'd made a beeline for her singles group friends once they'd gotten there, but she hadn't had a choice about a ride home, which had included a stop at the grocery store for supplies.

It was all too, too domestic. And Sam had been entirely too appealing during the grocery story visit, brawny arms straining his golf shirt, thoughtfully discussing salad options with the deli clerk, whose name he remembered and whose children he asked about.

And since Sunday dinner was, quote, the most important meal of the week, here she was helping to cook it, or at least dish it up. Though she didn't see the point of setting the table and putting deli food into serving dishes when all Mindy wanted was to play in the pool.

Through the window, she studied Sam and Mindy, side by side on the deck while Sam grilled chicken. He was talking seriously to her, explaining the knobs on the gas grill and putting out a restrictive arm when she came too close.

Sam. What a character. He might be the head of an empire, able to boss around his employees and make each day go according to plan, but he wasn't going to be able to control everything that happened in his own home. Not with a kid. Kids were never predictable.

And he couldn't control her, either. She had to maintain some sense of independence or the cage door would shut on her, just as it had almost done with her former fiancé. Encouraged by her father, they'd gotten engaged too quickly, before they knew each other well. Once Frank had found out what she was really like, he hadn't wanted her. And she'd been guiltily, giddily happy to get free.

She wasn't the marrying kind. And this stint in a housewifely role was temporary, just long enough to help her family financially.

From the front of the house, she heard a female voice. "Yoo-hoo! Surprise!"

Susan spun toward the sound, accidentally flinging a spoonful of macaroni salad on the floor in the process. "In here," she called. Then she grabbed a paper towel to clean up the dabs of macaroni scattered across the floor.

"Who are *you*?" asked a voice above her.

"It must be some of the hired help, Mama," said a male voice.

Susan paused in her wiping and looked up to see a yacht-club-looking, silver-haired couple. She gave the floor a last swipe, rinsed her hands and then turned to face them as she dried her hands on the dishtowel. "Hi,

I'm Susan. Mindy's summer nanny. Who are you?" She softened the question with a smile.

"I didn't know he was hiring someone," the woman said, frowning. "He should have asked me. I know several nice young women who could have helped out."

"Now, Mama, maybe there's a reason he wanted to do things his own way." The man looked meaningfully at Susan. "We're Mindy's grandparents," he explained. "We like to pop in when we can on Sundays."

"That macaroni salad is from Shop Giant?" the woman asked, picking up the container and studying it. Then she walked over to the refrigerator, opened it and scanned the contents.

Susan took a breath. There was no reason to feel defensive of this kitchen; it wasn't hers. "Yes, Sam picked it up on the way home from church."

"Oh, men." The woman waved a perfectly manicured hand. "They never know what to get, and with Sam so busy… Are you in charge of the cooking? Because I'd recommend Denise's Deli in town, if you don't have time to make homemade."

Susan's stomach knotted and she flashed back to her mom trying to please her dad with her culinary skills. It was a role Susan had vowed to avoid, so why was she feeling as if she needed to make an excuse for not having labored over doing all the chopping and boiling herself? For a family that, after all, wasn't her own?

The door from the deck burst open. "Grandma! Grandpa!" Mindy shrieked. She flung herself at the man.

He bent to pick her up. "Oh, missy, you're getting too heavy for an old man!"

Sam followed with a plate of grilled chicken breasts. "Hey, Ralph, Helen. I thought you two might stop by."

He had? Why hadn't he warned her?

"We can slide a couple of extra places in at the table. Susan, would you mind…"

"Consider it done," she said drily, adding just one place setting. And then, as soon as both grandparents were occupied with Mindy's excited explanation of the grilling process, she grabbed Sam's arm and pulled him into the playroom that adjoined the kitchen. "Look, since it's a family meal, I'm just going to leave you to it," she said. "Everything's ready to go here, and I've got a new thriller from the library that's calling my name."

"You have to eat," he said, frowning. "I'd like it if you'd stay."

"They seem a little…overwhelming," she admitted. "I'd feel more comfortable if—"

"Come on, Miss Susan, you forgot to make a place for Grandma! I got the extra placemats."

"Just stay for dinner," Sam said as Mindy tugged at her hand. "Then you can take off all afternoon."

"But—"

"I'm paying you to be here."

Clenching her teeth, Susan helped Mindy add another place setting to the table.

They all stood around it, and Sam said a prayer, and then they took their seats. Susan busied herself for a couple of minutes with bringing over food and fetching drinks, but then that was done and Sam urged her to sit down.

"Oh," the grandma, Helen, said, "are you eating with the family?"

Susan raised an eyebrow at Sam. "Not my idea."

"Susan's agreed to eat with us. Mindy needs a female role model."

"Oh, right," the older woman said. "At least until..." She gave Sam a meaningful look.

"Right," he said.

So was something in the works, then? Was Yacht Club Grandma cooking up a girlfriend for Sam? That would be ideal, Susan told herself as she helped cut Mindy's chicken breast. It would take her off the hot seat and out of a role she obviously wasn't suited for.

Amidst the clanking silverware and clinking glasses, there was a noticeable absence of small talk. Finally, the awkward silence was broken by Mindy's grandfather. "What *are* you?" he asked Susan.

"Hey, now, Ralph..." Sam started, a flush crossing his face.

Susan drew in her breath and let it out in a sigh. "It's fine," she said to Sam. She'd been answering that question all her life, but the questions had gotten a little more frequent since she'd moved from California to the Midwest.

Mindy looked alertly from one adult to the next, sensing the tension.

"I meant no offense," Ralph said, lifting both hands, palms up. "I'm just curious. You look a little..." He broke off, as if he was trying to think of the word.

As a person who blurted out the wrong thing herself fairly often, Susan thought it best to cut off his speculation. "I'm half-Japanese."

The older man snapped his fingers. "I thought so! You look a little bit Mexican, but I was guessing Oriental. Your mom's Japanese?"

Yes, he was a blurter. But that was so much more comfortable than his wife's sputtering disapproval. She smiled at him. "Nope. We don't fit the stereotype. It's my dad who's Japanese."

"Your English sounds just fine," the older man said reassuringly.

"I hope so!" Susan said, chuckling. "I was born in California."

Helen made a strangled sound in her throat, whether regarding California, Japan or her husband's line of questioning, Susan wasn't sure.

"California," Mindy broke in, "that's where earthquakes are, and Hollywood."

"You're right!" Susan smiled at Mindy. Hooray for kids, who could break through adult tension with their innocent remarks. She took a bite of macaroni salad. Not bad. She'd definitely choose Shop Giant's brand over anything she could make herself.

"Mommy was from Ohio, like me," Mindy informed Susan. "You're sitting just where she used to sit."

Everyone froze.

Wow. Susan's stomach twisted. She hadn't meant to intrude, hadn't wanted to take anyone's place. Should she apologize? Offer to move? Ignore the remark? Suddenly, the food tasted as dry as ashes in her mouth.

"Mindy," Sam said, taking the child's hand in his own, "honey, saying that might make our guest feel uncomfortable."

He was right, it did...but that wasn't something Mindy should have to worry about. Just like that, Susan's own discomfort melted away as her training clicked in. Stifling a child's natural comments about a loss was a way to push grief underground, causing all sorts of psychological issues. "That's probably kind of sad for everybody," Susan said quickly. "Did your mom like to cook out?"

Mindy looked uncertainly at her father. "I think… she liked to lie down the best."

Susan's throat constricted. Mindy had only been four when her mom died. She couldn't remember much of what had happened when she was younger, of course.

Couldn't remember her mother as a healthy woman.

"Oh, no, Marie *loved* cooking of all kinds." Helen's eyes filled with tears. "You just don't remember, honey, because she was sick."

Ralph was staring down at his plate.

This wonderful family meal was turning into an outright disaster. The grief of parents who'd lost their beloved daughter was *way* beyond Susan's ability to soothe. She met Sam's gaze across the table. *Do something*, she tried to telegraph with her eyes.

Sam cleared his throat and brushed a hand over Mindy's hair. "I remember how Mom loved to make cookies with you," he said. "At Christmastime, you two would get all set up with icing and sprinkles and colored sugar. Mom let you decorate the cookies however you wanted."

Susan breathed out a sigh of relief and smiled encouragingly at Sam. He was doing exactly the right thing. "That sounds like fun!"

"Did I do a good job?" Mindy asked.

Sam chuckled, a slightly forced sound. "There was usually more frosting and decoration than cookie. You were little. But Mom loved the cookies you decorated and always made me take a picture."

"I remember those pictures!" Mindy said. "Can we look at them later?"

"Of course, honey." Sam leaned closer to put an arm around Mindy and give her a side hug, and Susan's heart melted a little.

"That reminds me, I want to take some pictures today," Ralph said, "maybe out by the pool."

The conversation got more general, then, and the awkwardness passed.

Later, Susan insisted on doing the dishes so that the family could gather out by the pool. But after a couple minutes, Helen came back in. "I didn't want you to put things away in the wrong place," she said.

"Oh…thanks." That was a backhanded offer of help if Susan had ever heard one.

"Marie always had this kitchen organized so perfectly, but every time I come it's more messed up."

Susan's hands tightened on the platter she was washing. "I'm sure it's hard for Sam to manage the house along with his business."

"It's not Sam's job to manage." The remark sounded pointed.

Susan lifted her eyebrows at the woman, wondering where this was going. "If not Sam's, then whose?"

"Well, I just hope you're not thinking it's *your* job."

"Of course not!" Susan burst out. Where did Helen get off, coming over and criticizing the help? She wasn't Susan's boss!

She glanced over at the older woman and noticed that her eyes were shiny with tears, and everything started to make sense. Helen didn't want the kitchen arrangements to change, because she was trying to preserve her daughter's memory. But inevitably, things would get moved around, and sentimental treasures misplaced. Life had to go on, but for a grieving mother, every change must feel like losing another piece of her daughter. "Look, I'm sorry," she said, drying her hands and walking over to give the woman she barely knew a clumsy little pat on the arm. "It's a loss I can't even imagine."

"It's just hard to see another woman in her place," Helen said in a wobbly voice.

"I'm not trying to take her place," Susan said, feeling her way. "No one can do that, but especially not me. I'm just here for the summer."

"You're just not the kind of woman Sam and Mindy need."

Susan blew out a breath and plunked the platter down on the counter. Grief was one thing, but outright rudeness was another. "Did you...did you want to talk, or would you rather be alone?"

"Alone," Helen croaked out, dabbing at her eyes with a tissue.

"Sure. You go ahead and put stuff away wherever you want. I've got some reading to do." Half-guiltily, she fled the kitchen and made her way to her apartment via the front door, the better to avoid Sam and Mindy and Ralph.

Helen was right. Susan *wasn't* the kind of woman Sam and Mindy needed. But why that truth felt so hurtful, she didn't have a clue.

Chapter 5

Sam pulled into his driveway the next Friday afternoon, right after lunchtime. It would be good to get out of this monkey suit and work the rest of the rainy afternoon at home. He had a little planning to do on the summer picnic he put on for his employees, but it was all fairly low-key; Mindy could interrupt without bothering him.

And he had to admit to himself that seeing Susan was part of what had drawn him home. Not really seeing her, he told himself, but rather, seeing how she was interacting with Mindy.

He'd been so busy the past week, catching up on all the work he'd put off during the no-nanny period, that he hadn't spent a lot of time at home. Mindy seemed happy and Susan had said things were going well. He knew they'd visited the library and gone to the park with a couple of other kids. One day, Mindy had had her friend Mercedes over to play.

Sam was feeling pleased with the solution he'd come up with for Mindy's summer. She seemed to be thriving under the supervision of an active and engaged nanny.

Susan herself seemed guarded, but he had to assume she'd get more comfortable as the summer went on. That Sunday dinner with Ralph and Helen had been awkward, but that was because they hadn't understood that Susan was only a temporary fixture in the home. Next time would surely be better.

When he got inside, the sound of a busy, humming household met his ears, confirming his satisfaction with the arrangements he'd made for Mindy. He stopped in the kitchen to look at the mail, and the sound of voices drifted his way.

He heard his nephew, Xavier, explaining the finer points of Chutes and Ladders to Mindy. That meant Xavier's little sister, Baby Emmie, must be here, too, but he didn't hear baby fussing or cooing; apparently she was sleeping or content.

The low, steady murmur of women's voices let him know that his sister-in-law and Susan were both in the room with the kids.

"I know I can talk them into it," Susan was saying doubtfully. "The payment will just be a week late, maybe ten days. It's tips versus wages, that's all. I expected to have a little more money by now."

"Troy and I could probably loan you the—"

"No! Thanks, but I'll be fine."

Angelica made some sound as if she was comforting a baby, which she probably was. "What's your mom going to do with your brother away?"

"Enjoy her freedom. And I'm hoping I can send her a plane ticket later in the summer."

"That's so nice she's coming to visit you!"

"Oh, she's not visiting me," Susan said, sounding alarmed. "I want her to be able to go to New York to see some shows, or to a nice spa. Coming to see me would be nothing but stress."

"I doubt that. You're her daughter! Or...are things bad between you?"

Sam took a step closer and leaned on the counter, eavesdropping unabashedly. Mindy and Xavier argued a little in the background. Sam could smell the remains of a mac-and-cheese lunch. He saw the telltale blue-and-white boxes in the trash and shook his head, a grin crossing his face. Susan hadn't claimed to be a cook.

"I'm...a bit of a disappointment to her."

"I'm sure—"

"Don't feel bad, it doesn't bother me anymore. I know she's really just upset about her own life. She had a vision for me to do a better job than she did, to be a perfect wife who made her husband happy, but I'm not falling into line."

"Well, considering that you don't have a husband at all—"

"Exactly." They both laughed.

There was a little more murmuring and the sound of a baby fussing, then some quiet shuffling.

Sam felt bad about eavesdropping, knew he should say hello to let them know he was here, but if Angelica was feeding the baby, he didn't want to intrude. Quietly, he grabbed a fork and the pan of leftover mac and cheese and picked at it, thinking about what Susan had said.

Wages versus tips. Of course, she'd been expecting to make speedy cash as a waitress. He needed to bump her paycheck forward rather than waiting the customary two weeks to pay her.

"You should just ask Sam to advance you the money," Angelica advised as if she was channeling his thoughts.

"No way! That wouldn't be right. This is a job, and you don't ask for special favors in a job."

Sam got himself a glass of water, making some noise about it, to warn everyone of his presence.

"Daddy!" Mindy called, and ran to him.

"Hey, sugar sprite. Having fun?" He swung her up into his arms, feeling that odd mixture of joy and concern that was fatherhood for him.

"Yeah! Xavier is here!"

"Go back and play with him," he said, putting her down. "I'm going to change my clothes, and then I'll want to talk to Susan a couple of minutes."

He'd move her payday up, no matter whether she protested or not. And as he trotted up the stairs, an idea came to him: he'd send her mother a go-anywhere ticket. It was a benefit of his airline program and frequent flyer miles; it wouldn't even cost him anything. And it would help out proud, independent Susan.

Which, for whatever reason, was something he very much wanted to do.

"No!" she said twenty minutes later. "I'm sorry you overheard that, but I don't need any special favors."

"It's not a favor, it's just a change in pay date." He for sure wasn't going to tell her about the ticket he'd just told his assistant to send to her mother. That would go over about as well as rat poison.

"Why are you doing this?"

"To help you out," he said patiently.

"I don't need your help!" She banged open the dishwasher and started loading dishes in. Thankfully, they were plastic ones; the china wouldn't have survived her violent treatment.

He cocked his head to one side. "I thought someone was hassling you about a late payment. If that's not the case..."

"Oh, it's true, but I can talk some sense into them. Probably."

"What's the problem? The car?" Maybe now was the time to offer her the services of his car dealer.

"No!" She scanned the now-empty counter and slammed the dishwasher shut. "My car is paid for. It's...it's my brother."

"What's wrong?"

"His camp. The last installment for this special camp I want to send him to, it's due Monday. It's why I'm working this summer. He'll just love it, and he needs the extra stimulation. And my mom needs the break." She let out an unconscious sigh, and Sam felt the strangest urge to put an arm around her.

She was a little thing to be bearing the burden for an entire family, but she didn't complain; she just accepted the responsibility. Exactly what he would have done in the same situation. Admiration rose in him, along with a strange little click of connection. Maybe he and Susan weren't as different as he'd initially thought.

"Will your first paycheck cover the payment?" he asked her.

"Just about exactly."

"Then give me the number and I'll have the money wired today."

Relief warred with resistance in her dark eyes. "But it's not fair—"

"Look," he said, "it's nothing I haven't done for other people who work for me. I take care of my employees. Go get the information."

She drew in a breath and let it out in a sigh. "All right. Thank you, Sam."

The wheels were turning in his brain now. "In fact…" he said slowly.

"What?" she asked warily.

"Do you want to earn some extra money this summer?"

She laughed, a short sound without humor. "Always. I need to send some money to my mom. And I'd love to pay for an extra course toward my master's."

"And maybe buy a new car?" he needled.

"Sam!" She put her hands on her hips. "I know my car isn't pretty, but it runs fine."

"It runs loud. And smoky."

"It's fine." She turned away. "If you're through insulting my stuff, I'd better go help Angelica with the kids."

"She's fine. Wait a minute. Listen to my proposal."

The corner of her mouth quirked upward as she spun back around. "What proposal is that?"

Their eyes met, and held, and something electric zinged between them.

The breeze through the window lifted a strand of her hair, but even as she brushed it back, she still stared at him. He could see the pulse in her neck.

His own pulse was hammering, too.

Wow.

They both looked away at the same time. "So what are you thinking of?" she asked in a businesslike voice, grabbing a sponge to wipe down the already-clean counter.

He cleared his throat and leaned forward, resting his elbows on the kitchen island. "I'm having my annual summer picnic for my employees, and the woman who usually plans it for me is out on maternity leave. How are you at party planning?"

She laughed. "I'm a whiz with the elementary set, but I've never planned an adult party in my life."

He should definitely get someone else, then. "You could get Daisy to help," he heard himself saying. "And it's a family picnic, so we always try to make it fun for the kids. I'd pay you what I normally pay Trixi, the one on maternity leave. She gets overtime for the extra work."

"Really?" She frowned, bit her lip.

"Of course," he said, watching her, "you'd have to work pretty closely with me."

There was a beat of silence. Then: "I'm already working way too closely with you."

"What?"

She clapped her hand over her mouth. "Oh, wow, did I say that out loud?"

"Susan." He sat down on one of the bar stools to be more at her level. She was so petite. "I hope I'm not making you uncomfortable in some way. That's the last thing I intend."

"No!" She was blushing furiously. "No, it's not that,

it's just… I don't know." She turned away, staring out the window.

He came over to stand behind her, a safe couple of feet away. "I know this is pretty close quarters for two strangers. But I want you to know that I'm very pleased with your work, Susan. I think we can stop thinking of the nanny job as a trial run. I'd like for you to stay all summer."

She gripped the counter without looking at him.

"I haven't seen Mindy so happy since…well, since she was a baby and her mom was healthy."

She half looked back over her shoulder. "Really?"

The plaintive sound of her voice was so at odds with her feisty personality that he felt a strange compulsion to touch her shoulder, to run a hand over that silky hair, offering comfort.

The super-independent, super-confident teacher evidently had some vulnerabilities of her own. It almost seemed as if she hadn't received much praise, although he couldn't imagine why, when she seemed to be so good at everything she did.

Well, everything except cooking.

And why was his hand still moving toward her hair?

Just in time, he pulled it back. That wouldn't do at all.

He was getting a little too interested in Susan. She was too young, too independent, totally wrong for him in the long term, even though she was turning out to be an amazing summer nanny. He needed to get on with his program of finding Mindy a real, permanent mom. And he needed to do it soon.

He'd make sure to get back on the dating circuit right away. There were a couple of women he'd seen once and then left hanging. He'd give them a call. His secretary, who was of necessity a little too involved in his life, had a niece she wanted to fix him up with, and Mindy's Sunday school teacher had handed him her phone number along with Mindy's half-completed craft last week.

He just needed to get himself motivated to do it. He'd been too busy. But now that Susan was in place—Susan, who was completely inappropriate for him—he'd jump back into pursuing that all-important goal.

He forced himself to take a step backward. "If you're interested in the extra job, I'd appreciate having you do it. It would be easy, because you're here in the house anyway. But if you're not comfortable with it, by all means back off and I'll find someone else."

She studied him, quizzical eyes on his face, head cocked to one side. "I can give it a try," she said slowly.

And Sam tried to ignore the sudden happiness surging through him.

"When will we get to the lake, Daddy?"

Sam glanced back at Mindy, bouncing in her car seat, and smiled as he steered into the parking lot by Keystone Lake. "Hang on a minute or two, and we'll be here and out of the car."

As Mindy squealed her excitement, Sam felt tension relax out of his shoulders. Now things were falling into place.

He pulled into his old parking spot, surveying the soothing, tree-surrounded lawn with satisfaction. He'd grown up with Saturday trips to the lake, and he and Marie had brought Mindy here most summer weekends when she was small. He'd meant to continue the tradition, but it had fallen by the wayside…until now.

They'd play on the blanket, and have a nice picnic, and spend family time together. The only thing missing was the woman beside him. But Susan had agreed to work today in exchange for a weekday off next week. She'd fill the role temporarily, until he could get on his larger goal of finding a new mom for Mindy.

"It's a little cold for swimming," Susan said as she helped Mindy undo the buckles. "But there's a lot to do at the lake aside from swimming."

Sam's arms were loaded down with the picnic basket, blankets and a couple of lawn chairs, but looking around the stuff, he could see Mindy's lower lip sticking out.

"I want to swim!" his daughter said.

Susan nodded comfortably. "Okay. You can. I'm not going in that lake until the sun comes out, but I'll watch you."

Sam came around to the side of the car where Susan was bent over, gathering an armload of beach toys. "She can't go in the lake. It's too cold."

Mindy had already taken off for the water.

Susan pressed the beach toys into his already overloaded arms. "She'll figure that out for herself!" she called over her shoulder as she raced after Mindy. "Relax, Sam!"

Sam gritted his teeth, dumped the gear on a picnic table and hustled after them.

Mindy was already up to her knees in the water. She looked back toward the shore, her expression defiant.

He opened his mouth, but Susan's hand on his arm stopped him. "It's called natural consequences," she said. "If she goes in, she'll get cold and come out quickly. No harm, no foul. And she learns something."

"But she'll catch a cold!"

Susan shrugged. "I actually think colds come from viruses, but whatever. A cold never hurt anyone."

"For a nanny, you're not very protective."

"For a successful entrepreneur, you're not much of a risk taker."

They glared at each other for a minute.

"Come in, Daddy!" Mindy called.

"No way!" He looked at his shivering daughter and took a step forward.

"Then I'll come out," Mindy decided, and splashed her way to the shoreline.

Susan gave him an I-told-you-so grin. "What are you waiting for, Dad? Get her a towel. She's freezing!"

As Sam jogged off toward the beach bags, he couldn't help smiling. A trip to the lake with Susan was never going to be dull.

After Mindy was toweled off and building a sand-castle under Susan's supervision, Sam set up the colorful beach tent they'd always used to protect Mindy's tender skin. Then he rummaged for the tablecloth, but it was nowhere in sight.

Nor was the picnic. Had Susan forgotten to pack it?

Don't be controlling, he reminded himself. Maybe she thought packing food for a Saturday beach trip was beyond her regular duties. They could always call Daisy and ask her to bring something, or as a last resort, could get something from the junk food stand at the other end of the beach.

Noticing that several children had gathered around Susan and Mindy, he strolled down to see what was

going on. The little group had already created a somewhat complicated castle with the help of Mindy's multiple beach buckets and molds.

Mindy held a bucket with her half arm and shoved
sand in with her whole one, attracting the attention of
the two visiting boys.

"How come you only have one hand?" one of the
boys asked Mindy.

"This is how I was born," she answered simply.

"That's weird," the child said.

Color rose on the back of Mindy's neck, and Sam
opened his mouth to yell at the kid, and then closed it
again. He was learning from Susan that he needed to
wait and watch sometimes, rather than intervening, but
when someone made a comment about his kid, it was
hard. Natural consequences and learning better social
skills were all well and good, but insults, not so much.

He looked at Susan to find her watching the kids
with a slightly twisted mouth.

"Yeah, it's really weird," said the other boy, and they
both started to laugh.

"That's enough!" Susan stepped toward them and
squatted down, a protective hand on Mindy's shoulder.

"It's bullying," Mindy said. "Right, Miss Hayashi?"
She'd automatically reverted to Susan's professional
name, maybe because bullying was something they
talked about in school.

"Very good, Mindy. You're right." Susan turned a
steely glare on the two young offenders. "And bullies
can't play. Goodbye, boys."

"Aw, I didn't want to play with her anyway," said one
of the boys. He jumped up and ran toward the water.

"I didn't mean to be a bully," the other boy said, looking stricken. "I'm sorry."

Susan looked at Mindy. "What do you think? Can he still play, or would you rather he goes away?"

Mindy considered. "He said he was sorry."

"Yes, he did."

"He can play," Mindy decided.

"Thanks!" And the two of them were back to building a castle as if nothing had happened, while the other boy kicked stones on the beach, alone.

Susan stood and backed a little bit away, keeping her eyes on the scene as another little girl joined the group. She ended up right next to Sam.

"You did a good job handling that," he said to her, sotto voce. "I want to strangle anyone who teases my kid."

"Believe me, I felt the same way." She smiled up at him.

There was that little click of awareness between them again. She looked away first, her cheeks turning pink.

He needed to nip that attraction in the bud. He needed to start dating, before he did something silly like let Susan know that he found her…interesting.

As he was casting about in his mind for a new subject, Mindy looked up at them. "I'm hungry," she announced.

"Well, I think we forgot a picnic," he said tactfully.

"No, I brought stuff." Susan said. "Come on over, we'll have lunch."

"I'm hungry, too," said the little girl who'd just joined in the group.

"Me, too!" The little boy stood up and brushed sand off his hands onto his swim trunks.

"Tell you what, go ask your mom or dad if you can share our lunch," Susan said easily.

"Do we have enough?" Sam hadn't seen evidence of *any* food, so the thought of sharing was puzzling.

"Oh, sure," she said as the children ran toward their separate families. "It'll be fine."

He didn't see how, but he followed Susan and Mindy, curious to see what she came up with.

From the bottom of the bag of beach toys, she tugged a loaf of whole wheat bread, a tub of peanut butter and a squeeze bottle of grape jelly. "Voila," she said as the other two kids approached. "Let's play 'make your own sandwich!'"

"Yay!" cheered the kids.

Sam frowned at the splintery picnic table, thinking of the neat checkered tablecloth Marie had always brought to the lake. "It's not very clean."

She was digging again in the toy bag and didn't hear him. "Hey, Sam, grab me one of those beach towels, could you? Oh, there we go." Triumphantly, she produced a small stack of paper cups.

He handed a towel to her and she spread it over the table. "Everybody, take a cup. We'll wash hands and then get water from the drinking fountain." She looked at Sam. "Coming?"

"So lunch is…peanut butter sandwiches and water?"

She seemed genuinely puzzled. "You were expecting caviar?"

"No, but maybe… Never mind." He didn't elaborate on checkered tablecloths and homemade chicken salad and cut up melon in a special blue bowl, but for a second, his whole chest hurt with missing his wife.

Mindy was tugging at his hand. "Come on, Daddy, I'm hungry!"

The next fifteen minutes were a blur of helping a bunch of primary-school-aged kids make messy PB&J sandwiches and chatting with the parents who came over to check everything out. Both families, it turned out, knew Susan from the school, and showed respect for her and interest in her summer plans.

Finally the kids headed back to the water with one of the other families, and he and Susan collapsed down onto the picnic bench. Susan cut the sandwich she'd managed to make for herself and offered him half.

To his surprise, it actually tasted good.

"What I wouldn't give for a cup of coffee," she admitted.

"I could buy you one at the refreshment stand, since you provided the lunch," he offered.

"Well, technically you provided it. But if you'll buy me a coffee I'll follow you anywhere."

"Anywhere?" he asked lightly as they stood up together.

"Maybe." She had the cutest way of wrinkling her nose.

And he needed to watch it, or he'd be getting those romantic feelings for her again. He pulled himself together, checked one last time on Mindy, and then led the way to the concession area.

They were halfway across the grassy lawn when a young guy tossed a ball straight at Susan.

Sam stepped forward, ready to slug the guy, but Susan had already caught the ball and tossed it back, laughing. "Hey, Hunter," she said. "What's going on? Enjoying the summer off?"

The twentysomething guy rose to his feet, shirtless and in surf-style jammer shorts, and pushed his sunglasses to the top of his head. "I'd be better if you'd join the teachers' volleyball league," he said. "Every Wednesday. It's fun."

"Oh, well, I don't think so, but thanks."

"What are you doing for fun this summer?" the guy asked. Focused on Susan, he was completely ignoring Sam.

Sam restrained the urge to move closer and put a protective arm around Susan. No way could she be interested in this guy, right? He was much too young and silly.

He's Susan's age, his inner critic reminded him.

"I'm at the lake! That's fun, right?" She gestured toward a couple of people who'd headed down toward the water. "Your friends are leaving you. You'd better catch up."

"Hey, good to see you. I'll give you a call." He jogged off.

Susan rolled her eyes. "And I'll block your number," she muttered.

Relief washed over him. "You don't like him?"

She shook her head. "He's fine, but he just won't take no for an answer."

Curious now, Sam fell into step beside her. "That must be a problem, guys hitting on you."

She laughed. "No, not usually, but Hunter is fairly new in town. He doesn't know my reputation."

"What's your reputation?"

"I'm known as a cold fish." She kicked at a rock

with a small, neat bare foot, toenails painted pale blue. "Or, sometimes, too mouthy and assertive. I don't get asked out a lot."

"That surprises me," Sam said, tearing his eyes away from those delicate feet. "Does it bother you?"

She shook her head. "Not really," she said. "I'm not looking for love. I'm one of those people who's meant to be single, I think."

Sam knew with everything in him that this warm, funny, kid-loving woman was meant to be a mother. And a wife. "That surprises me, too."

"Why?" she asked.

"Well, because you're…cute. And a lot of fun."

"Thanks," she said drily. "I didn't know you cared."

He lifted his hands. "I didn't mean I cared like *that*…" He felt heat rising up his neck.

She studied him sideways. "It's okay, Sam. I really have no expectations in that area. I'm not angling for a date with Rescue River's richest bachelor."

She seemed to be telling the truth, and to his surprise, he found that refreshing. A lot of the women he dated did have expectations. They liked him for his big house and his money and his CEO position. Not so much for who he was inside.

"So tell me about *your* love life," she said, seeming to read his mind. "Since I don't have one."

"Not much to tell on my side, either," he said.

She made a small sound of disagreement in her throat. "Daisy says you date women just like your wife."

He felt his face redden. "Daisy has a few too many opinions."

She chuckled. "I know what you mean. And there's

nothing wrong with having a type. What was Marie like?"

He smiled, remembering, for once, with enjoyment rather than pain. "Beautiful, though she always worried about her weight. Loved being a mother more than anything else."

"I'm sure Mindy was a joy to her."

"That she was." He thought some more. "Marie was…a perfectionist. Wanted her home and her flowers and her family to be just picture-perfect."

She nodded. "How did she deal with Mindy's disability, then?"

He frowned, thinking. "She didn't want to highlight it, but she loved Mindy just as she was."

"That's good," Susan said. "Sounds like the two of you were…in sync. Perfect, loving parents."

"We were." They'd reached the food stand, and he ordered them both coffees. "We were in sync, that is. Perfect, of course not. Nobody is."

"Some people try harder at it," she said as she stirred an inordinate amount of sugar into her coffee.

She was making him think: about his history, his relationship with Marie, his views on how life should be lived. In the past year of dating, no other woman had really got him to examine his life.

He wasn't sure if he loved it or hated it. Yet another thing to think about, but not today. "What about you?" he asked. "You seem driven in the career area of your life. Wouldn't you say you try to be perfect there?"

She shook her head. "I'm in elementary and special ed. Aiming for perfection doesn't work for us."

He eyed her narrowly. "Excellence?"

"As a teacher, I try. In my personal life…I pretty much ruled that out a long time ago."

"That's cryptic." He paused, giving her space to respond, but for whatever reason, she didn't.

They strolled together back toward the picnic table. "Mindy's having fun," Sam said, pointing to her as she splashed in the lake with her new friends. "Thanks for making this happen."

"I didn't. It was your idea."

"I know, but…for whatever reason, I don't tend to do stuff like this alone with Mindy."

"Why don't you?"

"It just doesn't seem…right. Not without Marie."

"It doesn't seem perfect?"

"I guess not."

They strolled together more slowly. "Somehow," she said, "I don't think it was just Marie who was the perfectionist. But I'll do my best to keep things together for you guys this summer, until the right woman comes along."

Chapter 6

Back at the house, after a quick dinner of beefaroni stirred up by Sam, they watched an hour of TV. All sprawled together on the sectional sofa, Sam on one side of Mindy and Susan on the other.

Like a family. Too much so. Susan was hyperaware of Sam's warm arm, curved around Mindy but brushing against her. Of the smell of his skin, some brisk manly bodywash or deodorant he used. Of the carefree way he threw back his head and laughed at the cartoon antics on the TV screen. She liked seeing this carefree, boyish side of him. He didn't relax enough.

And wherever that wifely thought had come from, it needed to go right back there.

As the show ended, Mindy slumped to her side, asleep.

"Poor kiddo, she's exhausted," Susan said, stroking Mindy's soft hair.

Sam slid his arms underneath her. "I'll carry her upstairs. C'mon, Mindy. Time for bed."

"Miss…Susan…come," Mindy ordered sleepily.

"Do you mind?" Sam asked.

Did she mind playing the mother role, hanging out with this sweet father and daughter and falling for them more each day? "No problem," she said, and followed Sam up the stairs.

While Sam helped Mindy get ready, Susan looked around the big bedroom, really paying attention to its décor for the first time. With a Noah's Ark theme, it had a hand-painted border, and the bed was shaped like an ark. Ruffly curtains portrayed cheery pairs of animals, and a mobile dangled above the bed. It was a gorgeous room…for a three-year-old.

It made sense that Sam hadn't redecorated; that had to be the last thing on his mind, and the room was fine. But noticing all the things in this house that had frozen, at the point where a loving mother had gotten too ill to update them, made sadness push at Susan's chest.

Once Mindy was in her pajamas with teeth brushed, she was awake enough to want to talk. "That boy today was a bully," she said seriously. "Wasn't he, Miss Susan?"

Susan nodded. "He was. Did he hurt your feelings?"

"Yes. I don't like the way my arm is." Mindy held it up to look at it critically. "I wish I had two hands like other kids."

Susan glanced up in time to see pain flash across Sam's face. It must be hard to see your child suffering. And it didn't look as if Sam knew what to say.

But suddenly, Susan remembered how her own mother had talked to her about looking different. "You know," she said, "when I was a little girl, I wished I had round eyes instead of Japanese ones," she said.

"Your eyes aren't round," Mindy agreed, "but they're pretty."

"Thank you! But I still wished I looked like my mom. Even my brother came out looking more white, with round eyes. But I got my dad's Japanese look. For a while, I really hated it."

Mindy nodded, trying to understand. "What did you do?"

Susan laughed. "I did eye exercises every night, hoping I could make my eyes round. But of course, I couldn't."

"Sometimes I pull on my arm," Mindy confided, "so maybe it will grow longer."

"Mindy!" Sam sounded horrified. "That won't work, and it could hurt you."

Mindy's lip pouted out. "It *could* work."

"My eye exercises never did," Susan said. "But my mom bought me a poster for my room. It said, 'Be Your Own Kind of Beautiful.' There were pink butterflies on it." She smiled, remembering how happy the special attention from her mom had made her.

"I like butterflies. Can I have a poster like that?"

Susan raised her eyebrows at Sam, pretty sure that he'd order one before midnight struck.

"Of course you can, sweetie," he said.

"What really helped the most," Susan said, "was knowing God made me the way He did for a reason. My mom kept telling me I was part of His plan."

"God made everyone," Mindy agreed doubtfully.

"That's right." Susan patted Mindy's arm. "Also, getting some more friends who looked like me helped a lot, too. I could see I wasn't alone, or strange."

"Nobody else has a short arm," Mindy said.

"Oh, yes, they do. In fact, when we go to the library next week, we'll see if Miss Fern can order us some books about kids with limb differences."

Mindy's eyes were closing. "'Kay," she said. "Can you sing for me, Miss Susan?"

Sing? Susan couldn't restrain a chuckle. "Oh, honey, you don't want me to sing. Maybe Daddy could sing for you."

"Mommy and Daddy...used to sing...together."

Susan drew in a breath and let it out in a sigh and looked at Sam. So much grief in this house. So much healing to do. So many ways she'd never live up to the perfect Marie, not even as a summer nanny. "Go for it, Dad," she said.

Sam cleared his throat, his face closed. "We'll sing tomorrow, sweetheart."

Susan thought to flick on the little music player beside the bed, and some lullabies, meant for a younger child, poured out.

A quiet moment later, Mindy was asleep.

With a glance at each other, Sam and Susan rose at the same moment and tiptoed from the room. As they walked quietly down the stairs, she glanced up at him. "Sorry I can't sing."

"You bring other strengths," he said. "That really helped, what you said to her about wanting to be different from how you are."

"She should definitely meet other kids with limb differences." Susan felt relieved as they eased into a more businesslike topic. "I'll do a little research to-morrow, see what's out there. Angelica said something about a camp for kids with special needs."

"Great. But hey," he said, putting a hand on her shoulder, "did you really want your eyes to be different, or was that just for Mindy's benefit?"

"I wanted it. Every little girl wants to look like her mommy."

His grip tightened on her shoulder, and he turned her toward him. One hand cupped the side of her face, and his thumb touched the corner of her eye with a gentle caress. "I, for one, think your eyes are beautiful just as they are."

Susan went still, but inside, her heart was pounding out of control. She stared up at him, unable to speak.

He smiled, his own eyes crinkling. "Thanks for today."

"It was good to be with you and Mindy."

They were frozen there, in a moment that seemed to last forever, looking at each other. Lullabies sounded quietly from upstairs, and Susan breathed in the soap-and-aftershave scent that was Sam. She tipped her head a little to feel more of the hand that still rested on her cheek.

And then the front door opened, letting in the most unwelcome sound in the world. "Hey, yoo-hoo!"

It was Helen. Susan stepped back guiltily. Sam let his hand drop.

And they came down the steps double time, but not before Mindy's grandmother had appeared at the landing and seen them, her husband close behind her.

And not before Susan caught sight of the giant portrait of Sam, Mindy and the perfect Marie, directly at the bottom of the stairs.

"Just let me know what it costs," Sam said, and Susan looked at him, puzzled.

"That camp for special-needs kids," he explained.

"Oh!" Susan nodded. "You're fine with her going?"

"Sure, fine," he said, trotting the rest of the way down the stairs, obviously having no idea of what he'd just agreed to.

"Mindy isn't special needs." Helen eyed them suspiciously. "What's been going on?"

Way too much, Susan wanted to say as she followed Sam. Too much emotion for a little family that wasn't hers and never would be. A family that had a perfect woman always in the background.

She was starting to see that she might be able to fit into a family, that she might have something to offer, despite her lack of domestic skills. Part of that was Sam's appreciation for what she offered to a child like Mindy.

But she wasn't what he wanted. He wanted another Marie.

And he wasn't what she wanted, either, she reminded herself. She didn't want a businessman like her dad and her ex-fiancé, who would have overly high expectations and just throw money at any problem that arose.

"Sam," Helen said, "we stopped over to invite you to the Fourth of July picnic next week at the country club. There's someone I want you to meet." Her voice was rich with innuendo, and she was practically waggling her eyebrows at Sam.

"Mindy and I always go," Sam said, looking uncomfortable. "Surely you didn't come here just to invite me to that?"

"Oh, my, no. Come on, sit down." Helen led the way to the kitchen and pulled a sheaf of papers out of her large purse. Susan, feeling unwelcome but unsure of what to do, followed along behind them.

"There's all this paperwork for the Little Miss Rescue River Pageant. It's got to be filled out this week. I thought I could help you get Mindy signed up." She held up a brochure portraying a little girl dressed in a super-fancy evening dress.

"A beauty pageant?" Susan couldn't keep the derisive squeak out of her voice.

But Helen didn't seem to notice. "Yes, it's so much fun. I'm on the planning committee, and we've been busy setting up a wonderful show." Her voice was animated, her eyes lively.

"Oh, it's a big to-do," Ralph contributed.

Susan looked at Sam. Was he on board with this?

Thankfully, he was shaking his head. "It's a great event, but I'm not sure Mindy's ready…" He trailed off and sat down at the counter.

"But she's about to turn six, which is the lower age limit. I'm so happy that she can finally join in the fun!" Helen's voice was determinedly peppy, as if she was getting ready to run right over Sam.

And Sam, the big tough businessman, looked about to cave.

Susan jumped in. "I don't think that would be good for Mindy."

All eyes turned her way.

"Why on earth not?" Helen glared at her.

Could the woman really have no clue? "Beauty

pageants force little girls to dress in age-inappropri-
ate clothes and focus only on their appearance. There's
research that shows they foster eating disorders and an
unhealthy dependence on external validation."

"You could use a little more focus on *your* appearance," Helen said, eyeing Susan's cutoffs and T-shirt
with disdain.

Ouch! Susan clamped her mouth shut to avoid saying something she couldn't take back, and surprising,
unwelcome tears pushed at her eyes. Her self-image
had improved since the days when she'd hated the way
she looked, but it still wasn't perfect.

"Hey, hey now." Sam held up a hand. "Susan, Mindy
and I dressed for a day at the lake, and we look it. Nothing wrong with that."

Helen muttered something that might have been
"Sorry."

Susan made a little sound in her throat that might
pass for "okay." But it wasn't. She didn't like Helen
one bit.

"Let's keep the focus on Mindy," Sam went on. "I
just worry, Helen, that with her hand—"

"She could carry something to cover it if she
wanted, or wear gloves," Helen said. "You know what
a mix the pageant is. Everything from casual and relaxed to hairpieces and fake teeth."

"Exactly! It's a huge fake thing." Susan thought of
the little girl sleeping upstairs, pulling on her hand to
try to make it look like other children's. "It's an out-
dated ritual, and it would be bad for Mindy. Have you
ever watched *Tiny Tot Beauty*?"

"Susan, it's not that kind of thing." Sam looked dis-
tinctly uncomfortable.

She understood. It was hard for him to stand up to Mindy's overbearing grandmother. But she herself had no such qualms. "Have you seen what pageant people are like? What can those parents be thinking, pushing their little kids into that high-glamour lifestyle? I mean, I'm sure this small-town pageant isn't as bad as the big pageants you see on reality TV, but it's a step in the wrong direction."

The room was silent around her.

"Right?" she said, looking at Sam.

"Susan," he said quietly, "Marie was in pageants."

"Yep," Ralph said, nodding. "Those big ones. There wasn't reality TV back in those days, but I've watched the shows. They pretty much tell it like it was for us."

"Oh." Oops. Susan blew out her breath, her face heating.

Helen didn't say anything. Not in words, anyway, but her glare said it all.

Without meaning to, Susan had shot daggers at the woman they all loved so much. The woman Sam had adored and still did. The mother little Mindy aspired to look like and never would. Never would even see again.

They were all looking at her.

When would she ever learn to shut her mouth? "I'm sorry. I'm sure I...don't know everything about pageants. In fact, I probably know a lot less than anyone else in this room, so..." She trailed off into the silence.

The doorbell provided a welcome distraction. "Let me get that," she said.

"She certainly makes herself at home in your house," Susan heard Helen say as she left the room.

"Got some opinions, too," Ralph said.

As she hurried to the door, Susan's face felt as if it was on fire.

She opened it to a welcome sight: Daisy.

"Hey girl, I knocked on your apartment door and when I didn't find you, I figured you must be over here." She squinted at Susan. "Looks like you could use some girl talk."

"More than you know. Let me grab my stuff." She hurried into the kitchen for her beach bag, cell phone and keys as Daisy chatted with Helen.

Five minutes later they were drinking sodas in Susan's tiny living room. "How's it going?" Daisy asked. "You surviving the dragon lady?"

"She didn't like me before," Susan said, "but after tonight, she hates me." She told Daisy about the beauty pageant fiasco. "So if there was any hope of our getting along, not that it really matters, it went out the window tonight."

"She thinks you're after Sam," Daisy said, nodding shrewdly.

"What? Why would she think that?" Even as she spoke, Susan felt her face flush, remembering that moment on the stairs.

If Helen hadn't come, would he have kissed her?

Would she have let him?

Daisy eyed her suspiciously. "What's going on?"

Susan shook her head. Daisy was her best friend, but no way was she going to share the occasional moments of strange attraction between her and Daisy's big brother.

Instead, she turned the topic back to the pageant Helen wanted Mindy to enter.

Daisy rolled her eyes. "I'm with you. Pageants are

pretty ridiculous most of the time. But the Rescue River one isn't so bad."

Susan couldn't restrain her curiosity. "Was Marie really a pageant kid? Like on *Tiny Tot Beauty?*"

"Yep. She was way into it, through middle school at least. I'm sure there are some pictures around." Daisy cocked her head to one side, thinking. "In fact, Helen might have been in some pageants, too, back in the day."

Susan groaned. "So it's a family tradition, and I interfered with it with all my big California ideas. Sam's probably getting ready to fire me right now."

Daisy laughed. "Sam can take it. In fact, I think you're good for him. He looks more relaxed than usual. Even seems to have a bit of a tan."

"We were at the lake today," Susan explained, and told her about their day.

Daisy crossed her arms and studied Susan, her expression curious. "Sounds pretty cozy. How do you feel about Sam, anyway?"

"He's a good employer, and we're getting along better than I expected."

"Are you sure that's all there is to it? I mean, Sam's incredibly handsome, and has a great big heart, and he's also the richest man in town. Any chance of you falling for him?"

"No!" Susan held up a hand to stop Daisy's protest. "I don't date, remember? I'm committed to staying single so I can focus on my career. Plus," she added, "if I were going to go out with someone, it wouldn't be one of those classic business types. I like quirky, creative guys, and Sam's anything but."

"Does your dad's treatment of your family have to affect you forever?" Daisy asked bluntly.

"My dad's... What do you mean?" She didn't like the way Daisy was looking at her, as if she was a social work client. A troubled one.

"Our childhoods have an impact," Daisy lectured, in full counselor mode. "You think Sam is too much like your dad, but he's not only a businessman. He's a brother and a dad. And he's very lonely."

"He misses his wife, I can tell that." Susan frowned. "Even if I *were* interested—and I'm not—it would be crazy to get involved with a family still grieving such a big loss. They'd rip my heart out."

Daisy looked thoughtful. "I know Sam seems obsessed with Marie, but appearances can be deceptive. He's trying to keep her memory alive for Mindy, and he's been too busy surviving to build them a new life. But I can see him changing, letting go."

Susan walked over to the kitchen and snagged the jumbo bag of spicy tortilla chips. "Don't you think they need some counseling?" she asked as she replenished the bowl on the coffee table.

"They've had it. Do you think I would've let them muddle through without help? But it's a process." Daisy grabbed a chip and munched it, thoughtfully, then spoke again. "And you have to remember that Jesus can heal. He can heal Sam and Mindy of what they lost when Marie died. And He can heal you from the way your father treated you."

Susan leaned her head back on the couch and stared up at the ceiling fan. She wanted to believe it. She wished for Daisy's faith. But it was a stretch right now. "I'm afraid to change," she admitted. "I've been committed to being a single schoolteacher for so long. I've felt like that's God's will for me."

"His will might be bigger than you can imagine right now. Maybe it involves getting married, having kids of your own *and* being a schoolteacher. Ever think of that?"

Susan *had* thought of it lately. Specifically in connection to Sam and Mindy. But the whole idea felt risky and dangerous and scary. "It's out of my comfort zone. What with my family and all."

"God kinda specializes in out-of-our-comfort-zone."

Susan thought about that. God had called her to work with special-needs kids—in the classroom, or so she'd thought. But she knew she was doing good for Mindy right now. Taking this job with Sam had been a risk, but she could see that it was paying off. At least for Mindy, which was the important thing.

"And," Daisy continued, frowning, "it might be time for Sam to take down a few pictures from the Marie gallery. I'll talk to him about it." She grabbed Susan's hand. "But you need to work on healing, too. You're not limited to your past. With God's help, you can have a bright future and you can have love."

"But I don't want—"

"Just think about it."

Night was falling, turning the summer sky to pinks and purples, sending a cool breeze fragrant with honeysuckle through the open window.

Susan heard a car door slam outside. Hopefully, that was Helen and Ralph, leaving.

"Promise me you'll think and pray about healing, okay? Not just so you can work something out with Sam, although that would be totally cool. But no matter what happens with him, I want to see you be happy and whole."

Susan hugged her friend. "Thanks for caring about me. I know Jesus can heal. I know it in my head. But I'm not quite there with believing it in my heart."

After that emotional night, Susan and Sam steered a little clear of each other, seemingly by mutual agreement. When Susan had a question about the company picnic she was planning, she mostly texted Sam and he responded with brief, impersonal instructions.

She did notice that Sam quietly took down some of the Marie pictures, replacing them with drawings Mindy had made, which he'd had beautifully framed, and more recent photographs of him and Mindy. The change, Susan was sure, was Daisy's doing; she must have had that talk with Sam.

He'd also spent a couple of evenings helping Mindy create a photo album of her mother and her, which Mindy had proudly showed Susan each morning after Sam went to work.

Susan was surprised and impressed. Sam definitely had a stubborn, bossy side, but he also was able to listen to his sister's wisdom and follow it, and his thoughtfulness with his daughter, his intelligent care of her, made him all the more appealing.

She found herself watching him sometimes, in a silly, romantic way that wasn't doing her heart any good at all.

She just needed to keep reminding herself that her goal wasn't to swoon over her boss's softer side. It was to fix her own family's problems while staying independent. She wasn't the marrying kind, and in a tempting situation like this, she had to keep that well in mind.

Sam had brushed aside her apologies about her awkward words to his in-laws, saying everything was fine. But it wasn't, Susan could tell. He'd been distant, and she felt bad about it. Who was she to judge how others lived their lives? Maybe there was some redeeming value in pageants she didn't understand. And in any case, it wasn't her business. She was just the nanny.

She and Mindy were finger-painting late one afternoon when her phone buzzed. She washed her hands and looked at the text message. From Sam, and her heart jumped.

Did you get my message before?

Susan looked and started to sweat.

Hate to ask but could you fix something easy for dinner? Job candidate here with wife and two active boys. Would like to invite them home. Nothing special, no stress. ETA 5 p.m.

No stress. Ha! She checked the message again. Yes, it did say they'd arrive at 5.

It was 4:15.

She drew in a breath and sat up straighter. Here was her chance to impress Sam with her domestic abilities and make up for being such a screw-up the other night.

No problem, she texted back. She'd disappointed him then, but she wouldn't do it again. She could get it done.

"Come on, Mindy," she said. "We have work to do."

* * *

When Sam arrived home promptly at 4:55, he had a little trepidation as he held the car door for Emily, his job candidate's wife.

"Wow, that's a big house!" cried one of the couple's twin boys. They were cute, freckle-faced redheads with energy to burn, probably a couple years older than Mindy.

"How many kids do you have?" the other twin asked.

"One, and she should be inside. Come on in."

Just then, Susan came around the side of the house. She wore neat shorts and a… Was that a golf shirt? He'd never have guessed she owned anything so plain and ordinary.

She didn't look like herself, quite; she looked… almost traditional. A thought crossed his mind: had she dressed that way for him?

Surely she wouldn't do that, but the very notion of it tugged at his heart. If she'd tried to look conservative for him, it was a totally endearing effort.

And she should probably remove some of her multiple earrings to complete the effect.

"Come around back," she said. "Everything's ready."

"I can get the drinks," Sam said, relief washing over him at her gracious greeting. Times like this, he really needed a wife, and Susan was acting like a good stand-in. He wanted to bring Bill in as CEO of his agricultural real estate division, which would free Sam up to focus on the land management side of the business—and to spend a little less time at the office. But Bill and Emily were city people, used to sophisticated

living, so he was going to have to sell them hard on
the virtues of Rescue River.

On the back deck, overlooking the pool, the table
was set with a red checkered tablecloth and there were
baskets of potato chips and dip. Retro, casual, but that
was okay. He'd only let Susan know today.

Burgers were on the grill, smelling great, and
through the open kitchen window, peppy jazz played.
Nice.

Mindy came out, carefully carrying a bowl of baby
carrots. A glass bowl, but Sam restrained himself from
helping her. She was adept with her hand and half arm,
and he was learning, from Susan, to let her do as much
as possible on her own. He introduced her to the boys
and the adults and she greeted everyone politely and
turned away. "'Scuse me, I gotta bring the dip."

Susan emerged with a bin of assorted soft drinks
on ice, and since everyone seemed to enjoy choosing
their own, he didn't even complain about the fact that
they were drinking from cans. It was a barbecue, he
told himself. Relax.

Susan looked extremely cute. She'd tied a barbecue
apron over her shorts and shirt and was concentrating
on the burgers. "Hey, I think these are done already,"
she said, and they all sat down.

Dinner was happening a little too quickly, and he
wanted to suggest that everyone needed to enjoy their
sodas and relax a bit before eating.

"Yay, I'm starving!" cried one of the boys.

"Me, too!" yelled his brother.

Their mother smiled, so Sam let it go.

It was make-your-own-burgers—again, a little too
casual for his tastes, but the family seemed fine with

it. Susan ducked back into the kitchen and emerged with a casserole dish which, when she opened it, contained macaroni and cheese that looked suspiciously like the kind from a box. He arched an eyebrow at her.

"Mac and cheese!" the boys shouted.

"I really appreciate your arranging this to be so kid-friendly," the job candidate, Bill, said to Susan.

She chuckled, a throaty sound that tickled Sam's nerve endings. "Casual and kid-friendly, that's my specialty," she said with an apologetic smile to Sam.

Sam offered up a quick prayer and then they all dug in.

Sam took a giant bite of hamburger. His teeth hit something hard and he tasted ice.

Quickly he put the burger down. "I don't think these are done. Better get them back on the grill," he said.

Susan's face flamed. "Oh, no, I'm sorry. They came right out of the freezer, but I thought, with the grill so hot…"

Bill grinned. "Mistake of a novice griller," he said.

"I don't like hamburgers," announced one of the boys. "I like hot dogs better."

"Me, too!" Mindy said.

"We do have some," Susan said hesitantly. "I'm sorry, Sam."

Sam slapped a mosquito and noticed Mindy and the quieter little boy were doing the same. "Couldn't you find the bug torches?" he asked Susan.

"I…never heard of bug torches," she said regretfully. "Look. I'll grab the hot dogs, and we'll put the burgers back on the grill. You guys go hunt down the bug torches because I, for one, am getting eaten alive."

Everyone got up from the table and went to their respective stations. Sam was shaking his head. If there had ever been a worse attempt at impressing a prospective employee, he didn't know what it was.

"Sorry," she whispered as she brushed past him. And even amidst his annoyance, he felt a rush of sympathy and patted her shoulder.

"Can I come in and help?" asked Emily, a very quiet woman.

Susan shrugged resignedly. "If you want. It's a huge mess inside."

"We'll come, too!" the ginger-haired twins said and rushed inside.

As they walked to the garage, Bill clapped him on the back. "Ask me sometime to tell you about my major disaster of a client dinner," he said.

When they got the torches lit, everyone was still in the house, and the sound of the boys' yelling rang through the open windows. With some trepidation, Sam pushed in, followed by his client. And stopped and stared.

The entire kitchen table was covered with paint pots and paper, and the two visiting boys were having a heyday with it. The mother, who seemed to lack discipline or authority, was scolding ineffectually, and the boys were ignoring her.

"Those are *my* finger paints," Mindy said, looking ready to blow.

Susan was arm-deep in the refrigerator. "I know there are some hot dogs in here somewhere," she was saying.

What a disaster!

The doorbell rang. "Mindy, could you or your daddy

get that?" Susan called, obviously glad to have found Mindy a distraction.

Sam started to follow Mindy, but when he saw who'd arrived, he went back to the kitchen to give himself time to take a deep breath.

He needed it.

His daughter came in a moment later with Sam's father, who'd started Hinton Enterprises as a small agricultural real estate firm fifty years ago. "It's Grandpa!" she announced.

Sam felt a rush of the inadequacy he'd grown up with. His father was hard to please and, since he'd met Bill earlier in the day, he knew this dinner should be impressive. Sam was making a mess of things.

"Boys!" Bill scolded, frowning at his own wife.

"What on earth is going on?" Mr. Hinton asked.

Sam blew out a breath, looked around and realized he was going to have to take charge.

But there was a touch on his arm, one that tingled. Susan. "Sorry," she mouthed to him.

And then she proceeded to take charge herself. "Boys!" she said in a firm, quiet voice accompanied by a hand-clap. "Finger paints are for after dinner. Mindy, please show your new friends how to wash their hands at the kitchen sink."

"Marie never would have allowed that," Mr. Hinton said in a voice that was meant to be quiet but wasn't.

Sam saw a muscle twitch in Susan's face. She was no dummy. She knew she was being compared.

She drew in a breath. "Mr. Hinton, here." She put two packages of hot dogs into his hands. "You're in charge of grilling these. Sam." She handed him two packages of buns. "Take these outside, along with your clients. Socialize. Do your thing."

She turned to the children, who stood quietly watching her, obviously recognizing that teacher voice. In fact, Sam thought, even his father seemed to recognize that voice. "Kids, you can play outside with Mindy's toys until dinner. After you eat your hot dogs…" She tapped a finger on her lips. "I think we've got some of Xavier's clothes here. You can put on swimsuits or shorts, and finger-paint for a bit, and then jump in the pool to clean up. If that's okay with Mom?" She looked questioningly at Emily.

"Of course. Thank you."

"Yay!" cried the boys, and all three kids rushed outside.

So the men bonded over how to re-cook half-frozen, half-burnt burgers with ketchup already on them, and they grilled up a bunch of hot dogs. The kids played while Susan talked with Emily, who gradually became more animated. Dinner was eaten half at the table and half by the pool, and Sam's father actually stayed to eat three of the hot dogs he'd cooked and then to sit on a chaise lounge by the pool, watching the kids play.

The sun peeked through the clouds on its way toward the horizon, turning the sky rosy and sending beams of golden light that, as a kid, he'd always thought seemed to come directly from God. Salted caramel ice cream topped with chocolate syrup from a squirt bottle made a fine dessert, to his surprise. As the evening grew chilly, Susan brought out a heap of old sweatshirts from the front closet, and everyone put them on and stayed outside, talking and laughing.

Gradually, Sam relaxed. It wasn't exactly orthodox,

but the prospective employee's family seemed to be having a good time.

When darkness fell and the kids climbed out of the pool, shivering, Susan wrapped them in towels and took all of them inside to dress, accompanied by the mother.

"I tell you what," Bill said as he and Sam stood on the front porch. "When I saw this big house, I thought, oh, man, too rich for our blood. We like to keep it simple. But this has been great." He pumped Sam's hand as his wife and tired children came out onto the porch. "I've made my decision. I like this town and this lifestyle. If you still want me after the way my kids have behaved, I'd like to come work for Hinton Enterprises."

Fifteen minutes later, Sam stood with his father, watching the family drive away. "That's the wackiest business dinner I ever witnessed," Mr. Hinton said, clapping Sam on the shoulder. "But whatever works, son." He gave Sam a squinty-eyed glare. "You're not thinking about marrying that Japanese girl, are you?"

"Her name's Susan," Sam said. "And no. Nothing like that. I have other plans for that side of my life."

His father nodded. "Best to get moving on them. That little girl of yours isn't getting any younger. Seems to me she needs some brothers and sisters to play with."

"Yes, sir, I'm aware of that." He knew the clock was ticking. And every minute he spent noticing the appeal of an unconventional schoolteacher with a knack for causing disasters, even if they did usually turn out just fine, was a minute he wasn't finding the proper sort of mother for his daughter.

Was a minute he spent *not* fulfilling his promise to Marie.

* * *

The next Friday, July Fourth, Susan helped Mindy dress in her new red, white and blue shorts and shirt to go to the country club picnic. The day had dawned bright and hot, perfect weather for a picnic.

She was *not* looking forward to this.

She didn't need to spend the time with Sam, who'd been surprisingly kind about her disastrous efforts to cook dinner for his job candidate's family. He hadn't had a lot to say over the past few days, but she sensed that his attitude toward her had softened.

Which made him even more appealing. But she had to guard her heart. She didn't need to fall for a guy who wanted something altogether different in a woman. She wasn't going to put herself through that again.

"I'm bored," Mindy announced.

There was still an hour until it was time to leave, so Susan took her charge downstairs and looked around for something to occupy her. They'd spent enough time in the playroom, and the formal living room had too many breakables to be a good play area.

"Let's check our seedlings," she suggested, and they went to the kitchen window. To Mindy's delight, tiny, bent plants were appearing in the soil they'd put in an egg carton.

"They're not very green," Mindy said, poking at one with her finger.

"They need more light. Let's find another window to put them in."

They each took an egg carton and wandered around the mansion's downstairs, looking for the perfect spot. It occurred to Susan that she'd never been inside the sunroom. Even though she'd seen it from outside, the blinds had always been drawn. "Come on, Mindy," she said. "Let's try in here."

Mindy emerged from the formal dining room, saw Susan's hand on the doorknob of the sunroom. "No!" she shrieked, dropping her egg carton. "Don't go in there!"

Susan spun back toward the little girl, less concerned with the dirt and seedlings now soiling the cream-colored carpet than about Mindy's frantic expression. "Hey," she said, putting down her egg carton and kneeling in front of Mindy. "What's wrong?"

"Don't go in there, don't go in there," the child said anxiously, her eyes round.

"Okay, I won't," Susan promised. "But why?"

Mindy's face reddened and her eyes filled with tears. "I don't like that room."

"Okay, okay. Shh." She pulled Mindy into her arms and hugged her until some of the tension left her body. "Come on, we'd better save our plants."

Mindy looked down, only now realizing that she'd dropped her egg-carton planter. "Oh, no, they're gonna be broken."

"I think we can save them," Susan said. "And I have a good idea about how. Come on, you can help."

Forty-five minutes later, the little plants were replanted in some old cartoon character mugs Susan had discovered in the back of a cupboard. The mess was cleaned up, though Susan was going to have to tell the cleaning service to give that area of the rug a little extra attention. And Mindy was calm again, paging quietly through a library book about plants.

As for Susan, she had to get ready. In a weak moment, she'd agreed to go to the club herself, at Daisy and Sam's insistence, so she put on her own faded "Proud to be an American" T-shirt to pair with her standard denim capris and sandals. She pulled her hair up into a ponytail and added a little mascara and blush, and at Mindy's insistence, tied a red, white and blue ribbon into her hair.

But as Sam backed the car out of the driveway, Susan couldn't help looking toward the sunroom that was visible from the side of the house.

Why was the door always closed? Why was Mindy afraid of the sunroom?

When they reached the country club, Mindy tugged Susan along, chattering a mile a minute, while Sam gathered blankets and lawn chairs for the fireworks later. "C'mon, Miss Susan! We all sit at one big long table. The grown-ups on one end and the kids on the other."

Susan decided instantly on her strategy. "Can I sit with the kids?"

Mindy slowed down a minute to consider. "I guess you could," she said doubtfully. "Xavier likes you, and he's the biggest cousin, so he's kind of the boss."

Susan smiled at the thought of a soon-to-be-second-grader running the show. She adored Xavier, had been his first-grade teacher last year, had helped him catch up and cheered him on in his struggle with leukemia, a struggle he'd now won.

"And there's gonna be Mercedes!"

"I know! She's great." Susan was so happy for Fern and Carlo, Mercedes's foster mother and biological father, who'd fallen in love during a snowstorm over the winter and who were planning to get married soon.

"Put your stuff down here," Mindy ordered, gesturing to the promised long table on one side of the busy dining area, "and then we can go play. Look, there's Mercy!"

Susan waved at Fern, who was sitting at the table chatting with Angelica, Xavier's mom. Behind her, she heard Sam's deep voice, greeting people.

She glanced back to see that he'd paused to talk to a group of men clad in golf shirts. The preppy crowd. Of course. "I'll keep an eye on the kids," she said to Fern and Angelica, and followed the small pack of cousins before either woman could protest.

Staying with the kids would keep her from spending too much time with handsome Sam.

She watched them jump through the inflatables and play in the ball pit, all under Xavier's leadership. When he'd gotten them all onto a little train that circled the club's giant field, she sat down on a long bench under a tree to wait for the train's return.

A slight breeze rustled the leaves overhead, cooling Susan's heated face. From the bandstand, patriotic songs rang out over the chatter of families. The aroma of roasting corn and hot dogs tickled her nose, reminding her of holidays in the park in her California hometown.

Self-pity nudged at her. Holidays were meant to be experienced with family, and a lot of people here in Rescue River had a whole long tableful of relatives.

She missed her mom and brother, Aunt Sakura and Uncle Ren, and her cousins, Missy and Cameron and Ryan. They hadn't gathered often, but when they did, they'd always had a good time.

Now Uncle Ren had passed away and her cousins were scattered all over the country. She bit her lip and forced herself to concentrate on the buzz of a nearby bee, the beauty of Queen Ann's lace blooming beside the bench, the sight of Miss Lou Ann Miller carrying a tray of decorated cupcakes to the church's booth.

And of course, she wasn't alone long. No one ever was in Rescue River. There was a tap on her shoulder, and Gramps Camden, her buddy from the Senior Towers, sat down heavily beside her on the bench. With him was a weathered-looking man whom she'd occasionally seen around town but didn't know.

And that, too, never lasted long in Rescue River.

"Bob, meet Susan Hayashi. Susan, Bob Eakin. World War II Gliderman."

The thin old man held out a hand and gave her a surprisingly strong handshake. "And present-day librarian," he added with a wink. "Don't ever stop working. That's what'll kill you."

Since the man had to be in his nineties, if he'd fought in World War II, he must know what he was talking about. Susan shook his hand with both of her own. "I'm glad to meet you."

"He runs the library at the Towers," Gramps explained. "Don't worry, he was in Europe in the war, so he's not gonna have any problem with your people."

Susan smiled at the elderly man. "Thank you for your service, and I don't just mean that as a cliché," she said. "One of my great-grandfathers fought for Japan, but another was in an internment camp and eventually fought for the United States."

"Oh, in the 442nd?" His eyes lit up. "I was just reading about them. My buddy Fern brought me a new book about the various regiments."

"I can't believe you know about that! I'd love to borrow it sometime," she said. "I like history, but I don't know much about that period."

"Shame what we did to Japanese Americans back then," Mr. Eakin said. "We've learned better since. Is Rescue River treating you well?"

Susan nodded, her feeling of loneliness gone. "You're nice to ask. It's a great town. I love it here."

Gramps Camden studied her approvingly. "You fit right in. But how's your summer job with that Sam Hinton? Is he being fair to you?"

"I'm doing my best, Mr. Camden," came a deep voice behind them.

Susan spun around at the sound of it, her heart rate accelerating.

"Don't creep up on people, Hinton," Gramps complained. "We're having a nice conversation. You just leave well enough alone."

Sam ignored the older man. "Brought you some appetizers," he said to Susan. "I didn't mean for you to get stuck watching the kids all day. Come on back and sit with the family."

Gramps snorted. "She doesn't want to listen to your dad give her the third degree, and I don't blame her."

Susan looked at Sam with alarm as she accepted the plate. "Is your dad going to give me the third degree? Why?"

"Because he's like his son," Gramps jumped in, "a millionaire with no consideration for the common folk."

Susan looked up at Sam in time to notice the hurt expression that flickered briefly across his face. Now that she knew Sam better, she understood how unfair Gramps's accusations were. Sam treated his workers well and bent over backward to contribute to the town's well-being. "Sam's not as much of a Scrooge as I expected," she told Gramps, softening her words with a smile. "Maybe your information is a little bit out of date."

"The lady's right," Bob Eakin said, elbowing Gramps Camden. "Leave the man alone. He's done his share for Rescue River, just like we all try to do."

The kids' train returned then, and they all trooped back to the table.

Susan's plan of sitting with the children didn't hold water, though, because Helen was there and adamant about her own position as Mindy's grandmother. "I'll help her if she needs it," she insisted, sliding into the seat beside Mindy.

So Susan had to sit with the other adults. Which turned out to be okay. She stuffed herself with hamburgers and corn on the cob and potato salad, and laughed with Daisy and Angelica, and generally had a good time.

Mr. Hinton stopped by the table but demurred from eating with them. "I've got my eye on Camden. He's sitting a little too close to Lou Ann Miller, and I'd better make sure he doesn't bother her."

Daisy, Fern and Angelica exchanged glances. "Does Lou Ann have a preference for one or the other?" Daisy asked Angelica in a low voice.

"She's doing just fine on her own," Fern said. "I think she likes being single."

"Exactly," Angelica said, salting a second ear of corn. "I don't think she's wanting them to court her, but she can hardly say no if they put their plates down beside hers."

"Age cannot wither her, nor custom stale her infinite variety," quoted Fern's fiancé, Carlo, with a wink at Fern. "William Shakespeare, *Antony and Cleopatra*."

"He was in *one* play at Rescue River High School," Angelica said, rolling her eyes at her brother, "but he uses it every chance he can get. Makes him seem literary."

"I love it when you quote Shakespeare at me," Fern said, leaning her head on her husband-to-be's shoulder with an exaggerated lash-flutter.

Susan swallowed a huge bite of potato salad and waved her fork at the table of elders. "When I lived near the Senior Towers, I witnessed more drama than you see at a middle school. I wouldn't be surprised if those two came to blows over Lou Ann."

"That's for sure," Fern said with a quiet laugh. "When I go there for book group or to replenish the library cart, things can get pretty lively. Even Bob Eakin has his lady friends, and he's over ninety."

Sam was there, on the other side of Daisy, and it seemed to Susan that he watched her thoughtfully. At one point, as Angelica was apologizing for Gramps Camden's crotchety attitudes, he broke in. "I'm sorry you had to deal with all of that," he said. "I hope the older guys treated you okay."

"Mr. Eakin's going to lend me a book about Japanese who fought for the US in World War II," Susan said. "It's no problem, Sam. I always got along with older relatives."

"Maybe so, but watch out for Mr. Hinton, Senior," Angelica said in a low voice, grinning. "He's a tough nut to crack."

Another remark about Sam's dad. Hmm. After his

appearance at the disastrous dinner she'd tried to cook, she wasn't looking forward to seeing him again. Although, she reminded herself, it didn't really matter what he thought. She was just a summer nanny.

Still, right at this moment, Susan felt welcomed and affirmed, almost as if she was a part of the family. Which was strange...but nice.

As they all talked about how full they were—and made trips to the buffet for seconds—a tall, curvaceous redhead walked hesitantly toward the table, her four subdued kids following, all looking to be under the age of eight.

Susan's teacher radar went up immediately. Why weren't the kids looking happy in the presence of cotton candy and inflatables and face painters? Why the tension and caution?

Helen jumped up to greet the woman. "Fiona! Come on, right here. I have a seat for you, and we can squeeze in your little ones at this end of the table. Have you eaten?"

As she settled the woman beside Sam, Helen was practically glowing with excitement, and it all came clear to Susan.

Helen had an agenda to set Sam up with a replacement Marie. And here she was.

On Susan's other side, Daisy filled in the facts. "Fiona Farmingham. Just moved to Rescue River to escape all the gossip. Her celebrity husband just died, and it turns out he had a whole other family down in Texas."

Susan looked at the woman with sympathy. "Do the kids know?"

"Oh, yeah, they couldn't help but hear about it. Apparently, they got teased pretty bad. Fiona is Marie's distant cousin, so she knows the town. She's hoping Rescue River will be a fresh start."

"Looks like they need one."

But as sympathetic as she felt, she couldn't help feeling jealous as Sam and Fiona talked, egged on by Helen. Even after the rest of them had stood up, Sam and Fiona talked on.

Helen came over to share her triumph with Susan and Daisy. "They're hitting it off, I think," she said in a confiding voice. "Look what lovely manners she has. And she was a stay-at-home mom, and she knows just how to keep a big house nice. She was kind of Marie's role model in that."

"You doing some matchmaking, Helen?" Daisy asked bluntly.

"Sam needs a wife, and Mindy needs a mother. It should have been Marie, but since it can't…well. I hope he'll find a woman who's as like her as possible." Helen's eyes shone with unshed tears.

Susan stuffed down the feelings of hurt and inadequacy prompted by Helen's words. This was good. This was what she wanted: to keep a distance from Sam, which his serious dating of another woman would do. This would be good for Mindy, providing a mother figure and ready-made siblings.

"She's built like a model," Daisy complained in Susan's other ear. "And look, she's just picking at her food. It's hard to like a woman like that."

But Fiona soon excused herself from Sam and came over to talk to them. "Are you guys the moms of these kids?" she asked, her voice throaty and surprisingly deep. "Because I'm fairly desperate for mom friends. I had to leave a lot of people behind when I moved, and I don't know a soul here except for Helen. Well, and I've met Mindy a time or two."

Fern, who was unfailingly kind and accepting, started chatting with Fiona about her daughter, who was the same age as Fern's daughter, Mercedes. Angelica joined in the conversation, and Susan had to admit: the woman was lovely. When she squatted down to see what the kids were doing, she greeted Mindy happily with a hug, reminding the little girl that they'd met before. Soon, she'd engaged all the kids in conversation, introducing her own, encouraging the kids to play together.

As Fiona sat back down with Sam, now surrounded by her children and Mindy, Susan ground her teeth and gave herself a firm talking to.

This was right; this was what everyone, herself included, wanted. Fiona was good with Mindy and was the type of woman Sam needed, way more than Susan herself was.

She swallowed the giant lump in her throat.

She needed to leave them to it.

She excused herself from the others. She was left out anyway. Daisy had gone to see Dion and everyone else was talking. She pulled out her phone and shot Sam a text: Not feeling well, found a way home. There. That sounded breezy.

Then she slipped away and out the side door of the country club.

She'd achieved her goal of staying independent, she told herself as she started walking the two miles toward Sam's house. And it was just her own stupidity that had her feeling teary and blue about it. She'd get over it. She was meant to be alone. This was how it was to be, and it was just going to have to be good enough.

Chapter 7

After Susan left the table, Sam tried to focus on Fiona, new in town and someone his mother-in-law wanted him to get to know better. "She's perfect for you and Mindy, Sam," Helen had whispered as Fiona approached the table. "I know, four kids is a lot, but you have the resources. And she's happy to stay at home. Wouldn't that be wonderful for Mindy?"

The hard sell had made him feel resistant, but Fiona was a genuinely nice woman. They chatted easily about the small liberal arts college they'd both attended, although in different years, about how Rescue River was a great place to raise a family, about people they knew in common, since Fiona was related to Marie.

There was something shuttered in her eyes, some distance, some pain. Still, she was pretty, with her long, wavy red hair, tall as a model but with pleasant curves. Obviously smart.

Sam's attention strayed, wondering where Susan had gone. He scanned the crowd down by the band's tent, where the sounds of pop music emerged alongside patriotic favorites. Checked the food area, where the fragrance of barbecue and burned sugar lingered.

No Susan, though.

"Look," Fiona said, "I get the sense that Helen is trying to push us together, but don't feel obligated to stick around and talk. I'm not in the market for a relationship. I'm just trying to straighten out my life after my husband's death."

He snapped back to focus on her. "I'm sorry for your loss. I faced that and I'm dealing with it, but it's not easy when you had a great relationship and high hopes for the future."

She stared off across the field where people were starting to stake out spots to watch fireworks. Craned her neck, perhaps to see her kids, who were over at the face-painting station with Mindy, under Daisy's supervision. Then she turned back to him. "Be glad if yours was a clean break, Sam," she said, her voice surprisingly intense. "Not everyone has that. In a way, it's harder if the loss was…complicated."

He cocked his head to one side, looking at her and wondering about her story.

One of her children ran to her, a girl of seven or eight, and whispered something in her ear. The two talked in low tones while Sam thought about what she had said.

Thinking about Marie.

It had, in fact, been a clean break. He'd never had

any reason to doubt her faithfulness or her love. They'd been genuinely happy together. And right up to the end, her faith had been strong, had guided him even, kept him on a positive path.

It was only after her death that he'd strayed away, mentally, from his faith. Had gotten angry with God about what He'd taken away, not just from Sam himself, but from a little girl who'd sobbed for days as if her heart was breaking—which it surely was—about the loss of her loving mama.

But Mindy had only positive memories of her mother. She'd been well-cared for, and even though the loss had been terribly, terribly hard on her, she hadn't ever questioned her mother's love. She had more moments of joy than pain, these days. Nothing like the skulking, furtive demeanor of the mysterious Fiona's kids.

Marie had been everything a mother should be.

And maybe, just maybe, rather than exclusively feeling bitter about losing her, he should feel grateful to have had a faithful, loving wife.

Fiona's daughter ran off, and she turned to meet his bemused eyes.

"Are you doing okay?" he asked, feeling awkward. "Do you need someone to talk to?"

She waved a hand. "Don't worry about me. I have a strong faith and an appointment with the pastor here. I'll be fine. We'll be fine." Her face broke into a genuinely beautiful smile. "God's good even when times are hard."

"That's…true." And he wasn't just saying it. Maybe it was time for a change. Maybe he needed to not only get to church each week, but get right with God.

"You've made me think," he said to Fiona. "I appreciate that."

"Sure, Sam. Nice talking to you."

The obvious ending of their conversation turned on a light bulb for him: his "find Mindy a mom" campaign was going to be harder than he thought. Because right here in front of him was a perfect woman. Exactly what he would have wanted, had he filled out an order form.

And he had zero interest in her, romantically.

She pushed back her chair, holding out a hand to briskly shake his, and he could tell she felt the same way about him, so there was no guilt. There might even be a friendship, one of these days; they seemed to have some things in common. "Your kids are welcome to swim in my pool anytime," he said. "Mindy would love the company."

"Thanks, that's nice of you." She smiled at him, but her mind was clearly elsewhere. Her eyes held pain and secrets, and Sam resolved to get Daisy on the case.

He walked around for a while, enjoying the companionship of old friends, watching the kids run around in small packs, relishing another piece of pie. But something was missing: he couldn't find Susan. Mindy was still with Daisy, who hadn't seen Susan in a while.

Finally he thought to text Susan, but when he pulled out his phone and looked at it, he saw her message.

He frowned. She'd gone home? How, when she'd ridden over with him?

Sam asked around to see whether anyone had noticed her leaving. "I think she walked," a teenager told him offhandedly.

Walked home? That was close to three miles, mostly

on deserted country roads, and darkness was falling. Not good.

He shot her a text: Where are you?

She didn't answer.

He turned to find his mother-in-law at his elbow. "How did you like Fiona?" she asked.

"Can you watch over Mindy tonight and make sure she gets home?"

"Of course!" A wide smile spread over her face. "You liked her, then? Are you taking her home?"

Had she lost her mind? Sam shook his head distractedly. "Fiona is lovely, and we have nothing going on romantically. She seems to need a friend, so if you're wanting to help her out, that's probably the direction to go. Introduce her to some of the local women, something like that."

"But if you're not going to take Fiona home," she asked unhappily, "then why are you leaving?"

"Susan walked home, and I need to check on her."

Helen put a hand on her hip, her forehead wrinkling. "Now, why would anyone do something like that? That's just strange."

He ignored the judgment. "I'll see you when you get home with Mindy," he said, turning toward the parking lot.

"But you'll miss the fireworks!" Helen sounded truly distressed. "That woman is a terrible influence on you. She's not even patriotic!"

"Later, Helen," he called over his shoulder.

After catching Mindy long enough to explain that she was to leave with her grandparents—which appeared to be fine with her, she was having such a good time with all the kids to play with—Sam got in his truck and started driving, thinking about what Helen had said.

Susan *was* different. She was independent and outspoken and didn't always say the proper thing.

But as for patriotism… Sam thought of her interactions with the older veterans and chuckled. She'd had those guys eating from the palm of her hand. She was every bit a proud American, as evidenced by the words on her obviously well-worn T-shirt.

He drove slowly along the country road, windows open. A gentle breeze brought the smells of hay and fresh-plowed soil that had always been part of his homeland experience. Crickets chirped, their music rising and falling, accompanied by a throaty chorus of frogs as he passed a small farm pond.

The sky was darkening, and up ahead, he saw the moon rise in a perfect circle, like a large round coin in the sky.

Even with the moonlight, it was still too dark. Too dark for a young woman to be out alone, a woman unfamiliar with the roads. Could Susan have gotten lost? Could something bad have happened to her?

As he arrived at Main Street in downtown Rescue River, concern grew in his heart. Where was she? Had something happened? He'd been studying the dark road the whole way and hadn't seen her, but could she have fallen into a ditch or been abducted?

Finally he spotted a petite form just sinking onto a bench, a couple of buildings down from the Chatterbox Café. Susan.

She was taking off her sandals and studying one foot, and when he stopped the truck in front of her, she looked up.

She wasn't as classically beautiful as Fiona. Her hair was coming out of its neat ponytail, and her shoulders slumped a little.

He'd never been so glad to see anyone in his life.

He jumped out of the truck and strode over to her. "What were you thinking, walking home?"

She squinted up at him. "Umm…I was tired?"

"You walked two miles on rough country roads. Of course you're tired." He sat down beside her and gestured toward the foot she'd been examining. "What happened?"

"Blister," she said. "I'll live."

He sighed and shook his head. "Wait here a minute."

He trotted over to his truck, fumbled in the glove box and returned with the small first-aid kit he always carried. "Let me see that."

"Why am I not surprised that you have a first-aid kit?" she asked, but she let him take her foot on his lap.

The skin had broken and the blister was a large, angry red. He opened an antibiotic wipe and cleansed it carefully, scolding himself internally for enjoying the opportunity to touch her delicate foot.

"Ow!" She winced when the medicine touched the broken skin.

"Sorry." He patted her ankle. "Now we'll bandage you up."

He rubbed antibiotic ointment over the hurt spot and pressed on a bandage. "There," he said. He kept a loose grip on her foot, strangely reluctant to let it go.

Without the daytime bustle, Main Street felt peaceful. The streetlights had come on. Overhead were leafy trees, and beyond them, stars were starting to blink in the graying sky.

Down the street, the lights of the Chatterbox Café clicked off.

Susan looked at him with eyes wide and vulnerable above a forced-looking smile. "Didn't you want to stay and talk with the wife Helen picked out for you?"

He felt one side of his mouth quirk up. "Was it that obvious?"

"Kinda. She seemed really nice."

"Yes, she is." He squeezed her foot a little tighter. "And no, I didn't want to stay. Not when I realized you were missing."

"I'm sorry."

"Hey." He touched her chin. "I wanted to come find you."

"How come?"

The question hung in the air between them. He looked at her lips.

Which parted a little, very prettily, and then Susan pulled her foot off his lap and twisted it around her other leg, looking nervous. "Sam…"

He brushed back a strand of hair that had tumbled down her forehead. Her skin felt soft as a baby's.

He breathed in, and leaned forward, and pressed his lips to hers.

Susan's heart pounded faster than a rock-and-roll drumbeat as Sam kissed her. Just a light brush of the lips took her breath away.

She lifted her hands, not sure whether she meant to stop him or urge him on, and her hands encountered the rough stubble on his cheek. Intrigued, she stroked his face, getting to know the planes and angles she'd been studying, without intending to, for days.

What did this mean? And why, oh why, did it have to feel so good? She drew in a sharp breath, almost a gasp, because he hadn't moved away. His handsome face was still an inch from hers, and this felt like every forbidden dream she'd ever had, coming true.

"Close your eyes," he said in his bossy way that, right now, didn't bother her in the least.

And he leaned closer and pressed his lips to hers again, just a little harder.

Susan's heart seemed to expand in her chest, reaching out toward his. Everything she'd admired about him, everything she'd been drawn to, seemed alive in the air around them.

There was a booming sound, a bunch of crackling pops, and she jerked back as Sam lifted his head. At the same time, they both realized what it was.

"Fireworks!" Sam exclaimed, a grin crossing his face. "How appropriate." He studied her tenderly. "Was that okay?"

Was it okay that he'd rocked her world? Was it okay that his lightest touch made her feel as if she was in love with him? "When I kissed my boss, I felt fireworks," she joked awkwardly to cover the tension she felt.

He looked stricken as the fireworks continued to create a display above their heads, green and red and gold. "Oh, Susan, I'm sorry."

"For what?"

"I was forgetting for a minute that you're an employee. That was completely inappropriate."

Amidst the popping and booming sounds, his words were too much to process. She was still reeling from how his kiss had made her feel, and she couldn't think why he was looking so upset.

Unless he wished he hadn't done it.

"Come on," he said, and pulled her to her feet. He didn't hold her hand, though; as soon as he was sure she was steady, he stepped a foot away. Too far! her heart called, wanting her to grab on to him. But she squashed the feelings down.

A minute later, she was in his truck and headed to his house. He drove like a silent statue, a muscle twitching in his jaw.

He pulled up in the driveway and stared straight ahead. "We'll talk tomorrow. Again, I apologize."

She looked at him, confused. Clearly she was being dismissed.

Was he angry at himself for having let his feelings go out of control? Did he even *have* feelings, or had that been just a guy thing, driven by testosterone rather than his heart?

She wanted to ask him about it, but suddenly, there was no closeness available for such a discussion.

And she was just a little too fragile to push it tonight, when her lips still tingled from his kiss, her fingertips still remembered the way his strong jaw had felt beneath them.

She'd have to face what had just happened, but not tonight.

The next morning, Sam was in his office trying to put out a few fires before his employee party when there was a hesitant knock on the door.

"Come in." He tried to ignore the way his heart leaped, but it was next to impossible. His heart knew it was Susan; Mindy wouldn't have knocked, and who else would be in the house? And his heart was very interested in being near the woman who'd kissed him back so sweetly last night.

Sure enough, it was her. Dressed in another faded red, white and blue T-shirt and short jeans and wearing a worried frown. When their eyes met, she blushed and looked away. "We have a problem."

"What's wrong?"

"I just talked to Pammy. The one who's doing the kids' entertainment for the party? Only…she can't do it."

"What do you mean?" He felt relieved that she was all business this morning. Maybe that would help his racing pulse slow down.

"They had a death in the family and they all have to rush down to West Virginia to the funeral. And since it's a family-run business, that's pretty much everyone."

He blew out a breath, thinking of all his employees with families. They looked forward to this event as a time when they could kick back and relax, bring the kids, knowing it would be fun for everyone.

"Any ideas?" he asked. Because if there was one thing he'd learned about Susan, it was that she was good in an emergency.

"As a matter of fact, yes!" A smile broke out on her face, and Sam's mouth went dry. When she was excited about something, she was pretty much irresistible.

"What's the idea?" he asked, his voice a little hoarse.

"Let's get dogs from Troy's rescue to come be the entertainment."

"No." He shook his head. "That won't work."

"Why not?"

"Dogs, instead of a clown and a dunking tank and carnival games?"

She waved a hand impatiently. "Kids like real things better than all that," she said. "If you don't believe me, ask Mindy which she'd rather see."

"Oh, I know what Mindy would choose," he said, mock-glaring at her. "She's been on me nonstop about getting a dog. It's almost like someone put her up to it." He stepped closer.

Susan's eyes darkened and her breathing quickened. "That's an argument for another day," she said primly. "And it proves my point: kids love dogs."

"It's not safe," he explained, stepping back from her dangerous appeal and half sitting on the edge of his desk. "There are liability issues. If someone got bitten, it would be on Hinton Enterprises, and bad PR as well. And more than that, I like to take care of my employees, not put them at risk."

Susan nodded, sinking down to perch on his leather client seat. "Can't we post a warning? And Troy wouldn't bring any dogs who weren't friendly."

Sam shrugged. "A warning might solve the liability issue, but..."

"But you don't like change," she said.

He opened his mouth to argue and then closed it again. "You're right, I don't. We've had Pammy do the kids' entertainment for ten years."

"But sometimes, change has to happen," she said gently. "Pammy can't help it that she's unavailable this year. Her grandma passed."

Troy felt like a heel. "I'll send flowers," he said, making a note to himself.

"Write down, 'Puppy for Mindy's birthday,'" she suggested.

He looked up at her. She was messing with him! "Don't you ever take anything seriously?"

"Yes. Like the fact that an only child like Mindy needs a pet."

"We don't have time for a puppy."

"People manage!" She waved a hand. "There are dog walkers. Doggie day cares. Daisy was saying that new woman in town, your special friend, might start one."

"We're losing focus. Isn't there an easier way to entertain kids? You're the expert in that. Think of something!" He stood and started pacing back and forth in front of his desk, filled with restless energy.

"Yes, and I had an expert idea," she said. "The dogs. Let me go with it, Sam. It'll work great, you'll see. You won't be disappointed."

She didn't get it, how important this business, these people, were to him. How he wanted things to stay the same for them, wanted them to be safe. He stopped directly in front of her, crossing his arms. "No."

"It's community service," she teased, cocking her head to one side. "Helping animals. Doesn't that make Hinton Enterprises look good?" She edged neatly out of the chair and went around behind it, creating a barrier between them. She leaned on the back of the chair, her eyes sparkling.

He frowned away the energy her smile evoked in him. "You sure you didn't have training as a lawyer?"

"Just four or five dogs," she said, ignoring his question. "And Troy would be there the whole time."

Sam felt as if he was losing a business negotiation,

which never happened. But then again, he never sat across the table from a negotiator like Susan.

She raised an eyebrow at him. "Embrace the change, Sam. Sometimes, it can be a good thing."

He sighed. "If Troy can be there the whole time," he said grudgingly, "I guess we can give it a try."

Chapter 8

Susan slipped out midmorning and power-walked to the park in downtown Rescue River. Hopefully, the materials to set up for Sam's work picnic would be here. Hopefully, Daisy would be, too, to help her.

Hopefully, Sam wouldn't be anywhere nearby.

She didn't need the distraction of her boss, kisser *extraordinaire*.

Last night had been amazing, wonderful. Her heart, which she kept so carefully guarded beneath her mouthy exterior, had shown itself to be the marshmallow that it was and melted.

And as a result, Sam's coldness and dismissal afterward had bludgeoned said heart.

Back to the old way, the independent way. She'd decided it last night, and kept herself busy putting out fires and getting the new kids' entertainment orga-

nized this morning. Their little argument had fanned
the attraction flames a bit, but she'd stayed businesslike and she was proud of it.

As she got to the park, she was glad to see that the
large tent was up and the tables there. Sam spared no
expense for his workers, but at the same time, he didn't
want it to be overly fancy. He just wanted everyone to
feel comfortable and have fun. So her job was to add
a touch of down home to the whole thing.

"Hey!" Daisy strolled toward her, yawning.
"Where's the coffee?"

Knowing her friend, Susan had stopped at the
Chatterbox and picked up two cups. "Here's yours,
black with sweetener." She handed it over.

Daisy sank down on a bench beside the tent while
Susan opened all the boxes.

"Here's our centerpieces," Susan said, holding up a
bunch of kids' tractors. "Sam had me order enough so
that every kid can take one home. We'll march them
along the green runners so it looks like they're, you
know, on a farm."

"Sweet." Daisy took a long drink of coffee.

And it *was* sweet. Sam was good to his employees.
An amazing boss, an amazing man. A real catch.

Just not for her.

To distract herself from the sudden ache in her heart,
Susan looked around. There was a father and son tossing a softball while a nearby mom spread a red-and-
white plastic tablecloth over the picnic table. At one of
the park's pavilions, two pregnant women sprawled on
benches while their husbands fired up the park's grills
and a couple of babies played at their feet.

And there was Fiona, the new mom in town, pushing her youngest on the swings while her other three children kicked a ball nearby.

Susan had talked to her mom this morning. Apparently Donny was doing well at camp, but her mom sounded not so great. Surprisingly lonely. She'd even asked about how Susan was doing and how she liked her new job, whether she needed anything. It was an uncharacteristically maternal call, and Susan wondered what was going on with her mother.

Thinking about her family made her miss them. Susan sighed. "Holidays can be hard for us single folks."

Daisy didn't answer, and when Susan glanced over, she saw that her friend's eyes were filled with tears.

"What's wrong, honey?" Susan asked, sinking down onto the bench beside her.

Daisy shook her head. "I'm so tired of being single, but I just can't get into dating."

"Not even Dion?"

Daisy stared at her as if she'd grown two heads. "No!"

"Why not?"

"We're friends. I don't want to mess up a good friendship by trying to go romantic."

"But friendship is a good basis—"

"No way."

"Keep praying about it," Susan said, because obviously her friend wasn't open to discussing the topic further, "and I will, too."

"Pray about yourself while you're at it," Daisy advised, "because you and Sam have some major vibes going on between you."

Heat climbed into Susan's cheeks. "It's obvious?"

"To me, it is, because I know both of you so well," Daisy said. "What's going on between the two of you, anyway?"

Susan contemplated telling her best friend about the kiss. For about ten seconds. But Daisy was protective of her brother and Susan wasn't at all sure about how she felt about it, so she clamped her jaw shut and got busy unpacking tractor centerpieces.

"Susan? Are you seriously not going to answer?"

"Nothing's going on," Susan said firmly.

A welcome distraction came in the form of Xavier, who jumped into Daisy's lap. A minute later, Angelica appeared with baby Emmie in her arms, breathless. "Hey, guys," she said.

"Where's Mindy?" Xavier asked.

"She'll be here soon, with her dad. Which makes me think we'd better get more done."

"Oh, Sam will be worrying, all right," Daisy said.

"Hey," Angelica said. "Is Mindy all set for camp?"

"I think so," Susan said. "It's next weekend, right?"

"That's right," Angelica said, "but when I mentioned it to Sam, he didn't seem to know anything about it."

"I told him," Susan said. "He wrote the check. I'll talk to him about it." But uneasiness clenched her stomach. The camp was one Xavier was attending for a week, with Angelica, and they had a special program where younger siblings and relatives could come for a weekend. She and Angelica had discussed it, and while she'd explained the details to Sam, he'd been distracted. She'd been surprised when he said it was okay.

Hopefully, this was just a little misunderstanding she could clear up quickly when he arrived, and then she could fade into the background and refill bowls of potato chips and play with Mindy.

They soon had the tent decorated in patriotic, farm decor. Just in time, because the caterers arrived to put out the food, all-American hot dogs and hamburgers, plus a taco bar and tamales.

She and Daisy sank down at a picnic table with cold drinks.

"I'm sweating already," Daisy said.

"Me, too." Susan fanned herself with a napkin.

"Any thoughts of getting work done?" came a stern voice behind them.

The hairs on Susan's arms stood on end. Sam.

Daisy raised her eyebrows at Susan, ignoring her brother. "Somebody's cranky. Wonder what's wrong with him?"

He kissed me and he regrets it. Susan shrugged. "Who knows?"

Mindy, who'd come with Sam but stopped at the swings where Xavier was, ran up to them. "Daddy, Xavier says I can ride with them to camp. And I'm going to stay in a tent!"

Sam looked down at her and then his face focused. "Camp? What camp?"

Mindy looked worriedly at Susan. "I'm going to that camp with Xavier. Right?"

"Right," she said reassuringly, and turned to Sam. Best to get this over with now. "It's that special-needs camp. Xavier goes every summer, as a cancer survivor. They have a program for kids with limb differences. We talked about this."

"No, we didn't. When is it and where?"

"It's next weekend, or at least, Mindy's part is only for the weekend. In West Virginia."

Sam's eyes widened. "She's not going to sleepaway camp in West Virginia. She's five!"

"Daddy! I'm almost six!" Mindy drew a big six in the air to make sure everyone understood.

Susan squatted down. "I'll explain it all to Daddy. You run and keep Xavier company, okay?"

"Okay," Mindy said doubtfully, and ran off.

Sam's face was tight and closed as she led him over to a quieter part of the park.

"We talked about this. It's a done deal." Even as she spoke, guilt clutched at her. Sam had been distracted with Helen's arrival, the evening after they'd gone to the lake. He'd gotten a phone call when she'd been explaining the details, and he'd signed the check amidst a lot of other household expenses.

He shook his head. "I didn't okay her sleeping away. She's way too young."

"They have programs for younger kids who go with relatives. Angelica's going." She paused for emphasis. "Sam, I think it'll be good for her. She needs to meet other kids with limb differences."

"No."

Susan drew in her breath and counted to ten. "She's going to be very disappointed. She wants to go with Xavier. And Angelica will be there the whole time."

"Parents can go?"

She nodded, knowing exactly what he would say.

"Then I'll go."

"Sam." She touched his arm. "Troy and Angelica think it'll be best if you don't go."

"Troy and Angelica aren't Mindy's parents. And neither are you."

That truth hit her like a whip to the heart. She needed to watch herself, because her feelings as Mindy's nanny had begun to overflow their professional boundaries. It was all too easy to love the little girl. Easy to care too much about Mindy's dad, too, who was currently glaring at her, intent on putting her in her place.

She swallowed her hurt feelings. "I know that! I'm just someone who cares about her and has a role taking care of her. And who knows what kids with special needs, need."

He glared. "If I'm not going, then Mindy can't, either."

She threw up her hands, exasperated. "Fine. It's your money you're wasting. And it's you who can explain to Mindy why she can't go. I'm going to…" She looked around. "Set up the salt and pepper shakers at a perfect angle because I'm sure the control-freak boss of Hinton Enterprises will come in and redo it if I don't."

She spun and stormed into the tent.

Soon Sam was back in charming boss mode, and Susan watched him and marveled at his self-control. He'd been furious at her five minutes ago, but now he was all professional.

And it was clear his employees loved him. They crowded around him, and teased, but with respect; they listened to everything he had to say.

There was a moment when she thought the dog thing was going to be a disaster. Just when he'd stood to make his traditional speech, a squirrel had run past the dog crates and the dogs had gone haywire with barking, drowning out whatever Sam was saying.

But Sam responded graciously, with a joke, while Troy got the dogs under control, and then Sam continued his speech without a hitch.

Several people expressed interest in adopting dogs. And the local paper had come to cover the event and snapped more pictures of the dogs than anything else. Undoubtedly, there'd be a feel-good story featuring Hinton Enterprises in the paper tomorrow.

The downside, if you were looking at it from Sam's point of view, was that Mindy fell in love with a little black-and-white mutt with a bandage on one leg. While Mindy cradled it, Troy explained to Sam how it was non-shedding and, at three years old, already housetrained. "It'll probably always have a limp, though," Troy had said.

"It's got a hurt paw, like me," Mindy had said, cuddling the dog.

Susan's heart squeezed, and she looked up at Sam. The raw love for his little girl that shone out of his eyes almost hurt. She had a feeling that Mindy would end up with that little dog as a birthday present.

As the party went on, Sam seemed to let go of control a little bit and relax. The children played with the dogs and enjoyed the park and the play equipment, running hard, making up games. That gave the adults space to linger over their plates of food, talking and laughing. Aside from a few teenagers, no one seemed to have their cell phones out.

It was an old-fashioned type of picnic that could have just as easily taken place fifty years ago. A perfect kind of event for an old-fashioned, close-knit community like Rescue River, and Susan was proud of her part in organizing it.

Until the topic of Sam's being single came up. "We think Mr. Hinton needs a girlfriend," said Eduardo, a good-looking, thirtysomething groundsman at Hinton Enterprises. He sometimes moonlighted for Sam, helping with the landscaping around the house, and seemed to hold a privileged position among the Hinton workers; right now, he was sitting at a table with Sam and five or six other employees.

Sam's father, who'd been sitting at an adjoining table with Susan and Daisy, spoke up. "That's exactly what he needs. But not just a girlfriend, a wife."

"And a mama for his little girl," one of the older secretaries said.

"Hey, what about Susan?" someone said, and the group at the picnic table turned to look at her. "She's single, and she already takes care of Mindy."

"Good call," Eduardo said. *"Muy bonita."*

Totally mortified, Susan stared at the ground. She knew she should come up with some kind of a joke to make the moment go by easily, but for the life of her, she couldn't think of one.

"You people need to stick to business, and so do I." Sam's voice was strained.

"But Daddy," Mindy chimed in, climbing up into Sam's lap, "I *do* want a mommy!"

The images evoked by those sweet words made Susan's cheeks flame and her heart ache with longing. To be wanted, needed, cherished. To finally have a real home.

She stole a glance at Sam's clenched jaw. Obviously, his employees' suggestions hadn't induced the same images and longings in him. And he wasn't finding the gentle jokes funny, either.

If only the ground would open up and swallow her.

Sam stood under a giant oak tree in the Rescue River Park, talking to a group of five or six longtime employees who didn't seem to want to leave.

Even while he listened and laughed with them, he couldn't help watching Susan.

Apparently, she'd recovered just fine from that awkward moment with his employees. She was tying garbage bags and helping to carry heavy food trays to the truck. When a little boy ran up crying, she squatted down to listen, then took his hand and walked back to the tent to find the tractor he'd left on a table.

As he watched, Eduardo approached her, spoke for a minute, then gave her a friendly handshake that, to Sam's eyes, went on a little bit too long and was accompanied by a little too much eye contact.

He tamped the jealousy down. He didn't want Susan as a long-term part of his life, so why feel bad when other men admired her? She was totally inappropriate for him. Just witness this whole ridiculous camp situation. His blood pressure rose just thinking of Mindy going to camp.

Marie would never have allowed it.

But Marie's gone, and you have to move on.

That new voice inside him was unfamiliar and unwelcome, but Sam was honest enough to know that it spoke truth. He had to stop focusing on Marie, had to let her go.

But if he did that, would his life be as it had been for the past twenty-four hours—crazy and emotional?

Going from the intense excitement of kissing Susan to the low of feeling guilty, like a bad boss hitting on his employee? Angry about the camp. Embarrassed by his workers' jokes.

He didn't want such an exciting life, couldn't handle it. He wanted life on an even keel. Stable. Comfortable.

As he bid goodbye to the final couple of workers, his father approached. He'd stayed in the background during the picnic, letting Sam have center stage, but Sam had been conscious of him, as always. Though his father's health didn't permit him to run Hinton Enterprises anymore, he'd started the company and cared about its success, and Sam always respected his opinions.

"What did you think?" he asked his dad.

His father clapped him on the back. "Another good picnic," he said. "You have a way with the workers. They like you."

"Thanks." He knew what his father wasn't saying; the workers liked Sam better than they'd liked his father. Personality difference, and maybe the struggles of starting something from the ground up. His father wasn't an easy man to get along with.

Sam knew he wasn't always easy, either, but he at least could laugh at himself—usually—and listen to other people's ideas, talents his father had never mastered.

Since his father was so hard to please, his approving remarks about the event felt good.

They turned together to stroll back toward the almost-empty tent. Just in time to see Mindy run to Susan, hug her legs and get lifted into her arms.

"Looks like those two are close," Mr. Hinton remarked.

Sam nodded slowly. "It sure does."

"You worried about that?" Mr. Hinton asked.

"A little," Sam admitted. "But Mindy needs women in her life. She's attached to Daisy, and now to Angelica, but those two aren't always around. Susan fills in the gaps, that's all."

"Are you sure that's all?" His father's thick eyebrows came together, and though he was a good head shorter than Sam, his expression was enough to make Sam feel ashamed, as if his father had seen that moment under the street lamp.

"It has to be," he said. "Things couldn't work between us."

Mr. Hinton nodded, looking relieved. "I didn't think she was your type, but I was starting to wonder. Figured you'd do the right thing." He shook his head. "Back in my day, races didn't mix. Oh, we always had a lot of different colors in Rescue River, but for marrying, they stuck to themselves. Times might be changing, but it's hard for me to keep up."

"Dad," Sam said automatically. "What a person looks like doesn't matter, you know that. We're all of the same value to God."

His father frowned at him. "Never thought to hear you spouting religion at me."

Sam laughed. "Surprise myself sometimes," he said.

As his father walked off, Sam sank down on a park bench rather than interrupting the moment between Mindy and Susan. He needed to think.

He probably needed to pray, too, but this wasn't the time or the place.

Still, under the stars, he thought about his goal of finding a mother for Mindy and made a decision.

He wouldn't try so hard to replace Marie anymore. It wasn't working, and it wasn't possible.

But a woman like Susan wasn't possible, either. He wasn't the man to handle it.

Instead, he'd focus on being the best single dad he could be.

People did that. Look at his employee, Eduardo; he'd been a single parent for years. And several other dads at Mindy's school were going it alone.

Anyway, Susan was way too young for him.

He'd go forward single and let Mindy's nurturing needs be filled by his female relatives, by teachers, by the church.

It wasn't what Marie had wanted, and looking up into the starry sky, he shot an apology her way. "I'm sorry, Marie," he whispered. "I don't think I can keep my promise, at least not right now."

He let out a huge sigh as sadness overwhelmed him.

The quest to remarry had helped him get by, had given him a goal. Without it, emptiness and loneliness pushed at him like waves lapping the shore.

He had to find his center again, his stability. Had to get right with God. Had to learn to go on alone.

It was the only thing he could do, but it didn't feel good. Just for a minute, he let his head sink down into his hands and mourned the loss of a dream.

The next morning, Sam broke all of his own Sunday morning rules, flipping on a mindless TV show for Mindy and handing her a donut. Then he ushered Susan into his office.

She was wearing close-fitting black pants and a jade-green sleeveless shirt that showed off her tanned, shapely arms. Jade earrings swung from her ears, giving her a carefree vibe. But her expression was closed tight.

During the night, he'd gotten over some of his anger about the camp situation. He probably hadn't listened carefully enough to what she'd been telling him. Half the time, when Susan talked to him, he got caught up in her honeysuckle perfume and her shiny hair and her lively, sparkling dark eyes; it wasn't surprising that he might have missed some of the details she'd shared with him.

Now that he'd made a new commitment to staying single, maybe he could pay more attention to what she had to say.

And today, he just had to keep a cool, professional distance, make her see reason and get her on his side, so that she could help him explain to Mindy that she wouldn't be going to camp.

"Sit down," he said, ushering her to the same chair she'd sat in the day he'd interviewed her. Thinking of that day almost made him chuckle. When he'd suspected she'd be a handful to work with, he hadn't been wrong.

She perched warily on the edge of the seat. "We only have half an hour before we should leave for church," she said. "Or at least, I'm going to church. Are you?"

He nodded. "There'll be time. He spread his hands and gave her a friendly-but-impersonal smile. "I guess when I agreed to Mindy going to camp, I wasn't really listening," he said. "I'm sorry about that, but I really do think she's too young to go."

Susan nodded, and for the first time he noticed that there were dark circles under her eyes. "I lay awake thinking about it, and I want you to know I feel bad about what happened. I should have made sure I had your full attention about such an important decision."

Relief washed over him. This wasn't going to be as hard as he'd feared. "I'm glad you see it my way."

"Well, but I don't exactly see it your way," she said, flashing a smile at him. "You were wrong, too, not to pay attention about your child's summer plans. Now Mindy has a spot at the camp and some other child doesn't. It wouldn't be right to back out."

He hadn't thought of that. "I'll pay for the place," he said, waving his hand in an effort to dismiss her concern. Wanting to dismiss it himself, and not quite succeeding.

"It's not just that, Sam," she said quietly. "Mindy needs this camp. She needs to go where other kids with limb differences are. She needs to see what's possible for her and what's positive. For example, why doesn't she have an artificial limb?"

"We tried that when she was little. She hated it."

"From what I've read, that's common," she said. "But now that she's a little older, she might want one. And I'm sure the technology has advanced. It's something she can learn about at the camp, get a feel for it, see some kids with artificial limbs and others managing without."

He had to admit, Susan had a point. "In that case, maybe she should go. And—" he said to cut off Susan's expression of victory. "I should go, too."

She bit her lip and shook her head, looking regretful. "I thought of that. I mean, of getting you a space there, too. The problem is that the camp is entirely full. There are no more spaces for adults. I checked online last night, and they texted me a confirmation this morning. No more space."

He frowned. "Then she can't go."

"Sam." Susan leaned forward. "Why don't you want her to, really?"

The question floated in the air.

"I wish you hadn't talked to her about it so much," he heard himself blustering, knowing he was avoiding giving her an answer.

She nodded slowly. "I'm sorry. I should have made sure you understood what you were signing." Her voice was contrite. "And the last thing I want to do is cause Mindy to be disappointed. I...I really have no vested interest in this happening, Sam. For what mistakes I've made, I apologize."

Her accepting responsibility took the wind out of his sails. "I made mistakes, too," he said grudgingly. "I get too caught up in my work and don't pay attention to other people enough. You're...not the first person who's told me that."

"Anyone can get distracted," she said with a shrug. "So you're not perfect."

"That's it?" he asked. "You're not going to yell at me?"

She looked amused. "No. Should I?"

He settled back and stared at her, then down at his desk. That was new to him. Susan admitted her own mistakes, and she accepted that he made mistakes, too.

Hashing things out with someone like Susan, openly flawed, was actually a little more comfortable than arguing with someone practically perfect, like Marie.

Guilt washed over him. The very thought that there was something as good as, even better than, being with Marie seemed disloyal.

"Hey." Susan grabbed an old ruler that was sitting on the edge of his desk and gave his hand a light, playful whack. "What's going on in there? You never answered my question. Why are you so afraid to let Mindy go to camp with her aunt and cousin?"

He grabbed the ruler, pointed it at her and met her eyes. "I do have my reasons, young lady."

She lifted an eyebrow, waiting.

"The main reason is..." He started, then paused.

"Spill it."

He looked out the window, watching the leaves rustle in the slight breeze. "The main reason is that I don't like her to be so far out of my sight."

"Out of your control, hmm?" She was laughing at him. "Get used to it, Dad. She's growing up."

He smiled ruefully. "I'm not ready for that."

"Are you really going to be so lonely?" she asked in a teasing voice. "If it's too much to face alone, I can keep you company."

"Oh, is that so?" His whole body felt sharp with interest and surprise and...something else.

A pretty pink blush flamed across her cheeks. She picked up his tape holder and studied it with intense interest.

His hand shot out to cover hers. "A date? Maybe at Chez La Ferme?"

She dropped the tape holder and tried to pull her hand back, but he held on until she met his eyes.

"Are you asking me out?"

"Would you go?"

Their eyes met and held. Their hands were pressed together, too, and it didn't seem like either of them was breathing.

Then she pulled back and looked away, and he let her go.

"Now it's you who hasn't answered my question," he said, barely recognizing his own throaty voice. "Will you go out with me?"

"I don't…I don't know."

He leaned forward, not sure if he should press his advantage or retract the question. He knew what he *wanted* to do, but was it the right thing? "I shouldn't be asking you out when you're an employee. I don't mean to put any pressure on you, at all. You have your job whether you say yes or no. Nothing would change."

Her dark eyes flashed up to meet him. "Thanks for that," she said. "I appreciate your being so careful, considering that I'm just a temporary nanny. And… well, it's true that I don't have plans for the weekend."

Triumph surged through him, but he tamped it down.

"And I've never actually eaten at Chez La Ferme."

"So what you're saying is…" He prompted.

"Yes," she said, her voice a little bit breathy. "Yes, I'll go out with you."

And she stood, spun and hurried out of the room, leaving Sam to wonder what on earth he'd been thinking to ask Susan out.

Chapter 9

The next Friday afternoon, Susan climbed the stairs to her over-the-garage apartment, arguing with Daisy the whole way. Quiet Fern was following along, shaking her head.

"It doesn't make sense for me to get all dressed up. This is Sam! He's seen me in my sweats, in my ratty jeans, without makeup…"

"But you're going to Chez La Ferme," Fern said hesitantly. "That's super dressy, right?"

"Exactly!" Daisy said, her voice triumphant. "You can't wear ratty jeans to Chez La Ferme."

"They fired me once, what more can they do to me?" Susan asked as she opened the door. "Come on in. Not like I have a choice about it."

"I'm sorry, Susan," Fern said, looking stricken. "If you don't want us here…"

"Fern. You're fine. It's *her* I don't want." Susan flung an arm toward her best friend. "Because she's got some kind of an agenda that I don't share."

Daisy ignored her, walked over to the refrigerator and pulled out sodas.

"Make yourself at home, why don't you?" Susan said sarcastically. But the truth was, she was glad to have the other two women around. She was way too antsy about her date with Sam tonight.

Why had she offered to keep him company? Why had he jumped on the idea and upped the ante to a real date at Chez La Ferme? Maybe it was just something to do, and after all, he did sort of own the restaurant. Maybe this was all just business.

She'd run into Daisy at the library and made the mistake of confiding the reason for her anxiety. Daisy had taken one look at her and insisted on coming back to help her get dressed. Since Fern was leaving work at the same time, they'd talked her into coming along.

Now, Susan tore open a bag of BBQ potato chips and started pouring them into a bowl, only to have Daisy snatch the bag away. "No. Uh-uh. You're not eating those and then going on a date."

"Why not?" Susan asked.

Daisy and Fern looked at each other and burst out laughing.

"What?" Susan looked from one to the other.

"It's just," Fern said, still chuckling, "if you would happen to get close enough to kiss…"

"Your breath would reek like a third grader's," Daisy finished.

"We're not getting close enough to kiss," Susan said as heat climbed up her face.

"Here." Daisy found a bag of pretzels and tossed it to her. "Have these instead. Fern and I will eat the stinky chips."

"Well, actually," Fern said, blushing, "I think I'll stick to pretzels, too."

Daisy's eyebrows shot up. "Plans with Carlo tonight?"

"We like to watch movies on Friday nights, and it's my turn to pick."

"What are you watching?"

Fern grinned. "*Casablanca*. What's not to like? There's manly war drama for Carlo and romance for me."

"Fine," Daisy said, grabbing the bag of chips. "So I'm the only one without plans. I get the whole bag. Now, what are you wearing tonight?"

"I don't know." Susan looked at the pretzels but had no appetite. She took a sip of diet soda instead. "I have, like, one fancy dress, and I haven't worn it in a year at least. I don't know if it even fits."

"Let's see it," Daisy ordered.

Susan walked back to her bedroom and pulled out the turquoise silk. With a mandarin collar and buttons up the front, it fit snugly and had a perfectly modest hemline...until you noticed the slit that revealed a little leg.

But was that too dressy? This was Sam. She rummaged in her closet and pulled out a plain black skirt. She carried both garments out. "I'm thinking the skirt," she said.

Both Fern and Daisy said "no" at the same time.

"Wear the blue one," Daisy ordered.

"It's gorgeous," Fern agreed.

"But it's Sam, and it's Rescue River. Won't I feel way out of place?"

"You used to work at Chez La Ferme, right? Don't people dress up to go there?"

Susan thought back and nodded, reluctantly. Even Miss Minnie Falcon had worn a beaded dress when she'd come to the restaurant, and most of the men wore suits.

"What's Sam wearing?" Fern asked.

Susan shrugged. "I don't know." Truthfully, they hadn't seen much of each other since that weighted conversation that had led to this date. She wouldn't have thought they were on, except he'd sent her a text message confirming the time. And he'd washed his sleek black sports car and parked it in the driveway, so evidently they weren't going in her car. As if, Susan thought, giggling a little hysterically.

"I'll text him," Daisy offered.

"No!" Susan grabbed for her phone.

"Why not?"

"I don't want him to think I care what we wear!"

"Because..."

"Because I don't want it to seem like a real date!" Her voice broke on the last word and she sank down onto the couch, focusing on pinching a thread off the blue dress while she pulled herself together.

"Hey," Daisy said, coming to sit next to her. "You sound really upset. What's wrong?"

Susan swallowed the lump in her throat. "My dad sent me this dress because he said I had nothing decent to wear on dates with a real good prospect. So that's where I did wear it: on dates with my ex-fiancé."

"Oh." Daisy nodded.

"You were engaged?" Fern asked, her voice sympathetic.

Susan waved her hand impatiently. "Ancient history. It didn't work out because he wanted a dishrag of a wife. Like all businesspeople." She shot a glare at Daisy. "Like Sam, so don't go matching me up permanently with him."

"Who said anything about that?"

"Nobody!" Heat clamped into Susan's cheeks. Nobody had said anything about a permanent connection between her and Sam, so why had she mentioned it? What was she thinking?

"Don't you want to get married someday?" Fern asked quietly.

"No!" Susan said. "Marriage sucks the life out of women."

"It doesn't have to," Fern said. "I'm really looking forward to marrying Carlo."

Way to put your foot in your mouth, Susan. "I'm just going on my mom's example. I'm sorry," Susan apologized. "What you and Carlo have seems wonderful. But for me...for women in my family...marriage is the path to destruction."

"Nothing like being melodramatic," Daisy said, looking up from her phone.

"I'm not being melodramatic. I'm afraid I'll lose myself and then he'll leave! Just like what happened to my mom."

The comment hung in the air.

"Oooh," Fern said. "That does sound scary."

Daisy shook her head. "The past doesn't have to repeat itself. You're a completely different woman from your mom." Her phone buzzed and she glanced down at it. "Sam's wearing a suit, by the way."

"You asked him?" Susan practically shouted.

"So you should wear the blue dress. Go put it on, since you're not going to eat."

Susan drew in her breath and let it out in a sigh, then did what her friend said.

Buttoning the cuffs of a new dress shirt—cuff links would probably be excessive for a woman like Susan—Sam looked in the mirror and thought of his teary departure from Mindy just a few hours ago.

Oh, Angelica had comforted her, all too well. It made him realize how much Mindy needed a female figure in her life. And while he wanted to go forward with his plan to be single, this whole camp thing had put him back in doubt. Mindy needed a mom.

And there was the additional question: with Mindy gone, what was he supposed to do with himself this weekend? He didn't even get to go pick Mindy up because Troy was going to the camp to visit Xavier and had offered to bring Mindy home.

I'll keep you company, Susan had said in her throaty voice. He used water to tame his unruly hair and then decided he should shave after all, and took off the shirt so he wouldn't get anything on it. Man, he was acting like a teenager. He'd been on so many dates. Why was this one such a big deal?

Because it's Susan.

Susan, who was completely inappropriate for him. Susan, who wouldn't fall into line easily with any of his plans, for Mindy or otherwise. Susan, who was way too full of opinions and ideas of her own.

Susan, whose hair was like silk and whose laughter was like jazz music, rich and complex.

Susan, the very thought of whom made his heart rate speed up.

He had it bad.

Susan sat back in her soft and comfortable chair at Chez La Ferme. "You really want to hear that story?" she asked.

"I'm curious why your engagement ended, but if you don't want to talk about it, it's okay. I want this evening to be fun for you, not bringing up unpleasant memories."

"No, it's okay." Susan was surprised at how comfortable she felt. Oh, there'd been a few awkward moments at first, like when he'd come to her door. She'd seen Sam in a suit before, but tonight, knowing he'd dressed up for her, she found him devastatingly handsome.

And when he'd seen her, he'd offered a simple "You look great," but the way his eyes had darkened had sent the heat rushing to her cheeks.

Men didn't usually look at her that way, as if she was gorgeous. It took some getting used to, but...she *could* get used to it. Could learn to love it.

Even so, she'd gone into the meal with her guard up, determined to keep her distance. But Sam, with his pleasant, non-threatening conversation, gentle questions and self-deprecating jokes, had ruthlessly displayed his charm, causing her to drop that guard right back down.

"So, your engagement?" he prompted.

She'd keep it light, in line with the rest of the evening. "We actually broke up in Infinite. That super-exclusive department store in LA?"

He looked surprised. "I'm familiar with it."

"Well then, you can imagine the scene. Frank, his mother, the high-powered registry consultant and me, in their bridal registry salon." She squirmed, remembering. "Not my kind of place."

"You seem more the casual type."

"Exactly. But he and his mom and the consultant were trying to get me to register for formal china and super-expensive linens, stuff none of my friends could afford." She shook her head. "I saw my mom's life flashing before my eyes, you know? Trying to live up to somebody else's dream, trying to make a man happy when he couldn't be pleased."

He nodded, actually seeming interested in her rambling story. "What did you do?"

"Well, I...I'd read about how you can just have charitable donations at your wedding instead of gifts."

"That's usually something older couples do, right? People that already have what they need to set up housekeeping?"

She shrugged. "We had what we needed. Especially compared to the kids who could benefit from donations to Children International, which is the group I decided I wanted our guests to donate to. Frank made plenty of money."

"Okay..."

"So I...kind of stood up and said we were done at Infinite, that we weren't going to do a bridal registry after all."

He arched an eyebrow. "I guess that didn't go over well."

"It didn't." She reflected back on the scene, the horror on the saleswoman's face, the identical disapproval on Frank's and his mother's. "It wasn't that they didn't like charity, it was that such things weren't done among their friends. We ended up yelling—well, I did—and I got kicked out of Infinite, and Frank was totally embarrassed, and then he didn't want to marry me anymore."

"And were you heartbroken?" he asked, the tiniest twinkle in his eye.

"No." She'd been hurt, of course, and her mother had been furious, but mostly, she'd felt relieved. "It made me realize how different we were, and that I could never have made him happy." And she was done talking about it and wanted to change the subject. "I ate too much tonight. That was really good."

He waved for the check and smiled at her. "I overdid it, too. Maybe we need a walk?"

"Sure."

"Was everything okay, you guys?" Tawny, their server, asked as she handed Sam the check. "It's so great to see you guys here! I can't get over it. And I'm learning how to stand up for myself better, Susan. What you did to that one jerk really made a difference to me."

Sam's pen, signing the check, slowed down, and he glanced up at Susan and raised an eyebrow.

She felt herself blushing. "I'm glad," she said, smiling at the girl, who did seem a little more mature than at the beginning of the summer. "You did a good job tonight. You're a better waitress than I'll ever be."

"Aw, thank you!"

Tawny hurried away as Max, the restaurant owner and Susan's former boss, approached their table. "I trust everything was satisfactory, Mr. Hinton?"

He looked up, winked at her. "Ask the lady."

Which put her former boss in the position of having to treat her as a valued customer. Ha! It felt so gratifying that she had to be gracious about it. "It was fantastic, Max. And it's a lot easier from this side of the table. Tawny's a good waitress."

After another minute of small talk, Sam made some subtle sign of dismissal and turned to Susan. "Ready for a walk?" he asked with just the faintest hint of wolfishness.

Suddenly, she wasn't sure, but she didn't want to let her nerves show. "Sounds good."

He held her elbow as she stood and helped her drape her lacy shawl around her shoulders. "How are your shoes?" he asked, looking down.

She held one out for him to see and was glad she'd painted her toenails to match her dress. "Wedges. Very comfortable."

"Good." He ushered her out of the restaurant with a hand on her back, nodding to a couple of patrons.

"You know," she said as soon as they were out in the parking lot, "we might've just started a whole lot of gossip."

"I didn't see Miss Minnie Falcon," Sam said with a smile.

"No, but that lady with the white updo? That's one of Miss Minnie's best friends. She'll describe us, and the news will be all over the Senior Towers." She frowned. "Not to mention that Tawny's a talker."

"You think people are that interested?"

"In you, yes. Everyone cares about who the local millionaire takes to dinner." By unspoken agreement, they'd started strolling away from town, down a dirt road between two fields, one planted with corn and one with soybeans. The rural fragrances blew on a warm breeze, pungent.

"I've taken a good number of guests to dinner there," Sam said. "It shouldn't be that noteworthy."

"Good to know I'm part of a crowd." She meant the remark to be a joke, but it came out sounding hurt.

He heard it, clearly, and put an arm around her shoulders. "I can truthfully say I've never had more fun." He squeezed her to his side. "You're a great conversationalist. I really like being with you."

"Thanks." Timidly, she put an arm around his waist, and her heart rate shot into the stratosphere, so she let it drop, pretending she'd just meant a quick hug. "I had a good time, too." She hesitated, then added, "I'm glad we're friends."

He turned to face her and took her hands in his. "Is that what we are, Susan? Friends?"

She looked up at him, noticing the way the moonlight highlighted the planes of his face. "Aren't we?"

He drew in a breath. "I'm…trying to figure that out." He looked to the side, across the cornfield, for a long moment and then looked back at her. "The thing is, I can't seem to get around this feeling I have for you. I've tried. I've told myself we're opposites, that it wouldn't work. I've tried to connect with women who are more my type. But it's not working, and I've got to admit to myself…" He leaned in. "I've got to admit, I'm falling in love with you."

Susan's heart fluttered madly, like a caged songbird, and she couldn't seem to catch her breath. This was the moment she'd never thought to have. Shouldn't she be thrilled? Why did she feel so confused?

She replayed what he'd said in her mind.

"I know you're your own woman and think your own way," he went on, "but I'm wondering if you might put some of that aside for Mindy and me."

The mention of Mindy pushed Susan's questions away for a minute. Mindy was a wonderful little girl, so easy to love.

But Sam… She looked up at him, biting her lip.

His smile told her he already knew what her reaction would be.

Because after all, when did the poor teacher from a messed-up family say no to the handsome millionaire?

He leaned down as if he was going to kiss her, and she took a giant step back. Back from him, and back from the confusion he was causing her.

Having her hands free from his felt better. Safer. She propped one on her hip. "So you overcame your scruples and fell in love against your better judgment? And I'm supposed to be grateful, and give up being my own woman, and put my own needs and plans aside?"

"I didn't mean it that way." Behind him, clouds skittered across the moon.

Her heart was still pounding, almost as if she was afraid. But she wasn't afraid, was she? She was angry. "Haven't you ever read *Pride and Prejudice*?"

Her tone pushed the romantic expression from his eyes. "No."

"Well, if you had, you'd know that this type of a declaration leaves a little bit to be desired," she snapped.

He shook his head as if to clear it. "Wait. I did something wrong, and I have no idea what it is."

"Seriously, Sam?" She put her hands on her hips. "You practically told me how bad you feel about…"

She couldn't say it. Couldn't acknowledge that he'd said he was falling in love with her.

Couldn't *believe* it.

"Wait a minute." He put his hands on her shoulders, trapping her. "I'm not saying I was right to try to date a certain type of woman. I'm just saying that getting over my past tendencies has been a process. And at the other side of the process…" He bent his head to one side and a crooked smile came onto his face. "At the other side of the process, was you."

She bit her lip. "I wasn't just standing here waiting for you, Sam. I'm not going to fall into your arms just because you've figured a few things out."

"And I wouldn't expect you to." He squeezed her shoulders, then let them go and took her hand, urging her to walk a little further. "I know it'll take time and courtship and compromise. I'm just hoping we can do that, is all."

And drat if she didn't still hear that certainty in his voice. She could read his thoughts: *there's no way Susan could say no to me.*

She walked along the dirt road beside him, fuming. This was exactly why she didn't want to get involved with a man. All this scary emotion, all this confusion. All this feeling of hearing his words and trying to interpret what he meant. It made her stomach hurt.

Best to just be alone. She'd always said it, always known it about herself, and here was exhibit A.

She walked faster.

Until she felt a hand on her shoulder, pressing down, stopping her. "Susan. Wait."

"What?" she asked impatiently without turning around.

Sam stepped in front of her so she couldn't proceed. He looked down at her. "What I really want," he said, "is to kiss you."

She opened her mouth to refuse, and she was going to, for sure. But then she saw that a muscle was twitching under his eye.

Was he nervous?

Sam, the millionaire, nervous?

She cocked her head to one side, looking at him. He'd certainly put on a good show of being the dominant, successful male, but now that she studied him, she could see other signs. The hand he brushed through his hair. The slight uncertainty in his eyes. The way that when his hand reached out to touch her cheek, she could see it trembling just a little.

Now that was different. Sam was so accustomed to putting on a show of confidence in the business world that maybe he didn't know how to conduct himself in the personal world. Maybe he was used to pushing and acting cocky because that's what worked in doing deals. Maybe he didn't know how annoying that trait was when you were trying to declare your feelings to a woman.

"Do you...do you have any of those feelings for me, too?" He was still touching her cheek. And there was still a slight quiver in his hand. "Look, I don't pretend to understand you, or to know exactly how to make this work—"

She reached up and pulled his face down to hers and kissed him.

At least she started to. She started to assume the leadership role, but he quickly took it back, and their connection was a give and take, sweet and intense and…electrifying.

Susan didn't want it to stop, but she felt as if she might pass out if it went on, so she took a step back and stared at him. "Wow."

He nodded slowly, never letting go of her eyes. "Wow."

Then he pulled her to his side and put an arm around her shoulders and they walked together in the direction of the car.

Just like before, only everything was completely different.

Everything was new.

Driving home, the air in the car felt pregnant with possibilities. Susan had never felt anything like those moments with Sam. Not when she was engaged; not on any other dates. Not ever.

And the slight bit of insecurity that he'd shown made her feel as if she knew him better than ever before. That she'd gotten to know another side of the arrogant millionaire. A side she liked better. A side she wanted to know better.

When they pulled up to the house, she wondered if he'd kiss her again. Wondered if her heart could stand it, or if it would race right out of control.

But there was no chance to find out. Because there, sitting in the glow of the headlights, was a familiar figure. "Sam?" she asked, hearing the shrillness at her own voice. "What on earth is my mother doing here?"

Chapter 10

Still reeling from the intensity of kissing Susan, from the emotions that swelled his heart, Sam climbed out of the car, looking from Susan to her mother and back again. Two more different women could scarcely be imagined.

Where Susan looked funky and individualistic, her mother looked perfectly proper. Hair in a neat, curly style, impeccable makeup, nails done.

He opened the car door for Susan and reached down to help her climb out. Sports cars weren't always the easiest for women to navigate in a dress.

"I'm sorry to just show up here," Mrs. Hayashi said, hurrying toward them, then stopping a few feet away. "I tried to call when I got in to Columbus, but I couldn't get through."

Susan fumbled in her purse for her phone. "I'm sorry, Mom. It was off."

"You've been out? Somewhere dressy?" There were questions in the older woman's voice. "What have you gotten on your shoes, Susie?"

Susan looked down, and so did Sam. "We took a walk," Susan said, coloring deeply.

The two women still hadn't hugged.

Mrs. Hayashi shot him a quick glance, and heat rose in Sam's face, too. Of course, a mother would wonder where her daughter's employer had taken her, and why, and what his intentions were.

If only he knew the answers.

The moon cast a silvery light, making jewels across Susan's dark hair. A chorus of cicadas chirped in rising and falling waves, punctuated by a dog barking somewhere down the road. New-mown grass sent its tangy summer smell from next door.

"Well, I'm forgetting my manners." The woman approached Sam and held out her hand. "I'm Madolyn Hayashi, Susie's mom. It was so kind of you to send me that airline ticket—"

"You *sent* her an *airline* ticket?" Susan's jaw dropped.

"I had the extra miles," Sam tried to explain. "And I overheard you talking about how you wanted to do that. I just thought I could speed it up a little and give you a nice surprise."

Susan shot him a glare, and he had the feeling that, if her mother weren't here, she'd have kicked him. "Mom," she said, "I was going to send you a ticket next week. I've been saving. You didn't have to take his."

"It was no problem." Sam wasn't sure what he'd done wrong. Was Susan upset that he'd sent her mom a ticket without telling her? Or was it that she didn't want her mom around?

"It was supposed to be for you to take a vacation," Susan went on. "For you to do something relaxing, now that you have a break from Donny."

"Oh, honey, I wanted to see you, not go to a spa!" Almost hesitantly, she stepped closer.

And then the two women lurched into a hug that started out awkward and then lingered long enough to get close. "I missed you so much," Mrs. Hayashi said finally, stepping back to hold Susan's hands. "Especially since Donny's away. I started thinking about things, things I've done wrong."

"Mom…" Susan's face twisted in a complicated expression of love and exasperation and sorrow.

"I know our relationship hasn't been the best, and I wanted to see you, to try to fix things. I had the means, thanks to your boss, so yesterday I just packed up my things and called the airlines, and today…here I am. You don't mind, do you?"

"Mom, I'm glad you're here," Susan said, her eyes shiny in that way Sam was learning meant she was trying not to cry. "If this is where you want to be, I'm glad you came."

Sam had been listening, arms crossed, and thinking at the same time. Susan's mother's words made him reflect about parenting: how quickly it all went by, how little time you really had with your kids. Look at Mindy, away at camp. The first of many times she'd wave and run away. She'd go farther and farther in the years to come.

Susan and her mother had a chance to renew their relationship, right now. And suddenly it came to him, brilliant in its perfect simplicity. "Tell you what," he said, "for once, you *can* have it both ways. There's a spa and resort just an hour away. I have an ownership interest in it, and I'd like to get you two a room and some spa treatments there. You can go pamper yourselves and reconnect."

And the side benefit was that he could figure out what on earth he was doing, kissing Susan.

"No way!" Susan turned away from her mother to face him, hands on hips. "You've already done enough for us, Sam. We couldn't possibly accept."

"I want you to," he said. Even more than with Marie, who'd grown up wealthy, he found he liked providing special things for Susan, who wasn't so used to it. Susan didn't expect people to do things for her; she almost had the reverse of the entitlement mentality he'd seen among so many of his younger workers. "Just take me up on the offer in the spirit it's meant. No obligations, no strings. I just want you to enjoy some time with your mom."

"No!" She was shaking her head. "It's not… We're not…" She lifted her hands, palms up, clearly at a loss to explain.

"Susie." Her mother put a perfectly manicured hand on Susan's shoulder. "It makes him feel good to do it. Men like to do nice things for women."

Susan's eye-roll was monumental, and for just a minute, he could completely picture her as a teenager.

"Let him help us," Mrs. Hayashi urged.

"Besides," Susan went on, twisting away from her mother in another teenager-like motion, "what about Mindy?"

"I just decided I'm going to take a week off to spend

with her. Take her to the zoo, hang out at the pool. I miss her like crazy, having her away for the weekend, and I want to spend some extra time with her."

"That is so sweet," Mrs. Hayashi said. "I think that's wonderful."

Susan obviously didn't share the belief, but the slump of her shoulders let him know she realized she was defeated.

Good. She didn't get enough pampering in her life, that much was obvious.

And time off work would let him do some thinking about where his life was going and what he was doing. He might even go to that men's prayer breakfast Dion and Troy were always bugging him about.

Yes, a week off might give him some more perspective on his life.

"Daddy, I'm gonna listen to Mr. Eakin's story, okay?" Mindy said two evenings later.

"Sure, that's fine."

It was the Senior Towers open house, and the elders had gone all out to get the community to stop in and see what went on there. There were storytelling and craft booths, a used-book sale and a table set up to match senior volunteers with community needs.

Sam had relished spending the day with Mindy, hearing her exuberance about her camping experience, sharing simple summer pleasures like swimming and cooking out and the playground in the park.

At the same time, he had to acknowledge that it was hard to keep a five-year-old entertained. Especially one who was getting super excited about her upcoming birthday. He had a renewed respect for teachers and day care workers and nannies.

And for Susan.

In fact, he'd been thinking a lot about Susan.

Without her, the house was quiet, maybe a little lonely. There was less color and excitement.

He realized that he missed her in a completely different way than he'd missed Marie.

Marie had been stability and deep married love. She'd been the mother of his child. And her death had ripped a hole in his heart and in their home, one he and Mindy had been struggling to fix ever since.

Susan was excitement and spice. Her absence didn't hurt in the same way that the loss of Marie had, of course, partly because they knew Susan was coming back, and partly because his and Mindy's relationship with her was just beginning. It wasn't at all clear where it would go.

A lot of that, he realized, depended on him. There was something between him and Susan, something electric. But could he let go of the past for long enough to experience it and see where it led? Could he let go of at least some of his plans for a life as similar as possible to what he and Marie had planned together, what they'd always wanted?

"Sam Hinton." A clawlike hand grasped his arm, and he turned to see Miss Minnie Falcon, his old Sunday school teacher, glaring at him.

"Hey, Miss Minnie," he said. "How are you doing?"

"I'd be more at peace if I knew what was going on over in that mansion of yours."

"What do you mean?"

"I heard you took that nanny of yours out on a

date." She looked at him as if he'd pocketed the Sunday school funds.

"I heard the same," came a male voice, one he dreaded because it was always critical and negative. Gramps Camden had issues with Sam's father, but didn't seem to be able to make a distinction between the generations. He always took his ire out on Sam. "Hi, Mr. Camden," Sam said, restraining his sigh.

"What are your intentions toward our Susan?" the older man asked. "I hope you're not taking advantage. She's a real nice girl."

"Yes, she is," Miss Minnie agreed. "Very active in the church. Very helpful, and has a mind of her own."

"Which I wouldn't have figured you to like," Gramps said. "Your father never did."

"Hey, hey," Sam said, trying to still the gossip. "We went out for a friendly dinner. That's all."

"At Chez La Ferme?" Minnie sounded scandalized. "Why, you probably spent over fifty dollars on that dinner. That's hardly something you do with just friends. Or should I say, it's hardly something a poor schoolteacher can afford."

"But a rich businessman can," Gramps said. "Question is, why would he want to?"

"Are you courting her?" Miss Minnie asked.

Sam looked from one to the other and felt a confessional urge similar to one he'd felt years ago, in Sunday school. He gave up trying to say anything but the truth. "I don't know," he admitted. "We're so different. I don't know where it could go, but I do like her."

"How's she feel about you?" Gramps asked. "I warned her about your family. She's probably on her guard, as well she should be."

Sam thought, momentarily, of the way her eyes had softened as he'd leaned down to kiss her. "I think she's as confused as I am."

Miss Minnie frowned. "We've all got our eyes on you, young man."

"And as the man," Gramps said, "it's your job to get yourself un-confused. Figure out what you're doing. Don't string her along."

The old man was right, Sam reflected as he collected Mindy and headed home. The whole town of Rescue River knew what was going on, and he didn't want to cause gossip or hurt Susan's reputation.

He needed to make some decisions, and fast. Before the decisions made themselves for him. He just didn't know what to do.

Susan stood in the giant Rural America Outlet Store with her mother, looking through the little girls' clothing section.

Susan held up a colorful romper. "Mindy would look adorable in this!"

Her mother eyed her speculatively. "You've gotten close to her."

"Even being away for these few days, I've really missed that child." Susan couldn't wait to find out how Mindy had done at camp and to hear her stories of her week with her daddy.

"So get it," her mother said after feeling the fabric and squinting at the price tag. "It's a good bargain. But we should also get her something fun and glittery. Maybe a nail polish set." She led the way out of the clothing department and toward the makeup aisles.

"That's too grown-up," Susan protested, following

along past counters of jewelry and watches. "She's only five."

"Turning six, right?" Her mother smiled back at her. "Little girls that age love girly stuff. Even you did, back then."

As they reached the nail polish rack, Susan extended her freshly pedicured foot, showing off her new sparkly pink nail polish. "I did well with the girly stuff this week, didn't I?"

"Kicking and screaming, but yes." Her mother handed her a set of pale colors in a cartoonish box obviously meant for little girls. "What about these?"

Susan studied it. "Well, Sam will shoot me for buying it, but you're right, Mindy will love some nail polish."

"Then let's get it." Her mother took the polish set from her, checked the price and dropped it into their basket with the satisfied smile of an experienced bargain hunter.

The fun of shopping together was one of many rediscoveries Susan had made during the week. They'd gotten spa treatments and giggled through yoga classes and cried through the sappy chick flicks they both loved. In between, they'd done a little bit of real talking: about Donny, about Susan's father and about the mistakes they'd both made during Susan's stormy adolescence.

One conversation in particular stood out—the one about when Susan's father had left.

"I held on to him long after the love had died," her mother admitted, "with guilt about leaving me with you kids, and with pressure about how he didn't make enough money. I wasn't a good wife, Susie, and after he left, I tried to sway you kids against him."

"You tried so hard to make him happy, though," Susan had protested. "All those Japanese dinners, all your own needs suppressed."

"Which was my choice," Susan's mother declared. "I should have gotten a job and a life, especially after Donny was in school. The truth is, I was depressed and anxious, and I took it out on all of you."

Susan had hugged her mother. "I took out plenty on you, too," she said. "Some of the things I said to you as a teenager! I'm so sorry, Mom."

"Oh, every teenager does that, especially girls. I don't blame you for rebelling."

After that, they'd kept things light, but the tension and awkwardness that had hindered their connection for years was mostly gone. Susan felt better about their relationship than she ever had before, and for that, she was grateful to Sam Hinton.

Twenty minutes after they'd paid for their purchases, they were back at Sam's house, sneaking their bundles past the pool where Sam, Mindy and Mindy's grandparents were setting up for the birthday party that would occur later that day.

"Now, take the time to wrap these nicely," Susan's mother urged as she poured them both sodas. "You know, you really ought to get some decent dishes. You're an adult woman."

"Mindy will rip through this paper in two seconds. It doesn't matter how it looks."

"A nice package, as nice as the other guests bring, will impress Sam, though," Mom said. "You know, you just might get him to marry you. He's got that look in his eye."

"Mom!"

"He's a great catch," her mother said, coming over to kneel beside the box of wrapping paper Susan was rummaging through. "Look how wealthy and how generous with his money. A good father. You should consider it, sweetie."

Susan felt as if she was choking. "I don't want to do what you did! Look how that turned out!"

Susan's mother's face went sad. "Oh, Susie, it was so complicated between your father and me. You're not going to have the same situation—"

"I don't want to have a marriage that explodes and causes all that pain. I made a decision to stay single, and I'm sticking to it." She was, too. No doubt about it. What had happened between her and Sam, that night of their date, had been temporary insanity.

"Don't be stubborn. You're just like your father in that regard. Just…" Her mother looked off out the window and sighed. "Just choose the right man, the man who truly loves you, who looks at you like you're made of precious gems." She stroked Susan's hair. "And then communicate with him. Don't lose yourself like I did."

"So can I wrap the gift the way I want to?" Susan asked in exasperation.

"It doesn't hurt to show your softer side. You do have one."

So they wrapped the gifts in pink paper, elegantly, to rival Rescue River's finest. And then her mother brushed Susan's hair for her and put a little braid in it.

"You were always the best with my hair, Mom," Susan said, leaning back against her mother's stomach. "I'm so glad you came."

"I'm glad, too." Her mother placed a kiss on top of her head. "And now I'm going to the airport. My van is coming…" She consulted her phone. "Oh my, they're out front now."

"You're leaving already? So soon?"

Her mother clasped her by her shoulders. "You're on your own, you're on your way. You don't need me."

"But I don't want you to go," Susan said, feeling unexpectedly teary.

Sun slanted through the windows. Outside, car doors slammed and excited kids' voices rang out. It sounded as if a lot of people were coming to Mindy's party, and Susan wondered when Sam had planned it. And how he'd managed without her.

Her mother pulled her to her feet. "You have a party to get ready for. Go do that. And come for a visit soon, okay?"

"I will," Susan said. "Let me help carry your bags."

Her mother waved the offer aside. "I only have one bag, and I left it downstairs. Go get ready for your party."

Susan opened her arms, and her mother came to her in a fierce hug that made them both cry a little. And then her mother gave a jaunty wave and hurried down the stairs.

Party noise drifted through the screen door, and all of a sudden, Susan didn't want to be out of the action anymore. She needed to be a part of this important day in Sam and Mindy's life.

She changed into shorts and a sleeveless blouse, and hurried down the stairs, and immediately understood how Sam had gotten the party planned so fast.

Helen was greeting the well-dressed parents and children, and Ralph was directing a truck containing two ponies to an appropriate unloading spot—the pad behind the garage, where Susan kept her car.

Susan walked slowly toward the gathering, holding her nicely wrapped gift, which suddenly seemed cheap. Uncertainty clawed at her, and then she saw Mindy.

Mindy spotted her at the same time and started running. What could Susan do but kneel down and open her arms?

"There you are! I knew you'd come back in time!" she crowed, loud enough for everyone to hear. "Grandma and Daddy said you might not, but I knew you would!"

"I wouldn't miss it, sweetheart," Susan said, burying her nose in the sweaty, baby-shampoo scent of Mindy's hair.

"Guess what! I got my new little dog! Only," Mindy said frowning, "Uncle Troy said we had to shut her upstairs in her crate cuz the party's too much excitement for her. But that's only while she's a new dog."

So he'd gotten her a dog. *Good job, Sam.* "I can't wait to see her! Maybe after the party."

"You know what?" Mindy said in a serious voice, as if she was figuring something out. "You know what I really want for my birthday?"

The intensity of Mindy's voice had most of the others quieting down to hear.

"What, honey?" Susan asked.

Mindy put a hand on her hip and touched Susan's face with her half arm. "I want *you* to be my new mommy!"

Chapter 11

Sam heard his daughter's words ring out, clear as a bell. *I want you to be my new mommy.* So, apparently, did everyone else at the party, because a hush fell over the yard.

He knew who his daughter was talking to without even looking. Susan.

The silence was replaced by the buzz of adult conversation that seemed to include a fair share of gossip and curious glances.

He looked toward where he'd heard Mindy's voice and saw that Susan had squatted down in front of her, talking quickly, smiling and laughing, redirecting Mindy's attention to the modest gift in her hand, to the clown who was setting up shop in the driveway.

We have a clown? Sam thought blankly.

Mindy was smiling and laughing as Susan talked to

her, so that was all right. Mindy's words had to have been embarrassing to Susan, since everyone had heard, but as usual, her focus had gone immediately to Mindy and making sure she was okay and handling it.

In the direction of the pool area, he heard the sound of sniffling and turned to see his mother-in-law fumbling for a napkin and wiping her eyes. She wasn't one to break down, especially when she had a party to run, but Mindy's words had obviously struck a nerve.

They'd struck a nerve in him, too. Trust a little kid to lay out everything so baldly and clearly. She wanted a new mommy. And she'd decided she wanted Susan.

Which had to go totally against Helen's grain. He strode over to see what he could do for his grieving mother-in-law.

Former mother-in-law.

As he bent to put an arm around Helen, he caught Susan studying him, her eyes thoughtful.

Sam blew out a breath. Everything was coming to a head now. Mindy, Helen, Susan. It was an emotional triangle he couldn't figure out how to manage, couldn't fix. He, who could easily run a complex business, had no idea what to do, no idea how to arrange his personal life.

"Helen, you don't want to make a scene in front of all of these folks," said Ralph, patting his wife's arm and looking every bit as confused as Sam felt.

"You get those ponies set up," Helen snapped at her husband. "I have to talk to Sam."

After making sure that everyone had access to food and drink, and that Lou Ann Miller was supervising any kids who wanted to swim, Sam led Helen to the shelter beside the pool house. Bushes blocked it from the rest of the house and there was some privacy.

"Hey," he said once he'd got her seated on a picnic bench and found her a can of soda and a napkin to blow her nose. "You're going to be okay." He was terrible at this, terrible at comforting. He remembered all the times he'd tried and failed to comfort Marie. The one thing he'd been able to do to make her feel better, at the end of her life, was the promise. The promise that now dragged at his soul.

"You promised!" It was as if Helen read his mind. "Sam, you promised you'd marry someone like her, someone who would fulfill her legacy. And instead you've come up with…that woman."

"I don't know where the relationship with Susan is going," Sam said truthfully, all of a sudden realizing that he did, in fact, have a relationship with her.

"That woman can't cook, she wants to work rather than staying home, and she says the wrong thing all the time. She's so…different."

"That's for sure," Sam agreed. "Susan is different."

"Marie would hate her!"

Sam thought about it and decided that, yes, it was probably true. Marie would at least be made very insecure by Susan. But Marie *was* insecure, and that was what had made her such a perfectionist. And her insecurity had everything to do with her mother's demanding standards.

He didn't want to raise Mindy like that.

"She'd be a horrible mother. And you promised you'd marry someone like Marie."

Sam sighed heavily. "It's true. If I want to keep my promise to Marie, I…I can't marry Susan." As he said it, he felt trapped in a cage made of his own beliefs, the beliefs he'd always held about what made a good marriage, a good home, a good life.

Desperate for freedom, he lifted his head from his hands…and saw Susan and Mindy standing in the shelter's gateway.

And from the look on Susan's face, she'd overheard every word.

She squatted down and whispered something to Mindy. As Mindy ran toward him and Helen, Susan turned and left, almost at a run.

"Come on, Daddy, the kids all want to ride ponies and swim and nobody knows what to do!"

He had to take control of his child's party. He stood and walked out, feeling dazed, looking for Susan. But she was nowhere to be seen.

Susan's world spun as she thought about what she'd overheard. *I can't marry Susan.*

Marie would hate her.

She fell backward on her bed, staring up at the ceiling, eyes dry, stomach cold. She lay there for a long time while the sounds of the ongoing party drifted up to her.

It's fine, she told herself. It wasn't as if he'd proposed.

But if he'd made some kind of promise about what kind of woman to marry—and who made that kind of promise, anyway?—then what was he doing kissing her?

It was like her dad, saying one thing and doing another. Men were so unreliable.

And what of what Helen had said, about how bad

she was at household duties? Hadn't she proven that to be true?

Just like her ex-fiancé, Sam didn't want a woman like her.

Her foolish dreams crashed down around her and she squeezed her eyes shut, willing herself not to cry. She was a strong woman, and she would survive this. After just a little period of mourning.

Her phone buzzed with a text from Daisy. Where are you?

Susan ignored it. Clicked off her phone.

The ache in her chest was huge, as if someone had dug a hole there with a blunt shovel. It hurt so much that she couldn't move, couldn't think. *God, help*, she prayed, unable to find more words.

In response, she felt a small soothing rush of love.

She'd always gone to church, read her Bible when there was a study group to push her, talked over her questions with friends like Daisy. She'd felt God's call for her vocation as a teacher. She knew she was saved.

But she'd never thought much about being loved by God. She'd never *felt* it, not deep inside. Now, the small soothing trickle grew to a warm glow.

Her father had only loved her conditionally, and he'd abandoned her. They spoke rarely by phone, and only at his instigation. Never when she needed him.

Her heavenly Father was different. He was here, waiting for her to reach out. *Rest in me*, He seemed to say.

Her hurt about Sam didn't evaporate. In fact, knowing God loved her seemed to unfreeze the tears, and they trickled down the sides of her face and into her hair. She'd never have a future with Sam and Mindy, and the cold truth of that stabbed into her like an icicle, letting her know that somewhere inside, she'd been nursing a dream to life.

Now that dream was pierced, deflated, gone.

Finally, a long while later, she dragged herself out of bed and looked out the window. Most of the kids were inside, no doubt eating birthday cake. The clown was packing up to go. He'd removed his red wig and rubbery nose, but his smile was still painted on.

She watched him pack his clown supplies into his rusty car trunk. He looked tired.

Could she keep a smile pasted on in the face of what she'd heard?

No.

She pulled out her suitcase and hauled a couple of boxes out of the closet. She opened the suitcase on her bed.

She'd started to dream, to hope. Crazy, stupid hope.

And a little girl would suffer because of it. "I want you to be my new mommy," Mindy had said earlier today, and the words, and the notion, had thrilled Susan way too much.

But she could never, ever be Mindy's new mommy. Because Sam had made a promise.

She opened her dresser drawers and started throwing clothes randomly into the suitcase, blinking against the tears that kept blurring her vision. From the open window, she heard car doors slamming, adults calling to one another. The parents were starting to arrive. The party was almost over.

She heard steps coming up the porch stairs, double time. "There you are!" Mindy said, rushing in. "Come see all my presents!" Then she seemed to notice something on Susan's face. She stopped still and looked around the room. "Whatcha doing?"

Susan's heart was breaking. Rip the bandage off quickly, she told herself. "I have to go away," she said.

"But you just got back from a trip."

"No, I mean…I can't stay here anymore."

"Why not?"

Why not indeed, when she loved this little girl almost as much as she loved her difficult, obstinate father? "It's just not working out. But I'll still see you lots, honey. I'll see you at school."

"I don't want you to go."

Susan couldn't help it; she knelt to hug the little girl. "I'm sorry, honey. I don't want to go either, but it's for the best."

Mindy's shoulders shook a little, but she didn't sob out loud. So she was starting to learn self-control. Growing up more each day.

Susan hugged the child tighter, but she struggled out of Susan's arms and ran down the stairs without looking back.

"Whoa there!" came Sam's voice, drifting up through the windows. "C'mere, sweetie. What's wrong?"

Panic rose in Susan at the thought of facing Sam. She needed to get this done fast. She'd just take a few things for now and send for the rest, because staying to pack and move would be too painful. Maybe this way, she could avoid seeing Sam or upsetting Mindy again.

She didn't even have an idea of where to go. Maybe to the little motel in outside of town, until she could figure something else out. Maybe she could go spend the rest of the summer with her mom, drop in unexpectedly just as Mom had done on her.

Heavy steps climbed the wooden stairs, and there was a knock on the open screen door. "Susan?"

She sucked in a breath. Sam. She'd moved too slowly, lost her chance of easy escape. "Come in," she said, feeling as if she was made of stone.

"What's going on here?" he asked, stopping at the door of her bedroom.

"I'm leaving."

"Why?"

What could she say? Because I've fallen in love with you and staying will break my heart? And Mindy's heart, too, because it can't be permanent?

Men were not dependable. She'd always known it, but for a while, Sam had seemed to defy the norm. But he'd proven, too, that he couldn't be trusted, that she'd be better off alone.

"It's just not working out," she said, and found the strength from somewhere to snap her suitcase closed.

He stood in the doorway as if he was frozen there.

She had to leave now or she'd never be able to. "Excuse me," she said, and slipped sideways past him. She trotted out the door and down the stairs.

Sam didn't know how long he stood there after Susan left. But finally standing got to be too much of an effort and he sank down onto her bed. Collapsed down to rest his head on her pillow. Inhaled her scent of honeysuckle, and his throat tightened.

Why had she gone? Was it just that she was flighty, transient, easily bored? Had his and Mindy's life proven too dull for her? Now that she'd earned enough money to send her brother to camp and make things up with her mom, had she gotten everything she could out of him?

But that *wasn't* it. Or at least, it wasn't all. She'd overheard what he'd said to Helen, and it had hurt her.

Having her gone had been bad enough when it was just for a week, but the expression on her face when she'd left had suggested that this time, it was permanent. She'd left for good.

Maybe she was oversensitive. Maybe he'd been right: he needed to stick to his kind of woman. Someone solid and stable and from his background. Someone who valued home and family over excitement. Someone who was in it for the long haul.

But the idea of finding someone else, a clone of the stable, boring blondes he'd dated over the past year, made him squeeze his eyes shut in despair.

He didn't want that. But he'd made a promise.

He was well and truly trapped.

"Hey, Sam!" He heard voices calling outside the window at the same time his cell phone buzzed.

He didn't have the energy to pick it up, but his wretched sense of duty made him look at the screen. Daisy. He texted back a question mark, having no heart for more.

Is Mindy with you? she texted.

He hit the call button, and Daisy answered immediately. "Do you have Mindy?"

"No. She was down on the driveway a few minutes ago."

"Well, everyone's gone, and I don't see her anywhere."

Sam stood and strode to the window. He scanned the yard. He didn't see her, either.

He did see Susan's car. Susan and Daisy were standing by it together. So she hadn't left yet.

"I'm on my way down," he said, and clicked off the phone.

Susan followed Daisy back into the house she'd thought she was leaving forever.

"Maybe she just fell asleep somewhere," Daisy was saying. "Or maybe Troy and Angelica took her home? Would they do that? I'll call them."

She was starting to place the call when Susan put a hand on her friend's arm. "I think I know why she's missing," she said. "It's my fault."

"What?"

So she filled Daisy in on the skeleton details of how she'd been packing and Mindy had found her and gotten upset.

"I'm going to want to hear more about this later," Daisy said, "but for now, let's find Mindy."

A quick survey of the house revealed nothing. They'd already checked the pool, of course, but they went back to look around the pool house. The place where Susan had heard about Sam's promise. Where he'd broken her heart. But there was no time for self-indulgence now.

My prickly independence hurt a little girl, she thought as she searched the woods at the edge of Sam's property. *I need to do something about that. If only I hadn't just run up and packed, Mindy wouldn't be missing.*

They checked in with Sam, who was white-faced

and tight-lipped, searching the property lines as well. Phone calls were made, and within minutes Fern and Carlo, Troy and Angelica came back, with Lou Ann Miller to watch Mercy and Xavier.

"I shouldn't have jumped into packing," Susan lamented as she, Fern and Angelica walked back into the fields behind Sam's property, calling Mindy's name. "I always think I'm just going to run away. If I hadn't done that, she wouldn't be missing."

Fern patted her arm. "Don't forget the time Mercy went missing. Only it was the dead of winter out at the skating pond. I totally blamed myself, but I've come to realize these things happen. We'll find her."

"It's true," Angelica said, giving her a quick side-arm hug. "Don't blame yourself. We all make mistakes with kids."

"You guys are the best," Susan said, gripping each of their hands, not bothering to hide her tears. She couldn't even pretend to be an island now. She needed her friends.

They met up with the men and Daisy in front of the house. "She just can't have gotten far," Troy was saying. "Look, Angelica and I will head to the surrounding houses."

"We'll check the library and the downtown," Carlo said, "just in case she took off running."

Sam shook his head. "I have this feeling she's somewhere in the house. I'm going to search this place from top to bottom. But let's get Dion involved, just in case."

At that, Susan's heart twisted. Everyone else looked half-sick, too, reminded of what could happen to missing little girls.

Daisy made the call to Dion, and then she, Susan

and Sam started methodically going through the house. Susan realized anew how huge it was, how many spots there were for a little girl to hide. They searched each floor together, checking in with the other searchers.

Dion came in his cruiser and drove the neighborhoods.

The basement yielded nothing, and the main floor didn't, either. Susan thought she saw a head of blond hair in the playroom, but it was just a doll.

Upstairs, they went through Mindy's bedroom and all the closets, and then started on the spare bedrooms. Nothing.

But as they headed back downstairs, Susan heard a sound, like a sob, behind the sunroom door, that mysterious door that always remained closed.

"Did you hear that?" she asked.

"What? Where?"

Susan indicated the closed door.

"She wouldn't go in there," Sam said. "She's scared of it, because—" He broke off.

"Didn't you ever change it?" Daisy looked at Sam.

"Not yet," he said, and opened the door.

Inside was a beautiful, multi-windowed sunroom with wicker furniture and a rattan carpet, decorated in rust and brown and cream. Autumn colors.

In the center of the room was a hospital bed.

In a flash it came to Susan: this must be the place where Marie had died.

There was a bump in the covers of the bed. And there, sleeping restlessly, with the occasional hiccupping sob, was Mindy. Her new little black-and-white dog slept in her arms.

They all three looked at each other. Daisy bit her

lip, tears in her eyes. "You have to get rid of that bed, Sam. You have to open this place up."

He nodded without speaking, and from the way his throat was working, Susan could see that he could barely restrain tears, himself.

"Thank the Lord we found her." Daisy hugged both of them.

Sam picked Mindy up and carried her to her bedroom while Daisy and Susan called the others.

"Now, what's this about you packing? Why were you leaving?" Daisy asked as they walked out to meet the others.

Fern fell into step beside them.

"It's time for girl talk," Daisy told her. "Susan was thinking of leaving."

Fern winced. "I remember when you guys talked sense into me," she said. She beckoned to Angelica, and the four of them headed into the living room, which looked to be the most secluded place right now.

"It's not that I need sense talked into me," Susan said, sinking into one of the formal living room chairs. She was too broken down to lie or conceal her feelings. "I love him. And I love Mindy. But he's never going to be able to commit to someone like me. I heard him say it." She shrugged. "I guess I'm just too different from him, not his type."

"Do I look like Carlo's type?" Fern asked. "I'm a librarian, and he's a mercenary, or at least he used to be. What could we have in common? But love is strange."

Angelica leaned forward and took Susan's hand. "It's hard to trust in men after you've been hurt," she said. "But it's so, so worth it."

"Just stay a little longer," Daisy urged. "Talk to Sam."

Susan wanted to take in what they were saying, but her heart was aching and her head was confused.

They talked a few minutes longer, and then Troy and Carlo called from the foyer and everyone started to leave.

Susan stayed, alone, sitting on the couch in the gathering darkness, too drained to move. "Thank You for letting us find her, Father," she prayed. "I'm sorry I'm so messed up. Please, help me to change so I can find love and do what's important."

She sat without tuning on a lamp, listening to the murmur of Sam talking to Dion on the porch, feeling alternating waves of sadness and God's healing love wash over her.

Finally, she curled up on her side on the narrow couch, tucked a hard, uncomfortable pillow beneath her head, and fell asleep.

Chapter 12

Sam sank down onto the wicker armchair on the front porch, waving to Troy and Angelica as they drove away, tooting their horn.

Only Dion remained, his cruiser parked out on the street. "You okay, my man?"

Sam stared out at the night sky. "Not really."

"Rough day." Dion sat down in the other chair, propped his hands behind his head and put his feet up on the wicker coffee table. "Now's the time you wish for a woman to bring you a tall iced tea."

"Tea's in the refrigerator," Sam offered. "I think."

"Exactly. That would require effort."

They sat together for a few minutes in a comfortable silence.

"Sorry I made you search the streets," Sam said finally. "Mindy never goes in the sunroom."

"The room where your wife died?"

Sam nodded. "I...just keep the door closed."

Dion nodded, tipping the chair back on two legs. "I did that for a while myself. At the house we shared, and in my heart."

"And you stopped? How?"

Dion shrugged, still staring out into the gathering darkness. "Time, man. Time, and prayer." He leveled a stern look at Sam. "You've had enough time, but you could use some help on the prayer side."

"I'm coming to the men's breakfast," Sam protested.

"Which I'm glad of. But you might need a private consult with the Lord."

Sam smiled at the terminology. "I know I do."

"Marie was a good woman," Dion said, and then paused.

Sam knew a "but" was coming. "But what?"

"But I'm guessing she must've been a little hard to live with."

A few weeks ago, that remark would have surprised him and roused his defenses. Now he just nodded. "She was pretty tense."

"Grew up that way, I guess."

"Exactly." Sam thought about his in-laws. Marie had never really broken away from them enough to have her own life. Everything had been colored by their insistence on perfection, on image. It wasn't that they were bad people, just a little misguided about what was important. "They were...controlling."

"Sounds like someone I know."

"What?"

"Look in the mirror, my man." Dion gave him a

look. "Everyone knows you're a dominant alpha-jerk. It's a wonder you have so many friends."

He knew he was controlling, but he'd never put it all together like that. "Is that why Marie married me?"

Dion spread his hands, palms up. "I hate to say it, but she kind of married her mother."

"Hey!"

Dion stood up, clapped him hard on the back. "Think about it, my man. How long you gonna force yourself to live in the past? Don't you remember you can be a new creation?"

And he waved and headed down the long front walk to his cruiser.

Restless, Sam stood and went inside. He checked on Mindy, who was sleeping peacefully, her new little dog beside her. The rule he'd made, no dogs in bed, was obviously not going to stick.

And then he went downstairs to the room where they'd found her. Marie's room. Or Mommy's room, as they'd called it when Marie was alive.

He sat in the chair where he'd spent so much time, right beside the hospital bed where she'd lain as the strength had slowly left her body. Talking to her, trying to cheer her up, reading with her, watching the house and garden shows she'd loved.

Even though the shows had bored him to tears, he'd kept watching them religiously for the first year after her death, because he'd felt closer to her that way. But, he realized, he hadn't seen one in six or eight months.

Dion was right. There came a time to move on.

He leaned forward, elbows on knees, hands clasped together. It was a prayer position, but he wasn't talking to God, not yet. He was talking to Marie. Telling her how sad he was that their dream hadn't worked out. How sorry that he'd been a controlling replica of her parents, that he hadn't encouraged her to spread her wings and fly. Letting her know that he couldn't keep the promise he'd made.

After a while, he stopped telling her anything and just sat. Just invoked the Lord's presence, asking for help. Confessing his sins there, too.

And as he sat, in prayerful meditation, a realization came to him.

Marie was with Christ. He'd prepared for her a room in His mansion. He'd promised that He'd see her face to face.

Oh, Sam had known that, but he hadn't *known* it. Hadn't really felt it.

Marie was happy now, happier than she'd ever been in life. Free of her failing body. Free of her insecurities. Free to love.

Marie had moved on to a new life, one he couldn't even imagine.

And likewise, she hadn't been able to imagine that he would move on, that life would change, that Mindy would grow beyond toddlerhood and would maybe need something, and someone, new. Maybe Sam would, too.

With the promises of Christ, Sam could move on, just as Marie had.

He sat until the tears had mostly stopped falling. Grabbed a tissue from the box Marie had always kept by her bed, a box that hadn't been used or changed out since she'd died.

He wiped his face and blew his nose and felt like an idiot, but a cleansed one. A healed one.

He took a deep breath, opened the door wide and went to find Susan.

Earlier, he'd seen that Susan's car was still behind the garage apartment. She hadn't left with Daisy, so she must have gone back to stay in her apartment. Which was good, because he had things he wanted to say to her.

But the apartment was dark, and she wasn't there, and fear gripped his heart.

What if she'd found another ride, sometime when he wasn't looking? What if she'd left? Left, before he could tell her all the things he wanted to tell her?

He walked back into the house, exhaustion hitting him hard. It had been a long and stressful day, full of fear and joy, sadness and closure. What he wanted at the end of this long day—at the end of any long day— was to be with the woman he loved. But she wasn't here.

As Sam walked through the house, hoping to hear Susan's voice, he seemed to see it with new eyes. It had been Marie's pride and joy; she'd loved inviting her friends here, serving tea, hosting her book club. At one time, the place had been his dream, too, full of stability and love, a home base that ran as smoothly as a business.

Now, it felt empty, lifeless, sad. Was this even the house he wanted to live in? Was it the right place for Mindy to grow up, formal as it was and full of sad memories?

Desolation gripped him hard.

He felt like just collapsing into bed, but he had responsibilities. He finished his walk-through of the house, just as he did every night, shutting off lights, locking doors, checking to make sure nothing was amiss. He picked up some cups and a few stray cup-cake wrappers that remained from the party. Feeling utterly alone.

And then he saw her.

Curled up on the couch like a young girl, her fist at her mouth, silky black hair spread over her shoulders. In sleep, the determination and spark and movement weren't there, and she looked totally vulnerable.

Totally lovely.

Joy was surging in his heart that she hadn't left him, that she was still in the house. She was still in reach. There was a chance.

He pulled up an ottoman and sat beside her, but just watching her sleep felt creepy. So he touched her arm, patted her awake. "Hey."

She opened her eyes slowly, and Sam got a momentary vision of what it might be like to watch her wake up every day. His heart ached with longing to be the man who saw that, who was there with her.

"I fell asleep," she said, looking around. "What time is it?"

"It's late," he said. "Ten or so."

Susan stretched and pushed herself up into a semi-reclining position, propped on pillows, rubbing her arms.

"You're cold," he said, and looked for an afghan or throw. Finding none, he went to the front closet and found one of his sweatshirts. "Here," he said, tucking it gently around her shoulders.

She blinked. "What time did you say it was? And hey, are we even allowed to put our feet on this couch?"

"We are now," he said.

She grabbed her phone and studied it. "If I go now, I can get a seat." She started to stand up.

"Wait. What seat?"

"On a plane to California," she said, putting her feet down and brushing her hands over her messy hair. "There's this online standby thing, and it looks like I have a seat if I can claim it by eleven. I've got to go."

He put a hand on her knee. "Susan. Wait."

"If you're going to yell at me, don't bother. I already know I made a mess of things." She was fumbling for her shoes, checking her phone again, looking anywhere but his face.

"What did you make a mess of?"

She stopped fussing and looked at him. "It was because of me that Mindy hid," she said. "She found me packing and got upset. I think she felt like it was another mother figure leaving her alone." She shook her head rapidly. "I'm so sorry I did that to her."

"Why were you packing to leave?" If it was because she didn't care, then he had to let her go.

"Because," she said slowly, "Because I heard what you said to Helen. That you could never marry me, that you made a promise."

"Ah." He took her hands. "I was afraid that was the problem." And he explained about the promise.

"You're right that I'm never going to be that person," she said. "And I don't want to break Mindy's heart. Or mine. I need to go now, before we get more attached."

"Wait." He shook his head slowly. "I've realized something now. That promise is something that helped me to grieve, stopped me from moving on too soon. But it doesn't hold now. It's like the old law and the new."

"What do you mean?" She sounded troubled.

"Susan, one thing you've helped me see is that I needed to change. I don't have an easy time with change, never have. I'm the steady, boring, rock-solid type."

One side of her mouth quirked up. "Never boring. And steady's not so bad."

"Steady is okay, but I've seen that change is part of life. There's a new way. I'm a new creation."

She raised an eyebrow. "You mean like a new creation in Christ? You're talking religious, and that's not like you."

"It's like me now," he said. "I've recommitted. I've stopped blaming Him for what happened. With God's help, I'm back."

"Oh, Sam, I'm so happy for you!" She threw her arms around him.

Susan felt happy for Sam and more peaceful for herself, but she still had to get going. She talked to Sam for a few minutes, hearing about his conversation with Dion, glad to know he was getting right with the Lord.

But seeing his handsome face lose some of its tension, seeing the light in his eyes that hadn't been there before, just made him more attractive.

"Look," she said finally, "this is wonderful, but I really have to go. If I start driving in the next ten minutes, I can get to the airport just in time to catch this flight."

His lips tightened, but he nodded and followed her to the door. "Your purse, your phone?" he said, looking out for her, making sure she had what she needed.

She swallowed hard as she walked out of the house, because this was truly goodbye. "I'll send for my stuff," she said.

His hands clapped down on her shoulders, turning her to face him. Behind him, his giant mansion shone in the moonlight.

The mansion that had become home to her.

Looking up at him, thinking of Mindy in the house behind him, just about broke her heart.

"I don't want you to go. I want you to stay."

She shook her head. "It's just hurting Mindy," she said. "And me."

"Why is it hurting you?" he asked, touching her chin to make her look at him.

He was going to make her say it, but what did it matter now? She was already hurting and she was leaving. "Because I've fallen in love with you and Mindy. With this life we're playing at. I want to have it for real, but I can't."

"Why not? Susan, what you just said makes me the happiest man in the world." He sank down to his knees. "I want to marry you. I don't know how or when, I know Mindy and I have a little more healing work to do, but I think we can do it with your help. I want you to be Mindy's new mommy. And my wife. Especially my wife."

"But your promise to Marie…"

He shook his head. "I've made my peace with that. With her. I'm not held to it anymore."

"For real?" She wanted to believe it, but she wasn't sure she could trust him. Was he just saying that? Could people really heal from a loss like the one he and Mindy had sustained?

"I am completely, totally sure." He swept her into his arms and carried her over to the lawn swing she'd insisted they get.

"Sam!"

"No near neighbors to see," he said. "And I want to prove to you just how much I love you."

He cradled her against his chest and kissed her tenderly, and Susan's last shreds of doubt wafted away on the gentle night breeze. Eagerly, she kissed him back and then stroked his hair and looked into his eyes.

"Does that mean yes?" he asked, sounding a little insecure.

She laughed out loud. "When does the nanny ever say no to the millionaire?"

"This is a serious moment!" He shook his head, then traced a finger along her cheek. "And I take nothing for granted."

"I'm sorry," she giggled, her heart almost bursting with joy, her soul singing. Daisy had been right: God's plan for her, for all of them, was bigger and deeper and richer than their human minds could imagine. "I'm just so happy. And it's totally a yes."

Epilogue

"I can't believe you let her do a beauty pageant," Susan said as she and Sam approached the Rescue River community center, hand in hand. Mindy ran ahead of them, wearing a poufy pink dress and scuffed cowboy boots.

Sam chuckled. "It's a different kind of pageant, you'll see."

Susan looked around at other families approaching with their daughters of various ages. Some were dressed in customary pageant gear, but others wore shorts or jeans. Susan noticed one girl in a traditional Chinese cheongsam dress and two other girls, one looking Indian and the other redheaded, wearing matching saris.

"The main rule is that the girls wear what they like. Mindy feels beautiful in that dress. But they're not judged on how they look."

"Then what are they judged on?"

"You'll see."

"I'll take your word for it," Susan said, snuggling closer to Sam's side. "I know it makes her grandma happy, so I'm glad we're here." In the two months since they'd declared their love for each other, Susan had been learning a lot about compromise and communication—and about being loved for exactly who she was.

"Look," Mindy cried, "They have crafts! And I see Miss Fern!"

Sam and Susan followed Mindy to an area where several tables stocked with art supplies were set up. The directions, printed large and bold, instructed participants to make art about something they wanted to do when they were older.

"Hey," Fern greeted them as she pulled out a huge sheet of paper. "You've got plenty of time, honey," she said as she handed it to Mindy. "Make whatever you like, just something you want to do when you're older. There are other art tables with other topics, when you're done here. Do you want a smock to cover that pretty dress?"

Mindy plunged her arms into a smock and sat down beside Fern's daughter, who was vigorously painting.

"Looks like Dad's one of the judges again," Sam observed, looking toward the stage where the judges' tables were being set up. "Last year, he almost came to blows with Gramps Camden."

Helen approached, brushing a hand over her granddaughter's shoulders before turning to Sam and Susan. "We put Lou Ann Miller in between. We're hoping that keeps everyone on good behavior. Hi, Susan."

"Hi." Susan returned the wary greeting and then,

impulsively, hugged the older woman. They were starting to forge a relationship, but it would be a slow process. "You were right," Susan said, determined to do her part. "She does look beautiful in her dress, and this is a great event for girls."

When they released the hug and stepped back, Helen's eyes were shiny. "I just want Mindy to be happy," she said. "And I want to be a part of her life."

"Of course you do. You're a huge part of her life, and you always will be."

After an hour of mingling and following Mindy from art table to art table, the formal ceremony began. Susan sat back and listened, impressed, to the girls of all ages talking about the required topics, sometimes displaying art to go alongside. Finally, it was Mindy's turn, and as she walked confidently up to the stage, Sam gripped Susan's hand.

It was as if she could read his mind: he was nervous for Mindy, wanting her to do well, wanting her to feel good about it. Susan felt the same way. She loved the little girl more each day.

"Something I did that was hard," Mindy said into the microphone, speaking clearly, "was I went into my mommy-who-died's room. I used to be scared in there but now I'm not cuz I have my puppy." She held up a picture of Bonz. "I went in there and was brave to tell my mommy who died that I want a new mommy, and she said it was okay."

There was a collective sigh and a spontaneous round of applause.

"And something I like to do," Mindy said, "is hug people. I can hug just as good as anybody else even though I just have one hand."

Another collective "aww."

"I want to show that, for this pageant, but I have to get my daddy and my Miss Susan to come up here," she said, "cuz they're gonna get married."

Gasps and murmurs filled the room, and Sam looked at Susan. "Guess the secret's out. You game?"

"Of course." It had been an open secret, really; in a town like Rescue River, you couldn't hide a relationship very well.

So they went up front and Mindy proved that she could, indeed, hug as well as anyone else. And as the applause swelled for the three of them, standing there hugging each other tightly, Susan felt the invisible Master who'd been guiding them together from the beginning, and looked up through tears to offer praise.

* * * * *

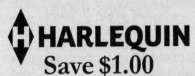

HARLEQUIN

Save $1.00

on the purchase of ANY Harlequin book
from the imprints below.

*Heartfelt or thrilling, passionate or
uplifting—our romances have it all.*

PRESENTS INTRIGUE

DESIRE ROMANTIC SUSPENSE SPECIAL EDITION

LOVE INSPIRED

Save $1.00

on the purchase of ANY Harlequin Presents, Intrigue, Desire,
Romantic Suspense, Special Edition or Love Inspired book.

Valid from June 1, 2023 to May 31, 2024.

52617414

Canadian Retailers: Harlequin Enterprises ULC will pay the face value of this coupon plus 10.25¢ if submitted by customer for this product only. Any other use constitutes fraud. Coupon is nonassignable. Void if taxed, prohibited or restricted by law. Consumer must pay any government taxes. Void if copied. Inmar Promotional Services ("IPS") customers submit coupons and proof of sales to Harlequin Enterprises ULC, P.O. Box 31000, Scarborough, ON M1R 0E7, Canada. Non-IPS retailer—for reimbursement submit coupons and proof of sales directly to Harlequin Enterprises ULC, Retail Marketing Department, Bay Adelaide Centre, East Tower, 22 Adelaide Street West, 41st Floor, Toronto, Ontario M5H 4E3, Canada.

U.S. Retailers: Harlequin Enterprises ULC will pay the face value of this coupon plus 8¢ if submitted by customer for this product only. Any other use constitutes fraud. Coupon is nonassignable. Void if taxed, prohibited or restricted by law. Consumer must pay any government taxes. Void if copied. For reimbursement submit coupons and proof of sales directly to Harlequin Enterprises ULC 482, NCH Marketing Services, P.O. Box 880001, El Paso, TX 88588-0001, U.S.A. Cash value 1/100 cents.

5 65373 00076 2   (8100)0 12532

© 2023 Harlequin Enterprises ULC

HSERIESCOUP0623

Get 3 FREE REWARDS!

We'll send you 2 FREE Books plus a FREE Mystery Gift.

FREE Value Over **$20**

Both the **Love Inspired®** and **Love Inspired® Suspense** series feature compelling novels filled with inspirational romance, faith, forgiveness and hope.

YES! Please send me 2 FREE novels from the Love Inspired or Love Inspired Suspense series and my FREE gift (gift is worth about $10 retail). After receiving them, if I don't wish to receive any more books, I can return the shipping statement marked "cancel." If I don't cancel, I will receive 6 brand-new Love Inspired Larger-Print books or Love Inspired Suspense Larger-Print books every month and be billed just $6.49 each in the U.S. or $6.74 each in Canada. That is a savings of at least 16% off the cover price. It's quite a bargain! Shipping and handling is just 50¢ per book in the U.S. and $1.25 per book in Canada.* I understand that accepting the 2 free books and gift places me under no obligation to buy anything. I can always return a shipment and cancel at any time by calling the number below. The free books and gift are mine to keep no matter what I decide.

Choose one: ☐ **Love Inspired**   ☐ **Love Inspired**   ☐ **Or Try Both!**
                Larger-Print   **Suspense**   (122/322 & 107/307
                (122/322 BPA GRPA)   **Larger-Print**   BPA GRRP)
                                       (107/307 BPA GRPA)

Name (please print)

Address   Apt. #

City   State/Province   Zip/Postal Code

Email: Please check this box ☐ if you would like to receive newsletters and promotional emails from Harlequin Enterprises ULC and its affiliates. You can unsubscribe anytime.

Mail to the Harlequin Reader Service:
IN U.S.A.: P.O. Box 1341, Buffalo, NY 14240-8531
IN CANADA: P.O. Box 603, Fort Erie, Ontario L2A 5X3

Want to try 2 free books from another series? Call 1-800-873-8635 or visit www.ReaderService.com.

*Terms and prices subject to change without notice. Prices do not include sales taxes, which will be charged (if applicable) based on your state or country of residence. Canadian residents will be charged applicable taxes. Offer not valid in Quebec. This offer is limited to one order per household. Books received may not be as shown. Not valid for current subscribers to the Love Inspired or Love Inspired Suspense series. All orders subject to approval. Credit or debit balances in a customer's account(s) may be offset by any other outstanding balance owed by or to the customer. Please allow 4 to 6 weeks for delivery. Offer available while quantities last.

Your Privacy—Your information is being collected by Harlequin Enterprises ULC, operating as Harlequin Reader Service. For a complete summary of the information we collect, how we use this information and to whom it is disclosed, please visit our privacy notice located at corporate.harlequin.com/privacy-notice. From time to time we may also exchange your personal information with reputable third parties. If you wish to opt out of this sharing of your personal information, please visit readerservice.com/consumerschoice or call 1-800-873-8635. **Notice to California Residents**—Under California law, you have specific rights to control and access your data. For more information on these rights and how to exercise them, visit corporate.harlequin.com/california-privacy.

LIRLIS23

HARLEQUIN
PLUS

Try the best multimedia subscription service for romance readers like you!

Read, Watch and Play.

Experience the easiest way to get the romance content you crave.

Start your **FREE TRIAL** at
<u>www.harlequinplus.com/freetrial</u>.